PRAISE FOR STEPHEN WHITE'S ELECTRIFYING THRILLERS:

The Best Revenge

"ANOTHER PAGE-TURNING THRILLER . . . TIGHTROPE-TENSE PLOTTING, THREE-DIMENSIONAL CHARACTERS, INTERESTING SUBPLOTS AND WHITE'S USUAL INSIGHTS INTO LIFE'S LITTLE IRONIES."
—*The Denver Post*

"White moves from strength to strength . . . [with] A SURPRISE ENDING THAT IS FOR ONCE WORTHY OF THE TERM."
—*The News & Observer* (Raleigh, N.C.)

"It is up to [psychologist Alan] Gregory, as usual, to save the day by uncovering dangerous inner secrets. He does it with speed, sensitivity, and panache, making *The Best Revenge* WELL WORTH A FEW HOURS ON THE COUCH."
—*The Orlando Sentinel*

"Another extraordinary suspenseful novel featuring Psychiatrist Alan Gregory . . . [White] adroitly juggles the themes of justice, revenge, and the personal need of victims to feel resolution . . . [with] SURPRISES IN STORE UNTIL THE VERY END." —*New Mystery Reader Magazine*

"GREAT CHARACTERS AND SATISFYINGLY CAMOUFLAGED TWISTS." —*The Charlotte Observer*

Featured Alternate Selection of Book-of-the-Month Club, Literary Guild, and Doubleday Book Club

Warning Signs

"INTRIGUING . . . BRILLIANT . . . A highly recommended read especially for those in between fixes
of Jonathan Kellerman." —*Ireland on Sunday*

The Program

"PSYCHOLOGICAL SUSPENSE AT ITS BEST."
—Bestselling author Jeffery Deaver

"[A] darned good storyteller . . . his novels are
subtler and more graceful than your run-of-the-mill
thriller." —*The Denver Post*

"Clever and involving . . . SMART, STEREOTYPE-
DEFYING THRILLER." —*Los Angeles Times*

"[A] stand-out." —*The Miami Herald*

"White's narrative skills are so strong that we
never argue with what he offers."
—*The Drood Review of Mystery*

"SUPERB . . . DETAILED CHARACTERIZATION,
FAST-PACED PLOT AND ACTION-PACKED
ENDING." —*The Tulsa World*

"Memorable characters, non-stop tension, and
twisty plot . . . AN IRRESISTIBLE READ."
—*Alfred Hitchcock's Mystery Magazine*

Also by Stephen White

And coming soon in hardcover from Delacorte Press

BLINDED

STEPHEN WHITE

THE BEST REVENGE

A DELL BOOK

THE BEST REVENGE
A Dell Book

PUBLISHING HISTORY
Delacorte Press edition published February 2003
Dell mass market edition / December 2003

Published by
Bantam Dell
A Division of Random House, Inc.
New York, New York

This is a work of fiction. Names, characters, places, and incidents are
either the product of the author's imagination or are used fictitiously.
Any resemblance to actual persons, living or dead, events, or locales is
entirely coincidental.

Library of Congress Catalog Card Number: 2002067593

ISBN 0-440-23742-4

Manufactured in the United States of America
Published simultaneously in Canada

OPM   10   9   8   7   6   5   4   3   2   1

This one's in memory of Peter Barton

There are two tragedies in life.
One is not to get your heart's desire.
The other is to get it.
—George Bernard Shaw

If the desire to kill and the opportunity
to kill came always together,
who would escape hanging?
—Mark Twain

PROLOGUE

1997

If Kelda James hadn't been wearing inch-and-a-half heels and the toilet paper roll hadn't been empty, Rosa Alija would probably be dead.

At about ten-twenty that morning Kelda had excused herself from her fellow FBI agents and followed directions to the rest room—down the long hall, go left, last door on the right. The bathroom was a step up from what she had expected to find, given the tacky condition of the rest of the building. She was relieved to see that the sink was reasonably clean and the toilet seat wasn't stained with yellow coins of urine. The only problem was that there was no toilet paper on the cardboard roll.

Kelda stepped back out into the hall to retrace her route and retrieve her shoulder bag and its stash of tissues, but noticed a closet marked "Utility" adjacent to the bathroom. The knob on the door wasn't locked and she found herself staring into a space about six feet square. A window was mounted high on the wall, dividing the small room in half. A jumble of brooms and mops leaned against a cracked porcelain sink on one side; the opposite side was stacked with particleboard shelves piled high with what appeared to be a lifetime supply of paper towels, soap, disinfectants, and toilet paper. Kelda reached onto an upper shelf for a fresh roll of toilet tissue and reflexively glanced over the sill and out the window as she rotated back toward the door.

The window overlooked the alley behind the building. Across the alley was the back of a single-story light-industrial building not noticeably different from the one that Kelda and her FBI colleagues had just raided.

Except for the hand.

Kelda was sure that for a split second she had glimpsed a hand in a window of the building across the alley. In her mind she was already considering it to have been a tiny hand, a child's hand.

She approached the utility closet window, stood on her toes, and peered again at the building across the alley. No hand. She raised her fingers to the sill to hold herself up and examined the distant window in detail. The bottom edge of the cloudy pane was streaked with parallel vertical lines that could have been made by fingers.

Tiny fingers. Child's fingers.

"Oh my God," she said.

• • • •

Fresh out of the FBI Academy, Special Agent Kelda James had been in the Denver, Colorado, field office for all of five weeks. Her initial assignment was to a squad that investigated white-collar crime, and that morning she had been ordered to accompany three other agents— all male, all senior to her, all somewhere between significantly and maximally apprehensive of her skills— to serve a federal warrant and raid a company called Account Assistants, Inc., on Delaware Street in Denver's Golden Triangle neighborhood. The company did contract billing for medical practices, and the raid was intended to collect evidence of suspected Medicare fraud.

For an FBI white-collar crime squad, this was routine stuff.

Prior to entering the FBI Academy, Kelda had earned her credentials as a certified public accountant and had spent a few years investigating fraud for an international insurance company. Her role in the raid of Account Assistants, Inc., was to cover the back door as the raid started and, later, to use her forensic accounting background to help make certain that the agents didn't fail to retrieve any records that they might ultimately need to press their case against the firm.

Most important, though, she knew that her primary responsibility was to remember at all times that she was the new guy, or in FBI parlance, "the fucking new guy." Her primary responsibility was not to screw up.

Later in the day, after she and the other agents had finished collecting the evidence and had transported the boxes back to the Denver Field Office, Kelda figured that she—the fucking new guy—would be the one who would be assigned to spend the next few weeks sitting at her Bureau desk examining the mind-numbing details of the service and billing records, trying to use Account Assistants, Inc.'s own numbers to prove the fraud case that had spawned the warrant and the raid.

It's what she did. And she knew she did it well.

That was what she was contemplating when she saw the hand flash across the window a second time. But as swiftly as it appeared in the window, the little hand disappeared again.

A more experienced agent might have gone back to her squad, reported what she'd seen, and asked one of her colleagues to accompany her across the alley to investigate the fleeting hand. A more experienced agent—one who wasn't a bookish young woman with an accounting degree whose colleagues called her Clarice behind her back—would have been less concerned about the scorn she would suffer if she pulled a fellow agent—or two, or three—away from important work to search the back of an adjacent building because she *thought* that *maybe* she had seen a child's hand in the bottom of a window.

Kelda could only imagine the relentless ridicule she would endure from her fellow agents after word spread in the field office that she had begged for assistance in checking out what would probably turn out to be nothing more nefarious than an unlicensed day-care facility.

Kelda moved out of the utility closet, closed the door, and took three steps farther down the hall to a door that was marked "Exit." An hour and a half earlier she'd stood in the alley on the other side of this very door in case any of the principals of Account Assistants, Inc., tried to flee out the back as the FBI team announced the raid and the warrant was served by the agents who entered the building through the door at the front.

She checked the inside of the exit door for an alarm: She couldn't spot any electronic devices attached to the heavy door that would announce that she had opened it. She stepped outside, propped the door open with a softball-sized piece of concrete, and then jogged across the alley to the window with the streaky glass and the disappearing tiny hand.

Two days before, six-year-old Rosa Alija had vanished from the playground of her elementary school's summer day camp near Thirty-second and Federal on Denver's near west side. The other children on the playground told police conflicting tales of a van or truck that was gray or brown and one man was white or two men who were black or two men and a woman who were all kinds of different combinations of races and colors who had waited for a child to chase a ball into the field adjacent to the school and then, when Rosa Alija had been that child, had scooped her up, covered her mouth, and carried her away in the van or truck.

Some of the child witnesses reported that Rosa had kicked her legs and cried. Others maintained she was already dead by the time she got to the van.

No adult reported seeing a thing.

And no one had seen Rosa since. The girl's frantic parents, an independent landscaper named José Alija and his receptionist wife, Maria, waited in vain for a ransom demand. But neither the police nor the local FBI office expected to hear from Rosa's abductors. The Alijas weren't the type of family who were chosen for a kidnapping for ransom.

Rosa Alija had been taken for some other purpose.

Denver mobilized in an unprecedented fashion to find the girl. Hundreds of citizens—Hispanic, white, black, Native American, Asian—searched the city for little Rosa. Posses of private citizens scoured the banks of the South Platte River and Cherry Creek. The huge expanse of rail yard between her school and Lower Downtown was searched, and the interior of every last boxcar in the yard was examined. Her picture was featured on the front page of both daily papers, and the quest to find her dominated the local TV and radio news.

Bloodhounds tracked her route away from the school. The dogs seemed confident that her abductor had taken her down Speer Boulevard after the kidnapping, but the hounds lost the scent near the spot where Speer intersected with Interstate 25. The cops knew that once Rosa's abductors had her on Denver's main freeway, they could have taken her anywhere.

Anywhere. The Rocky Mountains, the Great Plains, the Great Basin. North to Wyoming, south to New Mexico. Anywhere.

Even into the back room of a light-industrial building in one of Denver's transitional urban neighborhoods.

The bottom of the window in the building across the alley was level with the top of Kelda's head. She listened for the sounds of children playing, but all she heard was the sough of distant traffic on Speer Boulevard; she heard nothing to convince herself that she'd stumbled onto a day-care facility. A moment's contemplation failed to suggest any other good reason that a small child would be scratching at the glass in a back room in a building in this neighborhood.

Kelda grabbed a discarded plastic milk crate from the alley and carried it back toward the window to check and see what was inside the building.

Before she had a chance to step onto the crate, she saw the hand again. It was reaching, groping, the fingers extended against the bottom edge of the pane, but they could only stay there for a second or two. Kelda imagined that every time the girl lifted her hand someone else was yanking it right back down.

Most of the doubt about what she had discovered evaporated from Kelda's mind. *Rosa Alija,* she was hoping. *It's Rosa Alija.* But even in her head, the thought was only a whisper. If hope was the balloon, reality was the ballast.

What if it's not?

For the first time since Kelda had graduated from the Academy, she withdrew her handgun from its holster with the clear understanding that she might be about to fire it. The Sig Sauer felt almost weightless in her hand as she stepped up onto the crate. Her confidence grew; Kelda's best days in training at Quantico were the days that her Sig weighed about as much as a glove. She knew instantly that this was going to be one of those days.

The filth on the glass and the dark interior of the room kept Kelda from peering inside. For a split second she considered returning to Account Assistants to collect her colleagues, but she was already fearing what would happen if she left the little girl alone for another minute. She decided that she would use her radio to summon the other agents the moment she was absolutely certain that she had indeed found the abducted child.

The building had a small loading dock that faced the alley. She pulled herself onto the narrow cement shelf of the dock and tried the big door. It was locked tight. She hopped back down and moved to the side of the building. The long cinder-block wall was interrupted by a solitary steel door that was secured by a hasp and padlock. Around the front, two old newspapers still in their delivery bags littered the sidewalk at the main entrance. A big "For Lease" sign hung in the window, and three or four flyers were stuffed in the mail slot. Kelda put pressure on the handle of the glass entrance door. It didn't give.

Whatever this place once was, it wasn't in business anymore.

She returned to the side door. The bolt on the lock was in place, but the hasp seemed to be beginning to break free of whatever was holding it to the cinder block. She searched the weeds behind her and found a rusty length of angle iron, jammed it behind the hasp, and began to pry the steel hasp away from the wall.

After two minutes of constant pressure, the fasteners securing the hasp gave way and the door creaked inward half an inch.

Kelda had made a hundred armed entries into buildings during her training at Quantico. Maybe two hundred. She knew the drill. She knew where to look, what to say, how to hold her weapon.

She also knew not to do it alone.

In one minute, she promised herself, she'd call for help. Right after she was sure that Rosa Alija was safe and that her kidnapper couldn't spirit her away to some new location before the cavalry arrived.

Once inside the door, Kelda turned left toward the back of the building and stopped. Her gun was in her hand. It was not pointed at the ceiling; it was pointed in front of her. Why? Because that's what the FBI had taught her. Why? Because, as one instructor had shouted at a classmate during a drill, "very few fucking UNSUBs are going to be waiting on the ceiling."

She listened for any indication that the building was occupied. She heard nothing, and the stale air she was breathing confirmed her impression that the building was probably not being used.

She paced silently across the empty loading area until she confronted a closed door. The door, she figured, should lead to the room with the window. With the same gentle squeeze she would use to compress a trigger, she put pressure on the knob. It was locked.

She thought she heard a whimper.

Kelda's heart was cleaving. *She thinks he's coming back, that's why she's crying.* Kelda swallowed, checked her breathing.

He could come back any second.

Any second.

Her breathing grew faster, shallower. She realized there was a possibility she hadn't considered: *Maybe he's already in there with her.*

Kelda retreated across the loading area and backed into the hallway. She keyed her handheld radio. She'd decided not to communicate any doubt about her discovery: she'd already wasted too much time—she couldn't afford to give the other agents a reason to delay.

"Gary?" Gary Cross was the supervising agent of her

squad. He was a fifty-year-old black man who seemed sincerely interested in helping her adjust to the curious culture of the FBI. He also seemed sincerely interested in making certain that no one else recognized how helpful he was being to her.

"Gary?" she repeated.

"Yeah? Where the hell are you? Get back here. We need you to look at something."

In a throaty whisper she said, "I've just stumbled on Rosa Alija. You know, the little girl who was kidnapped? I'm in the building directly across the back alley from you. The door on the west side is open. The girl's in a room that faces the alley. I need backup. Hot."

"What? You found Rosa Alija?"

His reply had been too loud. Cursing silently, Kelda fumbled with the volume on the radio. "Gary, please confirm. I have a feeling I'm not alone here."

She actually heard a clatter of footsteps before she heard him say, "We're on our way."

The door that led from the loading area to the adjacent room opened slowly. Kelda could hear it squeak. She couldn't see the doorway, though, from where she was standing; she had melded herself against the cheap walnut paneling that lined the hallway.

A male voice called out, "Who is it? Who's there?" He was breathing loudly through his mouth. She listened to his footfalls and knew that the man had taken two steps before he repeated, "Who is it? Is somebody there?"

She tried to analyze the accent. *What is it? A little bit of East Texas? Or is that more Louisiana?*

The man took another step. One more, she figured,

and he'd be able to see her where she was standing in the hall.

Kelda turned to face where he'd be after his next step, slid her left foot forward into an ideal shooting stance, and said crisply, "Federal agent! Get down! Drop your weapon!" Before the last words had passed her lips, a gunshot pierced the seam of the paneling across the hall from her. The hole in the wood was at chest height. After a half-a-heartbeat delay, two more shots followed. One was higher, the other was lower, inches from her waist. The shooter was covering his bases, bracketing his shots like a photographer unsure of the light.

She heard a shuffled step; she interpreted the noise to mean that he'd moved away from her, not toward her.

Intuitively, she was sure that he was retreating now, intent on barricading himself in the room with little Rosa. Kelda knew she couldn't permit that. The situation she'd walked into would be exponentially more difficult if the UNSUB could use the little girl as a hostage.

Staying low, she sprang forward, dove, and rolled across the loading area, finally coming to rest in a prone position eight feet away from where she'd been hiding in the hall. As she moved she heard more shots—two, three, four. She wasn't sure exactly how many. She did feel confident that none of them had entered her body.

Rolling to a stop, Kelda jammed her elbows against the floor, the 9mm poised and ready. Within a fraction of a second she fixed the man's torso in her sight and in rapid succession fired three times into the black-and-white target that she imagined was pinned to the center of his chest.

Each impact caused him to jerk a little, as though

he'd hiccupped. He didn't drop his gun right away. She released a fourth round and kept light pressure on the trigger until he fell. It took every bit of discipline she'd acquired in her training to refrain from emptying her clip into him.

The room, she thought, smelled like the range at Quantico.

It was as comforting as the aroma of a lover's sweat.

Two or three seconds passed. Through the haze of what she had just done she saw the silhouettes of two of her colleagues as they entered the building through the side door. She held up her left hand to them to tell them to wait where they were. "I'm okay, Gary," she called. "The UNSUB is down. Let me go in and get the girl." The reverberation of the gunshots still echoed in her head, so she couldn't hear her own words as she spoke, and wondered if she'd said them loudly enough for Gary to hear her.

Kelda stood and stepped over to the man she'd shot, keeping the Sig pointed at his head until she was able to kick his weapon farther away from his hand. The handgun the man had fired at her was a monstrous .45; she shuddered at the thought of being hit by one of the gun's slugs.

The UNSUB on the floor was slight. He wore new Adidas, a clean pair of jeans, and a white shirt with the sleeves rolled up to his elbows. His shirt was untucked and his belt was undone.

The man had fallen on his side, facing away from her, and she couldn't detect any sign that he was still breathing. His rimless eyeglasses sat cockeyed on his head. She didn't see much blood, just three dark circles

on the back of his shirt. She wondered if she'd somehow lost the fourth round that she'd fired, though she
couldn't imagine how that could have happened.

Her Sig at the ready, she crouched beside him and
checked his pulse.

Nothing.

Standing erect over him, she said, "Damn you. Don't
die, asshole. Don't you dare die."

In order to control an impulse to kick him in the face,
she stepped back away from the man. Then she inhaled
twice to quiet the echo of the exact same impulse. In her
peripheral vision she saw Gary move into the room like
a bishop striking from the corner of a chessboard.

"Get the girl," he said. His voice competed unsuccessfully with the echoes of the gunshot; he sounded
as though he was trying to get her attention across a
crowded bar. But she knew what he had said.

Three quick steps forward took her into the room
with the window that faced the alley.

Rosa was kneeling sideways on a mattress, wearing
only a pink T-shirt with a filthy picture of Big Bird on it.
The little girl's face was wound with duct tape. One of
her skinny arms was manacled to a chain that was
bolted to a D-ring that was anchored to the wall.

She was weeping.

"Hi, baby," Kelda said. "I'm here to take you home."

Kelda was weeping, too.

PART ONE

Taunting the Hangman

CHAPTER

I can just walk out that door? That's what you're saying?"

The warden held back a smile and said, "You can stay here if you'd like. But if you do, I'll have to start charging you room and board. I can pretty much guarantee you won't like the rates."

The two men were standing in the sterile public lobby of the Colorado State Penitentiary. The spacious front room of the modern prison was all concrete and light. Some tile. It only hinted at what was inside— "inside" meaning the other side of the security doors.

Just hinted.

A dozen steps away, near the guards who acted as the gatekeepers/ receptionists for the public, one of the warden's assistants leaned against the wall.

From where the warden stood near the front doors,

the tall, electrified chain-link fences were visible through the glass, and above them coiled rows of concertina sparkled with the earliest indication of a summer dawn. Beyond the fences, miles of high prairie loomed. Beyond that, the Rocky Mountains hovered ominously.

Tom Clone's mind wasn't on the far horizon yet. He found himself examining the details of the room. He was uncomfortable with its unfamiliarity, and with its spaciousness. He said, "How do I get somewhere? I mean somewhere else besides here?"

"Your lawyer's sending someone to get you. I would guess they should be here anytime now."

"So that's it?" Clone asked the warden. He fingered the collar of his new knit shirt with his left hand and touched the money in his pants pocket with the fingers of his right. "After thirteen years here, I sign some papers, get a hundred bucks and some clothes from Kmart, and then I'm . . . gone? That's it?"

"You want a brass band maybe? Some dancing girls? With a little more notice, maybe . . ."

"That's not what I mean."

"Most guys don't get the ride from their lawyer, Tom. All they get is a cold seat in a big bus to Pueblo or Denver." *Usually get themselves a round-trip ticket, too,* the warden thought, but he didn't say it. He was pondering the question of whether—no, when—he'd be welcoming Tom Clone back again.

"Most guys who leave here aren't innocent, Warden."

The warden shrugged. "You ask them, they'll tell you they are. Don't ask them, most of them will tell you they are anyway."

"But most guys who walk out that door don't have

DNA tests on the murder weapon to back up their contention."

The warden considered his reply before he said, "I suppose they don't, Tom. I suppose they don't."

The inmate's sharp eyes read the time on the warden's Timex. "Why is this happening at five o'clock in the morning? Why not during the day?"

Completely deadpan, the warden said, "What? You wanted to sleep in? Damn, I hate it when the guests don't make their requests clear. We try so hard to please." He made a compassionate face. "Other than this one early wake-up call, you weren't disappointed with anything else during your stay, were you?"

"It's a serious question, Warden. I've never been released from prison before, but I'd be surprised to learn that it usually involves a personal visit with the warden and an opportunity to watch the sun rise."

"Well, if it's a serious question, then here's a serious answer. Once I actually received the order from the judge in Park County last night, I knew you were going elsewhere. Getting you out of here at dawn was my idea. Why? Because I don't want to give the press a chance to get themselves organized for your release, which they still think is scheduled for sometime this afternoon. As far as I'm concerned you can have your dog-and-pony show with the ACLU and the Innocence Project someplace else besides in my prison."

Tom didn't expect the honesty. He lifted his eyebrows involuntarily.

"As a general rule," the warden continued, "I'm not a big fan of commotion. You may have noticed over the years that we don't hold too many unnecessary group functions around here."

Tom Clone's eyes swept the big room again before they settled back on the warden. There was a time when Clone might have appreciated the sardonic nature of the man. But thirteen years living alone in a concrete room on death row had dulled his sense of irony. Anyway, the warden was a stranger to him, and Tom wasn't sure what to make of him. He'd noticed that the entire time they'd been talking the big man's tongue was busy in his mouth, as though maybe he had a poppy seed stuck someplace he'd rather not have one, and he'd really like to have a toothpick.

The warden looked away for a second or two before he returned his gaze to Clone. "Tom? You don't mind that I call you Tom, do you? Good. Listen, if you're waiting for an apology from me—and I'm beginning to suspect that you are—don't waste your energy. You won't get one. The courts told me to lock you up, and I did that. And now the courts have told me to let you go, so I'm doing that. I make it a practice not to apologize for doing my job."

Tom said, "How'd you know that's what I was thinking?"

"It's what I'd be thinking if I was standing in your boots." Both men looked down. "Or your cheap sneakers, as the case may be."

Tom Clone laughed. He heard the noise as though it had come from someone else. He thought, *That was my first laughter as a free man,* and said, "So what else might I be thinking?"

"Scared thoughts. Unless you're a fool, if you're not scared already, you'll be scared soon. Something tells me you're not a fool. You'll be scared soon. You can bet on it."

"I've been watching my back for thirteen years, Warden. Fear is nothing new for me."

"Not that kind of scared. Though that kind won't go away for a while, either. I'm talking scared that life's passed you by. Thirteen years is a long time to be institutionalized. Back then, you still had a life ahead of you; you were a hotshot kid who was about to become a doctor. Now you're an old-timer. You're used to this place. To us, to our ways. To being a small man in a small world."

The warden pointed out the door. "You don't know shit about what's outside that door anymore, and people on the outside are going to hear where you've been all this time and they're going to treat you like a con. That's scary to you already, or it damn well should be."

The words made him nervous, but Tom shook his head stubbornly. "I'm leaving here an innocent man. It's going to be different for me out there than it is for other people who walk out that door."

"Maybe. Maybe not. Some people may believe you're innocent, but most won't. Sorry, but that's just the way it is. Look, that there's your ride, I bet." He pointed at a green Buick sedan that was pulling into the otherwise empty visitors' lot half a football field away. "Good luck, son. You'll need it more than you know." He pushed the door open. "Now grab your duffel and get out of here before somebody up in Park County comes to their senses."

Tom hesitated as though he didn't trust what the man had said. Finally, he leaned down, picked up the blue canvas bag that was filled with his few personal belongings, and began to walk away. As Tom Clone cleared the front door and took his first steps outside as a free man, the warden's assistant sauntered forward and stood beside his boss. "How about twenty bucks?"

The warden replied, "I said I'll do up to fifty. But it's your call, Hank. If I were you, I'd save my money."

"Twenty's fine, Warden."

The concrete path that led through the gate in the fence ran about fifty yards to the parking lot. Almost exactly halfway down the path, Tom Clone tossed his duffel far ahead of him and immediately sprang forward. He took a little hop, picked up some speed, and launched himself into a cartwheel. When he completed the cartwheel—which he accomplished with some skill— he leaned backward and then, with an additional little push of his strong legs and a fluid thrust of his arms, he finished with a nicely executed back flip.

He planted the landing well. Only one little extraneous hop.

The warden held out his hand; the assistant warden carpeted his boss's palm with a twenty-dollar bill. "How did you know he'd do that?"

"For the last month, since the rumors started about him getting out, that's how he's been spending his hour a week in the yard. Cartwheels and back flips. Cartwheels and back flips. Over and over again. I figured we were going to have a little recital as he left."

The assistant shook his head and said, "Damn. I think these guys can't surprise me anymore and then . . ." He let the morning breeze carry the thought across the high prairie.

Eyes still on Tom Clone, the warden said, "I can't tell you how glad I am that there weren't any news cameras here to see him do that. I would have had to watch his gymnastics twenty more times on the news.

There would have been a thousand e-mails and everybody including the governor would have been calling wondering how we could have allowed him to do that."

"That's why we were up at four o'clock in the morning? So the press wouldn't see him play Olga Korbut?"

"Nadia Comaneci. But yeah, that's the only damn reason."

Tom Clone finished his back flip and pumped both fists into the air. Before he could shriek in exaltation, he heard a woman's voice behind him.

"Tom Clone? Mr. Clone?"

Even before he turned toward the sound, he was drinking in the novelty of the melody of a female voice that didn't belong to a guard. He reflexively inhaled, hoping the woman was wearing perfume. The morning breeze carried her scent. He wasn't disappointed.

The woman he faced was lovely. She was silhouetted against the mountains, but he could tell that her dark hair was tied back behind her head and that her face was adorned with little makeup. She wore white jeans and had on a claret-colored leather jacket that was zipped up to her throat.

He inhaled her perfume again.

"Mr. Clone?" she said once more.

He nodded and thrust out his hand. She didn't touch it. She kept her free hand by her side, while the other stayed atop the leather bag that hung from her shoulder.

Finally, he spoke. He said, "Yes, I'm Tom Clone."

"Hello," the woman said. "I'm Special Agent Kelda James of the FBI. Your attorney asked me to come to get you this morning. I'm your ride out of here. Welcome back to freedom."

Upon hearing her name, his impulse was to rush in and hug her, but he sensed her reticence and held himself back. He'd had a lot of recent practice with restraint. "Kelda James. My God, you're the one who . . . who—"

"Yes," she said. "I am that one."

He stepped forward and hugged her. Despite her stiffness at the embrace, the contour of a female body against his was almost overwhelming to him.

"Thank you," he said into her hair. "Thank you, thank you."

"Please let go of me, Mr. Clone. Please."

He did, and took a step back from her as well. Her voice carried that kind of authority.

"Those are all your things?" she asked.

"Yes," he said. "I donated everything else to Goodwill."

The lines of her mouth softened into the slightest grin. "Let's go, then," she said.

CHAPTER

1989

Martha Reese was red-eyed and her lime green apron was stained with cherry juice and almost perfectly parallel drools of her own vomit. She was shaking so badly that water was sloshing out of the cup she tried to hold in her hands. The cup was decorated with pictures of the Car Guys from NPR. The guys were laughing.

"I came over here for a cup of sugar, I swear. I know it sounds like a cliché but it's true. I bought a bucket of sour cherries this morning from a roadside stand out on the highway—you know the one by the turnoff to town?—and I was busy making pies and I totally misjudged how much sugar I'd need, and I just flat ran out. It happens, it does, even to experienced bakers.

"I knew the Greens were visiting their kids in California, but the lights were on at their place and the house sitter's car was out front, so I walked down the road to try to borrow some sugar. Nancy doesn't bake, but I'm sure she has sugar. I mean everybody has sugar. Maybe not diabetics, I suppose, but that's not the Greens. They're not diabetics. I'm telling the truth. I promise."

A young sheriff's deputy sat across from her on a hard teak chair on the front porch of the Greens' house. It didn't even cross the young cop's mind that Mrs. Reese wasn't telling the truth about the cup of sugar and the Greens not being diabetics.

Only a couple of hundred yards or so separated the cabin that Martha Reese shared with her husband—"It's really a house. I don't know why everybody calls them cabins"—and the Greens' home. The evergreen forest was sparse on the county road between the homes, and a dry spring had left the lane especially dusty. Summer hadn't even officially arrived, yet Park County was already a tinderbox. The neighbors were talking about what they could do to make sure that illegal campers or kids with fireworks didn't set the whole mountainside ablaze by the Fourth of July.

Martha was a few pounds overweight—"Okay, maybe twenty"—and regretted not driving up the hill for the sugar. As she climbed up to the Greens' place she was struggling to keep her breathing even and was more than a little embarrassed about the sweat that was dotting her upper lip and dripping in a rivulet down her spine. The sun had sunk behind the Divide but the early evening temperature was still in the seventies.

"Some people might not consider that warm, but I do. For us up here, that's a little warm for the evening."

She and Nancy Green weren't close—"They're more modern people than us. But we get along, you know?" The Greens and the Reeses were good mountain neighbors. They shared plowing expenses in the winter and pooled their resources to get deadwood cleared from the land around their homes in the summer. Nancy Green was comfortable stopping by to borrow Italian parsley—"I probably shouldn't admit this, but I didn't even know what it was. Why can't the Italians just use regular parsley?"—and Martha was comfortable going up the hill for sugar when she ran out while baking sour cherry pies.

Martha dreaded the final steep climb from the road up the driveway to the Greens' house. At the base of the driveway she actually considered going all the way back to her house and getting her car. But she didn't.

The Greens didn't have a regular doorbell; they had one of those speakerphone systems attached to their telephone. The apparatus made Martha uncomfortable. She was never quite sure what to do—"Am I supposed to lean over and speak into the little box or can they hear me if I speak regular?" She just didn't know. Nor did she understand why someone would want something like that living up in the mountains. It wasn't as though anybody but neighbors ever knocked on anybody's doors up in Park County. "You know as well as I do that we don't get too many Mormons or Jehovah's Witnesses walking around up here trying to get you to read their funny books. It just doesn't happen. I suppose we aren't worth the effort, or something."

Martha hit the button on the speakerphone but no

one answered. She hit it one more time, but again, no reply. She wondered, of course, if maybe she was operating the thing incorrectly, so she went ahead and knocked, using the heavy brass knocker that said "The Greens" in raised letters that looked a little Gothic. After waiting a few minutes for a reply, she decided to check out behind the house. The Greens had a spa—"We call them hot tubs around here. But Nancy calls theirs a 'spa.' Who can figure, right?"—on the big deck behind their house, and Martha wondered if the house sitter might be using it, though lolling around in a swirling pool of hot water was about the last thing that Martha could have imagined doing right then. Martha had met the house sitter, a nice enough girl named Ivy, a couple of times but didn't know whether she was a hot-tub-on-a-blistering-summer-evening type of person.

Martha followed the path on the south side of the house—"I've been here before and that's the best way to get to the back"—and climbed the cedar stairs to the big deck. She paused at the top of the stairs and admired the view to the east—"It's a much nicer view than ours. You wouldn't think a couple of hundred yards would make such a difference, but it does. We see mostly treetops from our cabin, but the Greens have a view with a capital *V*."

The spa wasn't being used, though. Without a breeze to mask the sound, Martha could tell that the water wasn't even gurgling beneath the fancy gazebo-type thing on the far corner of the deck. She peered through the wall of windows that led outside from the back of the house.

"I knew right away something was wrong. Why? Simple. The water was running in the kitchen sink. I could see it from the window. It was just running right down the drain. Nobody was standing there using it; it was just running. The sliding glass door was open, so . . ."

Martha kicked her favorite Merrell clogs off her feet—"Nancy has a thing about shoes in her house, like she is part Japanese or something. Not that I have anything against the Japanese, believe me, I don't"—and hustled over to the sink to shut off the water.

"I didn't see Ivy at first; my eyes were on the sink. Yours would have been, too. They would have. The water was just running and running. It gets your attention, something like that does."

What happened on the way from the back door to the sink was that Martha stepped in Ivy's blood.

"It was still just the slightest bit warm and it just squished right up through my toes. I didn't know it was blood, of course. If I'd known that . . ." She didn't finish the thought. "I thought something warm was spilled on the floor, like hot chocolate or soup or something like that. I did think soup for some reason, I don't know why, but I kept going for the sink. I really wanted to turn off that running water. None of us have enough faith in our wells that we'll waste water like that, especially when it's been so dry out like it has been this spring. Every time one of us has to drill a new well, we have to drill deeper than the last one did. The well we dug summer before last had to be drilled 262 feet deep. I don't have to tell you how much that cost us, do I? I didn't think so."

The Greens' sink was on the other side of their kitchen island—"We don't have an island in our house. Just a sink built into the counter below the kitchen window. The regular way, you know." Martha shut off the water and grabbed a big handful of paper towels to wipe up the hot chocolate or soup or whatever it was that Ivy had spilled on the floor. She was guessing that Ivy must have been taking a shower or something. "That's when I saw the footprints—turned out they were my own footprints—across the kitchen tile. I realized right then and there that I'd stepped in blood. I don't know of one single kind of soup that would leave footprints that color. Maybe beet soup. But beets and I don't get along, if you know what I mean. Who makes beet soup, anyway? Russians do, right?"

Martha reported that when she recognized exactly what it was that she had stepped in, she tried to scream but couldn't get the sound to escape her throat. She thought about going for the phone to call 911. She thought about running back out the door. Then she looked up and saw Ivy and she fell backward against the island. "That's when I knocked that big bowl on the floor. It's where Nancy kept her fresh fruit. In that bowl. That's why there are plums all over the floor. I did that. The plums, I mean. I'm so sorry."

She had to make herself look at Ivy again. "She was sitting in the corner behind the kitchen table on one of those big chrome chairs that Nancy has in her breakfast nook. Her head was hanging off to the side because somebody had cut right through her neck all the way to the bone. I could see the bone."

Martha was surprised that she didn't faint. "I should have fainted, don't you think? Seeing something like that? I'll probably have nightmares for the rest of my life. The whole rest of my life."

The young deputy who had been first to arrive at the Greens' house in response to Martha's frantic call to 911 just let her talk and talk. He didn't know when the detectives would arrive to take over, but he wasn't at all eager to go back inside the house anyway. He'd already seen all he wanted to see. He held his hat in his hand and he nodded almost the whole time that the woman spoke.

Martha sipped from the water she held in her hands and asked, "Is it all right if I clean between my toes, Officer? Or is that considered evidence?"

CHAPTER

3

June 1989

A girlfriend of Ivy Campbell's who was in nursing school at the medical center had told her about the deal: twenty dollars to sit through an interview with a medical student who was practicing basic interviewing skills during his senior psychiatry rotation. She'd spend sixty to ninety minutes answering questions about her life—that was it. Math wasn't her strong suit, but Ivy figured she would be making at least thirteen or fourteen dollars an hour, way more than the seven-thirty she was making at the new mall in Cherry Creek. The medical school interview would be videotaped, but the tape would be destroyed at the end of the semester. Her confidentiality, she was promised, was assured.

For Ivy, twenty bucks meant a night out drinking with her girlfriends or a concert ticket at Red Rocks or, if she went early enough in the season, a lift ticket at

Copper or Winter Park. She could spare a couple of hours for that.

She arrived at the Health Sciences Center at Ninth and Colorado in Denver a few minutes early for her two o'clock appointment and found her way to a sterile classroom on the third floor of a brick building that didn't seem anywhere near as close to the library as she'd been told.

A woman greeted her in the classroom, checked her in, and explained that her interviewer hadn't arrived quite yet.

Ivy smiled, pointed to the clock on the wall above the blackboard, and said, "In two minutes the meter starts running, right?"

The woman who had checked her in was a skinny black woman in a horizontally striped dress and black-framed glasses. She shook her head disdainfully. "These med students, let me tell you, I think one of the first things they learn in medical school is how to keep people waiting for them. They go through life like everybody's sitting reading an old *People* magazine with nothing better to do than wait for them to show up."

Ivy liked the woman immediately. She smiled again. "I don't mind the waiting as long as I'm being paid. You're on the clock, too, I bet. Hi, I'm Ivy," she said.

"Bertha." She bowed about thirty degrees from the waist. "I'm a department secretary. Trust me, this isn't my normal gig. I'm filling in for a friend who talked an ob-gyn resident into a free ultrasound of her baby."

"Cool. What department do you work in?"

"Psychiatry."

Ivy lifted her eyebrows.

Bertha said, "Yeah. Exactly. Oooh, I hear footsteps. It may be our young doctor, only a few minutes late."

The young "doctor"—white lab coat and all—walked right past the open door of the classroom before he doubled back, poked his head inside the door, and said, "Is this where I'm supposed to be?"

Bertha sighed.

Ivy replied. "Cosmically speaking, the answer to that question, I think, is always yes."

Bertha almost choked as she swallowed her laughter. She covered herself by looking down at her list. She asked, "You Clone?"

One hand went to the stethoscope that was hanging around his neck. He didn't seem to know how to respond. Ivy feared for a moment that he was going to need to check his white plastic nametag before he answered Bertha's question. Instead, he nodded.

Bertha said, "Good. This is Ivy Campbell. She's your interview. Ivy Campbell, this is Thomas Clone. He's your senior medical student." Ivy noted that Bertha emphasized the word "senior."

Bertha faced Thomas Clone. "A/V promises me the camera's all ready to go. Just hit 'record' when you're ready to start the interview. I'll be back in about an hour to get the tape. Any questions?"

Ivy said, "You promise you'll send me a check?"

Bertha shook the paperwork in her hand. "We will, Ivy, you have my word. You call me yourself if there are any problems. Anything else? Dr. Clone? No? Fine then. You two be good, now. You promise?"

Ivy said, "Later, Bertha."

"You, too, girl."

Clone's hand flew to his hip. "That's my pager. I

have to get that." His eyes flitted around the room. "There's no phone in here."

Ivy walked over to the video camera, hit the "record" button, and held her watch up to the lens for about five seconds. She said, "Do whatever you would like, Dr. Clone. As of now, we're on the clock." She sat on the chair that she guessed was intended for her and pulled a copy of *Entertainment Weekly* from her backpack. "I'll be here whenever you're ready for me."

Three or four minutes later Tom Clone rushed back into the classroom. He stopped just inside the door, composed himself, which included stuffing his stethoscope into a pocket of the lab coat, and walked over to Ivy. "Hello," he said. "I'm Dr. Clone. How do you do?" He offered her his hand.

"Hi, I'm Ivy Campbell." She didn't release his hand. After about ten seconds he realized that he was going to have to yank it away from her. He did and sat down on a chair five feet away.

"We're, uh, just going to talk a little bit about your life here, uh, today, Ms. Campbell."

Tom Clone was handsome enough, Ivy thought, in a my-God-he's-too-young-to-be-a-doctor kind of way. Nice shoulders. Good hair. Really, really nice eyes. "You can call me Ivy."

"Thank you, Ivy." He still hadn't actually looked at her for more than a few seconds.

"This is an unusual situation, isn't it?" she asked.

"I'm not sure what you mean."

"Usually when I go to the doctor—when anyone goes

to the doctor, probably—I'm kind of nervous, certainly more nervous than the doctor. But today, you're more nervous. Way more nervous. That's what's unusual."

"Um, yes, well. That may, um, be true." He flicked a glance her way. "Today, anyway. Now, would you like to tell me something about yourself?"

"Do you think I'm pretty?" She knew she wasn't giving him a chance. Nor did she intend to.

The trouble was, Tom didn't just think Ivy was pretty; Tom Clone thought she was gorgeous. Her fine hair was such a glistening mahogany color that it seemed to be radiating. Her eyes were so bright and deep, he felt as though he were looking into them the way he'd examine tropical fish in an aquarium. Her legs were so long—he didn't finish the thought. "Yes, um, well—why don't you tell me about yourself?"

"Do you like hamburgers and beer?" Ivy asked.

"Excuse me?"

"Ever been to the Cherry Cricket? It's in Cherry Creek, behind Sears? They have great burgers. Awesome, actually. Almost perfect burgers."

"Um. I, uh . . ."

"Are you allowed to ask me out to dinner? Like on a date? Even though we've done this interview thing?"

"I suppose. I'm—"

"Good. I was hoping you could. How about the Cherry Cricket this weekend? Saturday? Is nine okay?"

"Um, yes. Yes, nine's okay. I'm not . . . I'm not really sure it's something I should do but, yes, nine's okay."

"And then maybe we'll do a movie? But I pick, okay? I have a thing about movies. I get nervous."

"Sure. A movie. Yes."

"Great. My address is on the sheet that Bertha has. Pick me up. And don't be late, Doctor."

He looked puzzled.

"Bertha's the secretary who was here. You know, the black woman?" Ivy stood up and walked over to the video camera. She rewound the tape. "We're going to start all over, now, Dr. Clone. If you want to go back out the door and pretend you're just walking in again to start the interview, that would probably look best to your teachers. Don't you think?"

"Okay."

After he'd gone out the door and walked back into the room and repeated his introduction for the camera, she replied, "Hello, Dr. Clone, it's very nice to meet you."

Tom Clone continued, "We're going to spend a little while talking about your life here today, Ms. Campbell. Why don't you tell me about yourself?"

So she did, figuring that it would save them both some time on their first date.

CHAPTER

4

You have to put on your seat belt. It's the law now."

Tom Clone was flummoxed, totally flummoxed. The woman, the car, the perfume, the light. So much space everywhere. No guards, no shackles. No pale paint on concrete walls. He said, "What? Excuse me?"

"Your seat belt? Everybody has to wear them now. It's the law."

Now.

The word floored him. He was living *now.*

Not *then. Now.*

Tom looked down toward Kelda James's waist, saw the nylon strap stretched low across her abdomen, and noted the location of the latch beside the seat. He reached down between his own seat and the door and fumbled for his belt. It wasn't there. He felt like a fool. His last car had been a '77 Rabbit. He couldn't remember if it even had shoulder belts. He certainly couldn't remember wearing them.

"It's behind you. It comes across your shoulder. Here, like this." She removed her own belt and let it retract to its starting position before she reattached the buckle.

He mimicked her actions. "Thanks. There's so much I guess I don't know about. . . ."

"Yes," she said, confirming the thought, and started the car.

He stared back at the prison. "I wasn't even sure what the place actually looked like from the outside. When they brought me here after it opened in 1990, they did it at night. I barely remember seeing the building."

She glanced over at the shadowy complex and said, "Take away the fences, if you didn't know what it really was, it wouldn't look like much. Some kind of industrial complex."

He felt a chill crawl up his spine. "I know what it really is."

Kelda flipped open a device that was no bigger than a jumbo pack of Juicy Fruit and hit a solitary button with her thumb. He guessed the thing she was holding was a phone. Damn, they'd gotten small.

Seconds later she said, "Tony? Hope I didn't wake you but I thought you'd want to know that Tom Clone and I are driving away from the penitentiary as we speak." She paused and steered the car from the parking lot onto the street. "I think he's okay. Maybe a little overwhelmed by the suddenness of it all. You want to say hi?" She handed Tom the phone. "It's your lawyer. I think he'll be happy to hear your voice."

She saw him hesitate. "Hold the top part up by your ear. Don't worry about the other part. It won't actually reach your lips."

"Hello, Mr. Loving," Tom said. "I'm a free man, thanks to you."

The high prairie that fills the gap between the Front Range peaks of the Pike National Forest and those of the San Isabel National Forest is a desolate expanse that hasn't changed much since Native Americans were the only humans traversing the valleys. Late in June the landscape already reflected the aridity of summer, and the wind that gusted continually seemed designed by nature to suck whatever moisture it could from any living thing that had any water remaining in it. Despite the altitude, nobody of sound mind would mistake this land for mountain meadow. As a rule, meadows were green and lush. This long spread between Cañon City and Colorado Springs on the front porch of the Rocky Mountains wasn't.

With the exception of the tiny metropolis of Penrose—which isn't much of an exception at all—for the thirty-plus miles of Highway 115 that connect the prison towns of Cañon City and Florence with Colorado Springs, people reading maps don't have to check the key for any symbols at all. No towns, no cities, no tourist attractions. Nothing. The only highway signs by the side of the road are the ones that tell drivers how far it is to someplace else.

ROYAL GORGE 15 MILES

The only things that seem to grow naturally on that

high prairie are sagebrush and prisons. The years have proven that it's a hospitable environment for both.

Tom Clone finished his call with Anthony Loving as the Buick was approaching the edge of Florence. Kelda said, "Just fold it up. That shuts it off." He did and handed it back to her.

"I couldn't help overhearing," she said. "You don't want me to take you back to Cripple Creek?"

"No, there's nothing up there for me. Nothing but bad memories and injustice. Until I get settled into something and can afford my own place, I'm going to be staying with my grandfather. He lives in Boulder. Mr. Loving said he'd move the press meetings and interviews he has set up for later today up there. He said he thought you wouldn't mind dropping me at the bus station in Denver."

"I don't mind. It's actually more convenient for me than going over to Cripple Creek."

They were quiet until about five miles past Penrose, where the boundary of Fort Carson first rubs along the eastern shoulder of Highway 115. Then Tom said, "I can't get over the fact that anytime I want I can open the door to the car and just walk away. You don't know what that feels like."

She said, "If you decide to exercise that option, I hope you'll let me bring the car to a stop first."

He laughed. "I promise. You know I don't know how to thank you for what you did for me."

"Tony wanted to stay close to the courthouse, in case something came up at the last minute. The wheelchair makes it a struggle for him, anyway. When the warden called about the predawn release, Tony asked me if I was available. Thought I might be interested. I was. It's no big deal."

"I'm not talking about the ride this morning, although I'm grateful for that. I'm talking about what you did . . . for my case. Mr. Loving told me what you did to help me. I know that I wouldn't be . . . free . . . without you."

Kelda didn't respond at first—in the mirror she'd noticed the headlights of a car far behind her and then watched as they suddenly disappeared. She replied, "What you just said? That's thanks enough. Let's leave it at that."

Tom couldn't let it go. "Why did you do it?"

She squirmed and changed the position of her hands on the wheel. "I didn't do it for you, Tom. I was doing my job and it turned out that you were the beneficiary. I did it because it was the right thing to do."

"It wasn't the right thing for an FBI agent to do. You jeopardized your career for me."

She shrugged. "No, I didn't. I think the Bureau will get over it. Besides, I'm a little more bulletproof than most agents." She was making a reference to the insulation she had in the Bureau because of Rosa Alija, though she assumed that Tom Clone didn't know about Rosa Alija.

"What does that mean?" he asked.

"Nothing," she said.

"You helped a convicted murderer get off of death row? You think the FBI will forgive that? If that's true, then things have really changed since I got locked up." He paused. "I was running out of appeals, you know."

She shook her head in disagreement, but her eyes stayed focused on the rearview mirror. In the distance the pair of headlights reappeared, then flashed off again. "I don't know about that. Tony Loving seemed to think he still had a few appellate tricks up his sleeve. He wasn't convinced you were ever going to be executed. So it wasn't exactly like I had to rush right in there and pull the IV out of your arm."

Tom Clone shuddered at the image. "Mr. Loving's an optimist. Appellate lawyers have to be, I think. But appeals run out. They would have executed me, maybe later this year. Maybe next. Look what happened to Gary Davis. There were a lot of people who said he'd never actually be executed. Well, he was. Me? I thought I was running out of hope. But I didn't know about you."

"I did my job. I followed a lead. The evidence supported your release. That's all it was."

"Mr. Loving says there are a lot of people who are disappointed that I'm out."

Kelda said, "That may be true. But here's what I believe, Tom: For the death penalty to survive in this society, we have to stop using it on the wrong people. If I ended up helping you, that was my motivation. To try to protect part of our justice system. It wasn't about you."

"You support it? The death penalty?"

"I don't really want to go into that right now, if you don't mind."

He exhaled and said, "Okay."

Neither spoke for about a minute. Finally, Tom asked, "You're not working this morning, are you? I mean, it isn't actually the FBI that's giving me a ride home from prison, is it?"

"FBI agents are always working. We're just not always on duty. And I don't go back on duty until tomorrow. The Bureau has nothing to do with this, I assure you. If my SAC knew I was giving you a ride home from prison, he'd . . ." She let the thought slide away and checked the mirror again. The speck behind them was now definitely a car, and the car was closing on them so fast that Kelda glanced at her speedometer to assure herself that her Buick was actually maintaining its speed.

It was.

Kelda became concerned that the car behind her—she pegged it to be a Chevy Suburban, an old one—was going to ram her Buick from the rear, and she tensed to prepare to take an evasive maneuver onto the shoulder. But as the Suburban closed to about two hundred yards it switched into the other lane and shot past Kelda and Tom at a speed that she guessed was close to a hundred miles an hour.

Tom said, "Damn, what the hell was that?"

"I don't know," Kelda said. "Just some jerk." In half a minute the Suburban was once again a speck in the distance, this time in front of them, not behind them.

Thirty seconds later things started happening so fast that she wasn't sure whether she first lost control of the steering or whether she first heard the pop. Maybe the two events happened simultaneously. Regardless, her instincts took over. She turned the wheel in the direction she wanted the car to go, but the car had already begun fishtailing on the thin layer of sand and gravel on the highway. Within seconds the Buick had spun 180 degrees and Kelda busied herself trying to get control of the car. She found herself checking the road that had been behind her through the windshield, while in the rearview mirror she eyed the second approach of the Chevy Suburban that had zoomed past her only seconds before.

The Buick continued to skid until its two passenger-side wheels plopped off the shoulder onto the dirt. She braced herself—she feared that the car was going to flip.

Abruptly, the sideways movement stopped and the Buick came to rest on the dirt shoulder.

Tom Clone said, "Shit. That was some driving. Did we get a flat, or what?"

Kelda asked, "Are you all right?"

He nodded.

The Chevy Suburban was right on their tail now. It had crossed the road and stopped about a hundred feet away from the trunk of the Buick. As she had suspected, the grille identified it as an older model. It had once been blue, but the paint had oxidized to something that was closer to gray. The sun reflected off the windshield, obscuring the identity of the occupants. Kelda thought she saw the silhouettes of at least two people inside.

As the driver-side door opened, she reached for her handgun.

She had a feeling this wasn't a Samaritan.

CHAPTER

Fred Prehost was the lead Park County detective who showed up at the Greens' house the evening in 1989 that Ivy Campbell was murdered.

If you caught Prehost in a confessional mood over a beer some evening in one of his hangouts in Cripple Creek, he'd probably admit that the crime scene wasn't handled perfectly—not according-to-the-book perfectly—but he'd argue that, given the department's general lack of experience in dealing with violent crimes of that nature, the Park County Sheriff's Office had done a pretty darn good job of working up the murder of Ivy Campbell.

He'd tell you proudly that the neighbors who lived within a half-mile radius of the house were all interviewed before midnight the day of the crime. He wouldn't admit that given the density of the residential area in question, the canvass covered a grand total of nine families, nor would he mention that three of the nine weren't even using their Park County residences the night of the murder.

He'd boast that the land around the crime scene—a total of almost two acres—was scoured carefully for evidence by noon the next day, though he might not admit that the sheriff's deputies who walked the perimeter that had been delineated by Prehost and another detective named George Bonnet—whom everybody called Hoppy—didn't really know exactly what they were looking for while they were walking, and that they didn't collect a single piece of evidence that would ultimately be used at the trial.

Prehost would argue that the house itself was left largely undisturbed for the crime scene specialists from the Colorado Bureau of Investigation, who, he would point out repeatedly, didn't show up until *the next morning*. He certainly wouldn't specify what exceptions were included in the phrase "largely undisturbed." But he would emphasize the fact that the state criminalists seemed to take their sweet time getting themselves and their equipment to the scene.

Maybe by the time a couple of pitchers of Stroh's were empty, Fred Prehost might admit what he and the other Park County investigators didn't do correctly, and what they failed to find. One of the things they didn't do correctly was protect the dirt road and gravel driveway leading up to the Greens' home. At least a dozen different law enforcement and rescue vehicles had traveled the path up to the Greens' door by the time somebody considered that the road itself might be concealing some evidence.

What the Park County Sheriff failed to find was the murder weapon, whatever sharp object it was that had been used to almost decapitate Ivy Campbell. The coroner who did the post on Ivy Campbell's body narrowed the murder weapon down to a "large-bladed, sharp object."

Fred Prehost was confident that the "large-bladed, sharp object" was the Chicago Cutlery knife missing from the butcher-block set in the Greens' kitchen. But despite everything the detectives did to find it, the knife was never discovered.

CHAPTER

Kelda had her Bureau wallet ready in her lap when
the man who climbed down from the cab of the
Suburban arrived at the door of the Buick. The first
thing she noticed were the big rings he wore on the
pinkies of both hands. She noted that he was dressed in
worn dress trousers and scuffed black cowboy boots
and a white T-shirt that had only recently been in a
plastic bag that said "Fruit of the Loom." His rolling
biceps more than filled the sleeves of the T-shirt. A
brimmed hat like the stupid one her brother wore to go
fly-fishing shaded his face. She took a second glance at
the biceps and wondered about steroids.

She muttered to Tom, "We have company—that car
that sped past us a minute ago. Don't say anything. Not
a word. I don't trust this. I think this guy may have
spiked the road. That's why we got the flat."

"Why? What's going on?" he asked.

"Not a word, you hear me? I'm handling this."

Tom twisted around to look back at the Suburban. He said, "It's not just the driver. There's somebody else in that car. In the passenger seat."

She was staring at the rearview mirror. "I know. I see him, too. Now shut up."

She lowered the window in the door beside her seat. The morning air that blew inside the car bore only the slightest chill. After a moment's hesitation she decided to leave the engine of the Buick running. She was considering the likelihood that she might have to take off quickly and wondered how badly the car would handle with a flat front tire. Pretty badly, she concluded. Certainly not well enough to outrun an old Chevy Suburban that she had just seen cruising at close to a hundred.

The man leaned down and peered into the front seat. "You folks having a bit of car trouble?"

"Just a flat," Kelda replied in an even voice. "We'll take care of it. I have a jack and a spare. No problem." The man was so close to the door she couldn't see down to where he was holding his hands. That concerned her.

"Why don't you get on out of the car?" he said. "I'll see what I can do to help."

Kelda replied the same way she'd replied before. "I said we'd take care of it. Thanks."

The man leaned down a little farther and looked across the front seat at Tom Clone. Kelda thought the stranger's eyes hardened.

Without warning, the man thrust his hand toward her face. In the instant she prepared herself for the impact of his fist, she scolded herself for letting him get so close to her.

Those biceps.

But his hand stopped inches from her face.

He was holding a badge. But he was holding it so close to her eyes that she couldn't read it.

The man said, "Like I said before, ma'am, why don't you get out of the car. I'll see what I can do to help." Kelda didn't move. The man raised his voice. The menace in it, she thought, was practiced. "Do it now! In case you can't read, I'm a peace officer and I'm giving you an order."

She spun sideways on her seat and shoved her open ID wallet into his face before he could complete his smirk.

She barked right back at him. "And I'm a federal agent. My name is Special Agent Kelda James and I'm with the Federal Bureau of Investigation. Get the hell out of my face, Officer. I told you I don't want your help with my goddamned flat. Now, back off."

His chin dropped down half an inch and he stepped back, not in compliance, but so he could focus his middle-aged eyes to be able to read her ID.

He sneered. "It's 'Detective,' not 'Officer.' And I don't give a damn who you work for, I want you out of the car now. As I said, that's an order. I've identified myself as a peace officer and I expect my order to be obeyed."

She didn't budge. Her voice still even, she said, "I'm sorry but I missed it. Your wallet. I'd like to see your badge again, Detective." To Tom, she muttered, "Let me know if the car door opens up back there."

The man who had identified himself as a detective stepped another half step away from the Buick. With his left hand he reached behind his back.

Kelda knew he wasn't going for his badge. Her voice suddenly sharp enough to leave a paper cut, she rasped, "Don't touch that gun. It would be a big mistake."

He looked back at her to discover that a 9mm Sig Sauer was aimed at the center of his chest. "Hands on top of your head," she ordered. "Don't screw around with me. I promise I don't miss from this distance. And it's quite obvious you're not wearing a vest."

After a moment's deliberation he moved his hands slowly until his fingers came together on top of his head.

"So how many times have you fired from this distance?" he asked. His tone mocked her.

She thought about the little girl. About Rosa Alija. About the man she had killed that day. She said, "Exactly enough times to know that you're well within my range. I guarantee that from this distance I can empty this clip faster than you can belch, and still place every slug within three inches of your goddamned aorta."

A scent of recognition crept across his face. She thought he mouthed a profanity in reply.

She said, "Now take another half step back and lower your right hand so I can see that badge of yours again."

He did. His eyes were cold and the same dirty, gray-brown color as the snow that freezes into ice in the gutters in winter. His chest rose rhythmically, each inhale inflating the front of his T-shirt. He was menacing without even trying to be.

Kelda said, "Call back to your friend or whoever that is and tell him to get out of the car."

The man glanced back at the Suburban. "He's a cop, too. I think you're making a big mistake."

"Do I look like I care what you think?"

The man beside Kelda's Buick tucked his lower lip below his upper teeth, slotted the tip of his tongue between them and whistled, then gestured with his head. The second man climbed from the Suburban to join the roadside drama. He was slight and thin but almost as tall as the first man. His shirt was a dress shirt buttoned all the way to his neck, and he wore jeans that needed a few more washings to even approach a state where they were soft enough to wear comfortably. Even from that distance Kelda thought it was creepy the way the man's eyes bulged from his face.

When he was halfway between the two vehicles, Kelda said, "Tell him to stop right there. Not another step."

"That's far enough, Hoppy."

"I want his hands behind his head, too. I'm sure he knows exactly how to do it."

"The lady wants your hands up, Hoppy. She's kind of agitated. Go ahead and do what she says. In case you can't see from where you are, she has a cute little semi-automatic pointed at my chest."

Kelda said, "I think you're a little lost, Detective, aren't you? This part of the road is Fremont County, hell, maybe even El Paso County—I haven't really been paying attention to the road signs. But it sure as hell isn't Park County, which is what I read on your badge. You're a little out of your jurisdiction, aren't you?"

He seemed momentarily at a loss for words.

"Talk to me," she cooed.

"Makes no difference what county I'm in, 'cause I'm

not working. I saw a motorist in trouble. I stopped to help."

"That was going to be your rationalization for rousting me out of my car? Flimsy, Detective. Real flimsy. You want to stick with that? I have a witness sitting next to me, remember?"

She immediately regretted focusing any attention on her passenger.

The detective scoffed. "A witness, huh? Well, hell, let's talk about your little witness. I'm taking my hands down now and I'm going to put them on my knees. When I do I'd like you to point that little pistol of yours someplace else. You're beginning to make me nervous with it."

Kelda didn't respond as he lowered his hands, and she kept the Sig focused on an imaginary X over his heart. His eyes were now level with hers but he was looking past her, at Tom Clone.

Kelda couldn't tell, but Tom wasn't returning the cop's gaze; his attention was focused straight ahead out the windshield, back in the general direction of the Colorado State Pen.

The Park County detective flicked off his silly hat with his right hand. "Hey, Tom," he said. "Fancy meeting you here."

Tom Clone looked over. When he saw the red hair, his eyes closed to block out the memories.

CHAPTER

It was Alice Graham who initially led Detective Prehost to Tom Clone. Alice was a waitress at the Fossil Bed Café in Florissant who recognized the picture of Ivy Campbell in the *Rocky Mountain News* the day after she was murdered.

Alice had recognized the victim immediately. She was certain that she had waited on Ivy and a young man eight or nine days before. They had arrived in the café for a late breakfast, and the man had decided to use the opportunity of having her in a public place to break up with Ivy. Alice recalled that the girl didn't eat a thing during the meal. Her untouched breakfast consisted of two poached eggs, a toasted English muffin, and half a grapefruit.

Alice related to Detective Prehost that she thought the man had been unnecessarily cruel to the murdered girl, reciting the reasons he was dumping Ivy in great detail and repeating himself unmercifully in a manner that Alice considered belittling. The Fossil Bed is not a big restaurant, and even though Alice maintained that she wasn't eavesdropping, it was hard for her not to hear what was going on between the couple. She remembered thinking that if there were indeed fifty ways to leave your lover, this guy had chosen one of the worst. Maybe number forty-seven or forty-eight.

The man who broke up with Ivy Campbell was also one of only a handful of customers at the Fossil Bed Café to pay his bill that morning with a credit card. Alice remembered that, too, because after taking up her best booth for a couple of hours in prime time in the middle of tourist season, the guy at least had the decency to tip her well. It was her only fifty percent tip of the week.

The credit card voucher provided to the sheriff's office by Alice's boss at the Fossil Bed Café led Detective Prehost directly to Thomas Clone, a fourth-year medical student at the University of Colorado Health Sciences Center in Denver.

The case against Clone developed with surprising speed.

Although he denied even being in Park County the day that Ivy was murdered, a woman selling early sweet corn and apricots at a roadside stand a half mile from the house where Ivy died recalled seeing a man driving a car similar to Clone's Honda Civic stop on the shoulder opposite her stand to examine a map. She was closing up for the day when he stopped, so she knew that the time was about two-thirty, no later than a quarter to three.

Three days after the murder she called a local tip line to report what she had seen.

A day after that she picked a photo of Tom Clone out of a photo lineup. "That's the guy with the map," she told Detective Hoppy Bonnet. "Yep, that's him."

Clone's alibi for the time of the murder wasn't without flaws. He maintained that he'd attended a book signing at the Tattered Cover in Denver the evening of the murder. He even had a copy of the book *The Charm School,* by Nelson DeMille, that was inscribed to him, "To Tom, Best wishes, Nelson DeMille." The date was written below the signature. But the El Paso County medical examiner, who'd done the post on Ivy Campbell's body, had placed the time of death as early as five-thirty that afternoon, which would have allowed Tom Clone plenty of time to get back to Denver for a seven-thirty book signing in Cherry Creek.

Clone maintained that he'd broken up with Ivy over a week before—he admitted that he'd done it over breakfast at the Fossil Bed Café, but he insisted that he hadn't seen her since she'd asked him to come over to talk about their relationship three nights later. She wanted to try to work things out; his version was that she had begged him for another chance. He said he'd driven back up and they had talked in the Greens' cabin, but that nothing had changed and Tom had decided not to see her again.

"That was the last time you saw her?" Prehost had asked.

"Yes."

During that first interview with Detective Prehost,

who was accompanied by a detective from the local police department, Tom said he'd spent the afternoon of the murder studying at his little apartment in Cherry Hills, but he didn't think anyone had seen him there. His memory was that he hadn't left his home that day until the book signing at the Tattered Cover.

Tom's home in Cherry Hills was a one-bedroom caretaker's unit attached to a decrepit barn on a three-acre spread near the end of Vista Road, which sits on a high bluff above University Boulevard in suburban, rural Denver. Now that their kids were gone, the couple who owned the place spent twice as much time at their second home in Carmel as they did in their place in Cherry Hills, so they no longer kept horses in the barn. Tom's rent for the caretaker's cottage was negligible. In return for a great deal on his tacky apartment, he agreed to keep an eye on the main house and make sure that the various service people who were supposed to show up to do maintenance—the gardeners, the guys who plowed the snow off the long driveway, the woman who cleaned the pool—did indeed show up. He also collected mail and kept an eye on the front porch for packages.

Although his apartment was only fifteen minutes from the medical center, Tom felt as though he lived in the heart of the country. He knew he was the envy of his med student friends and considered the setup perfect. The way he looked at it, by living in Cherry Hills he was getting a taste of the life he'd have once he finished his radiology residency and set up shop reading MRIs at two hundred dollars a pop.

● ● ●

As laboratory analysis proceeded on the fruits of the crime scene search, the local media dogged the Park County cops, and the Park County cops focused more and more of their attention on Tom Clone. The forensics lab at the Colorado Bureau of Investigation identified hair similar to Tom's hairs in the guest room bed where Ivy had been sleeping. Semen from a secretor with Tom's blood type was discovered dried on the sheets. His fingerprints were picked up in a dozen locations around the house, including on three different items in the refrigerator.

During a subsequent interview with the medical student, Prehost, the young, agitated redheaded detective, said, "So you were there?"

"I told you I was there. Not that day, that week. I spent the night there earlier in the week."

"Did you sleep with her?"

"Not that it's any of your business, but yes, I did."

"That was three nights after you took her out to breakfast and told her that you didn't want to see her again?"

"Something like that."

"Something like that? Or that exactly? Which is it?"

"Three or four nights."

Prehost snorted.

"What difference does that make, Detective?"

"I'm asking the questions."

"The hell with this. I think I'd like a lawyer present if we're going to continue this conversation."

"Just like that?" Prehost said. "I ask a tough question or two and you want a lawyer."

"Just like that. I guess we're done unless I'm advised otherwise."

"We're not done, sonny. We're not done by any means."

Two days later Hoppy Bonnet had a brainstorm about the contents of the refrigerator in the Greens' kitchen. He'd taken the expiration date from the milk carton in the refrigerator—one of the three items that was marked with Tom Clone's fingerprints—to the local grocery store and asked what the earliest date was that the store had sold milk with that particular expiration date.

Bonnet had then confirmed the date with the dairy that had packaged the milk. The first date that the milk had been delivered for retail sale, it turned out, was the day after the last day that Tom Clone claimed he was in the Greens' house.

"How," Hoppy had asked Fred Prehost, "are his fingerprints on a carton of milk that didn't arrive in the stores until the day after he said he was last up in Park County?"

"Good question."

"The man is lying, Fred. Why is he lying?"

Three days later, three weeks after Ivy Campbell's murder, Prehost and Hoppy Bonnet arrested Tom Clone outside the auditorium where Grand Rounds was being held at the Health Sciences Center and charged him with first-degree murder.

CHAPTER

8

Prehost wasn't quite smiling as he looked past Kelda at Tom Clone, but she thought that his eyes were twinkling like an evil version of Santa Claus.

"Remember us, Tom? Me and Hoppy?"

Tom didn't answer.

Prehost said, "Just in case you're confused about what it means that you're off death row, here's what it means and here's all that it means: It means we're not done, Tom, you and me and Hoppy. I want you to know that. I have some advice for you. You want to hear it?"

Tom had resumed staring out the windshield.

"Cat got your tongue? Too bad. I'll offer my advice anyway. Here's what I think you should do: Check for us every day when you wake up. That's right, as soon as you open your eyes, and long before you begin to appreciate that you're not living in a cement room anymore, I want you to take a look around and make sure that we're not there watching you, waiting.

"And if I were you, I'd check my back all day long, and then do a real careful check every night before you go to sleep. Why? Because one time I'll be there, or Hoppy'll be there, right where you least want to find us. See, we're not going to rest until justice is done. And in my mind, justice won't be done until they take that IV needle out of your arm and they slide your miserable dead body into a big plastic bag. Sometime before that happens, me and Hoppy'll be there with a fresh warrant and an ice-cold pair of handcuffs."

Kelda said, "What the hell are you talking about?"

Tom answered her. "This is Detective Fred Prehost of the Park County Sheriff's office. He's the detective who led the investigation of the murder of Ivy Campbell. He's the one who arrested me. And out there?" He pointed at the skinny man standing on the shoulder of the road. "That's his sidekick, a man named Hoppy Bonnet. Mr. Bonnet thinks he's a genius."

Prehost said, "Yes, Special Agent, ma'am, I'm proud to say that I'm the one who put this man away back in 1989."

Kelda said, "And now you're threatening him?"

"No, no, no. Dear me, no. I don't make threats. Never felt much of a need to. I'm just telling him the way things are." She thought Prehost puffed up his chest just a little bit for her benefit.

"And how are things, Detective?" Kelda asked.

"Things are fucked up, Ms. Special Agent. That's how things are. When convicted killers get set free, in my book things aren't good. Especially when they get help they shouldn't have from people who should know better."

She knew that he was talking about her.

Tom said, "The DNA says I didn't do it. I'm innocent, like I always told you I was."

"The DNA is fucked."

"DNA doesn't lie, Detective."

"The eyewitnesses say you were there, Tom. Your fingerprints say you were there. Your lies say you were there."

Tom said, "Eyewitness testimony is unreliable. You know that."

Prehost countered, "Ivy's friends said she was frightened of you. Then you went ahead and proved she had a reason to be."

"And I told my mother the tooth fairy was going to come. Then the next morning there was a buck under my pillow. Is that evidence that she actually showed up, Detective?"

The detective shook his head. "The fat lady hasn't sung, Tom. You've been released pending a new trial, that's all. For now, the Park County DA has chosen not to retry the case. That means nothing is settled. Nothing. Given some time, who knows, I'm confident that I'll be able to change the district attorney's mind and you and me will get to do the same dance all over again."

Kelda asked, "Why don't you just let it go, Detective? Let the courts do what they're going to do?"

"You want to know why? Here's why: Because Ivy Campbell was a sweet kid. A really sweet kid. I only got to know her after she died. But I got to know her well enough to know that she didn't deserve what she got from this asshole. Why do I care? Because my heart says that someone needs to be concerned about jerks like this who prey on sweet young women who don't have a clue what they're up against."

"I'm innocent, Prehost. Get used to it."

"Ivy Campbell is still dead," Prehost told him. "I've been trying for over a decade and I haven't gotten used to that. So don't count on me suddenly getting comfortable with you being off death row. What girl's next, Tom? You picked out your next victim yet?"

"Someone else killed Ivy Campbell. Go find him. Leave me alone."

Prehost laughed. "We're not done, Tom. You and me. We're not done. The only finish line I'll recognize is the flat line on a monitor attached to your heart."

Kelda said, "That sounds like a threat to me."

"Really? Why don't you take it up with your FBI supervisors then, Ms. Special Agent. See if they want to investigate me for harassing this asshole. Maybe we can do a whole civil-rights-violation song and dance. I'm sure you're their very favorite special agent right now and your word about what happened out here today will carry just a ton of weight with the U.S. Attorney." He laughed again, turned, and took leisurely strides back toward Detective Bonnet, whose hands were still on top of his head.

"Come on, Hoppy," Prehost said, walking away. "And get your hands down, goddamn it."

Tom didn't take his eyes off Prehost.

A half dozen steps away, Prehost stopped and turned. He pointed a finger at Kelda. "You hang with this guy, you better watch your back. That's free advice. And that's good advice."

Beside her, Kelda thought Clone mumbled, "I could

kill that fuck. I swear." But she wasn't a hundred percent sure.

Less than an hour later the Buick was motoring up a tree-lined residential street on the southwestern side of Colorado Springs. "Is this area familiar at all?" Kelda asked.

Tom said, "No. It's sure pretty, but it's not familiar. I don't think I've ever been here." He took note of the elegant homes and big lots. "A lot of rich people in this neighborhood. Really rich people."

"That's the truth."

"Where are we going?"

Kelda said, "I need some breakfast. After all these years locked up, I'm sure you could use some real food. And after that little run-in with your cop friends from Park County, we could both use what some say are the finest Bloody Marys in the state of Colorado."

Suddenly, the patrician outline of the stucco front of the main building of the Broadmoor Hotel was visible through the trees. Tom said, "We're going to the Broadmoor for breakfast? I can't believe it."

"Believe it. It's what free people do. They eat when they want to, where they want to. Don't worry, it's my treat."

"Am I dressed okay?"

"You're dressed fine. This is still Colorado, people tolerate just about anything."

The hour hand on the clock in the lobby wasn't quite pointing due south when they walked into the hotel. At that early hour they were only the second couple in the restaurant, and the view from their choice window table extended from the placid lake in the center of the resort, to the emerald contours of the golf course, to the vaulting leap of Cheyenne Mountain, which seemed close enough to the hotel that Kelda thought she could hit it with a strong seven iron, and finally to the uncluttered morning sky.

The waitress was pretty, pleasant, and efficient. With Kelda's encouragement, Tom ordered a full breakfast—eggs, bacon, toast, potatoes, juice, and coffee. Kelda added waffles with fresh berries to his order and ordered a complete spread for herself—fruit, oatmeal, and an egg-white omelette. When the waitress asked, "Anything else?" Kelda said, "Yes, two Bloody Marys, please."

"Of course."

Tom sat back and fingered the silver cutlery. "It feels better than I'd dreamed. Being out."

"Blame it on the Broadmoor. This place has been known to distort reality a little bit."

"How about I blame it on you, instead? I'm just so happy to be free. I owe you so much for what you did."

"You can still say that even after our little visit from Detective Prehost?"

Tom nodded. "I half expected to see him sometime soon. I thought it would be later on at the news conference, actually. Didn't think he'd get in my face so quickly after I left . . . but I've prepared myself for the fact that there are going to be some people who are unwilling to accept my innocence. Prehost is definitely at the top of the list."

"You think that's all that was? He was expressing his unwillingness to accept your innocence?"

Tom managed a pinched smile. "No, that's not all it was. Prehost wants me dead. He won't be happy until I take the needle."

Kelda swallowed and looked away from him. Her eyes were focused on the lake as she said, "It's hard for me to imagine that he could find that outcome so . . . satisfying."

"For people like Prehost, it completes the circle, I guess. Things aren't complete for him yet."

"What about for you? How do you right the wrong that's been done to you? How do you complete the circle?"

"How do I get even with Prehost?"

"Yes. I guess that's what I'm asking."

"I don't know. Maybe some lawsuits. I don't know. I'm tempted to go there sometimes but . . ." He sighed. "I probably don't get even. I think I probably just move on."

"You can turn the other cheek? Just like that? Before, in the car, you said you could kill him."

"What? I didn't say that. Time will tell whether I can turn the other cheek, won't it? I am surprised that Prehost pulled this in front of you, though. That surprised me. It doesn't show much discipline. I thought he was disciplined."

"Well, he didn't waste any time getting in your face."

"His act didn't seem to faze you much. Weren't you . . . scared? The guy terrifies me."

"For some reason, people like him don't intimidate me. If they did, I never would have made it out of the FBI Academy. Female agents have to have especially thick skins. God knows that the Bureau has its share of self-righteous bullies. Fortunately, people like Prehost just get me riled."

"Won't he turn you in to somebody for pointing your gun at him?"

"No. He'd have to admit to spiking the road and harassing you. What just happened out there will become a story he embellishes for his cop buddies the next time he's at his favorite saloon. But he'll change it a little bit—in his version the girl won't get the draw on him, I can promise you that."

Tom sat back on his chair. "So what *does* scare you?"

Kelda found it an interesting question. She pondered it a moment before she said, "Bees. Some spiders. Failing. Mice, a little, but not so much."

"But not bullies with badges and guns?"

"Not them, no. I've never had a problem with them."

The Bloody Marys arrived. Tom lifted his glass. "To freedom, and freedom fighters."

Kelda acknowledged the compliment and touched her glass to his. The celery stalk and the tomato juice caused her to think about Christmas and long, white flannel nightgowns at dawn. As she sipped at the drink the fire from a healthy dose of peppers lit the back of her tongue.

They both looked at the mountains.

"God, this is good," he said.

"The Bloody Mary?"

"Everything. This moment. You, the drink, this place, the mountains. Everything is good. I haven't felt that for a long, long time."

Silence took over the space between them. "The dark, sometimes," Kelda finally said.

"What?"

"You asked what scared me. The dark does sometimes."

Her admission caused his breathing to pause and he wondered if his heart had added an extra beat to its routine.

The waitress arrived with their food. He was momentarily transfixed by the bounty that was placed before him. When he looked up from the table, Kelda was smiling at him.

Tom said, "You don't smile much. You should. It makes you even more attractive."

"Maybe," she said, "that's why I don't do it."

CHAPTER

9

Kelda and Tom had finally made it past the madness of T-Rex, the "transportation expansion" that was decimating seventeen miles of Denver's primary interstate corridor in honor of the vanity that building more lanes of highway might somehow result in less traffic, and they were skirting downtown on I-25 near the new football stadium.

Kelda said, "I think I'll take you to Boulder myself. It'll save you a bus ride on your first day out."

"You don't have to do that." He was trying to decide whether he liked the new stadium better than he'd liked Mile High.

"I know I don't. Look, I actually live in Lafayette. Going a little farther down the turnpike to Boulder is not that big a deal for me. I can run some errands while I'm there."

"Great, then, thanks," Tom said. A moment later he added, "You just decided, didn't you? To take me to Boulder. You were originally planning on taking me to the bus station, weren't you?"

"Just decided? No. I actually made up my mind back near Park Meadows."

She realized that Tom wouldn't know what, or where, Park Meadows was. The huge mall had been conceived long after his incarceration began.

He asked, "Why?"

"Why what?"

"Why did you decide to pick me up today?"

She checked her mirrors for Prehost's Suburban, something she'd done regularly since fixing the flat. "Just so you understand. . . . What I did over the past few months in Park County? With the evidence in your case? That wasn't about you. That was about justice. I was doing my job. There's no benefit to any of us in this country when we convict the wrong man, let alone when we execute him.

"Picking you up this morning? That was a combination of simple curiosity and me agreeing to do a favor for Tony Loving. And breakfast at the Broadmoor? To be honest, that was selfish; I wanted to treat myself. I really enjoy having breakfast at the Broadmoor, and I don't get down that way very often. Let's face it, asking you to wait in the car wouldn't have been exactly polite. But since we sat down to eat, I've begun to come to the conclusion that you may be a decent enough guy, so I've decided to do you a small kindness by driving you to your grandfather's house."

"Thank you for your honesty."

"You're welcome."

"What kind of name is Kelda?"

She shook her head and made a disappointed face. "Maybe some other time, Tom. The question is, like, so first-date-ish, you know what I mean?"

Tom Clone's grandfather lived on High Street, just off Fourteenth, at the end of the cul-de-sac that extended up from Casey School north of the Downtown Mall. The few blocks of High Street in Boulder hadn't been named on a whim by some pioneer who'd enjoyed a little too much whiskey. The precious strip of land enjoyed prime territory on the front shelf of a bluff above downtown, and the views to the south were special. The red brick of the old city, the vaulting faces of the Flatirons, the miles of greenbelt around Chautauqua. The Rockies.

The location was convenient, too. The charm of the Downtown Mall was within walking distance. Tom's grandfather lived mere blocks from the offices of the doctors who cared for his myriad health problems, and he could buy groceries, his favorite brandy, and fresh bread minutes from his front door.

Despite all that, the house that Tom's mother had grown up in on High Street was almost worthless.

But Tom's grandfather slept well at night knowing that the land on which it rested was worth a fortune.

You want to come in?" Tom asked Kelda.

"No, thanks. You and your grandfather need some time together. And I have to get back home to my cat."

She didn't have a cat, but the imaginary pet came in handy when she was in need of an excuse.

They stood in front of the house. Tom's duffel was at his feet. "Will you be at the press conference later?"

Kelda said, "No, I won't be there. Tony thinks that word is leaking out about my role in your release. Now that you're out of prison I think it's prudent for me to try to reduce my profile a little. This is a story I'd rather not become part of."

"Yeah. Tony told me that on the phone. I'm cool with that."

A whining drone increased in volume as a cherry red Vespa came into view from down the street.

Tom said, "There he is. He said he got a new scooter. I like it. Do you like it?"

"That's your grandfather on that scooter?"

Long gray hair flowed out from beneath a helmet that matched the bike. The driver raised a hand to wave before turning up toward the house.

"That's Grandpa. He's had a bum hip for years, so he's been getting around on a scooter since I was a kid. He's always been kind of a legend in the neighborhood. Gave us all rides when we were kids, let us drive it around parking lots on Sundays. He's a good guy."

"God bless him," Kelda said.

"Yeah," Tom said.

"What about the winter?"

"Snowy days cramp his style."

"I bet they do." She turned to leave. "Hey, good luck, Tom."

"Thank you. Thanks for everything."

Kelda stepped away from the awkwardness of their good-bye, slid back into the Buick, and watched through the windshield as an elderly man hobbled from the garage with the aid of a cane. His grandson saw him, too. Tom took a little skip and a hop before launching himself into the cartwheel/back flip combination that Kelda had first witnessed that morning just before dawn on the walkway leading up to the public entrance of the Colorado State Penitentiary.

She circled the end of the cul-de-sac on High Street and chanced a final glance in the mirror.

Tom was two steps from his grandfather, his arms outstretched. As Tom closed on him, the thin, frail man actually took a clear step back, away from his grandson. Their eventual embrace was cordial, but not exuberant. A pat on the back, good-to-see-you kind of hug. As a child, Kelda got warmer greetings than that after she returned from a sleepover at a friend's house. What did it mean that Tom Clone only got a pat on the back after thirteen years on death row?

She wasn't sure. Probably nothing.

When she finally returned her attention to the road, she thought she saw the tail end of an old Chevy Suburban descending Fourteenth toward downtown Boulder.

But she wasn't quite sure about that either.

Kelda didn't bother to watch the news coverage of Tom and Tony's press conference that afternoon.

The drive from High Street in Boulder to her old farmhouse in Lafayette took her only about twenty minutes. Recently she'd been getting the uneasy feeling that new tract homes were filling the fallow fields near her two acres so fast that they were literally going up overnight. She told herself that it couldn't be true.

Couldn't be. But she knew that it wasn't going to be long before she was going to have neighbors who were close enough to peer through her windows.

She parked the Buick in the shade cast by the two elms that were closest to her home, walked in the side door, and shut off her alarm. She flicked on the swamp cooler and began stripping off her clothes, sparing a moment to return the Sig Sauer to its temporary resting place on top of the highboy in her bedroom. She took a quick shower and pulled on a long T-shirt that was one of her few remaining mementos from the FBI Academy.

Kelda was ready to begin her ritual.

From the freezer in the kitchen she pulled six bags of frozen peas and carried them into her bedroom. The blinds on the window were closed against the relentless heat, and she left the light muted in the little room, though she did flick on the ceiling fan. On her bed she spread two bath towels and carefully aligned three bags of peas on each before folding the towels over to cover the plastic bags. She fluffed the pillows at the head of the bed before she propped herself against them, slowly lowering her legs onto the parallel rows of frozen vegetables.

Beneath each leg, one bag of peas pressed against the meatiest part of her calf, another against the underside of her knee. The final bag pressed against the terrain where Kelda's buttocks became her thigh.

She slowed her breathing, forcing herself to inhale more deeply than usual. At first she felt no temperature change on her legs; the insulation of the terry cloth temporarily prevented the peas from yielding their chill.

But as the seconds became minutes the cold began escaping the cotton, and she thought maybe she knew how addicts felt as the tip of the needle pierced their skin.

Usually she thought she felt the pain most intensely at the instant when she was on the threshold of relief. This was one of those times. She tried not to cry but soon the tears were tracking down her cheeks. She captured one salty drop with the tip of her tongue and realized she was thirsty. Getting something to drink meant getting up and going to the kitchen. The act felt impossible to her.

Impossible.

Instead, she cried some more and used her tongue to steal each tear as it meandered toward her chin.

She didn't think she'd be able to nap but she did. Her last remembered thought was about Tom's grandfather's red Vespa. She wondered if maybe she should get one—if they were as helpful for bad legs as they were for bad hips. And she wondered if they came in green.

When she awoke, the afternoon sun had just begun its descent toward the mountains. The air along the Front Range was calm, and the billowing clouds that could provide a canopy of relief were still tantalizing miles away over the Divide. The swamp cooler was losing its battle to make the tiny house temperate, and the rhythmic pulse of breeze from the ceiling fan washing over her bare skin offered the only respite from the heat.

Beneath Kelda's legs the peas had softened, and the

thunder and lightning in her lower body had diminished its burn and roar. She stood and carried the flaccid bags of peas to the freezer, carefully hanging the damp towels over the backs of kitchen chairs to dry. The clock above the door that led out to the service pantry told her it was just after four in the afternoon.

She mouthed a profanity at her forgetfulness and took quick steps toward the tiny bathroom. She crossed her arms in front of her and lifted the T-shirt over her head. She immediately turned her back to the mirror, looking over her left shoulder at a spot high above her scapula.

The patch wasn't there. Her heart skipped a beat and then she remembered she'd chosen a new location for the one she'd put on three days before. Kelda spun back around and without checking her reflection touched a spot on her right side, level with her navel. She slid a fingernail beneath the edge of the clear rectangular patch, grabbed the edge of the plastic, and ripped it off her skin. She dropped the solitary square inch of material into the toilet, and she flushed it away.

The telephone rang.

Kelda mouthed another profanity and half ran to the side of the bed. She sat on top of the comforter and crossed her legs before lifting the receiver.

"Hello," she said. It was her Bureau voice. She feared that the call was from somebody at the office wanting to harass her about what she'd been doing to help Tom Clone.

The line went dead. She hit *69 and waited to hear the number of the last telephone that had been used to call her home. But the phone company's system couldn't—or wouldn't—identify it. She logged the call in a notebook she kept beside the phone. It was the third hang-up she'd received in the past six days, since the rumors began surfacing about what she'd done to help Tom Clone.

Before she had a chance to stand up, the phone rang again.

She grimaced, cursing silently. "Hello," she said, again using her Special Agent incantation.

"Kelda? It's Tom, Tom Clone."

She mouthed yet another profanity.

"How did you get my number?"

"I asked Mr. Loving for it. He gave it to me. I'm sorry. I shouldn't have called, should I?"

Damn, Tony, she thought. *How about a little discretion? We had a deal, right? Jesus.*

"It's okay. What can I do for you?"

"Um, if this is a bad time . . . Look, I'm sorry. This was a mistake, obviously. I shouldn't have bothered you again. You've been so great already. I'll—"

She sighed. "What is it you want? Just tell me, please."

"My grandfather? He and I have been talking. He's come up with some conditions for me to live with him. They're okay, they're reasonable. I understand where he's coming from. Basic things. He wants me to start looking for work within a week or so, which is fine—I was going to do it anyway."

"Yes?"

"He wants me to talk to a lawyer friend of his about my options. I'd planned to do that anyway, too. And . . . he wants me to get some psychotherapy. Thinks I might have some issues to work through for some reason."

She ignored his attempt at humor. She said, "Your

grandfather wants you to go into psychotherapy?" A fly landed on her knee and immediately jumped up to her left breast. She flicked it away with the back of her hand.

"As you may have gathered earlier, my grandfather is not your typical eighty-year-old. He's real bright, real sharp, and he tries to keep up with the world. He says he's serious about the psychotherapy—that he doesn't want me to carry around any baggage from what I went through in prison. It's a pain, but he's doing me a favor, right? I'll humor him for a while. But I don't know who to go see. I wondered, since you live close to Boulder, if you know of anybody here, or even out your way in Lafayette. I'd rather have a recommendation than just go to somebody cold, you know."

"Tony doesn't know anyone you could see?"

"Mr. Loving said he doesn't know anything about anyone north of Denver."

Kelda said, "I know one guy, in Boulder. His name is Dr. Alan Gregory. He's good. Try him."

"You know his number?"

"Check the phone book. I'm sure he's there."

"Thanks," Tom said. "That's all I ever seem to say to you. I'd like to make it up to you at some point."

"That's not necessary. Low profile, remember? No grand gestures, please."

"I understand."

"Listen, I need to run. Good-bye, Tom. Good luck."

After hanging up the phone, Kelda opened her closet and punched in the code that unlocked the heavy door on her little gun safe. From inside the safe she pinched a small foil-lined pouch out of a flimsy cardboard box. She clenched the edge of the pouch between her teeth while she retrieved her Sig Sauer from the top of the highboy and returned it to its home in the safe.

The fly flew in with it.

She said, "Stupid fly," closed the door on the insect, and walked back to the bathroom. She ripped the pouch open, withdrew the solitary patch from inside, peeled the lining from the adhesive, and stuck the plastic square onto the firm skin of her abdomen six inches or so from her navel. This time the patch went on her left side.

After keeping pressure on the patch for half a minute with the palm of her hand, she pulled the FBI Academy T-shirt back over her head and ran her fingers through her hair. The narcotics in the patch were absorbed slowly; the fentanyl wouldn't make it through the membrane of the patch into her skin and from her skin into her bloodstream until sometime during the middle of the night.

Which meant that if she wanted to dull the pain, she'd go through a lot of frozen peas and Percocet by bedtime.

Out loud, she said, "Why the hell did I give him Alan's name? God, Kelda. Think, think."

She thought about the fly inside the safe, and noticed that the light that was seeping into the room through the cracks in the blinds was slightly gray. She concluded that the clouds that had been building above the Divide must have finally blown down from the mountains.

Maybe there'd be some rain. Maybe there would be an early beginning of the summer monsoons.

Maybe Tom Clone wouldn't call him. Or maybe Dr. Alan Gregory and Tom Clone wouldn't hit it off.

Right.

And maybe her pain would be gone by morning.

She walked over to the gun safe and punched in the combination. The fly burst out and immediately landed on the side of her highboy.

She swatted at it with her open palm and missed. It took off toward the window and crashed into the glass.

"Stupid fly," she said again.

The sky had darkened and the swamp cooler was finally beginning to catch up with the heat in the house by the time someone knocked on Kelda's door. She glanced at her laptop monitor and noted the time at the bottom right corner of the screen: 8:47.

Kelda lifted her legs from the bath towels and checked the condition of the peas. Definitely thawed, on the way to mushy. She yelled, "Coming," picked up the half-dozen bags, and returned them to the freezer. She opened the front door without bothering to check the peephole first.

She smiled. "God, I was hoping it was you."

The man who stood on her porch wore a faded yellow T-shirt with the sleeves cut off and a pair of Billabong board shorts that looked as old as he did. Even though his feet were adorned with flip-flops, he towered over her. He said, "Who else was it going to be? You shouldn't be on your feet, Kelda. You know that. Come on, find a place to lie down and I'll rub your legs."

She stood on her tiptoes and kissed him on the scruff on his chin. "Okay, I'll let you. Come on in, Ira."

Ira switched on Kelda's little stereo and slipped in a CD he'd burned for her. Mostly jazz, some electronic synthesized stuff he was trying to sell her on. They sat on the sofa in the living room, and she rested one of her legs on his lap. He reached across her body for the remote control and flicked on the TV across the room, which he tuned to ESPN. He muted the volume before he began his practiced ministrations on her thigh.

"That hurts so good," she said. "*SportsCenter*'s coming on?"

"Yeah."

"If you want to listen, too, it's okay with me. Maybe Mike Hampton pitched today. I think he's cute. Did you work this late?"

Ira was a veterinarian.

"I was done about six, six-thirty. I had to do an emergency operation on a—"

"I'm sorry, I don't want to hear about surgery on animals today. What have you been doing since you left the clinic?"

He touched the line of dew that was visible on his brow right below his hairline. "I've been doing what everybody in the state is doing. I'm waiting on the thunderstorms. God, we need rain, don't we? What's this—eleven straight days above ninety? It's too hot, even for me."

"I don't think the storms are coming early this year. Maybe by mid-July if we're lucky. But, I agree . . . it does feel some days like it's never going to rain here again."

"I'm still hopeful. One of those storms will blow out of the mountains and drench us. You have to have faith, darling."

Kelda lifted the T-shirt away from her sticky chest.

"Please, please, please. I don't want to talk about the heat, either."

"How about we talk about Tom? I saw a little bit of the news earlier. He's really out of prison."

As he spoke Ira's cheeks rose along with his eyebrows and Kelda thought, not for the first time, that he looked a little like Stan Laurel. "Yeah, he really is. I saw him in the flesh. There was a change in plans this morning. I was the one who picked him up at the penitentiary and drove him to Boulder." She didn't tell Ira about stopping for breakfast at the Broadmoor.

Ira paused the ministrations to her legs. "Seriously? Do you think that was a good idea? How did that happen?"

She slapped him lightly. "Don't stop rubbing when you ask questions—it interrupts the flow. His lawyer called late last night and told me that the judge in Park County had just issued the order for the release. He kind of asked me to help out. The prison warden wanted to get Clone out the door before dawn so the press couldn't make a fuss about the release. His lawyer's in a wheelchair, he figured I might be curious about the guy, so I made some suggestions and he asked me if I would pick him up."

"Yeah?"

"Then it got interesting. The detective who originally arrested Clone followed us away from the penitentiary. He spread some spikes or something on the road to give me a flat tire and then tried to intimidate Clone."

"What did you do?"

"I had my gun on him before he knew who he was dealing with."

"No?" Ira stopped rubbing.

"Yeah. Don't stop."

"Is he going to be trouble? The detective?"

She shrugged. "He's the least of my concerns. I'm much more worried about the reaction I'm going to face at work."

"Your boss knows that you helped the lawyer?"

"All he knows is that somebody leaked that lab report to the lawyer. I'm on the short list of suspects. I don't think he can prove anything, but . . ."

Ira was using his thumbs to circle the bone on her left ankle. "So why did you take Clone to Boulder? I thought he would be going to Cripple Creek to sue everybody he could find down there or that he'd be moving back to Denver. That's where he was, right, Denver? In medical school?"

"Yes. For whatever reason, he's going to stay with his grandfather in Boulder for a while until he adjusts to life outside."

Ira nodded. "Where in Boulder?"

"A little house on High Street. You know it? It's right above downtown. Terrific views of the Mall and Chautauqua."

Ira didn't respond. His skilled fingers moved from Kelda's feet up toward the territory where her quads closed in on her knee. "You still feeling okay about . . . everything you did, love?"

She smiled with her eyes. "Yes, I am. I still feel good about it. It was the right thing to do."

"Justice?"

"Yes, Ira. It is about justice. It's all about justice."

"Even if it ends up causing you problems at work? You'll still think it was worth it?"

"If I don't get a handle on this pain, Ira, my days in the Bureau are numbered anyway. I can't take any more medicine than I'm taking without being sedated. I'm just hoping that Rosa Alija will continue to protect me until I decide it's time to leave. Fortunately for me, the Bureau doesn't want to be perceived as mistreating one of its heroes."

"I hope you're right."

She winced and said, "That's a bit too hard."

He lightened up on the pressure and said, "You and I are still okay?"

"What do you mean?"

"Nothing's changed?"

"No, nothing's changed. We'll give things another month or so to cool off. Then we'll go. Everything's the same."

Her arms were crossed across her chest, the fingers of each hand curled over the opposite shoulder.

He noted the posture and jumped at an interpretation. He asked, "You're in between pain patches, aren't you?"

"They're not lasting the full three days anymore. And I changed this one a little late, anyway. The new patch will kick in soon. Before morning for sure. I'll be okay by the time I go back on duty."

He allowed his hand to migrate up the inside of her thigh.

Her breath caught in her throat. After a moment of indecision, she responded to him by sliding her toes inside his shirt.

"Why is it," she asked, "that there are only two things that totally distract me from my pain, and one of them is hot, and the other is cold?"

"Me and the ice?" Ira asked.

"Yes," she murmured.

"The thing about me and ice is, we're both hard," he said. "Maybe that's it."

"Maybe," she agreed. "Maybe."

PART TWO

Necessary Lies

The sign on the bricks beside the front door of our offices in the old Victorian on Walnut Street in downtown Boulder is simple. On top it reads "Alan Gregory, Ph.D." On the bottom it reads "Diane Estevez, Ph.D." Diane and I had toyed with the idea of putting "Clinical Psychology" on a third line below our names, but had gotten so caught up in an alpha dog argument about whose name should be on top that we neglected to resolve the question of whether we should list our profession on the sign.

The sign maker had resolved it for us. The result was that to someone strolling by on the street, our offices could easily be mistaken for the habitat of a couple of petroleum geologists.

A coin toss—actually, since this was Diane I was dealing with, it was best two out of three—had placed my name at the top of the sign. It was a contest she's made sure I've wished I'd lost ever since.

My four o'clock patient that summer afternoon was a woman whom I'd been treating for much too long who thought that there was actually a correct way to load a dishwasher. Not a preferred way to load a dishwasher, but a correct way. My private name for her was "the Kitchen Aid Lady." The details of her argument, I admit, had numbed me right from the moment she'd first revealed them many, many sessions before, but one of her more passionate protests had to do with an arcane concept she called silverware nesting.

We revisited the concept at regular intervals. I can't tell you how much I looked forward to it each time.

My patient adamantly believed that anyone who didn't load the dishwasher the correct way was ill informed or, more likely, an idiot. The idiot in question during our session that day was, of course, the Kitchen Aid Lady's husband. But she did not consider her spouse to be mentally challenged; in fact she considered his intellectual acumen one of his more attractive features. His failure to load the dishwasher correctly was therefore—no surprise here—an unmistakable sign that he didn't really love her.

His position, I gleaned from her newly refined comments that afternoon, was that there were many ways to load a dishwasher and that reasonable people could disagree on which method was best. He also seemed intent on not compromising on the issue, refusing to allow the measure of his love to be determined by what he considered to be a spurious dishwasher-loading assay.

My patient wrapped up her soliloquy that hot summer afternoon by asking me to cast my lot on the dishwasher-loading question. She didn't exactly ask; what she did was insist that I validate her position. Was I a proponent of her method—the correct one that took into account such issues as silverware nesting? Or was I a proponent of some radical or haphazard alternative method—like her idiot spouse?

Dodging the question adroitly—I admit that I hadn't paid enough attention during any of her previous recitations of the specifics of dishwasher-loading etiquette to make a rational choice between the various methodologies—I suggested that it appeared that she was, right then and there, doing the same thing with me that she was doing with her husband.

"What?" she asked. "What on earth are you talking about?" She was stupefied. She couldn't see the point I was making.

I repeated my gentle confrontation. That worked sometimes.

Not this time. She still didn't get it.

I spelled it out for her. "It seems to me that you've decided to equate your husband's love for you with his willingness to load the dishwasher according to your desires. Now, apparently, you've decided to equate my capacity to be a helpful psychotherapist with my position on the same question."

When I finished my interpretation I sat back and awaited the reward of her *Aha, you are so brilliant.*

It didn't come. Instead, she made a short guttural sound deep in her throat and appraised me as though I had just peed on the carpet. Finally, she asked, "Are you saying that if you load the dishwasher right, I'll think you love me?"

Despite my commitment to helping my patient with

her problems, at that moment I couldn't help but em-
pathize with her idiot husband.

I made a few notes, returned a couple of phone calls—
including one to schedule an initial appointment the
next day for a new patient, and packed up to leave. My
quasi partner in my clinical psychology practice, Diane
Estevez, walked out to her car a few moments after I
walked out to mine. Diane and I had been friends and
colleagues for enough years that I no longer remembered precisely how many years it had been. That was a
very nice feeling.

Although our clinical practices were separate enti-
ties, she and I co-owned the little Victorian house on
Walnut Street in downtown Boulder that housed both
of our offices and that of our tenant, a gnomic man of
Pakistani ancestry who for the past fifteen months or
so had used the upstairs attic/alcove for a business that
had something to do with security on the Internet. For
the first fortnight or so of his tenancy, Diane and I
had both tried to understand his business strategy, but
his broken English and our intact technological igno-
rance combined to make it clear we weren't ever going
to get it.

The early summer heat was stifling. A big tacky
thermometer with an oxymoronic enticement for ciga-
rettes—"Lucky Strike Means Fine Tobacco"—was nailed
up on the ramshackle garage at the rear of the property,
a structure that by all rights should have already been
blown over by any number of recent winter Chinook
windstorms. I walked halfway over to the garage—it
was as close as I liked to get to the thing—and eyed the

temperature. The gauge maintained that the air that was currently enveloping me was ninety-six degrees. And that was in the shade.

Diane opened the door to her Saab and stood outside to allow the thermal waves to escape from her leather seats. I did the same with my car, although my seats were cloth. "Hey," she said. "Haven't seen you much lately."

"Yeah, I've missed you," I replied. "My hours have been weird. Lauren and I have been juggling our schedules to try to spend more time with the baby. You and Raoul doing okay?"

"Yeah, yeah. He's traveling a lot for his new business. But we're fine. Grace is good?"

"Terrific. She's getting big. She's walking, talking—"

"Peeing, pooping." Diane's vision of parenthood had never been quite the same as mine. The bottom line was that she focused more on diapers than I did.

"That, too," I said. I threw my canvas briefcase into the car. "Diane, does the work get to you sometimes?"

"Therapy? That work?"

"Yes."

She flicked a glance at her watch, then spent a moment examining my face. She ordered, "Take off your sunglasses." I raised them obediently to my forehead and held them there. She said, "Just what I thought. You have time for a drink?"

I looked at my watch and considered her offer for a second or two while I wondered what she had seen in my eyes. "Yeah, that would be great. Let me call Viv and tell her I'll be a while."

"She's your nanny, right? I don't want to be interfering with a tryst with some mistress."

"Lauren and I consider Viv our goddess. But to out-siders, 'nanny' seems to be less controversial."

"You want to get something to eat? I've been fanta-sizing all day about eating my entire next meal at Emiliana and you can save me from myself. What do you say we walk over to Triana? Although it's not going to be as satisfying as the six-course dessert indulgence at Emiliana, I think I could go for some tapas and sherry as a consolation prize." She fanned herself. "Anyway, it's too hot for a full meal."

The full name of Emiliana was Emiliana Dessert House and Restaurant. My wife, Lauren, liked to say that they put last things first, right where they belong. To Diane, I said, "You like sherry?"

"No. I like beer. But it sounds better to say tapas and sherry. Don't you think it sounds better?"

"Is that what Raoul says?" Diane's husband's family was from somewhere close to Barcelona.

"No, he says snacks and beer. But I know he does it just to annoy me."

Triana was a couple of doors west of the Downtown Boulder Mall. Only a few years old, the restaurant con-sumed the century-old space of what for years had been Boulder's iconic used-book store, Stage House Books.

The bar was almost full when Diane and I arrived. She found a couple of seats at a tiny table that was in the precise location where in the building's Stage House days I'd once discovered a treasure trove of nineteenth-century political cartoons. Diane waved across the room at a waitress who couldn't have been old enough to serve us. She couldn't have been. To me, Diane said,

"I think it's too hot for sherry, so I'm going to get a beer."

She said it with a straight face. I was impressed. "Make it two."

She'd grabbed the little bar menu from the table. "Do you mind if I order the tapas?"

"Would it make any difference if I minded? Go ahead and order enough for both of us. And remember I don't like olives."

"I forgot. With you it's olive oil, *sí*, olives, *no*. I don't get it. What do you have against olives?"

"Do you really want to go there?"

"Probably not. So, what, are you burned out, Alan? Or are you just a precocious marcher in the midlife crisis parade?"

I'd had enough practice conversing with Diane over the years that I could usually follow the uneven terrain of the progression of her thinking without tripping over my feet. "Maybe. I don't know. I hadn't been thinking about it that way, but, shoot, it's a possibility." I'd never considered myself one of those people who were vulnerable to professional burnout, but I spent a few minutes recounting the story of my four o'clock appointment and the dishwasher-loading dilemma as a way of trying to elucidate for Diane whatever it was that I was vulnerable to.

"Raoul would agree with your patient. Sometimes I catch him rearranging the dirty dishes after I load the dishwasher."

"No, no, no," I protested. "The difference is that Raoul doesn't consider you flawed because of it and he doesn't consider your failure to learn different dishwasher-loading techniques to be a measure of your love for him."

"Wrong," Diane replied. "Raoul definitely considers me flawed, but he would consider me flawed no matter how the hell I loaded the damn dishwasher. He loves me anyway. Why does he love me anyway? Because I am much more lovable than I am flawed. That's what Freud said mental health was, by the way—the ability to feel worthwhile despite your flaws."

"No, Diane, Freud didn't say that. Freud said mental health was the capacity to love and to work. But otherwise, my point exactly. Good try."

She frowned at me. Diane didn't like being corrected, especially when she'd been caught fabricating quotes from dead people.

The waitress had arrived tableside in time to listen politely to the last few back-and-forths between Diane and me. She pretended to be unfazed by our interchange, however, took our order from Diane, and strolled away into what I still thought of as the nonfiction section of the restaurant.

"We both know it's not the dishwasher princess that's bothering you," Diane told me. "So what is it?"

"I prefer to think of her as the Kitchen Aid Lady. But the answer to your question is 'I don't know,'" I replied.

She laughed at me. "Boy, you sure gave that a lot of thought. Are you always this contemplative these days?"

I smiled at her. "I don't know what it is, Diane. I just don't." From experience, I knew that even if I didn't know, Diane probably had an opinion or two that she could spare.

"The diagnosis you blew last year maybe?"

"What?" I said.

The waitress returned with our beer. I drank a third of mine in one long draw. There is nothing like the first drink of cold beer on a hot day. Nothing. Unfortunately, that includes the second drink of cold beer on a hot day, so I made the first drink last as long as I could.

Diane drank half of her beer before she clarified her accusation. "The woman who got blown up on the street outside our office—remember her? Your, um, shall we say 'miscalculations'—is that too strong a word?—in that case allowed a few people to die, as I recall."

I sat back on my chair. "Well," I said, removing the knife from my chest and preparing to defend myself with it.

She reached across and rested one hand on my wrist and sipped at her beer with her free hand. "Do I have your attention now?"

"You bet, Diane."

"You've had some tough cases, dearest. That whole situation last year with the kids and the bombs, the whole witness protection thing you got mixed up with before that. Your practice has not exactly been something to envy. I sometimes think that there should be some kind of government-mandated caution sign on your office door. All of it has to have taken its toll on you."

I shook my head. Her argument didn't taste right. "I don't regret those cases. They're not what I think about when I have doubts about what I'm doing every day in my office. I end up thinking about cases like this woman and her dishwasher."

"What?"

"The one-step-forward, two-steps-back cases. You know, the depression that won't crack. The abused woman who keeps going back to her husband. The therapy that should last six months that isn't any better after a year. Those are the cases that make me nuts. The people who come into the office and dare you to help them change. They're the ones. It seems most days go by and I don't think I've done anything to help anyone get better."

"So? Me neither."

"And it doesn't bother you?"

"No, it doesn't. Okay, maybe a little, but I get over it." She wiped her lips with her cocktail napkin. "You know, I used to think it was my job to help people get better. Now I know I was wrong. My job is to help them get better equipped. The whole give-a-man-a-fish-and-he-eats-for-a-day routine, you know? And I bet you do that every day whether you give yourself credit for it or not."

"I don't know if sitting in that room listening to people is the best way to help them do that."

"But that's what we do, sweetheart." She had softened her tone in a way that was disarming. "Those are the bricks we lay. If you've started hating the bricks, maybe it's time to reconsider being a bricklayer."

"What?" I laughed.

She laughed, too. "I thought that was pretty good. I didn't even know it was coming, it just rolled right out of my brain."

"It was cute, I'll give you that. But seriously? I wonder if I'm making a difference, if what I do is truly important. I worry that I'm beginning to lack compassion. This woman, today, I had no empathy for what she's struggling with. I just wanted to take her by the shoulders, and . . . and . . ."

"Throttle her?"

We laughed together and finished our beers just in time for the arrival of the tapas. Diane had ordered so much food that it didn't all fit on the table. She yanked a free chair from an adjoining table and moved a platter of something onto it. She did it so quickly that I didn't get a clear look at what was on the platter. Before the waitress disappeared, Diane ordered another beer. I shook my head, declining.

Diane lurched first for the trout, which had made a not-so-seamless transition from swimming in a river with its head attached to swimming in a pool of olive oil, herbs, and white wine without its head attached. She swallowed a big mouthful before she said, "I could send you some custody work and court referrals. That would break the tedium for you."

"Ugh. Please, don't do me any favors. And leave some of that trout, if you don't mind."

She reluctantly shifted her attention from the trout to the eggplant and baby leeks. "You and Lauren have any vacations scheduled? Maybe getting out of town would help. Raoul and I found this great place where we stay sometimes outside of Sedona." She paused. "That's in Arizona."

I shook my head. "Diane, I know where Sedona is. But no, that's not a solution. We got away last month."

"And look at you now," she said, making a dubious face.

"Yeah, and look at me now."

"Well," she said as she sat back on her chair with a cute little drool of olive oil on her chin. "Then I think you'll just have to suck it up, Alan. I don't have a clue what you should do."

I eyed her for a moment before I said, "I really have missed you. We should do this more often. We really should."

She'd already returned her attention to the food. "I know. This problem-solving stuff? It's my forte. If we come back here and do this come autumn, I'll really truly order sherry and make it even more authentic."

We attacked the food with gusto for a couple of silent minutes. Diane broke the spell by saying, "Alan, you know I'll do anything to help you. Anything. A few years ago—after that patient was killed by her husband in my office—I had a rough time. I'm sure you remember what a disaster I was. Nothing really seemed to matter to me for a while after the shooting. Nothing. But I muddled through it. I kept working at it. Raoul helped, you helped, my other friends helped, and things, well, they just got better. That'll happen for you, too. Things will get better."

CHAPTER

**My wife, Lauren, must have recognized my growing
malaise before I did.**

Diane and I returned to our cars after stuffing ourselves with tapas at Triana. I drove straight home.

Lauren, Grace—our baby—Emily, our dog, and
Anvil, our foster dog, and I lived in a renovated caretaker's house that shared the few remaining acres of a
ranch that was high on the slope of the western-facing
hills of the Boulder Valley in a neighborhood called
Spanish Hills. My happy-hour respite with Diane had
spared me most of the after-work traffic, and I was home
twenty minutes after leaving downtown.

Although it wasn't totally dark outside, the night
was almost moonless and my headlights were necessary

in order to navigate the way down the dirt and gravel lane that led to our house. The beams illuminated the door to the garage just as I was fumbling on the console for the button that would activate the automatic opener. When I spotted the decorations plastered on the door, I immediately stopped the car. I was parked fifty feet or so shy of the garage, which left me just opposite the front of the house.

The front door opened and Lauren stepped out. She was dressed in a little cotton sundress that she called a rag and that I adored. She was barefoot. Grace was in her arms, waving, saying, "Daddy, Daddy," or more precisely, the toddler equivalent. The dogs were both on leashes and I could tell that it was taking most of Lauren's energy to keep them beside her.

The word "bucolic" came to mind.

Domestic visions like that one almost allowed me the luxury of denying the reality that my wife struggled with relapsing/remitting MS. Not quite, but almost.

I shut off the radio, lowered the window, and said, "Hi, sweets," as I gestured toward the garage door, which was crisscrossed with yellow ribbons and adorned with a huge bow that had been fashioned to look like a giant rose. I knew that my wife, who wasn't particularly craft-oriented, had received some significant help with the bow. I asked, "What's going on?"

Simultaneously, I was silently reviewing the gift-giving occasions of which I had apparently lost track— anniversary, no; her birthday, no; Valentine's Day, no. Christmas? Hardly.

Lauren smiled. Her anthracite hair had grown long enough that she could hook it behind her ears. Her violet eyes sparkled in the light reflected from my headlamps as she shook her head a little and said, "Open your present. Don't worry, you didn't forget anything."

"Open the garage?" I asked.

She nodded in one grand motion and said, "Yes."

I touched the button on the transmitter and waited as the garage door began to roll up its tracks. The huge bow was decimated just as the interior lights kicked on, and I saw that an unfamiliar vehicle had been backed into the place in the garage where I usually parked my car.

I recognized it, but I didn't. And then I did.

My first car had been a very used red-with-white-top 1964 Mini Cooper. I'd loved her. Absolutely loved her.

She hadn't loved me back, though.

In retrospect, I'd made the same mistake with the Mini that I would make years later with my first wife, the one who shared my bed before Lauren. I went for the flash and the feel and let the passion of love-at-first-sight overwhelm any objectivity I should have been able to muster.

I called my Mini Sadie. She was every bit as gorgeous and high-maintenance as my first wife had been. And just like my first wife, Sadie was an adorable girl who responded to a firm touch, but who, alas, had an aversion to rough roads.

I poured money into Sadie. Money I didn't have back then. Her weakness wasn't old Persian rugs—that was one of Merideth's, my ex's, many indulgences. Sadie's weakness was her electrical system. The wiring in my old Mini was inhabited with more gremlins and spooks than the tackiest B movie I'd ever taken her to the drive-in to see. No matter how much I invested in making Sadie content with the flow of her electrons, she was never satisfied. She consumed generators, alternators, solenoids, and wiring harnesses the way Madonna consumed lingerie. Where electrical components were involved, Sadie always seemed to be going for a good poker hand: One of something wasn't enough—she wanted two, three, four of a kind. Her house was never full, though. Never.

I left Sadie after three tough, expensive years. I sold her to an ex–Army Ranger, someone I hoped could find the fortitude to discipline her and make her toe the line. But I never forgot her.

Apparently Lauren had never forgotten my lame stories about my love affair with Sadie. Because sitting in the garage in front of me was the distinctive front-end grille of a brand-new, red-with-white-top BMW Mini, the incredibly-difficult-to-find, even-more-difficult-to-purchase, recently reincarnated version of my once-beloved.

I hopped out of my old car, took one step, and then I stalled. I wanted to move in two directions at once. I wanted to rush to the Mini and I wanted to rush over and hug my family. To Lauren I said, "You . . . you . . . how did you . . . they're so hard to . . . Is this mine? Is this really mine?"

She smiled.

"Why? What did I do to . . . ?"

"I thought you would like it. Do you? Do you like it?" she asked, and I made my decision, running toward her, not the car.

The dogs broke free of Lauren. My instincts told me to watch out for Emily, our big Bouvier des Flandres. I knew from experience that Emily could take me down at the knees with one exuberant sweep of her solid flank. But I should have kept an eye out for Anvil, too. Sixteen pounds dripping wet, Anvil was a miniature poodle currently groomed to resemble a small sheep. He was without an aggressive gene lurking anywhere on his strands of DNA. But Anvil was tricky the way ferrets are tricky.

I dodged Emily's playful greeting, shifted my weight, rolled my ankle a little—just enough to compromise my balance—and then I tripped trying to avoid Anvil. The crack I heard as I extended my arm to cushion my fall on the gravel warned me that something bad had happened as I hit the dirt.

The pain that exploded up my right arm confirmed it.

The humerus is the big bone that runs from the elbow up to the shoulder. Breaking it makes a lot of noise and causes a lot of pain. Trust me. The crack sounded like a gunshot in a closed room and the pain was enough to make me wish for my mother's shoulder to cry on.

In my case the treatment for a supracondylar humerus fracture involved immobilizing my arm in a cast that locked my elbow at a roughly sixty-degree angle. Over the next twenty-four hours I would learn that sixty degrees is the incorrect angle for almost everything that a human being might choose to do over the course of a typical day.

Think about it.

The ER doc who evaluated me at Community Hospital was a friend of mine named Marty Klein. After the orthopod he'd called in for a consultation had left the hospital to return to his family, Marty supervised the construction of the cast on my arm. Finishing up his project with the application of a bright red outer coat—based on the flimsiest of evidence, Lauren and I were both of the opinion that red was Grace's favorite color—he commented that the cast was going to severely hinder my participation in the summer bicycling season.

I nodded silently. I was already lamenting that fact. Bicycling was my Xanax. And summer was high season for my habit.

Dr. Marty added, "But there're two good things. One, you're lucky you don't play golf, and two, you're lucky that piece-of-shit car of yours is an automatic. If it was a stick, you wouldn't be able to drive it for a while."

I thought of O. Henry and launched into a maudlin, self-pitying explanation about the brand-new—I stressed the "yet-to-be-driven"—BMW Mini that was sitting in my garage. As I completed the story, Marty seemed almost as bummed as I was. He was a car nut; I didn't even have to point out to him that the Mini came with a standard shift.

He eagerly offered to come over and take me for a ride, though.

I wanted to cry.

I dread displaying visible injuries to my patients.
Even a simple Band-Aid on my cheek from a razor injury was likely to require an hourly—or more accurately, every-forty-five-minute—recounting of whatever
had caused the defacement. One patient out of three or
four would be sure to express doubt about my explanation that I'd cut myself shaving, and we'd end up going
back and forth about my denials that I didn't really
have malignant melanoma.

There was always a subset of patients who would
not notice whatever damage I was displaying on my
body. These were the patients whose own maladies or
characterological predilections had left them so self-
involved that they were either unable or unwilling to
register the Band-Aid that was on my face, or the jaw
that was swollen from my just completed root canal, or

the cherry red cast that was holding my right arm at an impossibly inconvenient angle.

Despite the fact that Lauren had encouraged me to take some time off work, I drove myself to the office the day after my poodle-induced tumble. The hours would pass more quickly, I was surmising, if I was occupied with other people's problems than if I was focusing solely on my own.

My schedule those days had me working late on Thursdays, so my initial appointment wasn't until ten. While I awaited my first patient's arrival my arm was still throbbing and the ibuprofen I'd been downing like Altoids after a tuna and onion sandwich was turning out to be an inadequate defense against my agony. It was going to be a long day.

Lauren had called Diane, told her about my humerus, and warned her that I was in the process of making some testosterone-induced masochistic statement by showing up at the office. Diane was actually sweet about it. She brought me coffee and a bagel and apologized profusely for filling me with the beer that she was certain had led to my accident. I reminded her that I'd only had one beer at Triana and assured her that I didn't hold her responsible for the tumble.

Good, she replied. Because she didn't either. She had just been acting polite.

I was already truly tired of having a broken arm by the time I welcomed my new patient at two forty-five that afternoon. We shook hands awkwardly in the waiting room—his right hand, my left—and I led him down the hall to my office, a walk that typically takes only about ten seconds. I spent the entire ten seconds berating myself for the slight mistake I'd made when I'd recorded my new patient's name in my appointment book the day before.

The man who took the seat opposite me wasn't Thomas Cone, which is the name that I'd written in on the 2:45 line in my book. He was actually Tom Clone, the man who'd just been released from the Colorado State Penitentiary after DNA testing had cast considerable doubt upon his conviction for a brutal murder that had taken place in Park County in the late eighties.

During our brief phone conversation the day before, had I even asked how he'd gotten my name?

I didn't think I had. Which meant I hadn't.

The previous day I definitely hadn't been on top of my game.

Ｈow can I be of help?" I said after Tom Clone seemed settled on the chair across from me. It was my stock opening line.

"Do you know who I am?" he asked. His voice was hopeful. It was apparent he didn't want to have to tell me.

"Yes, I do, Mr. Clone." *I didn't yesterday when you called, but I do now.* "I saw some coverage in the news."

"Then you can probably guess how you can be of help."

"I could make a guess," I said, "but my experience tells me that I'd probably be wrong."

He pursed his lips and exhaled through them. "This isn't exactly my idea. Coming here."

I waited, immediately concerned that Mr. Clone's

presence in my office was court-mandated, though I couldn't imagine under what legal circumstances that might have occurred. I took the opportunity to observe him. He was wearing what I guessed were new clothes. His shorts had cargo pockets on the legs, a fashion statement that wasn't being made when Tom had entered the Colorado penal system. His feet were clad in Tevas. Ditto.

I thought his body looked slightly puffy, as though he were still coming off an extended period on steroids. Something I'd learned during a consultation I'd done years earlier at Camp George West, a minimum-security facility in nearby Golden, was that inmates often grew pudgy during their time inside. The culprit was lack of exercise coupled with a less-than-ideal diet. An analogy came to mind and it felt right: Tom Clone looked like a frat boy who occasionally lifted some weights but had otherwise started to go to seed.

"I'm staying with my grandfather. As part of the bargain, he's insisting that I see somebody for therapy. He's a good guy, but he's stubborn sometimes. Hey, listen, I'm not saying it's not a good idea, but I thought you should know the circumstances of my being here."

I waited some more, wondered if I knew his grandfather, and wondered whether he might be the source of the referral.

"I guess since I have to do it, I'd like to make use of the time and get some help adjusting," he said. "It's so weird being here. Out of prison, I mean. I don't want to screw it up. There're a lot of people who would like me to screw it up."

I heard what might have been the rustling winds of paranoia, but reminded myself to allow the possibility

that my new patient's concerns were absolutely justi-
fied. "That sounds like a reasonable goal, Tom. Where
would you like to begin?"

Tom said, "You broke your arm."

"I tripped over my dog." After four prior attempts at
explaining my malady to patients that day, I'd distilled it
down to its essence.

He appeared to be about to say something else about
my arm, or my dog, or my klutziness, but he didn't. He
said, "Thirteen years. That's what they took from me.
They took thirteen years that I'll never get back."

The throbbing in my arm probably hadn't stopped.
But I suddenly wasn't noticing it. I was confident that I
was about to get a chance to do something that might
renew my faith in the value of this work I did. I was anticipating that I was about to hear something that I
hadn't heard in all my years in practice. I was about to
learn what it was like for a man to be incarcerated for a
crime he didn't commit, what it was like for him to sacrifice, involuntarily, a huge chunk of the prime of his
life to a miscarriage of our justice system.

I was about to learn firsthand what it was like for
him to watch his appeals dwindle like a winter's supply
of firewood while he waited for the final chill to arrive.

What it was like to sit on death row waiting for
someone to tell him "It's time."

But that's not exactly what Tom Clone began telling
me about. Instead, he began telling me about his ride
home from prison. More specifically, he began telling me
about his conversation with the warden and about the
woman who picked him up and drove him to Boulder.

He went into great detail telling me about an FBI
agent named Kelda James and the perfume she wore

and the white jeans that hugged her ass and the run-in that they'd had with sheriff's detectives from Park County and how fast she had filled her hand and the cop's face with the barrel of a Sig Sauer, whatever that was.

"When she pulled the gun on that asshole, I thought—sweet Jesus, I can say anything here, right? You can't tell anybody? Good. This isn't being taped, is it?" He twisted his head left and right as though he half expected to see a camera sitting on a tripod across the room.

I opened my mouth to explain the limits of confidentiality, but my explanation was quickly overrun by the continuation of his narration.

"When she had that gun pointed at his nuts, I was scared, sure, but I was also thinking this woman was the hottest female on the planet Earth. The way she took him down, stood him up, backed him down. Oh man! She never wavered, I swear. He tried to act tough but she had him pissing his boots.

"Sexy? Oh, let me tell you. After where I've been and what I've been through, that barely begins to describe the way she was. I swear my single goal right now is to find some way to get back in touch with that woman."

I wondered when he would stop to take a breath. I hadn't detected an inhalation from him for a while.

"First, she's gorgeous. I mean hotter-than-hot gorgeous with a body that shows no sign of her years—I mean, she's not exactly twenty-five anymore—and then she sends this guy packing and then the next minute she's down on her knees changing the tire on her car like she practices doing it every night when she gets home from work. I swear I've never seen a woman do something like that in my life.

"And then? And then—you'll love this part—she takes me to the damn Broadmoor Hotel for breakfast. She's the sexiest thing in the world and she's driving me up to the front door of this great hotel. I'm thinking I'm dreaming, this can't be happening. I'm an hour out of the damn penitentiary and this fox is taking me to a five-star crib.

"I can tell you honestly that breakfast was the furthest thing from my mind as we walked into that hotel lobby. Have you ever been there? It's like, oh my God, I just wanted to reach into my wallet, pull out my credit card, and get us a big suite overlooking that damn lake and those mountains. That's what I wanted to do. I didn't care what it cost." Abruptly, he slowed his soliloquy. "Problem was I didn't have a wallet, and I sure as hell didn't have a credit card. I'm stuck wearing these crap clothes they give you to leave the damn pen, and I don't even have a fucking wallet to stick my damn hundred dollars in."

He grew silent and for a few seconds his mind seemed to go somewhere I wasn't supposed to accompany him. I was about to point that out when he brightened and started talking again.

"Did I tell you about the cartwheels? I didn't, did I? Okay, okay. Here's that part. This is good."

He told me about the cartwheels. And the back flips.

And then he returned to his plans for getting back in touch with Kelda James.

The whole time, I remained oblivious to the pulsing

pain in my arm. I was too busy casting aside all my assumptions about who Tom Clone might be. Caution was imperative, I knew; I couldn't begin to fathom what this man had endured over the last baker's-dozen years. I was certainly prepared to discover that the man sitting across from me was a poster boy for post-traumatic stress disorder.

Before the time was up, Tom and I agreed to meet again the following Wednesday.

"Do you know," Tom asked just as the final moments of our session were approaching, "that I actually made it through all that time inside without a single tattoo? I'm proud of that." He held out his arms for my inspection, then rotated them so that I could examine both sides.

"Congratulations," I said. I don't know why I said it. Maybe it was because he seemed so sincere.

"Yep," he replied cheerfully.

CHAPTER

Kelda James was one of the reasons that I had started to work late on Thursday evenings. A month before, when she'd called me seeking an initial appointment, my Thursday schedule ended at five forty-five. But I'd agreed to see Kelda James at six o'clock. So now my Thursdays ended at six forty-five. Why did I agree to stay late for her? I figured that I had three reasons.

One: At some level, I suspected she wasn't going to be wasting much of my time lecturing me on the vicissitudes of dishwasher loading.

Two: She was an FBI agent and I thought it would be interesting to hear about her life. Number two was, admittedly, a rotten reason for agreeing to see a new patient. But there it was. I couldn't deny it. The truth was that, had Kelda James been a produce manager at Whole Foods or a marketing consultant at IBM, or spent her days disinfecting laboratories out at Amgen in Longmont, I might have referred her on to another therapist rather than agreeing to extend my workday.

Reason number three for agreeing to treat her even though it meant staying late? Reason number three was complicated.

If Lauren had spotted Kelda in my waiting room, she would have argued that reason number three was even more pathetic than reason number two. She would have maintained that reason number three I was seeing Kelda was that she was more than pleasant to look at.

I didn't even want to approach the entrance to that cave, so I didn't. I was self-aware enough that I knew I was at a stage in my career and my life where I could barely tolerate an increase in professional self-doubt.

So what was *my* reason number three for agreeing to treat Kelda so late in the day? Call it rationalization—Lauren probably would; Diane definitely would—but I had a suspicion that I was the right person to help Kelda James.

However burned out I was feeling, I wasn't burned out enough that I'd stopped caring about that.

The day after I broke my arm, Kelda was late for her appointment, not arriving until ten minutes after six.

During our very first session she'd warned me that she wasn't going to be punctual for therapy, that sometimes she'd cancel sessions at the last minute, and that at other times she would not even be able to cancel—she'd just not show up. Her work was like that. She didn't ask whether it was okay with me. She just wanted my consent that I'd live with it.

I'd thought about it for a moment that day and finally explained to her that I'd wait for twenty-five minutes for her to show up for her sessions. If she didn't arrive, during her next appointment we'd discuss her rationale for not showing up. If her excuse didn't involve FBI business, I would charge her anyway.

"Deal," she'd said.

Patients come in to see a clinical psychologist for a lot of reasons. Some are sent by others: Husbands by their wives. Teenagers by their parents. Employees by their bosses.

Or, as I'd recently learned, exonerated murderers are sent by their grandfathers.

But mostly people come to see people like me because they are in pain. The pain is usually not new. Typically it is pain that the patient has lived with and endured for months or years or even decades. The patients come in to see a psychotherapist like me because something has changed that has caused their tolerance of their pain to crumble. The pain has gotten just *that much* worse. Or they've decided they can't live with it anymore.

Something.

Kelda's motivation was a combination of the two categories. First, she was certainly in pain. There was no doubt about it. And second, she'd been sent to see me by someone else. Her referral to me was made by her Boulder neurologist, Larry Arbuthnot. What was unusual about treating Kelda was that her experience of her pain was more corporal than psychological. Larry was treating Kelda for chronic pain in her legs, and part of his willingness to continue to treat her while he searched for a diagnosis that would explain the agony she suffered was his insistence that she see someone like me to assess possible concomitant psychological components of her condition.

Patients being treated for what they consider to be purely physical illnesses usually don't like to hear that their physicians are thinking that there might be a psychological component present. Kelda was no different. She'd spent much of her first three sessions with me displaying resistance to the idea. I was already prepared to spend a fourth, and fifth, and a ninth and tenth session doing the exact same thing. It hadn't taken long for me to recognize that Kelda James's will was something to behold.

The only topic other than Kelda's physical pain that we'd covered in any detail during those initial sessions was the story of Rosa Alija. I remembered the little girl's name, of course, from the blanket news coverage of her kidnapping and rescue, and could have related the gist of her story myself. Rosa was the Denver child who'd been rescued by Kelda in dramatic fashion a few years earlier. I still recalled that one of my more cynical friends had commented, after her rescue, that Rosa Alija was "the metropolitan area's antidote to JonBenét Ramsey."

For some reason, people do tend to forget the names of heroes sooner than they forget the names of villains or their victims. But Kelda James had proven to be different. I think half the population of the metro area could still have identified her as the person who had rescued Rosa Alija.

Along Colorado's Front Range, Kelda James was a certified hero.

Not surprisingly, her impression of herself was different. She'd informed me, "I'm not a hero. I'm just an average person who was lucky enough to save a little girl. Some days I'm not even sure I qualify as an average person."

"How so?" I'd said.

"I'm sorry about how things happened that day. I'm sorry that I had to kill the guy. I wish I could do it all over again, and do it differently."

"How would you do it differently?"

She didn't blink. "I wish he wasn't dead."

I made a puzzled face. I was eager for her to keep talking.

She still didn't blink.

After all the years I'd been doing psychotherapy, sometimes I actually knew when to shut up. This was one of those times.

A few seconds later Kelda finally said, "Rosa still suffers. She'll probably suffer until she dies. Her parents still suffer. Their agony will never end. So why should that monster rest in peace?"

Oh.

Although the possibility of a psychological connection seemed so seductive, I reminded myself that the pain in Kelda's legs had developed years before she'd saved Rosa Alija. There couldn't be a connection, right?

I was almost convinced.

I asked, "And you?"

"What?"

"Do you still suffer, too?"

She blinked and looked away from me.

"It's not about me," she said.

"No? Well, this is," I replied, waving my hand between us.

I thought she shook her head, but the movement she made was so constricted that I wasn't totally sure. I thought at the time that she was daring me to start digging, and I admit that I was tempted to put a shovel in the dirt right then and there.

I didn't. I made a judgment that the alliance between this patient and this therapist wasn't secure enough yet.

Was my failure to heft the shovel evidence of clinical acumen? Or was it clinical cowardice?

As she left the office that day, I generously decided that the jury was still out on that.

It would turn out to be one of many things I would be guilty of misjudging regarding Kelda James.

The first words from Kelda's mouth in the waiting room the day after my run-in with my poodle were "Oh my God, Alan! What on earth did you do to your arm?"

I tried the CliffsNotes version. "I tripped."

"Are you okay? Does it hurt? When did you do it? How did it happen?"

"I just did it yesterday, Kelda. It's still a little achy, but I'll be okay when I get used to the cast. Come on back to the office."

Less than a minute later she settled onto the chair opposite mine and watched me struggle to lower myself into position. "We can cancel. Why don't you go home and take care of yourself? You must be miserable."

"Thank you for your concern, but I'm okay." My reply was intended to acknowledge her compassion and to redirect her to focus on to the reason she was in my office.

"You're sure you're all right?" The fact that Kelda couldn't distract herself from my broken arm was every bit as meaningful as was the fact that Tom Clone had barely noticed it.

"What happened?"

I told her about tripping over my dog. The story sounded sillier every time I told it.

She wanted to know if the dog was okay.

I decided to try being more direct with Kelda. "Yes, the dog is fine. What about you?"

She sighed and adjusted her position on the chair while the fingers of her left hand kneaded the muscles on the outside of her thigh. I wasn't certain she was even aware she was doing it.

"You asked me to try to remember when the pain started. What was going on in my life?"

"Yes," I said, although I hadn't actually asked her to remember. I'd suggested that it might be helpful for her to remember. I noted the slight translation she had made.

"You're sure you're okay?"

I said I was.

"I think, looking back, that the pain started when I was in Australia, living in Sydney. It may have been earlier but I think it was then. I think I told you about Australia. Didn't I?"

I shook my head.

"The insurance company I worked for when I first got out of college had an office in New South Wales.

One of my bosses in the accounting department was sent over to supervise an internal investigation of some fraud they suspected was going on in the Australian office. He asked me to come with him to Sydney to help with the investigation.

"At some level I knew he asked me to go only because he figured he could get me to sleep with him, but I was fresh out of school, I was twenty-four years old, and I thought, hey, what a great opportunity to get to see some of the world. So I went to Sydney, and ended up being there for almost six months. I loved Australia—just had a terrific time—and I learned most of what I know about forensic accounting while I was there. It was a wonderful period in my life."

Her affect didn't reflect her words. No joy sparkled in her eyes, and her wide mouth was set flat. Her right hand was doing the kneading now, higher on her leg, near her hip. She pushed her dark hair away from her face with her other hand before she rested the tip of her index finger on her upper lip.

"And that's when the pain began?" I asked.

"Yes, I think it was right around then. At first I thought it was just because I was doing so much. You know, activity-wise. The people I was hanging around with in Sydney lived for the water, and I wanted to try every single activity they were involved in. I was learning to surf and trying to learn to windsurf and I met a guy who had a boat and he was teaching me to wakeboard. When I wasn't in the water, it seemed I was out bushwalking with friends in the Blue Mountains. I assumed the pain in my legs was just because I was so active."

"Did you see a doctor while you were there?"

She shook her head. "I *dated* a doctor a couple of times while I was there. He was interesting. But no, I didn't go to see anybody for the pain in my legs. I thought it would go away."

I could have asked another question. A few came to mind. But my scorecard showed that I'd already asked one too many, and I was curious where Kelda was going to wander next if I didn't get in her way.

"When I was in Sydney I met another Kelda, too. A girl from Queensland. Her grandmother was from County Cork, just like mine. She's the only other Kelda I've ever met." She smiled self-consciously. "She reminded me of Jones. Same blond hair, same fair skin, same green eyes. Almost as skinny."

"Jones?" I asked.

Kelda's face softened. "Yeah, Jones. I haven't talked about Jones, have I? A friend from college. My best friend, really. My best friend ever. Joan Samantha Winslett." She crossed her legs. "The day we met I saw her name written on a class roster at DU. It said 'Winslett, JoanS.' The space was missing between the *n* of Joan and her middle initial *S*. When I saw it I read it out loud as 'Winslett, Jones.' She was standing next to me and thought it was hilarious. We became great friends; we were even roommates the last couple of years at school.

"Right from that first day I always called her Jones. No one else did. It was just our thing, part of our bond, I think. Anyway, the Kelda I met in Sydney reminded me of Jones."

Intuition, I've decided, is a combination of experience and attentiveness and maybe some other magical things that I haven't yet isolated. The amalgam, what-ever its actual components, was shouting at me that Jones wasn't just some old friend of Kelda's.

"Was?" I asked. "You said it *was* your thing."

"I did say that. Jones is dead. She died that same year while she was living in Hawaii. She was an artist."

The non sequitur *she was living in Hawaii/she was an artist* hung in the air between us like a mist that refused to settle.

I compared the time periods in my head. "Jones died while you were in Australia?"

Kelda looked back up at me, her eyes moist with tears. "I'm not ready to talk about Jones yet. Okay?"

The statement was poignant for many reasons. The most important was that it told me that Kelda was aware that talking about Jones was one of the crucial things that she and I needed to do.

"Of course," I said. "I'd just like to point out that when you started talking about the beginning of your pain, it didn't take very long for your mind to go to your friend, Jones."

The look she gave me was steely—some alloy of *You want to make something of it?* and *Please don't make me talk about her.*

It wasn't the first admonition that Kelda had com-municated to me. The first had come during our initial session and had to do with the fact that she wasn't us-ing her government health insurance to pay for her treatment; she was paying for the psychotherapy her-self. She admitted that the FBI wasn't aware that she was seeing a neurologist for chronic pain, nor were they aware that she relied on narcotics to function, and she certainly wasn't planning to make them aware that she was seeing a psychotherapist for issues that might be related to her pain.

She'd even admitted to me that she had devised a few different ingenious systems—including an old IV bag taped to her back with a tube down the crack of her ass—that had, so far, successfully allowed her to thwart the FBI's best efforts to discover the morphine derivatives in her urine.

She'd made clear to me that I wasn't to divulge either the fact of, or the nature of, her treatment to anyone. It could cost her her job if the FBI learned that she was taking narcotics on a regular basis.

I had assured her that I had no wish, and certainly no obligation, to inform the FBI about anything having to do with her psychotherapy.

Despite some gentle encouragement on my part, we didn't talk any more about Jones that day.

As the session came to a close, Kelda collected her things to leave the office, stood, and said, "I gave somebody your name. As a therapist, I mean. That guy who was just released from death row? Tom Clone." She stood. "You may have heard that the press has been speculating that it was an FBI agent who helped discover the evidence that got him freed from prison. Well, they're right, it was. I'm that FBI agent. I'm the one who found the knife you might have been reading about."

She took a step toward the door, then turned. "Hope your arm feels better, Alan. Next time try to step over the dog. I'll see you in a week."

● ● ●

I was halfway home, caught in traffic on South Boulder Road, when I stopped wondering about Jones and my arm began to hurt again.

It made me think about the Mini.

I didn't know at the time, of course, that it was the wrong association.

But it's the one that I made.

Kelda's route back to Lafayette would take her down Arapahoe Road, on a path parallel to the one that her therapist, Alan Gregory, was taking to his house. Before she headed home, though, she decided to run a couple of errands in Boulder—Liquor Mart to pick up some beer from Crested Butte that Ira liked, and McGuckin Hardware to get some material to fix the screen on her bathroom window. There was no sense heading east before she allowed some time for the local roads to lose some of their rush-hour inflammation.

Other than to notice that it pulled in just as she was walking into the store, she didn't actually pay much attention to the burgundy Toyota pickup that followed her into the Liquor Mart parking lot. After she bought Ira's favorite beer and left the store, she noted that the Toyota pickup turned from the lot onto Canyon Boulevard about ten seconds after she did.

Could be a coincidence, she thought. *Probably is.*

A few blocks east she turned right on Folsom and then immediately got into the far lane to turn left into the McGuckin lot. The pickup followed her onto Folsom but continued past her as she waited to turn. As the vehicle passed her she tried to get a look at the driver, but the sun visor blocked her view through the windshield, and the window tint kept her from looking into the pickup from the side. She thought that the driver of the truck was a man. The front license plate on the truck was missing. The one on the rear was obscured by a convenient splash of dried mud.

A half block farther ahead the truck eased into the left-hand turn lane at Arapahoe Road.

Had she been trying to do a one-vehicle tail—which she wouldn't: any experienced agent would argue that they're almost impossible to pull off unless the target is oblivious—she would have made the exact same maneuver that the pickup made before finding another route into the parking lot. She parked her car and ambled to the entrance to the hardware store, waiting just inside the door for the truck to reappear. A minute later she spied it as it pulled into the lot from the direction of Arapahoe.

This is no coincidence.

Errand accomplished, screen repair supplies in hand, she returned to her car and snaked through the lot until she could turn onto Arapahoe. When she pulled to a stop at the red light at Twenty-eighth Street, the truck followed her onto Arapahoe. After the light changed she lost sight of the tail for a couple of miles but spotted it again thirty blocks later. The Toyota was a dozen cars behind her.

Kelda lifted her Sig from her shoulder holster and set it on her lap. She edged her Buick into the right lane and slowed, hoping the driver of the Toyota pickup wouldn't notice the speed change. But the tactic didn't work. The truck stayed a few hundred feet back.

Three miles farther east, Kelda approached the left-hand turn onto 111th Street that would take her to her tiny ranch. She knew she didn't want to lead whoever was driving the truck back to her home, so she made a decision to bypass 111th and proceed up to 119th. She'd turn right instead of left and do some maneuvers to lose the tail in the residential clutter of the last decade's orgy of suburban excess as she doubled back between Baseline and Arapahoe. Then she would head home and try to sort out what was going on.

She accelerated gently as she approached 111th, keeping her eyes glued to her mirror as the distance increased between herself and the Toyota. Her impression was that the distance between the two vehicles was increasing much faster than she was accelerating.

Kelda was a couple of hundred yards past 111th, staring into her mirror, trying to make sense of the rapidly increasing gap between her Buick and the tailing Toyota, when the Toyota slowed and turned onto the road that led toward her home. Absently she touched the handgun on her lap and returned her attention from the mirror to the road just in time to see the blunt yellow end of a school bus light up in bright red orbs a hundred feet in front of her.

She slammed on her brakes but knew instinctively

that she wasn't going to be able to stop in time to avoid colliding with the back end of the bus. Escaping to the right shoulder was out of the question—that's where the kids would be exiting the bus. Her only choice was to swerve into the oncoming lane of traffic. She tried to process the data that was screaming at her: at least three pairs of headlights were approaching in the opposite lane. She would somehow have to swerve between two of the oncoming cars in the instant before she impacted the bus full of children.

The first car passed. Kelda's heart pounded as she recognized that an Impala full of teenagers had just driven past her. The last two pairs of headlights appeared tightly spaced, but she determined that the gap would have to be large enough.

The yellow wall grew closer. The red lights on the back of the bus flashed so brightly that Kelda could feel them as though they were pounding hard at her flesh.

Kelda's eyes locked onto the two child restraints she saw poking up in the rear seat of a Dodge minivan, and she began the sudden maneuvers she hoped would help her avoid an impact with the back of the bus.

The bus was only feet away when Kelda yanked the wheel of her Buick to the left and simultaneously lightened the pressure on her brakes. Instantly, her car bolted into the oncoming traffic, eluding the back of the school bus by inches and heading at a sharp angle across the lane of oncoming traffic.

The car hurtling at her was a new VW Bug that was painted a shade of yellow that nature reserved for bananas, birds, and tropical fish. The expression on the driver's face was one of complete incredulity. Kelda's appearance in the lane in front of her was so sudden that the young woman driving the VW didn't even process the danger she was in—only shock was apparent on her face.

In the next instant, Kelda recalled seeing the flash of yellow swim past her. But she wasn't immediately sure whether it was the mustard yellow of the school bus or the neon yellow of the VW that flowed by in her periphery. She didn't know for sure that she had escaped colliding with the onrushing vehicles until the left wheels of her Buick plopped off the macadam shoulder on the far side of Arapahoe Road.

She said, "Shit," and skidded her car to a stop, two wheels in the dust, two on the asphalt shoulder. Traffic continued to surge by in both directions as though nothing had happened. The flow of the road returned to normal long before Kelda's breathing did.

Kelda retrieved her handgun from the floor below the steering wheel and slid it back into her holster. She waited what felt like forever for a break in the traffic that was sufficient to allow her to pull back onto Arapahoe again.

She slowed after she completed the turn onto 111th, her eyes peeled for the burgundy Toyota truck. It wasn't there. As she accelerated toward the speed limit, an uneven ribbon of pink grays hugged the fractured tops of the mountains of the Divide to her left. Sunset was in its final moments. High above the horizon in front of her, stars had begun to pop into the black sky.

But there was no sign of the arrival of the monsoons.

Unlike Arapahoe, 111th Street wasn't a busy street. That night, traffic was even more muted than normal.

Few cars passed Kelda as she covered the final mile that would take her to the lane that led to her house. No headlights appeared in her rearview mirror. She checked every few seconds to be sure.

She tapped her brakes as she approached her lane. A car was coming her way from the north; she decided to wait until it passed to complete the turn. The car—a big SUV—zoomed past and she eased into a wide arc that would take her to the bank of mailboxes at the end of the lane. She moved the shift lever to "park" and pulled herself from the car to retrieve her mail. The adrenaline that had pumped into her veins was dissipating almost as rapidly as it had arrived, and as the hormone disappeared, the pain was returning to her legs. She felt deep aches in her calves and thighs as she walked up to the post that was topped with her galvanized mailbox.

A loud click pierced the night.

Kelda froze.

A heartbeat later her right hand snaked inside her jacket. A starter motor whirred and in a split second she heard the roar of an engine revving much faster than any manufacturer would have recommended. She looked down the lane and then back out on 111th, but she couldn't tell where the vehicle was parked.

A pair of lights flashed into her eyes from down the lane. Seconds later the glare boosted to bright and the roar of the motor began to quiet. She heard the crackling of tires on gravel as the car moved at a measured pace in her direction. She stepped behind the Buick and crouched down. Her Bureau training was almost instinctive; she was putting the engine compartment and the tire between her body and whoever was coming down the lane.

The burgundy front end of the Toyota pickup emerged from the illuminated dust that was hanging above the lane. The visor was still down on the driver's side of the pickup, and the tint on the glass was no more transparent than it had been earlier. The truck pulled even with her Buick and stopped. Kelda stayed low and held the Sig just out of sight.

Ten seconds passed. Fifteen. Finally, the window cracked open about two inches.

Kelda thought she smelled cigarette smoke emerge from the cab.

A voice that Kelda was certain was male said, "Evening, darlin'."

Prehost?

The window rolled back up and the truck turned south, back toward Arapahoe Road. Kelda watched it go until the two red taillights merged into a solitary pink dot.

From her car, she grabbed her big flashlight and a few plastic bags and paced down the lane toward the spot where the Toyota had been parked. She held the big light in her left hand and her 9mm Sig Sauer in her right. She swept the dirt path with the beam of her torch, trying to determine exactly where the truck had stopped. Twice she paused and crouched to examine cigarette butts in the brush by the near side of the lane. In each case the butts had already started to disintegrate.

A hundred yards down the lane a pair of headlights

flashed on. An engine rumbled to life. Kelda skipped off the line and hopped the little fence that lined her property. The Sig felt weightless in her hand.

The car approached. She could see the driver lean his head out the window. She crouched behind a fence post, and the Sig floated into firing position as though her arm were being lifted by a helium-filled balloon.

"It's me, baby. Ira."

She said, "Shit, Ira. You almost gave me a heart attack. A few more seconds and I would have shot you."

He pulled up opposite her and killed the engine.

She said, "What the hell were you doing down there?"

He shook his head in disbelief. "I came over to see you a while ago, and your car wasn't here but someone else's was. Some guy sitting in a truck seemed to be watching your house. I decided to see what he was up to, so I drove past him down the lane, parked my car, and pretended to go into Lucas's place. Then I watched the truck. Do you know that guy?"

"No. I was in Boulder seeing that shrink. I thought I saw this truck following me home but I thought I lost him. Apparently, I didn't. Did you get a plate or a clear look at the guy?"

"Negative on both counts. Obviously he knows where you live, Kelda. That can't be good."

"Tell me about it."

"What did he want?"

"He drove by real slowly and said, 'Hi, darlin'.'"

"That's it?"

"That's it. I think somebody was just letting me know that he can find me."

"Why? Does this have to do with Tom Clone?"

She shrugged. "I don't know. Maybe. Probably. Right now, I assume everything does."

"Was it one of the guys who hassled you on the way home from the penitentiary?"

"I don't think so. It could have been one of them, but if I had to guess, I'd guess not. The voice wasn't right."

"You want some company tonight?"

"I don't think so, Ira. I'm tired. I just want to freeze my legs and try to get some sleep."

"At least let me come in while you check the house."

"Ira? What are you going to do? You would faint if it turned out that there was someone in there. I'm better off doing it by myself. I'll be fine. Call me tomorrow, okay?"

After a moment, he answered, "Whatever you want."

She watched Ira drive away before she continued her search. She walked on until she was at least a hundred feet past her own driveway and spotted two more cigarette butts, one in the dirt, the other floating on top of some dried grass like a golf ball perched on a tee. Both were the same brand and both had filters. These two butts—one burnt all the way down to the filter, the other almost—weren't disintegrating from exposure to the elements. These were fresh. She stuck her right hand inside one plastic bag and used her protected fingers to lift the butts from the lane and drop them in a second bag.

Methodically, she walked a wide perimeter around where she was guessing that the Toyota truck had been parked. She crisscrossed the space in between the perimeter lines, her eyes on the lookout for any clue as to who might have been in the truck. But she ended her search after finding nothing but the two cigarette butts and some tire prints in the dust.

Flashlight in hand, she walked around the outside of her house, examining every opening for signs of forced entry. She flashed the beam on the entire length of the electrical line as it snaked from the post on the lane to her house. She did the same with the phone line and even examined the natural gas pipe that led into and out of her gas meter. She didn't see a thing that would indicate that whoever had been in that truck had approached her house or tampered with anything.

Kelda retraced her steps down the lane and retrieved her car. She parked it in the usual place beneath the twin elms.

Her legs were on fire by the time she slid the key into her back door and entered her house. The alarm sounded as it always did. Her Sig still at the ready, she shut the alarm down and searched the interior of her home as though she was certain that it had been invaded.

Ten minutes later she felt confident that there was no one there. And that no one had been there.

She stripped off her clothes, pulled on some short cotton pajamas, flicked on the swamp cooler and the ceiling fan, and shut all the window coverings before she grabbed two bath towels and six bags of frozen peas. She was only halfway done arranging the peas and towels on her bed when the phone rang. Caller ID said "Private."

"Hello," she said.

"Kelda? It's Tom Clone."

"Yes?" Her shoulders slumped.

"Is this a bad time?"

She mouthed a profanity, but said, "What's up, Tom?" She tucked the phone between her ear and shoulder while she completed the placement of the peas and the careful folding of the towels on her bed.

"I think somebody broke into my grandfather's house."

"What?"

"There's been some weird stuff going on since I got here. The past day or so especially. I'm thinking somebody's been in the house."

"Why don't you call the Boulder Police? I'm sure they'll be happy to help you out. Just dial nine-one-one."

"I don't really want to get involved with the police. I hope you can understand why."

The subtext of Tom's call was suddenly clear to Kelda. Involuntarily, her mind formed a picture of Ira. It developed slowly in her head, like an old Polaroid bubbling to life.

"I can't help you, Tom. I'm a federal agent. What you're describing is not an FBI problem, it's a local one."

"I'm not asking for your official help, Kelda. I'm just, I don't know, I guess I'm kind of paranoid. Wondered if you'd look around, unofficially. Let me know if you think I'm being crazy. I don't know who else to call."

Wistfully, she stared at the towels. Imagined the peas releasing their chill into her legs.

Ira.

She shook her head and sighed. "It'll take me at least twenty minutes to get there."

"I really appreciate it."

"See you soon," she said. With the same reluctance

that an alcoholic feels when recorking a bottle, she returned the six bags of peas to the freezer, leaving the bath towels in place on the bed.

Agony twanged in her legs as though the devil himself were playing the cello on her tendons. Before she pulled on some jeans and a soft gray T-shirt, she swallowed a couple of Percocet and wondered how the hell she'd make it through the night, let alone through her week.

As she walked out the door, she was careful to reset the alarm. She used the thirty-second delay to grab two bags of peas and a couple of kitchen towels. On the drive to Boulder she'd do what she could to freeze away the pain.

CHAPTER 15

The trip back to Boulder didn't take Kelda long. She'd given herself a headache trying to track the headlights that appeared behind her. She didn't think she'd been followed, but she really wasn't sure.

As Kelda parked her Buick by the curb near the end of High Street, the clock on the dashboard clock read 9:06.

Tom Clone was waiting on the front porch of his grandfather's house.

She hooked her purse over her shoulder and began to walk across the narrow lawn. She paused a moment to watch heat lightning illuminate the dark skies of the southeastern horizon like the last gasp of giant sparklers. The sky was clear to the west, which everyone but recent transplants knew meant that this would be another summer night without rain. One of the DJs she'd been listening to on the drive over said that there had apparently been a pretty good hailstorm up north around Greeley, but nothing near Boulder County.

"Thanks for coming, Kelda," Tom said. He stood, took a couple of steps forward, and extended a hand to her.

She stopped five feet from him, at the foot of a couple of flagstone steps. "Hi. So how's life outside?"

As he moved into the light, she could see that his hair was wet and concluded that he'd just stepped out of the shower. She made a conscious decision not to take it personally; she didn't want to think he'd showered just for her visit.

"Better than life inside." He touched his clothes—a pair of cargo shorts and a T-shirt—and swept an arm up toward the sky. "I can't get enough of all this. Do you know I'd forgotten what the night sky looked like? Or how a summer peach smelled. Or what beer tastes like. I'm serious; I'd forgotten what beer tastes like. But the high point so far was that ride home with you. I won't forget that for a while. I can still remember the way you looked and smelled when I walked out of that prison."

At his words, Kelda felt a chill in the base of her spine.

"That's nice," she said. "Listen, it's late. I have to get back home; I have a full day tomorrow. Why don't you go ahead and show me what it is that you're so worried about?"

"My manners," he said, ignoring her question. "Can I offer you something? A beer? My grandfather drinks Bud. There's plenty of that. Some orange juice, too, I think. Maybe something else."

"Nothing, thank you. Let's just get started."

"Of course, whatever you would like. Come on out around back. I'll show you what's going on." He led her around the west side of the house and through the gate of a chain-link fence. "I'm not accustomed to a world where I can open and close gates whenever I want to," he said. "But I think I'm going to like it."

Although the lights of downtown sparkled right below them, the back corner of the house was dark, dark enough that she couldn't see her feet. Kelda's mind wasn't far from the burgundy Toyota, and the darkness made her feel especially wary. "Will I need my flashlight back here?" she asked. "I have one in the car."

"No," he replied. "Wait."

She adjusted her shoulder bag and checked the slit that allowed her access to her handgun.

He reached up the wall and slid his fingers into a light fixture. The bulb suddenly flashed on and a harsh yellow light bathed both of them. "That's exactly how I found it tonight. With the bulb loose. Exact same thing on the other side of the house. Last night these lights were on. Grandpa grilled pork chops and sweet corn for us out here. The lights were both on. I remember."

"What else?"

"This way." The rear of the house had a cracked concrete patio and some lawn furniture that had somehow managed to get coated with rust despite Colorado's minuscule humidity. Tom crossed the patio and stood in front of a window that was a double-hung design, maybe two feet by three feet. "This goes to Grandpa's laundry room, just a little alcove off the kitchen. The screen's been cut. Look."

She stood next to him and could smell his scent.

She thought that he might actually be wearing cologne. She shuddered.

The screen had been sliced so that it could be peeled away from one corner. The cut was too straight to have been accidental. She guessed a razor knife. "Is the window locked from inside?" she asked.

"Kind of. There's one of those hook catches on it, but I was able to get it to give by sliding a putty knife in between the two sashes from out here. It would be easy to get inside if you wanted to."

Kelda stared at the window for half a minute more before she asked, "Anything else? Anything missing inside?"

"Not that my grandfather noticed. He's in bed now. He really wanted to stay up to meet you, but he gets too tired. He said he wanted to shake your hand and give you a kiss and say thanks."

Kelda smiled politely. "That's nice. Tell him thank you for me, but that it's not necessary. So it's just the loosened lightbulbs and the cut screen? That's it?" She tried not to sound dismissive, but she was pretty sure that what her words had ended up saying to Tom was *You brought me all the way to Boulder for this?*

"Yes, I guess that's it. I thought it was important. It looked like somebody had tried to get in and couldn't, or . . . maybe somebody had done the preparations so that they could get in tonight, or sometime soon."

"And why would someone want to get in, Tom?"

A sharp *craaack* snapped behind them, followed by the sound of running through the bushes at the back of the property.

Tom spun to the noise even faster than Kelda did. After staring into the night for a couple of seconds, he said, "The stupid raccoons are back." When he turned back to face Kelda, she had her handgun pointed into the darkness.

"Damn," he said. "You're quick with that thing. Where the hell did that come from?" With his eyes he checked her outfit for a holster and didn't find one. "Did you get that out of your bag that fast?"

"Raccoons?" she replied.

He couldn't take his eyes off the gun. "Do you always draw your gun this much? I'm with you twice and both times you're like Wyatt Earp or John Dillinger with that thing."

"Raccoons?" she repeated.

"Yeah. Grandpa said that he's only seen them come all the way up here two or three times in all the years he's lived here, but with the dry spring they've been wandering farther and farther from the creek looking for food. They're scavengers. They knock over trash cans and eat garbage."

She slipped the Sig back into her bag. "Is there a reason why someone would want to get into your grandfather's house? Does he have valuables? Collectibles? Antiques? Anything like that?"

Tom considered the question for a moment. She felt that he was taking advantage of the opportunity to stare at her. "He likes marbles. There's a whole section of wall in his den that's covered with marbles."

"But that's it? Just marbles?"

"Pretty much. I don't think whoever is doing this is after my grandfather's money."

She raised an eyebrow. She meant for her face to ask, *Then what the hell are they after?*

"There are people who don't like that I'm out of

prison. Who don't like that I'm off death row. We've gotten phone calls. My attorney has received threats against me and him."

Again, Kelda thought about the burgundy Toyota that had followed her home.

"I'm sure that's true, that there are people who don't agree with the decision to let you out of prison," she said.

"I think I have to consider the possibility that there may be someone who might try to break in here to get at me."

After a moment she said, "That can't feel too good."

"It feels like prison all over again. I'm out. I'm free, but I still have to watch my back."

"Well, I'd say you probably do have something to worry about then. I agree with your impression that someone's been tampering with the house in a way that is consistent with planning an intrusion. I'll repeat what I said to you on the phone: This is something to take up with the local police. I would guess that Tony Loving would be able to arrange some extra attention for the house in terms of patrols."

"Kelda? Look. Like I said, not everybody is happy about me getting out of prison. I'm including the local cops on that list. For right now, I'd rather fly below their radar, you know?"

She didn't want to debate police attitudes with Tom Clone. "Does the house have an alarm system?"

"No."

"You might consider it."

"My grandfather doesn't have that kind of money. He's worried about having enough to pay his property taxes. And I don't have a job yet."

"Then you might want to nail or pin the windows shut. That's the only way to really secure those old double-hungs." Kelda knew about double-hung windows. Her little house in Lafayette had them, too. "How are the locks on the doors?"

"They're shitty. Only one out of three even has a dead bolt."

"That's your first priority, Tom. Better locks on those doors."

"So I should go ahead and build myself a little prison? That's what you're suggesting?"

"That's not what I meant." Her legs were on fire. She wanted to leave Boulder and drive home to more frozen peas. "I changed my mind. I will take some of that orange juice, if you don't mind," she said as she lowered herself to sit on one of the old patio chairs. Sitting didn't eliminate her pain, but it changed it. Sometimes, when relief wasn't possible, the novelty of a fresh perspective on her discomfort was all she could hope for.

She didn't tell Tom that she needed the juice to wash down another Percocet. Or two.

"You okay?" he asked when he returned with the juice.

She cursed to herself. She didn't like it when people noticed her pain.

From someone else, the question might have sounded sympathetic, but for some reason, from Tom Clone, Kelda was left doubting the depth of his compassion. She was wondering if his sensitivity to her pain was something like the radar a bull elephant has for an injured foe or that a shark has for blood.

She tried to keep the wariness out of her voice as she asked, "What do you mean? I'm fine." She took the glass from his hand and held it to her lips. She'd swallowed a pill dry while he was gone, and it felt as if it was caught in her throat. She allowed the cool drink to flush it down.

"Do you know the last thing I did every night when I was inside?" Tom asked.

She suspected the question was rhetorical. She glanced at him over the rim of her glass, relieved that they were no longer talking about her pain.

"I tied my cell door shut. When I could steal one, a shoelace worked well. But mostly I used little ropes that I braided out of threads from my blankets or my clothes. But every night, I had to tie the cell door shut or I couldn't sleep." He stared at her eyes and nodded slowly. "That's right, believe it. I locked myself into my very own cell every night."

She wondered where he was going with his story.

"I'm confined in a fucking maximum-security penitentiary and my last act each night is the exact same one that almost every suburban homeowner does. I locked my doors to keep out the bad guys. Except in my case the bad guys weren't nickel-and-dime burglars; they were killers and rapists. The people who wanted into my cell at night were mad dogs."

She watched him, but didn't reply.

"You're having trouble being sympathetic, aren't you?" he asked.

"Um, no."

"My point is that I'm accustomed to going to bed scared. I did it every night I was inside. Every single night for thirteen years. And I don't want to do it anymore. I just don't want to."

"That's why this is so hard?" She gestured toward the

back of the house. "The lightbulbs and the cut screen? Because it means you're still going to bed scared?"

"Yeah. I feel like I'm hoarding shoelaces again. Weaving ropes. Tying my cell door shut."

"Was that the worst part inside? The fear?" Kelda surprised herself with the question, surprised herself how sincerely she wanted to know the answer.

"The worst part?" He pointed to the sky. "That's like asking which part of the night is the blackest. Black is black."

Almost involuntarily a tear formed in the corner of her eye. She turned away from him.

"What did I say? Did I upset you?"

She turned back. "No. I'm sorry. What you said reminded me of something." Kelda was thinking about Jones. Thinking about Jones talking about her fears.

"You're very pretty."

She shook her head in a narrow arc to try to make the compliment go away. She wouldn't admit it to him, but he still felt like an inmate to her, his flattery like a profanity shouted between the bars.

He took a step away from her before he spoke again. "I hated the sound the cell doors made when they were shut. I never got used to it. And I hated the footsteps in the halls. The echoes. Everything inside echoed. Everything. And meals? It was just slop in a trough.

"But it was all black. There was no worst part. No darkest part. All of it was black. I was on death row for a murder I didn't commit. How could there be a worst part?"

This was when she was supposed to say, "I'm so sorry." She didn't. She struggled to keep her fingertips away from the long muscles in her legs. She thought, *We all have our prisons*.

He was staring at her, waiting for her to say something.

She stammered out a reply. "You, uh, don't babble on about it, about the injustice, I mean. Not with me. Considering what you've been put through, I would think that you wouldn't be able to talk about anything else. Where's your rage?"

He looked away from her for a second.

Kelda opened her mouth to say something more, but Tom turned back, locked his eyes on hers, and spoke first. "I saw that Dr. Gregory today. How do you know him?"

Kelda hesitated, moistened her lips with the tip of her tongue. She thought she'd succeeded in keeping her expression neutral. "A friend sees him," she said. She stood and repositioned her shoulder bag to better handle the weight of the Sig. She added, "You really should call the police, Tom. For your grandfather's sake, if not for your own. What's going on here at the house, this could be a serious problem."

"I'll think about it. I promise."

He followed her out to the curb.

"I've been wondering," he said abruptly. "The call that you got about where to find the murder weapon? The knife? That just came out of the blue one day?"

"Yes," she said. Tom was silhouetted against the front porch light of his grandfather's house. She couldn't see his eyes. "Maybe someday I'll tell you the whole story."

"I'd like that," he said.

● ● ●

On the ride back to Lafayette, Kelda began to wonder about how the possible had become the inevitable and how justice and science had somehow become Siamese twins.

The whole way home she kept checking her mirror for the burgundy Toyota. She tracked a hundred pairs of headlights, but none of them followed her down 111th toward her little house.

She half expected to see Ira's car in front of her house or to find him sitting by her door with his daypack over his shoulder. She didn't want to explain about her trip back to Boulder.

She wouldn't have to; he wasn't there.

Kelda had taken the phone call ten months before.
It had come, just as Tom Clone had suggested, seem-
ingly out of the blue.

She recalled that the morning was cold for
September and the evidence of the season's always-
surprising first snow was lingering on the still-green
lawns of Denver. The thin coating of fat flakes that
coated the grass felt like an affront to everyone who
adored summer.

When the phone rang on her desk, Kelda was standing across the big office she shared with other agents.
She'd been talking with a friend of hers, an agent
named Bill Graves, whose desk was ten feet away. She
interrupted the conversation with Graves to take the
call.

She said, "Special Agent James." After listening for

a few seconds, she added, "Yes, this is Special Agent Kelda James. How can I help you?"

That was how it all began. She'd taken a phone call while standing beside her desk.

Three or four minutes later she turned to Bill Graves and said, "That was odd. Someone just called and told me that he knows where I can find the weapon that was used in an old murder."

Bill had returned his attention to a file on his desk. He looked up and said, "Really? Just like that?"

"Yes, just like that. Guy says there was some old murder up in Park County in 1989 and he says he knows where the murder weapon is hidden. Said he saw the murderer hide it."

"You get a name?"

"No, not from the guy who was on the telephone. He wouldn't say, but he gave me the victim's name. Dead woman was named . . ." Kelda glanced down at the notes she'd scribbled while on the phone. "She was named Ivy Campbell. Does it ring a bell? You weren't here in '89, were you?"

Bill shook his head. "No, I was still in Topeka. Why did this person call you? Why didn't he just call the local cops and tell them about the weapon?"

Kelda looked away from the other agent. Even though she trusted Bill, she was embarrassed about the implications of what she was about to say. "He says he doesn't trust the local cops, and that's why he called the FBI. He said he asked for me, specifically, because of . . . you know, the girl."

Rosa Alija. The girl.

Bill Graves nodded and sighed, as though he was disheartened by her reply. He knew precisely what girl

Kelda was referring to. With half a smile on his face he said, "That little girl is like an annuity for you, isn't she? She just keeps paying dividends year after year. Who would have guessed what those few minutes in that warehouse would do for you?"

Kelda heard the echoes of envy in his voice. She'd heard them before from other agents, but never from Bill Graves. She said, "Yes. It seems that way sometimes."

"Why did he call after all these years?"

"He said that he thinks the cops may have the wrong guy in prison for murdering this Ivy Campbell and he can't live with that anymore."

"You going to check out his story?"

"I don't think I should ignore it. I'll run it by the SAC. The guy was clear that he wants us to deal with the information he provides by ourselves. He said if we involve the local cops, he won't tell me where to find the weapon. I told him I had to get clearance before I could investigate anything. He's going to call back in a couple of hours to hear the decision."

Bill said, "It's a no-brainer, Kelda. The SAC"—Bill always broke convention and put the emphasis on the A. For him, the Special Agent in Charge was the s-A-c—"loves stuff like this, stuff that makes the locals look bad and us look good. Especially given all the bad press we've gotten lately. He'll tell you to check it out. Bet your lunch on it."

"If he tells me to check it out, then I'll check it out, won't I?"

"You said Park County, right?"

She nodded.

"Get me in on it, Kelda. I could use a day in the mountains."

Kelda picked up the phone, called the switchboard operator, and asked for an origination number for the call that had just been forwarded to her extension.

She took a call back in about a minute with the not-unexpected news that the call had come from a pay phone. The phone was in Colorado Springs, not too far from Park County.

Kelda spent about an hour on her telephone and on her computer getting her facts straight before she sent the SAC a concise e-mail about the chronology of Ivy Campbell's murder and the subsequent response of the criminal justice system. She highlighted the convicted murderer's recent efforts to gain a new trial. At the end of the e-mail, she described the anonymous phone call from the man who offered the tip about where the FBI could recover the weapon that had, purportedly, been used to slice Ivy Campbell's throat all the way to the bone.

The SAC's reply came back to her in about ten minutes. It was as cryptic as he was. *Do it.*

She e-mailed back asking if Bill Graves could accompany her.

The reply was almost instantaneous. *Yeah, take Graves. He has more experience collecting evidence than you do. Get a video record of everything you do while you're there. And I want to know exactly what you two find before any calls are placed to the locals.*

Almost exactly an hour after Kelda read the SAC's e-mail, the anonymous man called back. The agents were ready this time. A simple caller ID machine identified the source of the call as a pay phone in Woodland Park, about twenty miles east of Park County. The man on the phone listened to Kelda's assurances that the local police wouldn't be involved until after the search for the weapon, then gave her detailed directions to a rusted drainage pipe that was near a culvert about a hundred yards or so from Highway 24, not too far from Lake George.

The chill was still in the air at three-thirty in the afternoon as Kelda and Bill Graves drove from Denver to a location that the *Pierson Guides* map indicated hugged the boundary between Park and Teller counties. Bill was thrilled at the chance to get out of the city and up into the mountains and was eager to drive. He chose to avoid the interstate, taking 67 out of Sedalia, passing up through Deckers, and coming within sight of the intersection with Highway 24 a few minutes after five.

"God, I love it in the mountains in the fall," Kelda said as they neared their destination.

Bill shot back, "Check the calendar, my friend. It's still summer. It's not fall. Fall means winter's coming soon, and I'm not ready for winter."

"It snowed last night, Bill. Calling it summer doesn't make it summer."

"A few flakes. That's nothing. It's going to be in the eighties tomorrow."

"How about Indian summer, then? I love it up here during Indian summer. Can you live with that?"

"Yeah, as long as Indian summer lasts three months,

or even better, six. Do I go left or do I go right at the intersection?"

Kelda checked her notes. "If this is Highway 24 coming up, go right. Then we go nineteen miles and start watching for a dirt road on the left-hand side of the road."

A while later they both saw the dirt lane. "I turn here, right?" Bill asked.

"You turn here, *left*. Apparently there's a little clearing about fifty yards in. We park there."

The forests along most of Colorado's Front Range are commonly pine or fir. This one was mostly pine. Although no visible signs of the previous night's snow remained, the storm had left an unfamiliar moistness in the woods. After standing outside the car for ten seconds to gauge the temperature, Kelda shed her blazer and pulled a fleece jacket out of the backseat.

Bill collected an evidence kit and a video camera and tripod from the trunk of the car. Kelda grabbed a big flashlight and hung a 35mm Canon around her neck. He said, "We look like a couple of tourists from Kansas."

She laughed. "You are from Kansas, aren't you?"

"Yeah." Bill said it proudly, with the kind of conceit that usually accompanied people announcing their allegiance to Texas.

"Tell me something. Is your cousin really the governor, or is that just one of the stories you tell around the office?"

"No, my cousin is really the governor. Second-term Republican. Elected first back in 1994."

"Are you guys close?"

"We were as kids. He's a little bit older than me. I

followed him to Kansas Wesleyan for college. After I got my CPA, I worked with him for a while in the family trucking business in a little town called Salina."

"Yeah?"

"Yeah. We have the same name. When we were little, everybody called him Bill and they called me Billy."

"Billy? You? People called you Billy?" She had trouble seeing anyone calling Special Agent Graves "Billy." He stood six-two and was a chiseled 210 pounds.

"Yes. Me."

"Can I call you Billy?"

"I wouldn't recommend it."

"I'm still not sure if you're making this up."

He held up three fingers. "Scout's honor."

"Were you a scout?"

"No. But he was. The governor."

"Jerk."

Bill asked, "This is National Forest, right? Federal land? This whole area around here?"

"That's what the map says."

"I just wanted to be sure we have jurisdiction to do what we're about to do." He looked down the road. "So now what?"

Kelda shrugged and looked at her notes. "We walk up the road a little bit until we see a drainage culvert coming in from the west. He said that the culvert is really just a big galvanized pipe that goes under the road. He said all we'll really see from a distance is a dry creek bed."

Bill spotted the creek first. It was nothing more than a smooth contour of recessed barren ground. "That must be it, Kelda. It probably only has water in it during the thunderstorm season."

She glanced up briefly, nodded in agreement, and then continued reading from her notes. "Ten, twelve feet farther down the road there should be an old drainpipe that was part of the system that the culvert replaced. The guy on the phone said the pipe was small and that the entrance sticks up out of the ground only a few inches. It's bent now, and rusty."

Bill walked a few paces farther along the road and announced, "Here it is. Here's the rusty pipe, just like the man said."

Kelda was still examining her notes. "How big is it?"

"I don't know, four inches in diameter, maybe five."

"Big enough for a knife?"

He tilted his head to change the angle of his vision. "Sure, big enough for a whole set of knives."

Kelda said, "We should probably slow down and take some pictures before we go any farther."

Bill said, "Yeah." He pulled the lens cap from the video camera. "Did it cross your mind that this could be a setup?"

"You mean a wild-goose chase? Of course."

"No, that's not what I mean. I've been thinking that . . . this is a great way to get a couple of FBI agents out in the middle of nowhere. Let's make sure we're alone out here. That's all."

Dusk had just begun seeping into the forest, and the approaching night seemed to highlight the discomfort in Kelda's legs. The pain was reaching all the way from her toes to her hips. The tingling in her feet had degenerated into a burn. "I don't see anybody, Bill. I don't think it's really necessary."

"Humor me, Kelda. Give me the flashlight."

• • •

Five minutes later Kelda greeted him on his return from his trek through the woods. He'd covered a perimeter that led away from the culvert at a radius of about a hundred feet. "See anything?"

"Beer cans. Couple of old illegal campfires. Condoms, empty pint of tequila. What is this place, party central?"

She shuddered. "Not my idea of a great place for a romantic interlude. Come on, it's getting cold, Bill. Let's get this over with. I got pictures of everything while you were pretending you'd been a Boy Scout. Why don't I set up lights and do the video camera and you can decide how you want to proceed with the evidence collection."

Bill used the flashlight to peer down into the pipe. "If there's anything in there, it's probably more than a foot down the pipe. I'm not convinced we'll get anything. It may turn out that we're going to need to get some help getting anything out. Maybe it would even be best to excavate the whole pipe and take it back to Denver. The search would be cleaner that way."

"May I look?"

"Yeah."

Kelda took the flashlight and stared into the pipe. "There's something down there, I think. Look."

Bill leaned over the opening.

Kelda moved her head out of his way. They were so close that she could smell whatever it was he used on his hair. She said, "Move the flashlight around. See that shadow on the left-hand side? A foot down, maybe a little more? Well, something is causing that shadow."

"Yeah. Maybe."

"I think I can get my hand into the pipe."

Bill laughed. "Yeah, maybe you can. The question, of course, is whether you can get your hand back out of the pipe. If you don't, there will be a whole new Kelda James legend for the boys back at the office."

She scoffed, "Give me a glove. Let me try."

He handed her a glove. She pulled the latex onto her fingers and snapped it tightly around her wrist.

Bill stepped away, hit the "record" button on the video camera, and checked the composition of the framing of the shot. "We're rolling. Go for it anytime, Houdini."

Kelda paused, pulled off her fleece jacket, and rolled up the right sleeve of her shirt. Bringing her fingers together to make her hand as narrow as possible, she inserted it into the pipe. Her hand had disappeared almost to her wrist when she suddenly yanked it back out. She blurted, "Do me a big favor? Check again for bugs."

"Bugs?"

"Spiders. I don't like spiders. That pipe is a great place for a black widow or even"—she shuddered—"a brown recluse."

"A brown what?"

"Check for spiders, please."

He laughed, but he picked up a stick and used it and the flashlight to probe the opening for spiders.

"Not even a web, Kelda. Now go on, go fish."

She took a deep breath and reinserted her hand. It was almost twelve inches into the pipe when she felt the metal of the opening tighten on her forearm, near her elbow. She tried not to think about the creatures whose home she was invading. "I'm not sure I can get it in any farther," she said.

As the words left her mouth she prayed that Bill was too much of a gentleman to take advantage of the fat serve that she'd just hit over the net. Sardonically, he said, "That's too bad. I guess we'll have to come back out here tomorrow when we're better prepared. I still like the idea of excavating the whole pipe and cutting off a section. We'll use power tools. Or acetylene torches. That would be even better."

"Wait, wait," she whispered. "I feel something."

"What is it?"

"How the hell would I know what it is? My arm is stuck down a pipe full of spiders."

"You know, Kelda, my brother's a gastroenterologist in Topeka. Maybe we could get a flexible camera and a light like he uses for sigmoidoscopies and see what it is that's down there."

"This isn't somebody's rectum, Bill. It's a damn drainage pipe and I've got something hard between my fingers. I'm going to try and bring it up. Do you have gloves on? I'm going to need some help grabbing it if I am able to get this thing to come out. My fingers are going to cramp up in this position and I'm afraid I'll drop it."

"Two seconds," he said. He went back to the evidence kit and pulled gloves on both of his hands. "Kelda?"

"What?"

"You know, your butt is perfectly framed for the camera right now."

She cursed at him. There were maybe two men in the Denver field office that she would permit to get away with that comment. Bill Graves was one of them.

She turned half a step so her body was in profile to the camera.

He walked back to stand beside her. Slowly, she pulled her arm straight up from the pipe. She'd managed only about two inches when a dull thud sounded.

"Damn it," Kelda muttered. "Lost it."

"It's okay. We'll come back tomorrow with the right equipment. We'll get whatever it is. I'm thinking torches, maybe. That'd be fun."

"I'm going to try once more." Again, she lowered her hand all the way into the pipe. "I think I've got it. Yes, yes, I do. And I have a better grip this time. Here it comes. Here she comes." Slowly, her arm emerged from the pipe. "One second," she said, "get ready to grab it!"

"Got it," he said. "Good work, Kelda. Bravo."

Kelda shook her arm from the exertion of having clamped down so hard with her fingertips on the wooden handle of what turned out to be an eight-inch kitchen knife. Even through the crusted dirt it was apparent that the engraved handle read "Chicago Cutlery."

"Wow," Bill said. He was holding the knife by its wooden grip between his index finger and his thumb. The blade of the knife, which was pointing straight at the ground, was stainless steel and didn't appear to be rusted, but the whole knife was coated in an uneven red-brown layer of grime.

Kelda said, "Damn. Maybe Ivy Campbell *is* back from the grave. Is that dried blood, do you think?"

Bill leaned over, moving his eyes to within six inches of the knife. But he didn't respond to her question.

She said, "I bet it is. We'll know within a day or two."

"This won't get examined locally, Kelda. The SAC is

going to want to send this to the big lab in the sky. And since the crime in question has already been solved, and the perpetrator is on death row, I don't think it's going to be the highest of priorities for them."

Kelda knew that Bill was talking about the laboratory at FBI Headquarters. "Yes," she concurred. "You're right. The SAC will want to send it east. I'll get a bag for it. Then let's see if we can get anything else out of that pipe."

Bill said, "Want to get some dinner on the way back to town? Celebrate our find? There used to be a great bar in Morrison. And . . . if you promise to fill out the FD-620, I'll spring for dinner."

"You hang out in bars in Morrison?"

"Not hang out, exactly. But I've been once or twice. I have a Harley. I like to ride up there."

Bill placed the knife into a bag that Kelda was holding open.

"You have a Harley?" she said.

"I do."

"Is your cousin really the governor of Kansas?"

He laughed.

Indian summer was in rare form the September that Kelda and Bill found the knife.

But by the time that Kelda received the first report with the analyses of the weapon that she'd sent to the FBI laboratory in D.C., the daytime temperature was still hovering in the sixties, the glory of the annual metamorphosis of the aspen trees from emerald to gold in the Colorado Rockies was complete, Halloween had passed, and the stores were screaming, "Thanksgiving's almost here!"

She'd collected case records and laboratory samples from the original case files and evidence records from the original prosecution and shipped them along with the knife to the attention of the DNA Analysis Unit in Washington, but her FD-620 had specifically requested that the laboratory provide "all appropriate analyses."

The agent-examiner in the DNA Unit had reviewed the circumstances involved in recovering the knife and determined that it should also make the rounds of many of the other forensic laboratories on the third floor of the FBI Headquarters building at Ninth and Pennsylvania in Washington, D.C. Ultimately, Fingerprints, Toolmarks, Chemistry, and Hair and Fibers had taken turns examining the knife.

The report the lab provided back to the FBI's Denver Field Office was packed with insights about the weapon.

An attempt had been made to wipe the handle of the knife clean of prints, but two partials were recovered. A cursory attempt had also been made to wipe the blade clean of blood. No useful hairs or fibers were recovered from the weapon. Chemistry of residue from the surface of the knife was not remarkable. The toolmarks analysts found nothing idiosyncratic about the blade that could identify it as anything more than a likely weapon in the Ivy Campbell murder.

The first surprise in the report? The partial fingerprints were not consistent with the exemplars from Tom Clone.

The report saved the blood and DNA analysis for last.

Despite the UNSUB's efforts to wipe the blade clean of blood, traces remained on the knife blade. Modern forensic techniques permitted a wealth of analyses to be performed on the limited blood residue that was recovered.

Kelda and Bill weren't surprised to learn that the lab wizards had managed to isolate the DNA from the blood.

But they were surprised to learn that the DNA of two individuals was discovered in the blood residue on the knife. The analysis revealed that some of the blood was, indeed, Ivy Campbell's. The identity of the person whose blood ended up on the knife along with Ivy Campbell's was, of course, unknown to the FBI examiner.

But Kelda and Bill assumed it might belong to Ivy's killer.

Bill, look," Kelda said. She'd copied some pages from the records of the initial investigation of Ivy Campbell's murder. The page that she shoved in front of Bill Graves's eyes was the write-up of an interview that Detective Prehost had conducted with Tom Clone two days after the girl's murder.

"What?"

"You have a minute? I want to talk about the knife."

He marked a spot on a column of figures with his fingertip. "Huh?"

"Stay with me here, okay? We have blood from an UNSUB on the knife along with the victim's blood, right?"

"This is about the Ivy Campbell knife, right?"

"Right. The one we found? Remember? Hello. The big lab in the sky found the victim's blood and they found blood from an UNSUB on the knife."

"Yeah, I saw the report, too, Kelda. I've moved on. You should think about doing the same."

"Well, I've been doing a little more investigating. Just a little—come on, Bill. Anyway, here's what I know today that I didn't know yesterday: Two days after Ivy's murder, the detective from Park County who was investigating the murder—his name was Prehost, in case you don't remember—"

"I remember."

She put a second page in front of him. "Good. Two days after the murder, Prehost observed a cut on the heel of the thumb on Tom Clone's left hand. Look at the next page—Prehost even traced his own hand and drew in the precise location of the cut. I kind of like this guy, Prehost, the way he thinks, you know. In case you don't recall, Clone's the guy sitting on death row for the murder."

She was teasing him. He knew that, and she thought he liked it. "Yeah."

"At the time of the interview, Clone's explanation for the wound was that he cut himself at work. At the time, he was a med student who worked in various clinics at the Health Sciences Center." She placed another sheet of paper in front of Bill. "Now look at the third page."

Bill lifted the second sheet off his desk.

"Well, it turns out that Detective Prehost was thorough; he followed up on Clone's story. He interviewed the nurse who Clone said witnessed the accident at the hospital."

Bill made a "go on, go on" motion with his right hand.

"The quote-accident-unquote happened in a treatment room in the orthopedic clinic the day after Campbell was murdered. The nurse told Prehost that she helped Tom Clone clean and dress the wound on his hand, but she didn't actually see the incident occur.

She remembered he told her he'd slipped with an instrument or something. A scalpel, maybe."

Bill looked up at Kelda and smiled warmly. "This is sure a fun story but we're getting near the punch line, I hope."

She slapped a final sheet of paper on Bill's desk. "Prehost also talked to one of Clone's classmates who thought he'd seen a Band-Aid on Clone's hand the morning before the accident in the treatment room, but the witness wasn't one hundred percent sure. Now, what do you think of that?"

"You're thinking that Clone cut himself on the murder weapon and then tried to cover up the wound by faking an accident at the hospital?"

"Exactly. Watch this." Kelda turned and lifted a long, thin box from the top of her desk. She raised the lid off and exposed an eight-inch Chicago Cutlery French knife. "This is the same model as the one we found in the pipe. I found it at a garage sale. And it's the same model as the one missing from the kitchen where the murder occurred."

He sat back on his chair, finally acknowledging to himself that Kelda's intrusion was going to last a while.

"Clone's right-handed, by the way. But let's say he's getting ready to wipe the blood off the knife—he'd hold it in his left hand and use his right hand to do the wiping, right? I'm right-handed and I would." She demonstrated, first holding the knife by the handle and wiping the blade with an imaginary cloth, and then by the blade and wiping the handle the exact same way. "See, if he held it like this, blade down, the base of his thumb is exactly where the butt of the blade would be. If he wasn't careful, he could cut himself."

"That's what you think happened?"

"Yes. That's why his blood's not at the murder scene. He didn't cut himself until later, when he was trying to clean the knife. Maybe he even did it right where we were a few weeks ago, at that pipe."

"What's the point of all this? This Clone guy is already on death row, Kelda. How much worse can we make it for the guy?"

"He still has appeals left. Anything can happen in these cases, you know that. He's trying to get his lawyer to get him a new trial as we speak."

"So what do you want to do? See if Clone will volunteer a DNA sample so we can hang him with it? Something tells me that there are some Fourth Amendment issues that we should be considering here."

She sat on the corner of Bill's desk. Across from her a hinged frame held a picture of his daughter on one side; the other side—the side where his ex-wife's portrait had been—was empty. His wife Cynthia's affair was still an open wound for Bill.

"Kelda, we have a lot of unsolved cases." He gestured toward the top of his desk, which was cluttered with paperwork. "More than we have time for. I don't see any reason to waste any more time on one that's already been solved. I don't think the SAC will authorize another minute for you to waste forging yet another nail that's going to serve no other purpose than to secure this guy's coffin."

"Maybe Clone gave some blood or tissue samples during the initial investigation. We could send those back to the lab for comparison."

"Why? What's to be gained? The right guy has been convicted. He's on death row."

"We could short-circuit his appeals."

Bill raised his eyebrows. "Again, why? My experience is that the courts will do what the courts will do. If his appeals get out of hand, we can always play the trump card. Keep it up your sleeve for now. There're lots of bad guys out there who deserve our attention more than Tom Clone does."

"What he did was vicious, Bill. He sliced that girl all the way to the bone. You've seen the pictures."

"So that means we should convict him twice? That means we should kill him twice? Come on, Kelda. It's not like you to spin your wheels." He lifted a file from his desk. "Pull up a chair—we have money-launderers to catch."

She didn't move.

"Anyway," he said, "there's always the possibility that the blood on the knife isn't Clone's. The partial prints on that knife aren't Clone's. What are we going to do then?"

"What do you mean?"

"What if we go for a DNA match with the UNSUB's blood on the knife and it doesn't match Tom Clone? What then?"

"I hadn't thought of that."

"Well, I have."

"Look at the evidence against this guy, Bill. It's overwhelming. Everything points to Clone. Everything."

"If the prints on the murder weapon don't match and the DNA of that blood doesn't match, the rest of the evidence is crap. You know it and I know it. We already have a conviction. We already have a death sentence. Everybody involved thinks it's the right guy. We should be patient and let his appeals evaporate."

"What? You think running the DNA is just a roll of the dice?"

"No, of course not. I think there's a ninety-nine percent chance the UNSUB blood on the knife will match Clone's. But if I told you that there was a ninety-nine percent chance that you wouldn't be killed in the elevator as you left work today, I bet you'd take the stairs."

18

I eyed Tom Clone. He was slumped on the chair across from me in my office. The cocky energy that I'd witnessed during the previous week's session as he'd talked about his ride home from the penitentiary with Kelda James was absent. He appeared weary, and frustrated. I suspected that he was going to be one of those patients who offered the promise of surprise every time he walked through my office door.

"It's not going as well as I'd hoped. Being out of prison, I mean. People are more suspicious, less forgiving than I'd anticipated. I thought people would seem happier for me, you know? But everybody acts wary, like they're not really sure I should have gotten out at all. I'm not sure that all the news coverage my lawyer arranged was that good an idea."

Although nothing that Tom said particularly surprised

me, I still didn't know what to make of him. That alone made him interesting to me. I used my silence as bait.

He took it.

"The first few days were real exciting. I did lots of news interviews. But that gets old fast, you know? Talking to those people, answering the same questions over and over and over. It's okay with me that they're gone. Anyway, my lawyer wants me to keep a low profile now while he's making decisions about the lawsuit we're going to file. Hopefully there will be a lot of money coming my way. I want somebody to pay for what they did to my life."

Since he'd walked through the door I didn't think a minute had passed that he hadn't stolen a look behind him. He did it again right then. I tried to imagine what life was like when the ghost of somebody with a shank was always in your rearview mirror.

"I may take a job working as a pharmacy aide at the Kaiser clinic. You know the one. It doesn't pay much but I can walk there from my grandfather's house. It would give me something to do while my lawyer twiddles his thumbs and I decide about applying to finish med school.

"I think they'd have to take me back into school, don't you think? I mean, how could they not? They'd probably make me repeat some coursework; I mean, I would have to catch up on thirteen years of medical progress. There have been lots of developments. AIDS, biotechnology, this whole Internet thing, too. Who would have thought?" He nodded to himself, as though he appreciated the cogency of his own argument.

He looked around my office again as though he was seeing it for the first time. I watched his eyes scan the corners where the walls met the ceilings. "I thought of doing this years ago, you know that? When I was still at the Health Sciences Center, one of my supervisors suggested I consider therapy, and I really did think about it. But . . ." His voice trailed away.

"But?" I repeated after him. It was my first word of the session. I'd been tempted to query him about the supervisor's rationale for suggesting psychotherapy, but I decided instead to follow Tom's lead. Early on in treatment, the path of least resistance was sometimes the best path to take.

"I didn't want to get into all that shit with someone who worked at the same place I did. It didn't feel safe."

"What shit was that?" I asked, my voice absent of inflection. I often thought that if psychotherapists had been in the California gold rush, a strike into the mother lode would have been greeted, not with "Eureka!" but with a carefully modulated version of "I wonder if this is what we've been looking for."

"The stuff when I was growing up," he replied. "I'm sure you've read all about it. Or at least the public version of it. People like to make a big deal out of shit they really don't understand."

"No," I said. "I haven't read about it."

I actually hadn't. My tolerance of what the modern media considered "news" had been diminishing as I aged. O.J. had been the first straw, Chandra Levy one of the last. JonBenét had come somewhere in between. Perhaps the Gulf War and the September 11 travesties had deserved nonstop cable TV coverage. It was hard for me to believe that so many other things did. But I did find it interesting that Tom Clone assumed I was learning about his life through the media.

I said, "Tell me."

"My mom was bipolar." Tom put a big, fat period at the end of the sentence. It was his way of exclaiming, "Enough said."

When a patient turns the traffic signals in therapy from green to yellow, few therapists can resist the urge to put the pedal to the floor and run the light. I leaned forward on my chair just a little bit as I prepared to gun the engine. The gesture caused me to have to readjust the position of the arm with the cast on it. "Wow, that must have been something. What was that like for you, Tom? Growing up with a manic-depressive mother?"

I could tell that my questions had disarmed him a little. They didn't shake him; they just surprised him. I don't know what he had expected me to say, but I guessed it was probably some version of "Really? What was her disease like?" or "Really? Was she stable on lithium?"

"It wasn't all bad" is how he replied. "She and I had some great times when she was 'feeling good.' That's what she used to call her manic phases when I was little, you know. She'd say, 'I'm starting to feel good, Tom,' and all of a sudden she'd rush into my room and put both her hands on my face and tell me, 'You have two minutes to grab your stuff and get in the car,' and before I knew it we were off on a road trip to visit relatives in Illinois or we were going to the Grand Canyon or we were going to Las Vegas. That was one of her favorite places when she was 'feeling good.' She loved Las Vegas. But when I climbed in the front seat with her, I knew we could be going anywhere.

"I felt like the little kids in Peter Pan. I was off on an adventure to a land where my mother loved me."

• • •

I moved my arm into my lap, sat back on my chair, and said, "So when you were little, you liked the eggs?"

He looked at me as though I were nuts. "What?"

As my partner Diane would say, I had his attention. In explanation, I walked him through the penultimate scene in *Annie Hall*, where Woody Allen's character is explaining to a psychiatrist that when he was growing up he had a brother who thought he was a chicken, but that the family tolerated the pathology because "We liked the eggs."

Tom laughed. "Yeah, when I was little, there were times when I liked the eggs." He smiled at some memory. "When Mom was 'feeling good' we had a lot of fun. I didn't know she was sick back then. I just knew that this sad, quiet woman would suddenly become the most fun friend I had in the whole world. And I was the one in the center of her universe. Especially on those road trips. We had an old VW station wagon we used to take. I loved those times. I really did. It was so great to be with her—it was like she chose me to be her kid all over again. 'You're my best buddy, Tommy—my best buddy in the whole wide world!' she'd scream out the window of the car." Suddenly, Tom's smile diminished. "Yeah, I think you could say that I liked the eggs."

I said, "But at some point she would crash?"

The natural history of bipolar disease is loosely governed by the rules of gravity. What goes up with mania eventually comes down with depression. Usually the descent from euphoria into despair, like the crash of Newton's apple, leaves someone feeling bruised. Without the cushion of appropriate medication, bipolar phasing isn't a graceful process for the patient or anyone in close proximity to the patient.

"At some point she would crash. When I was older—what, sixth grade, maybe?—I could feel the crash coming a day or two or three before it happened. Her batteries would start to wear down, the sound around her would get quieter like the tornado was running out of steam, you know, and the frantic energy would slow, and then finally . . . finally she would start to weep, and she would start to see sadness in everything. She wouldn't talk as much. She'd cry at flowers. At traffic signs. I remember once that a 'Yield' sign left her weeping for hours. I thought that was all the sickness was—the sadness and the tears. I never considered that the good times were part of it, too, that everything was all tied up together.

"I thought that when she was 'feeling good' she was her true self. But then she'd crash.

"We'd get home somehow—but it was always an adventure. Broken-down cars, out of money, skipping on motel bills, caught shoplifting—you name it, it happened to us on those trips. By the time we got home she'd have lost whatever job she had and she'd disappear into her room. One of her sisters or brothers would show up to take care of her. Sometimes my grandfather would come, but not too often. Usually it was one of my aunts."

The old house creaked and Tom spun in his chair to track the source of the sound.

"And you?" I asked.

He returned his attention to me. "I went back to my life. My life as I knew it stopped when she was 'feeling good' and it started up again when we got back home.

She got worse as I got older. The manic periods weren't that different, maybe they were a little shorter and more intense. But the time before and after—the depression times—those were worse. Those were definitely worse."

I noted that he had said that the relatives arrived "to take care of her," not "to take care of me."

"Did it get harder for you, too, as you got older?" I asked.

Tom, I thought, wanted to talk about his mother. I was much more interested in hearing about the little boy who lived with her, but I doubted that was going to happen, at least not that day. I suspected that I was going to lose him soon. He would drift off into some area that was less tender for him than his memories of living with his mother's mental illness, and given that we were only in our second session, I would be inclined to allow whatever drift he required without attempting to reel him back in.

That was my supposition on what was about to happen. But that's not what happened.

Almost as though he was intent on proving me wrong, Tom said, "She killed herself when I was fourteen."

Reflexively, I replied, "I'm sorry."

Yes, for his loss. But I was also lamenting my assumption that talking about his mother was misdirection, not direction. I prepared to move from probing mode to some stance that would permit this man who had lost so much to explore whatever residual grief remained from his mother's suicide.

But Tom had other ideas. He shrugged and said, "I was relieved when she died. The craziness of living with her ups and downs was really starting to get to me. When she killed herself, it let me get off the roller coaster. The thing about roller coasters is that they're fun to ride for a while, but it's no fun when you don't have any control about getting on and getting off. Imagine living a life where someone can at any second yank you away from whatever you're doing and plop you into the front seat of the Twister. You know what that's like?"

He took a quick glance over his left shoulder to check for a shadow with a shank. Then he looked back at me.

My face was impassive.

He said, "I expected you to ask me how she killed herself. Everybody does. Everybody seems to want to know that."

"Do you want to tell me?"

He put an I-don't-care expression on his face and started picking at a scab on the back of his left hand. "She sliced her own throat, if you can believe it. My mother was really crazy. I think you'd have to be really crazy to slice your own throat. Don't you agree?"

I had a question at that point. I asked, "Were you the one who found her after she killed herself, Tom?" The image of a fourteen-year-old boy discovering his mother's body after she killed herself by cutting her own throat flashed across my consciousness and then vanished in a microsecond, as though someone had quickly changed the channel with a remote control.

He nodded. "Yeah. What a mess."

The scab popped off his hand and the wound began to bleed. A full red drop hovered above where the scab had been. He stared at the blood as he might gaze at an insect that had landed on his hand. He told me, "This is where you should be making the connection between my mother and Ivy Campbell."

"Pardon me?" I said.

"They both had their throats cut. That's quite a co-incidence, or so I'm told. Plenty of people have used it as evidence that my mother's suicide drove me to re-peat the act with Ivy. The shrinks who interviewed me before my trial sure thought it was important. What about you? You don't find some psychological diamonds to mine in those facts, Doctor?"

I found the challenge that Tom was making interest-ing. "I'm more than a little perplexed. The DNA testing says you didn't have anything to do with Ivy Campbell's murder, Tom. Right? So how could there be a psy-chological connection between that and your mother's suicide?"

My eyes found the clock that was on a table behind his chair. Our time was almost up.

He smiled at me in a way that made me uncomfort-able. "She was crazy, too. Ivy was. Not like my mom. Ivy had panic attacks. Ever been around somebody while they had a panic attack? It's not a pretty thing."

I didn't answer his question. Tom had just traversed the ground between telling me that he'd grown up with a mother with a severe mood disorder and telling me that he'd once been romantically drawn to a woman with another serious mental illness, so I encouraged him to keep talking. "Ivy Campbell had panic attacks?"

"Yeah. Suddenly she'd freak for no reason. She'd ac-tually hide in closets, pull all the clothes around her. She'd yell, she'd cry. She'd think she was dying."

"Would she want you around to soothe her?" I al-ready suspected that I knew the answer.

"Are you kidding? The way I knew the panic attacks were coming is that she'd kick me out. She wouldn't want me around."

"What was she like in between panic episodes?"

"She was terrific. She was exciting. She was a truly passionate girl." He smiled at some memory. "Ivy always made me want to dance."

I pondered my next move for the time it took me to inhale and exhale twice. Then I said, "You suggested that I might be interested in the parallel between how Ivy died and how your mother died. I find that I'm actually interested in a different parallel. It sounds as though, at least in this instance, you found yourself attracted to a woman with a mental disorder."

I paused solely for effect. But Tom didn't wait for me to resume.

"Like my momma?" he said. I suspected that he'd been waiting for me to say what I did. He pounced on my reflection and whacked it right back over the net like Andre Agassi slamming a perfect overhand.

"Yes, Tom. Like your mother."

His eyes lit up. "Well, that's something, isn't it?"

As I suspected at the beginning of the session, Tom Clone was going to offer me the promise of constant surprise.

19

My best friend was a cop. That was easily as astounding to me as it was to Sam Purdy that his best friend was a shrink.

Although we'd talked on the phone once, Sam hadn't seen me in the days since I'd lost the tussle with my poodle. I wasn't anticipating a whole lot of sympathy from him; it wasn't his nature to fuss over illness and injury. And the fact that a sixteen-pound miniature poodle was responsible for keeping me from driving my dream car for at least six weeks would amuse him no end.

He'd come over to our house after dinner. The rationalization for the visit was that Simon, his son, wanted to see Grace, our daughter. I knew that it was a ruse; the truth was that Sam missed me.

He and I were standing in the open door of the garage. Sam was holding a bottle of Odell's. I kept his favorite local beer in the house just for him.

I was admiring the Mini. Sam wasn't.

"Lauren was right about this? You really wanted one of these?" he asked. He was leaning over way too far, as though he needed to demonstrate that he couldn't see inside the diminutive car without almost getting down on his knees.

"I didn't know that I did but . . . yeah, I guess I really did want one, Sam. Lauren must have read my mind. I think she may be trying to preempt an incipient midlife crisis."

He grunted.

I took a few moments to explain to Sam about my first car.

He wasn't moved by the story of my adolescent fling with a British import named Sadie. He said, "Simon has a skateboard with bigger wheels than this thing. Maybe his scooter has bigger wheels, too. Shoot, you know what, I think I have a suitcase with bigger wheels than this thing."

"You're not an aficionado, I take it?"

Sam laughed. "My first car was a Pontiac GTO, Alan. Hurst shifter, twin carbs. My current dream car is a Lincoln Town Car or one of those Buick whatever-they're-calleds. The big ones." He gestured at the Mini. "If I sneezed inside this thing, I'd blow out the windows." Sam was a large man. When he was ignoring his diet, which was usually, he outweighed me by most of a hundred pounds.

"Want to know what's ironic?" I said. "I haven't

even driven it. I broke my arm the night Lauren gave it to me. It's been sitting in the garage the whole time."

"Why am I not surprised?" Sam asked.

Sam carried Emily's retractable leash in one hand and a fresh beer in the other as we walked down the dirt lanes that laced the hillsides adjacent to the house. Emily wasn't attached to the leash; she ran free in the dry grasses, following the scent of the red foxes or some of the other critters that roamed the undeveloped parts of the eastern rim of the Boulder Valley. The night was as dry as the day had been. I'd heard weather reports of thunderstorms full of hail near Pueblo, down south, but a high-pressure ridge that was parked in just the wrong place was still responsible for pushing the main channel of the monsoonal flow into Texas and Oklahoma.

What that meant in the real world was that it wasn't going to rain in Boulder County.

Sam was working on a task force that was trying to reduce the number of assaults that were disrupting the peace on the Hill, the student-dominated neighborhood west of the University of Colorado. Although he wouldn't say he was seeking my professional opinion— hell, when he was in certain moods, he wouldn't even acknowledge that what I did for a living constituted a profession—he was seeking my professional opinion. We talked about young kids away from home and drugs and alcohol and how best to influence the mix. I told him what I thought, but the truth was that the conversation didn't leave me feeling like a wizard.

After we paused to watch the sun make its final descent behind the Divide, we started back up the hill to the house. Sam wanted to corral Lauren and the kids and go out someplace for ice cream. He thought his wife might drive someplace and meet us.

We walked a few more steps and Sam said, "Simon told me that his friends say I have a unibrow."

"What on earth are you talking about?"

He leaned toward me and tapped the bridge of his nose. "See, my eyebrows run together above my nose. Simon says it's called a unibrow. I didn't even know there was a name for it."

"A unibrow, huh? And that's a bad thing?" I gazed at the shrub of hair that seemed to connect his eyebrows. I'd never noticed it before, but sure enough, there it was.

"I guess. His friends are telling him he's going to have one, too. He's kind of worried about it."

"Given the rest of the genetic bounty he's getting from you, I think it's a small price to pay."

He raised half his unibrow. "That was sarcastic, right?"

"So what did you tell him, Sam?"

"I told him that he'd inherited Sherry's eyebrows, not mine. It seemed to satisfy him for now."

"I assume he doesn't know about plucking?"

"Nope. He's blissfully ignorant about plucking."

"Well," I said, "I suppose that's one of the good things about being under ten."

"He asked me if I have a six-pack, too."

"Like beer?"

"No, like abs. He wanted to know whether I'm, you know, buffed."

I choked and ended up in a paroxysmal spasm trying to swallow my laughter.

"What did you tell him?"

Sam rubbed one hand over his rounded abdomen. His voice grew slightly defensive. "I told him what I have is better than a six-pack."

"Yeah? How's that?"

"I told him I have a whole keg. He seemed impressed."

"You're quick on your feet, Sam."

"That I am. That I am."

We continued walking. I used the ensuing silence as an excuse to change the subject. "What do you guys think about having Tom Clone living in Boulder?"

Two steps, then, "What guys? Are you talking about me and Sherry? Or me and the rest of the cops?"

"You and the rest of the cops. I'm wondering how the police feel about having Tom Clone in town."

"Why are you asking?" Sam was a detective; he couldn't keep himself from exploring questions like that. His job, like mine, was one that often left residue after hours.

"Just wondering."

"Yeah, right. You have a broken arm and a brand-new widget of a car that you can't drive, a gorgeous wife and a daughter who's cute as they come, and you're wasting your time wondering about Tom Clone? I'm not stupid. You're involved with him somehow. Don't tell me he's one of your, you know, your—"

"Sam, stop. Stop right there. Would I tell you if he was?"

Emily raced to within ten feet of us before plowing

back into the fields. I think she just wanted to make certain that we hadn't been attacked by foxes. Sam shook his head in disdain at my question and said, "I don't care that Clone is here. I just care that he's not there."

" 'There'? What does that mean?"

"I don't care that he's in Boulder. If he stays out of trouble, he's just another civilian as far as I'm concerned. I'm just not convinced he should have been let out of the penitentiary in the first place."

"I thought you were a proponent of DNA testing. Even if it means going back after conviction. It's one of your more progressive public-policy positions."

He glanced over at me to gauge my intent with the little dig I'd just sent his way before replying. "I am. But leave the DNA out of the case and this guy looks as guilty as they come, Alan. I can't think of a way he didn't kill that girl."

"So someone else got ahold of the knife after her murder and bled all over it? That's a stretch, Sam."

He eyed me suspiciously. "It's possible. Why are you defending him? The cops had eyewitnesses that put him there—that's plural—and they had enough circumstantial evidence to construct a skyscraper. They had motive. It's all there. The guy was just dripping guilt."

"I'm not defending him, Sam. I'm . . . I don't know what I'm doing. Barry Scheck has a book full of stories about people who were convicted with the same kinds of evidence. They were all wrongly convicted. If it weren't for DNA, they'd either be dead or still on death row."

"I'm trying to enjoy myself here and you want to talk about Barry Scheck? Why don't I just tell you about the last catheter your friend Adrienne shoved up my . . ."

Thankfully, he let the image of my urologist neighbor,

Adrienne, evaporate in the dry air. I was about to change the subject when he continued. "Well, I can't explain it. I just can't find a single hole in the case that they put together against this guy. Some of Scheck's cases? I've read his book. They were flimsy to start with. There were holes. But not this murder they had Clone for. I only know what I've heard from other cops, but Clone sure looks guilty to me."

"Didn't the prosecutors rely on a lot of eyewitnesses to make their case against Clone in court?"

"Yeah, they did. So what? Personally, I like eyewitnesses."

"But you know the data, Sam. Eyewitnesses are terribly unreliable informants about what actually happened."

"I don't really care about 'the data.' Want to know why I like eyewitnesses? Because juries like eyewitnesses. And that's good enough for me, because it's how our system works. Those cops nailed Tom Clone, Alan. They played by the rules and it was a good collar."

"Except for the DNA. And those partial prints that don't match. The DNA says someone else's blood is on the murder weapon."

"Yeah," Sam said while he kicked at the dirt. "Except for that. The DNA is a problem, I admit it. I don't pretend to understand it, but I admit it."

"And you're still not convinced about his innocence?"

His response was some dismissive sound that involved expelling air rapidly in a single burst from between his lips.

I asked, "Given what you know about the case, would you have been okay with him being executed?"

He shot a suspicious glance my way. "You sure you wouldn't rather talk about hockey or even, God forbid, the Rockies? Or how dry it's been this summer? I'll even talk about your funny little car some more if you want."

"I'll take that as a yes," I said.

Sam and I saw eye to eye on virtually nothing, politically speaking. We had an unspoken agreement to avoid discussing most public controversies. The pact had served us well over the years.

"Don't make assumptions about me, Alan."

I tried to spot Emily's dark mass mowing over the prairie grasses on the hill beside us. When I did see her, the appearance was more apparition than anything else. It reminded me of reports of sightings of the Loch Ness Monster. Emily was there—or was she?—and then she was gone.

"Really?" I said to Sam. "On some things, you're pretty predictable."

"Stop walking for a second," Sam said. I did. He looked me in the eyes. "What I'm about to say goes nowhere, you understand?"

"Sure."

He pulled a wrapped toothpick from his pocket— I guessed he'd lifted it from the last restaurant he'd visited—poked it through the paper sleeve, and stuck it in the corner of his mouth. Most of the wooden stick vanished under the umbrella of his mustache. "Fucking McVeigh," he said finally. "God forgive me, but I hate him and I hate what he did."

I thought of responding. I didn't. I couldn't begin to guess where the "Fucking McVeigh" segue was taking us, and I didn't want to be responsible for altering the course Sam was plotting.

Sam continued. "At the end—during the last few

months before he was finally executed—once McVeigh finally started talking about his crime, he said he blew up that building in Oklahoma City in order to punish those people he considered responsible for committing the quote-unquote reprehensible murders at Waco and Ruby Ridge. He felt that the responsible parties were the Feds and that the Feds worked in the Murrah Building, so that's why he blew it up."

"The kids in the day-care center, too?" I asked. "They were responsible for something?"

He glared at me but when he replied his tone was gently admonishing, not angry. "Don't get sidetracked there, Alan. Don't. It's an easy detour. But it's a dead end. The truth is that we would have tracked McVeigh down, convicted him, and executed him even if there were no children and no civilians in that building. The fact that he killed kids and innocent civilians gives us an excuse to hate him even more than we do—and I'm as guilty of that as the next guy—but we didn't turn the world upside down to arrest and convict this guy only because of the kids he killed. Take the children out of the equation and he's still a monster. Take the kids out of that building—and God, I wish I could go back and do just that—and McVeigh is still going to lie down on a cold table and take the needle."

Sam paused long enough to give me a chance to make the mistake of saying something in reply. I didn't.

"When it came time to rationalize his execution, the powers that be said that he needed to die because it was the only appropriate punishment for the quote-unquote reprehensible murders he committed in Oklahoma City."

Across from me, to the north, Emily suddenly popped up above the grass, twisted 180 degrees in midair, landed, and took off in the opposite direction. Her herding instincts were firing but some creature out there had her snookered. It was great fun to watch.

Sam let his words hang in the dry air for a few moments. I wondered if they were going to spin and do a one-eighty, too.

"It got me thinking," he went on finally. "We, the people, used the exact same argument to kill McVeigh that he was using to justify killing a building full of federal employees. Is that just some great cosmic irony? Or are we, as a society, teaching the exact kind of retribution that we say is so reprehensible? What gives us the right to decide who lives and dies? We killed McVeigh for making the exact same decision that we as a society want the freedom to make."

He made an I-don't-get-it face and said, "Huh? What?" while he kicked again at the dust. "McVeigh thought that what those federal employees in the Murrah Building did was reprehensible enough that they deserved to die. So he killed them. We thought that what McVeigh did was reprehensible enough that he deserved to die. So we killed him. Right?

"Well, what gives? Are we writing the rules and just don't like the fact that other people have decided to play by them, too? Or are the terrorists and murderers writing the rules and now we've decided to stoop low enough to play at their level? I'm no longer sure, no longer sure at all."

I found myself entranced by my friend's soliloquy.

He asked, "How do I teach this distinction to my kid? I can't figure it out. It's like telling Simon it's okay for a teacher to hit a kid but not for a kid to hit another kid. Well, I don't want him to think that. So do I tell him the government knows best? That because the government has said capital punishment is the law and the government is doing the killing, that somehow the Ten Commandments don't apply? I'm a conservative Republican, Alan. There's not a bone in my body that believes that the government always knows best. Not about taxes, not about religion, not about much of anything that comes anywhere close to my home or my family. Certainly not about who should live and who should die."

He started walking. I whistled for Emily and followed Sam back up the lane. As far as I knew, we were on our way to get ice cream.

He looked at me over his right shoulder and, in a voice that was stunning for its normalcy, he said, "I know you, Alan. I know where your mind is going. If you're even thinking about mentioning the World Trade Center to me, don't. Our response to the events of that day was self-defense. That was war. War is a different story, and . . . war has a different ending."

I took a step. He didn't; he'd stopped walking. I wasn't about to say anything about September 11 or the World Trade Center or the Pentagon. What happened that day *was* different. We were painfully learning all the ways that it was different.

In the same everyday voice, he continued. "Once we put him in jail and dragged him to court and convicted McVeigh, it wasn't war. It was justice. The same thing never happened with bin Laden because from moment one that was war. We can't mix them up, war and justice."

I knew he wasn't done.

Finally, he said softly, "I don't think our society could survive that."

CHAPTER

20

Kelda was on time for her appointment for the first time since I'd started seeing her for psychotherapy.

I started by rescheduling the following week's session from Thursday to Tuesday. Kelda agreed to a late-afternoon time. She didn't ask, so I didn't explain that I had to take Grace to the pediatrician for a checkup late in the day on Thursday.

Kelda used a minute or two of the remaining time to ask about my arm and my adjustment to my injury. I deflected her inquiries as well as I could without becoming rude. When it was clear that I wasn't inviting any further attention on my condition, she crossed her legs, ran her teeth over her bottom lip, and said, "I imagine that you want me to talk about Jones."

The only neutral response was no response. If I said I did, Jones would become my topic, not Kelda's. If I said I didn't, I ran the risk of dismissing something that might be important to her. I could have been obvious and told Kelda that we would talk about whatever she wanted to talk about. My silence said the same thing.

She uncrossed her legs, untied her hair, and threaded through it with her fingers before she sat back and re-crossed her right leg over her left. Then she smiled, laughed out loud, and said, "Jones was the first person I ever knew who shaped her pubic hair. She said it was an artistic statement." She shook her head in amuse-ment. "We'd be out somewhere and she'd pull me aside into a room or just off by ourselves and all of a sudden she'd drop her pants or lift her skirt and point to her crotch and say, 'What do you think, Kelda? Is this my best work, or what?' "

I was enamored as Kelda's eyes sparkled. The memory of Jones's shaved pubes lit her like stage lights. Something about her friend was the electricity.

"I don't know why I told you that, but that . . . that was Jones. She was always a step ahead of the world, always . . . out there a little bit. Have you ever been with one of those people whose face seemed to be in a never-ending smile? You know, someone who was like the opposite of the rest of us. Most of us have a normal face, and sometimes we smile, right? Not Jones. Jones's normal face was this big half-moon smile and some-times she would have to force herself to close her mouth and *not* smile. No matter how you were feeling, you ended up smiling back at her when you were with Jones. If things seemed dark, she always managed to light a different path for you."

Kelda uncrossed her legs and crossed her arms across her chest, curling her fingers around her biceps.

I didn't think I was observing a strategy to cope with physical pain. She was embracing herself in preparation for something she was about to tell me.

What? I didn't know. So I waited.

"And then she died," Kelda said. "And then Jones went and died. I don't think I've been the same since."

We lost touch a little bit when I went to Australia. I think she was kind of hurt that I would just pack up and leave Denver. Leave her. I thought she was being silly about the whole thing. For me, Australia was a lark, a chance to go exploring and see a piece of the world. Because of her fears, Jones couldn't do that, just pick up someplace and go. But it wasn't like we were fighting or anything. We exchanged a couple of letters during the first few weeks, and I called her once and woke her up because I misjudged the time difference. I didn't think much about her and me while I was there. I always thought that when I got back to Denver we'd be the same great friends we'd always been."

Kelda grew silent.

I said, "And then she went and died."

She sighed. "I didn't even know she was dead until I got home. After I'd been in Australia for a few months she sent me a letter, more of a change of address really, just a note letting me know that she was moving to Hawaii, to Maui, to be part of some co-op gallery. She had an opportunity to do art full-time. I was surprised— shocked is more like it—I didn't think that Jones could make that big a change in her life. But I thought, great, that I'd stop and see her on my way back to the States when I was done with my work in Sydney. I sent her a postcard or something telling her to watch for me one day soon on her doorstep, and I waited to hear back from her. But I never did hear back from her, and I didn't stop in Hawaii.

"I tried to reach her once more before I came home, but the letter was returned to me. When I finally got back to Denver, I called her parents in New Hampshire to try to find out where I could find her. That's when I learned that she'd died a couple of months before on Maui."

"What happened?" I asked.

"Do you know Maui?"

"No," I said. I'd been to Hawaii once years before, but hadn't spent much time on Maui.

"The island is shaped like a peanut, and she was living in the hills outside a little town called Paia that's on the side of the isthmus where the tourists don't tend to stay. Paia's an old cowboy town that's kind of been taken over by aging hippies and young hippies and windsurfers. A lot of artists have congregated there, too. It was a real little town, not a tourist place. She could find real people there; it was the kind of place where Jones could thrive."

I waited, wondering why the geography lesson had been important.

"Anyway, Jones fell—that's how she died. She went hiking one day by herself near some cliffs above the ocean outside of Paia on the road to Hana. It was low tide and somehow she fell about sixty feet onto some rocks, and she died. She crushed her head on the rocks."

I was still wondering why the geography lesson had been important. I was about to ask when Kelda continued. "There's a wonderful old cemetery outside of

Paia on this sloping hillside above the Pacific. It's a tiny graveyard, just a little wispy place below some sugar-cane fields that's dotted with gravestones and a few crosses. She's buried there.

"The wind blows hard on that part of Maui almost all the time; it's this constant, strong force that comes off the ocean. Not a breeze, but a real wind. A few years after she died—after I came back to Denver from the FBI Academy—I went there, to Hawaii, and I spent a few days in Paia and I visited her grave three or four times. On a clear day you can see the shoreline where she was hiking right from the cemetery.

"I was moved by it all. The cemetery, the cliffs, the ocean, the wind. The wind reminded me of Jones. Its power. Its energy. Since then I've thought about her every time I've felt a breeze wash over my skin. It's like a sign that she's visiting me, looking over me."

"You went to Hawaii to say good-bye?" I almost immediately regretted the presumptiveness of my words.

"Yes," she said. "To say good-bye. To say I'm sorry. And to make sure she was resting in the right place."

"Is she?"

Kelda nodded. "Yes, yes, yes." Her words were a hoarse whisper.

"You said that you went to say that you're sorry?"

"Yes. For losing touch with her, for not being as good a friend as I could have been, for not being with her when she went for that hike."

"I don't understand that last part, Kelda. You were sorry for not being with her when she went on the hike?"

"You had to know Jones, Alan. If I had been living in Denver when she decided to move, she would have begged me to go to Hawaii with her. And if I'd said no, she wouldn't have gone by herself. Jones had fears. Serious fears, phobia fears. They ruled her life sometimes. She was afraid of heights, of fire, of loud noises. She was always worried about someone breaking into her apartment. Even in Denver, she had more locks on her doors than anybody I knew. She had this weird thing about electrical wiring—she was always checking for electrical shorts and worrying about the wiring in the walls. She used to crawl around and sniff the electrical sockets to see if she could smell fire. And lightning? God, you didn't want to be outside with Jones on a summer afternoon.

"She told me once that if it wasn't for her fears—and the fact that she had one or two freckles too many—she'd be an almost perfect person. I don't think she was speaking from conceit—I know she wasn't—I think she was telling me that at some level her phobias and her fears kept her humble."

I didn't know which strand of the story to tug. I tried one almost at random. "But even though she was afraid of flying, she somehow got the nerve to get on a plane to go to Hawaii—a place she'd never been—by herself?"

"Yes, she did."

"Did that surprise you?"

"The whole thing surprised me. Jones wasn't an independent person. Sometimes I thought that her demeanor was so magnetic because she constantly needed to attract new people to be around her. People got fed up with her fears, and they got fed up fast. She wouldn't do *this* because of that fear. She wouldn't do *that* because of this fear. It was always something with Jones. Her friendships started quickly and they ended quickly. She burned through friends and she really burned through boyfriends." She shook her head. "Packing up and moving someplace where she didn't know anyone? That wasn't Jones. It just wasn't. Her fears were like anchors. They kept her from moving, they kept her from going anywhere.

"And she definitely wouldn't have made the move if I was in Denver instead of Australia. I would have talked her out of it."

"You would have talked her out of it?"

"Yes. That's sounds funny, doesn't it? I wouldn't convince her not to go. That's not what I mean. I'd simply point out alternatives, and help her see what she'd have to confront if she did go. That's all."

"In terms of her fears?"

"Yes."

I asked, "You mentioned something about regretting not being with Jones when she went hiking. What's that about?"

"Jones didn't tolerate her fears passively. She was constantly confronting them, you know, like inching up to things that terrified her. She thought if she desensitized herself that maybe the fears would go away. She'd light candles in her room and try to read by candlelight. The whole time she'd be sure her hair was on fire. She'd use an extension cord when she didn't have to, and every thirty seconds she'd feel it to see how hot it was.

"And my role? She'd count on me to tell her when she'd gone too far. Where things she was afraid of were concerned, she didn't have a sense of what was reasonable for her to do."

"Like walking too close to a cliff?"

"Exactly. Like getting too close to a cliff. I would have been the one who would have said, 'People who aren't afraid of heights wouldn't get any closer than this, Jones. It's not safe—this is as close as you need to get to the edge.' She wouldn't have a natural sense of that. She would think that she needed to get right to the edge and curl her toes over the rocks—that that was the only way to confront her fear, that that's what other people would do. Normal people.

"I have an image in my head of the last few seconds of her life. Of her approaching that cliff edge and that big strong wind blowing off the Pacific into her face. What I think Jones would have been doing is she would have been leaning into the wind. She would have had her arms out like the wings of a bird, letting the wind hold her up as she tried to look down over the rocks and the water. Her heart would have been pounding and the fear would have almost paralyzed her but she would have forced herself to do it, to get all the way to the edge. The picture in my head is that the wind . . ." Kelda exhaled in a little burst. "What happened is that the wind paused, just for a second, the way it does sometimes, and in that instant it stopped holding her up and she lost her balance and she toppled over and she fell."

I asked, "But if you were there, you would have warned her that she was close enough, and she would have backed off from the edge of the cliff? That's what you think?"

"I should have been the one to tell her she was too close to the edge or that the wind wouldn't really hold her up. It was one of the things that I did. It was my job as her friend."

"And you think it would have made a difference?"

She didn't answer.

"Do you think it's reasonable for you to feel responsible for her falling off that cliff?"

"Reasonable? God, no. But you wanted to talk about my pain, right? Well, the pain in my legs started right around the time that Jones moved to Maui. Maybe even the exact same week that she moved to Maui. I didn't even know that she'd moved, of course, but . . ."

"Are you suggesting a relationship between Jones's decision and the onset of your pain?"

Kelda's voice turned slightly mocking. "Are you going to allow me to get away without taking a look at that possibility, Doctor?"

I smiled.

Kelda said, "Are you wondering if she got help for her anxieties? Professional help?"

I nodded, although what I had actually been considering was the likelihood that Kelda really didn't understand the magnitude of her friend's anxiety. Kelda was describing a level of fearfulness that left me wondering about a significant underlying paranoia, and not just a strange pattern of multiple phobias. If Jones had been my patient, I would have tuned my antennae to the frequencies that were most sensitive to a complex presentation of post-traumatic stress disorder.

"Your friend had some serious problems," I said.

Kelda's eyes were unblinking as she responded, "The fears were definitely a problem."

"Not just the fears, Kelda. The way she reacted to you going to Australia. I suspect that other things might have been going on with Jones, too. Was she ever worried about things that weren't inherently dangerous?"

"What do you mean?"

"The things you describe—her fears of fire, electricity, lightning, airplanes—are all exaggerated responses to everyday things that have the potential to be dangerous but usually aren't. I'm wondering whether she was ever fearful of things that aren't usually considered potentially dangerous."

"You're talking about paranoia? People after her? Like that?"

"Sure," I said, grateful that Kelda had made the last hop on her own.

"Sometimes she would worry that people didn't understand her. That they were . . . trying to undermine her. There were some people she didn't trust, wouldn't want to be around. Like that."

I waited. *Go on*, I thought, *go on*.

"But that wasn't often. Mostly, it was the fears that we dealt with. Just the fears," she insisted.

"Phobias don't usually come in bunches like hers did. It's an atypical presentation."

"Funny. That's what my neurologist says about my pain. It's atypical. I don't care. It's still real."

I debated proceeding with my psychopathology lesson. Before I was even aware I'd reached a decision, I said, "Even if the phobias were all that Jones was dealing with, there are some medications that might have helped her, and there are a few therapeutic approaches—desensitization and even traditional psychotherapy, for example—that work for a lot of people. But yes, to get back to your original question, I was thinking that maybe she didn't have to suffer so much. That someone could have eased her pain."

"She sought help. She went to see different therapists at least twice while I knew her. In my opinion, she saw a couple of flakes, unfortunately. One guy she saw hit on her during their second session—asked her to go skiing with him for a weekend at his condo in Winter Park. And a woman therapist she went to see took her fire walking with a bunch of her friends out on some ranch near Parker."

I would have liked to say I was surprised. I wasn't. Anybody with an inclination could hang out a shingle as a psychotherapist in Colorado. Most consumers didn't seem to understand the distinction between a licensed and an unlicensed therapist, between a psychologist and a psychiatrist and a clinical social worker, between a competent professional and an unskilled quack. My impulse with Kelda was to apologize for the behavior of people I sometimes abhorred having to consider colleagues. Instead, I said, "Fire walking?"

Kelda said, "Yes. Fire walking. She aced it. It turned out Jones didn't have any phobias about prancing down a bed of hot coals."

CHAPTER

Kelda called Rosa Alija *"hermanita"*—little sister. The girl, a shy child, called Kelda *"hermana."*

Since Kelda had rescued Rosa, the two had never gone more than eight weeks without visiting, and they talked frequently by phone in between encounters. Kelda could rely on receiving an e-mail message from the girl at least a couple of times a week.

Rosa enjoyed all the visits. Kelda had taken the girl to Broncos and Rockies games, to the ballet, had even endured a trip to the Pepsi Center to see some boy band. But the visits that Rosa seemed to enjoy most were the weekend afternoons at Kelda's little piece of property in Lafayette. Rosa's mother or father would drop her by sometime during the late morning on a Saturday or after church on Sunday, always bringing something special along for Kelda. José would pull a shrub from the back of his pickup to plant in the long bed near the highway, or he'd spend twenty minutes lining the walkway with a tantalizing border of annuals, or he'd dig a hole for a sapling that would someday grow to replace one of the aging elms on the property.

When it was Maria who drove Rosa to Lafayette, she would offer a covered dish full of tamales or, Kelda's favorite, a basket of homemade *churros*. Once she took over Kelda's kitchen to make a huge platter of *chilaquiles*, which she said was her daughter's favorite meal.

Kelda ate more than Rosa did.

Rosa would spend the long afternoons in Lafayette exploring the fallow fields and repeatedly acting out some homesteading fantasy that Kelda never really understood. The girl was a natural athlete who was fearless in the trees. She would climb to limbs high in the elms. The dangerous heights made Kelda crazy. Rosa could spend hours on the swing that Kelda had hung from the big branch on the elm that was closest to the lane. The swing faced the mountains, and Rosa would swing higher and higher, kicking hard at the top of the arc as though she was certain she could reach out and tickle the glaciers on the northern slopes of Mount Evans.

Rosa was on the swing and Kelda was watching her from the kitchen window when Kelda spotted the microwave truck lumbering down the street near her home. Involuntarily the muscles in her jaw tightened. The familiar logo on the side of the rig identified it as being from Denver's Fox News affiliate.

A few summers before, all of Denver's television stations had done anniversary pieces on Kelda's rescue of Rosa. Two of the stations had sent crews to Lafayette during one of Rosa's visits to Kelda's home and had ultimately agreed to Kelda's restriction that they film the little girl only from the rear. Kelda, after consultation with the Denver SAC and with the Alijas, had agreed in return to brief interviews. But she set firm ground rules: She would answer questions about her current relationship with Rosa, but wouldn't discuss anything about the rescue.

She would say nothing about the shooting.

Nothing.

What she would talk about on camera was the man who had kidnapped Rosa. After years of delving into his background on her own time, Kelda knew more about the kidnapper than Boswell knew about Johnson. "Why is it so important to know him so well?" the reporters would ask her.

"Because it is," she would reply. "We have to know our enemy."

Each summer since, Kelda had been forced to deal with at least one TV station eager to reminisce about the dramatic rescue as the anniversary date approached. The truck on 111th Street meant to Kelda that this summer would be no different than the others.

"*Hermanita,*" Kelda called from the side door of her house. "Inside for a few minutes, please."

"Why?"

Kelda nodded at the microwave truck and the little girl immediately understood what was happening. Kelda said, "Don't worry, I'll go talk to them. I just made fresh lemonade. It's in the fridge. You help yourself, okay?"

"Can I pick some fresh mint to put in it first?"

Rosa was already running to the thick patch of mint

on the south side of the house. "You bet," Kelda yelled after her.

It took Kelda almost ten minutes to negotiate to a stalemate with the reporter who got out of the truck. The reporter ultimately used her cell phone to reach her producer, who asked to speak with Kelda.

Kelda took the phone and walked away from the reporter before she said anything to the producer. Once she was fifty feet or so down the lane, she said, "We're okay, right? No changes from what we agreed?"

The producer was a young man whom Kelda had dealt with twice before on Rosa Alija stories. He wore his ambition on his sleeve and because he was so brash about it Kelda found that she trusted him as much as she trusted anybody in the media.

He said, "We're okay on this, Kelda. Just tape, no audio. We'll only show the kid from behind. But . . ."

He let the word hang between them. "But what?" she asked.

"But . . . I'm running down a story that you might have had something to do with Clone's release from death row. Is that true? Were you really the one who found the knife that got him sprung from the pen?"

"Rafe, you know I can't comment on reports like that. Rosa Alija is human interest. Tom Clone is law enforcement business. If you have questions about that old case, take them up with Park County or with the FBI information officer."

"So the FBI is involved?"

"Uh-uh. I'm not going there with you."

"I'm doing you a favor here, with this shoot. I want you to remember me if this Tom Clone thing breaks open. Is that a deal?"

She said, "I know you're doing me a favor."

"Is that a deal?" he pressed.

"I said I know you're doing me a favor." She started retracing her steps back down the lane.

The producer said, "I'm going to take that as a yes."

"No comment. Hold on. I want to say all this out loud in front of your talent." Kelda approached the reporter, a pretty woman whose skirt was too short for a Sunday afternoon in Lafayette. Almost too short for a Sunday afternoon in Denver. Kelda held the cell phone out between them.

"Your producer and I have reached an understanding. Here it is: You can tape me outside the house, and you can tape Rosa from behind, but no audio and no interview. Not with me. Not with Rosa. No interview. And no copy and no shots that would identify the location of my house."

The reporter took the phone from Kelda. She had trouble finding a comfortable way to get it close to her ear over her big earring. Finally, she said, "That's the deal, Rafe?"

She listened for a moment to her producer, then folded up the cell phone and reluctantly gave instructions to the woman who was handling the camera. When Kelda asked, the reporter said that the piece should be ready to air by the following night at nine.

The news truck pulled away from her house about forty-five minutes later. Kelda sat on a lawn chair and watched the dust settle in the lane. Rosa crawled onto her lap and pressed her face into Kelda's breast. "*Hermana?*" she said.

"Yes."

"You killed him? The bad man? My father said you killed him."

In all the years that had passed, Rosa had never asked about that day. Kelda hoped she would have forgotten.

She hoped for peace in the Middle East, too.

"Yes, *hermanita,* I did. You don't have to worry about him ever again. I killed him."

The little girl pressed harder against her chest. "I'm glad he's dead, *hermana.*"

Kelda said, "I'm glad, too."

22

The fentanyl patches were designed to provide relief for Kelda's pain for seventy-two hours. After she'd kissed Rosa good-bye and tucked her into José's truck and yanked on her seat belt at least a couple of times, she walked inside and checked the calendar by the phone and read the notation she'd penciled in the previous Thursday at bedtime. It read "F—11:30p." The clock on the microwave told her it was only 3:31. That meant that the patch she'd put on Thursday night had been on her skin for only sixty-four hours. Yet she could already feel it failing. A fresh patch, even if she put it on right then, wouldn't provide relief until almost morning.

She popped a Percocet and washed it down with the rest of the lemonade from the refrigerator. There was enough mint floating in the pitcher to flavor the contents of a bathtub. Rosa's excess made her smile.

Kelda left a message on Ira's voicemail, suggesting he stop and pick up some Thai takeout for dinner before he came over. She set up her bath towels and her frozen peas, and spread out on the bed to take a nap.

When the rumble of thunder woke her, she glanced at the clock by the bed; it was a little after four-thirty. The light that was filtering into her room was grayer than usual. She listened for the melody of raindrops on the roof but wasn't sure if she heard a faint pattering or not. *Had the monsoons finally arrived?* Hopeful, she eased herself from the bed and walked to the western window. Between the trees, she could see a curtain of virga silhouetted against the sky between Lafayette and Boulder. But virga was to weather watchers what fool's gold was to a miner: Kelda could tell at a glance that the mirage of moisture would all evaporate before it reached the soil of Boulder County.

She picked up the phone and tried Ira again. When he didn't answer, she hung up without leaving another message and collected the bags of peas from the bed to return them to the freezer.

She was still craving *pad Thai*.

She took another Percocet instead.

Twenty minutes later she reached for the phone to try Ira one more time. But the phone rang before she got the receiver out of the cradle.

"Hello," she said.

The line was silent. With her free hand she depressed the button on the phone that would kill the call, and then hit *69. Once again, the phone company failed to identify the location of the caller. She noted the date and time of the call in the log she kept beside the phone.

After saying "What the hell," she picked up the local phone book and checked for a number. Finding it, she dialed. After two rings, a man answered. She thought she recognized his voice. "Have dinner with me," she said.

"Is this Kelda?"

"How many women do you have calling you out of the blue asking you out for dinner?"

"Not enough."

"How many would be enough?"

Tom Clone said, "If you're the woman doing the calling, one is enough. The answer is absolutely, you bet—yes! But I can't come to wherever you are; I don't have a car, Kelda."

"I'll come by and get you. We'll walk over to the Mall or something. I'll be there around six-thirty."

Days in Boulder are a little more compressed than they are in the nearby towns on the eastern plains of Colorado. Boulder's elevation above sea level is a tad more than a mile, while the nearby sun-shielding peaks of the highest reaches of the Continental Divide rise to over fourteen thousand feet. The difference in altitude between Boulder and the highest mountaintops, which are less than twenty miles away, is a fraction under two miles. As the summer sun sets in clear skies behind that two-mile-high wall of mountains, it casts quite a shadow. That's why day disappears early in Boulder and night seems to be in a hurry to impose its presence.

But on hot summer days spent waiting for the monsoons, the early nightfall and cooling shadows are a blessing to almost everyone. Even if the dry air holds no prayer of rain, as the evening sky above the Front Range glows in grays and pastels, in the high desert of Colorado there is always the promise of an overnight chill.

It was a few minutes before seven when Tom and Kelda walked down the hill from Tom's grandfather's house on High Street toward the nightlife of the Downtown Boulder Mall.

Boulder's Downtown Mall is a mall in the manner Americans thought of malls before the last quarter of the twentieth century. The Downtown Mall is a brick-paved, tree-lined promenade that traverses four blocks of lovely public spaces, with shops and restaurants in century-old buildings. Motor vehicles are prohibited— along with bicycles, dogs, skateboards, scooters, in-line skates, and anything else that the City Council's current whims determine are impediments to public enjoyment. On a warm evening in early summer the Mall and its adjacent streets are packed with people. The sounds of street musicians or buskers and their audiences overlap on the short blocks, and the outdoor seats at the Mall's cafés and restaurants are temporarily the hottest real estate in town.

Tom and Kelda scored a table at Mateo, a Mediterranean restaurant just off the east end of the Mall. She never told him that she was craving *pad Thai*.

As they sat down she said, "Don't worry. I'm paying."

He said, "Thank you, I'm not working yet. But I got

a job. I start Tuesday." He told her about the job in the Kaiser pharmacy.

"That sounds good, Tom. Congratulations. It's hard for me to tell, though—are you pleased with it?"

He was studying the menu. "I'm still having trouble getting used to the prices of everything," he said. "Hey, I have a question for you."

"Yes?" She was wondering why he'd ignored her question.

"Is this a date, Kelda?"

She let his words hang in the air. "I'll let you know when I take you back home, Tom. How's that?" She offered him a smile.

"I'll take that. You know, when you smile at me, I can feel it all the way into my bones." He smiled back at her.

She looked away.

"But why?" he asked.

"Why what?"

"Why me? You could have any guy you wanted, Kelda. Why are you sitting here with me tonight? Some guy who just got out of prison?"

"I don't know. And I don't think what you said is true. I'll turn it around on you—why did you say yes when I asked?"

"That's easy. Because you're gorgeous. Because you've been wonderful to me." He sighed and leaned back in his chair. "And because you're hot."

"Hot?" She exaggerated the query in her inflection as she tried not to choke on the word.

"What? Are you playing with me? Have you looked in a mirror lately? You're as hot as they come."

She blushed. "I think maybe you've been in prison too long."

"Kelda, I've definitely been in prison too long. One day was too long. But you . . . you . . . you make me want to dance."

A chill traveled the length of her spine and she felt goose bumps cause the tiny hairs on her arms to become erect. She smiled again. "I've never heard that before," she said. "No one has ever told me that."

"Well, then, they're crazy. As great as it is to be out of prison, the most alive I've felt since I got out has been the little bit of time I've spent with you."

"You're sweet, Tom. But I think you probably just have a thing for women who are constantly drawing their handguns."

He looked around. She wondered if her response had made him nervous.

"Have you seen our waitress?" he asked.

"This is Boulder. She's probably still at home getting dressed for work. Or is still up in the canyon stowing her climbing gear into her SUV. Don't worry, someone will come by before we starve." She leaned forward and lowered her voice. "And nobody really says 'waitress' much anymore. It's 'waiter' or 'server,' regardless of gender."

"I'm sorry," he said, frowning. "I bet that I make a lot of mistakes like that. The last few days I've felt like Rip van Winkle. People use words I've never heard, talk about things I don't know anything about. And TV? My God, what's on—"

"Where's your anger?" she asked abruptly.

He tucked his chin. "What do you mean?"

"You've lost a lot of years, Tom. They're just gone.

You'll never get them back. Where's your anger? You just seem like this mild-mannered guy, not like someone who's just been let out of prison for a murder that he didn't commit."

He shrugged. "What can I do? I'll try to get even in court. Tony Loving's optimistic. But whatever happens, I'll try to live my life well. As they say, that'll be the best revenge."

Again she tried not to react visibly to his words. She said, "I read the trial record, you know. You didn't even say anything when the verdict was read against you."

"What good would it have done?"

"You're always that rational?"

"I have a high boiling point. People used to tell me they thought I'd be great in the ER because I stay calm under pressure."

"You can put up with a lot?"

"In most circumstances, yes. It's served me well, I think. Impulsiveness doesn't go over well when you're inside." He checked behind him. Kelda thought he was looking for the waiter again.

She asked, "What does it take to get you angry?"

"I don't know. It happens. I certainly got angry a few times when I was in the penitentiary."

"You want to tell me?"

He thought about it for a moment before he said, "No."

"What about fear? What frightens you?"

"That's easy. Going back to prison. Being locked up. What about you?"

"What do you mean?"

"You. Anger. On our ride home. Did you really mean what you said to Prehost that day?"

"He was pushing me around. I told you I don't like to be intimidated. So I pushed back. That's who I am."

"Did you mean what you said to him, though? About shooting someone? Did you really do that?"

Before she could figure out how to respond, Tom went on. "You told him that you knew you wouldn't miss from that distance. He asked you how many times you'd fired from that distance. You said you'd done it before. Is that true? Have you?"

"Yes, I have." She touched the daisy that was in a small white vase on the table, wondering if it was real. It was. "When you were . . . in the penitentiary, did you ever hear about a little girl named Rosa Alija?"

He shook his head. "For some reason I had constant trouble with the delivery of the newspaper. I complained and complained, but it was never on the porch where it was supposed to be."

She smiled.

"Who was she? The girl?" Tom asked.

Without looking at him once, Kelda told him about being a rookie FBI agent and accidentally finding a little kidnapped girl in an industrial building in Denver's Golden Triangle and about rolling along a dirty floor and coming up firing and clustering three slugs in the center of a child molester's chest while he was trying to blow her to shreds with a gigantic .45.

"Wow. You weren't kidding."

"No, I wasn't kidding."

"What's an UNSUB?" he asked.

"It stands for 'unknown subject.' It's FBI lingo for a suspect."

"And you shot him?"

"I did."

"You killed him?"

"Unfortunately."

"Why unfortunately? It sounds like he deserved it."

She flattened her palms on the table. "Because he deserved worse. He was dead in seconds. That's why it was unfortunate."

"Gotcha," he said.

She thought his eyes said something else entirely. She said, "Can we change the subject?"

He reached across the table and with the tips of his fingers he touched her hand. "Okay, how about this? Back last fall, how come you were so sure that the knife you found was really the one used to kill Ivy Campbell?"

She had trouble keeping her surprise from showing. "What?"

"When the guy called you that day with directions on how to find the knife, why were you sure it was really the one? After all those years, why would somebody suddenly call the FBI about the murder weapon in a case that was all settled?"

She stammered, "I wasn't sure. I wasn't sure about anything until the laboratory results came back."

He closed his hand over hers and lowered his voice. Given his sultry tone, the words he spoke seemed bizarre. "Until that moment—until the lab results came back—did you think I did it? That I killed Ivy?"

"Yes, Tom. I did. There was a lot of evidence that said you did. And I didn't know you then."

He sat back a little, but kept his hand on hers. "Thanks. For being honest about that."

"You're welcome."

She watched him take a few deeper breaths before

he asked, "Are you a hundred percent sure right now—right this minute—that I didn't do it? That I didn't kill her?"

"If this is a first date, Tom, I swear it's the strangest conversation I've ever had on one."

"Please. I need to know. It's important that I know that at least one person believes that I'm innocent."

"What about your grandfather?"

"He'd like to believe it. Maybe he'll get there. Maybe he won't. He loves me. Right now that's all I can ask of him, I think. Please answer me."

He surprised her with his insight. She said, "The answer to your question is yes, Tom, I'm a hundred percent sure you didn't kill Ivy Campbell. Is there anything else?"

"Yes, there is." He raised an eyebrow. "Is this . . . a first date?"

She held her breath and nodded once.

His face broke into a wide grin. "Well, hallelujah. Since this is a first date, you said you were going to tell me how you came to be named Kelda."

She looked down at his hand touching hers. "Okay," she said. "Have you ever heard of the *Book of Kells*?"

"Something else I missed when I was inside? Like you saving that kid?"

"No, hardly. It's an old book, an old Irish book. It's a beautiful hand-drawn manuscript of the four gospels that was written around 800 A.D. The book is in Ireland, in the library at Trinity College in Dublin. My grandparents are from there and my grandfather was an amateur scholar who was always interested in the manuscript. The name was their idea. Kelda—it's in honor of the *Book of Kells*."

"That's certainly more interesting than 'Tom.' "

She closed her eyes and imagined jumping off a cliff. At the same moment, she turned her hand over so that her fingertips touched his.

"I guess," she said.

"A hundred percent sure?"

"Yes."

"Good."

"And I make you want to dance?"

"Yeah, and I'm not talking a waltz, either."

CHAPTER

23

Sam Purdy called my home a few minutes after nine. I knew immediately that he was on his cell phone and that he was attempting the call from one of the canyons of crappy reception that dot Boulder.

"Hey, Alan," he said after I answered. "It's Sam."

Sam was from northern Minnesota, a little town in the Iron Range called Hibbing. His accent had emigrated to Colorado along with him. Anytime he called, once I'd heard his voice on the phone, I had no need for further identification. "I know who it is," I said. "How are you doing?"

"I'm working." He said something else but all I heard was some crackling and the word "goofy."

"You're breaking up."

"What?"

"You're breaking up."

In a few seconds he said, "Is that better?"

"Yeah, a little bit. I didn't hear a thing you said before other than the word 'goofy.'"

"I'm with Lucy. We're finishing up working a home intrusion and assault in an old house on High Street. You know High Street? It's a little bit east of Casey Park. Nice street. I don't think I've ever answered a call up here before. Anyway, an old man was beat up. It's ugly."

Lucy was Sam's partner. I wasn't sure what to say about the news of the home intrusion and assault. I tried, "I'm sorry."

"I'm not asking for your sympathy. I'm calling to tell you that the victim is the grandfather of Tom Clone. I thought that, given the interest you showed when I was at your house the other night, you might be curious about it. Turns out that Clone is living here with his grandfather, but something tells me you already knew that."

"Huh," I muttered.

"What?"

"Nothing. What's goofy about it?"

"Goofy? What? I don't even remember what I was saying before. You have any thoughts that might make my evening any shorter? I'd like to get home before Simon graduates from high school."

Simon was, maybe, in the third grade. "You mean . . . thoughts about the assault?"

"Yes, I mean about the assault." Sam's patience, never exemplary, was fading with the cell signal.

"No, Sam. I don't know a thing that would help you. Why would I? Are you suspecting Tom Clone?"

"Now, why would you think that?"

"Don't be cute. You guys always suspect the family in domestic assaults. How is the grandfather?"

"He's unconscious. They took him by ambulance to Community. Tom Clone called this in himself, by the way. Believe it or not, he says that an FBI agent—a woman—was with him when he got here."

"Really?"

"Yeah, she's his alibi. He says they were on a date or something. Clone and this Fed. Go figure. Guy gets a free pass off death row and a week later he's dating a Fed."

"Really?"

"That's what he says. Haven't talked to her yet—he says she drove away before he went inside and found his grandfather—but I'll track her down." He paused as though he was expecting me to say something. When I didn't, he said, "Listen, you've been terribly helpful and all, but I think maybe I should get back to work."

Trying hard not to sound sarcastic in reply, I said, "Thanks for calling, Sam. I appreciate the heads-up. I do."

"Whatever. Tell Lauren I said not to get mixed up in this one. I'm already dodging microphones and cameras, and the media leeches don't even know who the victim is yet. Once they know it was Clone's grandfather, this one's going to be a real circus. But . . ." He paused. "Hey, since circuses are now illegal in Boulder, I'll have to think of another metaphor, won't I?"

Sam had been exceedingly amused when the Boulder City Council voted to ban circuses with animals from performing in the city. He told me he'd had a lifelong ambition to collar an elephant sometime in his career and it looked like he was finally going to get his chance.

Lauren was a prosecutor for Boulder County. As far as I knew, she wasn't carrying the beeper to catch cases that night for the district attorney's office, so odds were that she wouldn't end up prosecuting the assault on Tom Clone's grandfather.

That was the only good news I could glean from the events. Still, I told Sam I would pass along his advice.

After I hung up the phone, I checked to see what the local news channels had to say about the crime. The nine o'clock news programs had crews at the scene already, but the reporters didn't know much; in fact, as Sam had said, they weren't yet reporting Tom Clone's involvement in the incident. I clicked off the TV set and ambled into the nursery to kiss Grace's sleeping face.

The phone rang once more a few minutes before eleven. I'd just crawled into bed. Figuring it was Sam again, I answered by saying, simply, "Yeah."

After I listened to the greeting on the other end of the line, I replied, "Hold on. I need to change phones."

Lauren rolled my way and said, "What is it?"

"It's a patient. I'll get it in the other room. Go back to sleep."

"Okay," she murmured and rolled over the other way.

I picked up the portable in the kitchen and carried it into the living room. The sky was surprisingly black, with few stars, but below me the Boulder Valley was carpeted with twinkling lights. I was wondering how one of my patients had gotten my home phone number.

In an emergency, patients were instructed to call a number that activated my beeper. My home phone was unlisted.

"Yes, Tom," I said after taking a few seconds to capture my composure.

"My grandfather was assaulted tonight. Somebody broke into his house and beat him up."

As his words registered, the circumstance I found myself in perplexed me. I tried to decide whether I should pretend that I didn't already know about the assault. If I revealed to Tom that I'd received an early heads-up about his grandfather from a police detective, he would be suspicious about why I'd been called and might question whether I'd been indiscreet with Sam about his confidentiality. Impulsively, I chose to try to adopt a middle ground. But I knew my path was paved with banana peels. "How is he?" I asked.

"Not good. I'm calling you from the hospital. He's in the ICU. They hit the poor guy in the head. There's blood all over the hallway. It looks like he was trying to get down the hall to his room or the bathroom or something when they caught up with him and hit him. He doesn't move very fast."

"I'm so sorry."

The sound I was hearing suddenly changed. I thought he might have covered the phone with his cupped palm. "I think the police think I did it."

"Go on," I said.

Tom went into great detail about his interview with Sam Purdy. It did sound as though Sam thought that Tom might have done it. But with Sam you never knew; his whole posture could be a ruse. I'd once been on the receiving end of his interrogation skills. It wasn't a pleasant experience.

"Did you call your lawyer?" I asked.

"Yeah, sure. What? You think I'd call you first? Of course I called my lawyer. As soon as I started getting a weird vibe from that detective, I called him, got one of the other lawyers in his office. She talked to the detective on the phone and asked if I was under arrest. When the detective said no, I got back on the phone and this lawyer told me to shut up. Then she told me to tell the cops to get out of my house and to get a search warrant."

"Tom, what can I do for you tonight?"

"I don't know. I'm upset. I feel vulnerable, you know. I don't know why someone was in the house. Why they would beat up an old man like that, whether they might have been gunning for me. I'm afraid that the police are looking for an excuse to put me back in jail. I'm vulnerable. I feel like a fish in a barrel."

"I can only imagine."

"Maybe I should set up another appointment. Something sooner than the one we have scheduled. I need some advice on how to handle myself so that I don't get in any deeper."

"A big chunk of that advice will need to come from your lawyer, Tom. The part that has to do with the stress you're feeling—you and I can do that. But first things first: Are you okay tonight?"

"Yeah, I guess. I need to find someplace to stay. The police won't let me back in the house until they're done. I may just sleep here at the hospital. I don't have any money with me."

Was he suggesting that I offer him a bed? My reaction to the prospect troubled me almost as much as did the image of Tom sleeping downstairs from my daughter. I knew there was no way I would invite this man into my home. Not only because he was a patient, but also because I now reluctantly realized that I wasn't one hundred percent convinced about the events that had landed him in prison in the first place. I got lost for a moment considering the implications of my musings before I said, "I'm sure that your grandfather would be grateful that you stayed with him at the hospital. It will mean a lot to him to see the face of a loved one by his side when he wakes up."

Tom said, "Yeah, I guess."

I couldn't tell whether or not he was at all convinced. I said, "I'm curious about something. How did you get my home number, Tom? Although this certainly qualifies as an emergency, as I explained to you during our first session I usually hear from patients on my beeper."

Without hesitation, he said, "I called Information. You know, four-one-one. They gave me the number."

"Oh," I replied. "So you want to set up that extra appointment?"

A moment later, as I hung up the phone, I entertained the possibility that it was Kelda who had given Tom my home number. I had no illusions that phone numbers that were unlisted to the rest of us were actually unavailable to curious FBI agents. I also considered the possibility that Sam Purdy had scribbled the number on the back of one of his business cards and given it to Tom.

When he was in certain moods, Sam would have thought that such a prank was pretty funny.

What I wasn't entertaining was the possibility that Tom Clone had told me the truth about calling directory assistance.

There was a time early in my career when I might have marched straight to my closet, changed my clothes, and driven across town to Community Hospital to check personally on Tom Clone's emotional state. Most of the motivation for making such a humanitarian trip would have been the result of a grandiose sense of the psychotherapist's purview—early in my career I actually functioned under the mistaken belief that part of my job was to provide comfort in its purest form.

But two minutes after I'd hung up the phone, I wasn't pulling on a pair of jeans and preparing to drive across town. No, I was back in my bed, focusing more of my mental energy on the violation I felt at having my home phone number compromised than I was directing it toward compassion for Tom Clone's personal tragedy, or toward curiosity at the revelation that Tom Clone and Kelda James were developing a social relationship.

I didn't want to admit it to myself, but I was beginning to regret picking up Tom Clone's case at all. Why?

I was no longer at all certain that he was the victim of the justice system that I originally thought he was. At first, I'd been willing, even eager, to offer him the benefit of the doubt.

Now, no.

But that wasn't all. An honest appraisal would reveal that I was ambivalent about Tom Clone because he was tugging at me in ways that threatened my complacency. He needed me in ways that I didn't want to be needed.

What had Diane said to me? *If you've started hating the bricks, maybe it's time to reconsider being a bricklayer.*

Maybe it is time, I thought. Maybe it is.

I fell asleep pondering the reality that, other than my therapeutic abilities, I possessed absolutely no marketable skills.

CHAPTER

24

After they finished their dinner on the Mall, Kelda and Tom had walked down Pearl Street and Tom had tried to recall what buildings had been demolished and identify what buildings were new in all the redevelopment that had taken place during the nineties in the blocks adjacent to the east end of the Mall. She thought it was an interesting exercise for someone trying to make sense of what had happened in the world during all his missing years. They had coffee at Penny Lane because it was one of the few businesses that Tom remembered from the years before he'd been arrested and incarcerated.

While he stood at the counter picking up their drinks, Kelda turned her back to him and popped another Percocet into her mouth.

A little bit after nine, at Kelda's suggestion, they

strolled back up the hill to High Street. She stopped when they reached her Buick, which was parked on the street, one door down from Tom's grandfather's house.

He asked her, "Have you been limping?"

"Maybe," she said. "I worked out hard this morning. My muscles get a little sore sometimes."

"That's it? You're sure? You got quiet, too, when you started to limp. After we had coffee and started walking, you got quiet."

She opened her purse and reached inside for her car keys. She was surprised that he'd noticed the connection between her pain and her distraction. She liked to think she made it invisible to others, especially to people who didn't know her well. She replied, "I think you're imagining that, Tom. It's no big deal. My leg gets a little sore sometimes. That's all."

He shook his head. "I don't think that's all that's going on. Whatever, why don't you come on inside? Maybe my grandfather will be awake. He really wants to meet you."

"No, thank you, I don't think so. I'm going to head home. Maybe some other time."

He asked, "Why not?" and the resentful undertow in his tone caused her to step back involuntarily.

"What do you mean, 'Why not?'" She tried to force some playfulness into her voice. "I don't need a reason. I just don't feel like going inside with you. I'm tired, and I want to get home."

"I thought we were having a good time."

"We were." She stressed the second word.

"Is it whatever's going on with your limp? Is that it?"

"Tom, I said no. I don't know what things were like for you when you went to prison, but in the twenty-first century when women say no—especially this woman—you would be wise to heed them."

"Because you have a gun?"

She couldn't tell if he was joking, but hoped he was. "I had a nice time, Tom. Good night." She pressed the button on her key ring that unlocked her car door. She had to wait for him to step back before she had room to swing the door open. Her impression was that he forced her to wait an additional second or two. When he finally moved away, she lowered herself into the car.

Her breathing was rapid. His wasn't. She lowered the window and placed her left hand on the ledge of the door. "This was fun," she said, hoping to defuse the tension she was feeling.

"Yeah," he replied, and leaned down so that his face was opposite hers.

Don't, she thought. *Don't try it.*

He lowered his head and brushed her fingers lightly with his lips. His touch was like an electric shock. She repressed a flinch. "See you," he said, looking at her dashboard. "Hey, what time do you have?"

She glanced at the clock. "It's nine-twenty."

"Thanks. Good night," he said. "I'll call you. Assuming that's still okay in the twenty-first century?"

"Yeah," she said. "That's okay. Good night, Tom."

She made a U-turn in the cul-de-sac at the end of High Street and headed back toward Fourteenth. Her headlights were illuminating the silhouette of a Chevy Suburban that was parked along the curb on High opposite the grounds of Casey School. A man was sitting in the driver's seat, but she couldn't make out his features. As she turned the corner she decided that the Suburban was an older model and that the paint was dull blue or gray.

"Prehost," she said aloud. She hit her brakes hard and brought the Buick to a stop. She hadn't planned her next move. One option was to get out of the car and have a chat with the Park County detective, but she quickly decided against it. She wasn't sure what a confrontation would accomplish. Instead, she took a moment to memorize the license plates on the Suburban, then she glided down the hill toward Mapleton.

Four minutes later, as she turned onto Arapahoe to head home, Kelda used her cell phone to call Ira. "Hey, you," she said when Ira answered his phone.

"Hello, girl. I tried to get back to you earlier, but I kept getting your machine. I thought you might not be answering because you were freezing your legs. Hope I didn't wake you."

"No, I've been out, I had some things I had to do."

"Is the pain okay?"

"It's been better. If you're free now, I could sure use a massage."

He laughed. "Is that all I am to you? A good pair of hands? I'm not doing anything. Are you home? You sound like you're on your cell."

"I am, but I'm on my way home. Give me twenty minutes."

"You got it."

Ira was sitting on the wooden steps that led up to her side door when she pulled her car under the elms.

He had his ratty daypack beside him. That meant he was planning to spend the night.

The next morning she parked her Buick in its usual spot at work and took the elevator up to the FBI offices. Bill Graves spotted her as soon as she stepped off the elevator. He took her by the arm and hustled her away from the reception desk. "Come with me," he murmured.

"What?"

He checked the hallway around them before he asked, "What did you get yourself into last night, Kelda? The SAC is ready to take your head off."

She thought, *Oh shit, he's probably having a fit about the Rosa Alija anniversary piece on Fox.* She'd forgotten all about it and wondered how it could have aired already. She quickly decided to deny everything. "I didn't do anything last night, Bill. I don't know what on earth you're talking about."

"Well, apparently there's some Boulder police detective who wants to talk to you about an assault on Tom Clone's grandfather that happened last night. He called the SAC at home and told him that Clone's using you for an alibi. The detective wants permission to interview you."

She shook her head slowly and said, "Damn."

Bill took half a step back and asked, incredulously, "It's true? You were with Clone last night?"

"Not last night. A couple of hours yesterday evening. We had dinner. That's all. That's it." She grimaced. "Shit."

"The SAC is going to string you up if you really did

this. He doesn't need this kind of public attention right now. The Bureau doesn't need this kind of public attention right now. Everybody's under orders to make sure that the only publicity we get is good publicity. And everybody includes you, Kelda." Then, with obvious disdain in his voice, he added, "You had a date with Tom Clone? What the hell were you thinking? Haven't you jeopardized enough with what you've done for that guy?"

She didn't answer. She said, "Thanks for the warning about the SAC, Bill. You're a good friend." And she walked away from him.

A message in the middle of her blotter directed her to go to the SAC's office as soon as she arrived. She mumbled another profanity and tried to figure out how she was going to finesse this with him.

One word came to mind.

Prehost.

Ten minutes later she returned to her desk and grabbed her shoulder bag. She gestured to Bill Graves with a slight movement of her head. He stood and followed her to the elevator.

"Let's get some coffee," she said.

"Is it a good career move for me to be seen with you right now?"

"Ha, that's funny." The elevator arrived and they stepped in. An Asian woman with an infant in a baby carrier was already in the car.

"So?" he said.

"Patience, Mr. Governor's Cousin." She lowered her voice to a whisper. "We're not alone."

"I don't want coffee, Kelda."

"Then at least wait until we get outside the building, okay?"

"I don't have much time. I have calls I'm waiting for."

"Shush, we won't be long." As the elevator opened she grabbed his hand and led him outside onto Stout Street. The Federal Building was on the edge of Denver's downtown business district, and she turned toward the I. M. Pei–designed pedestrian mall that bisected downtown on Sixteenth Street.

"I've never seen him so angry," she said as they reached a red light at the corner of Eighteenth and Stout.

Bill laughed and said, "The SAC? That's because you weren't involved the day that Smith and Jorgensen dropped that surveillance on the—"

"No, you're right, I wasn't part of that. Listen, Bill, I need to ask you something. Has anyone been following you?"

"What?"

"Any strange phone calls? Hang-ups at your house? I'm talking basically since about the time that the press seemed to get wind of Tom Clone's impending release from prison."

"Kelda, what on earth—"

The light changed. Bill's feet seemed permanently affixed to the sidewalk. She almost had to yank him off the curb to get him to cross Eighteenth Street. She lowered her voice. "I've been seeing this car, this old blue Suburban, and another car, a burgundy Toyota pickup, around me for the last few days. Since Clone's release, maybe even a few days before. Thursday, the Toyota was on the lane by my house in Lafayette when I got home."

"Yeah? Anybody do anything threatening?"

She thought of Prehost and the flat he caused on her Buick in the middle of nowhere. His badge in her face. The size of his biceps. "No, no. Nothing like that. What about you?"

"No. But I haven't exactly been watching for tails, either. Maybe I should." He grunted. "And you've been getting phone calls, too?"

"Hang-ups. A few. I've star-six-nined all of them. Nothing ever comes up. I've been guessing that this all has to do with what we did with the Tom Clone case."

"Why you and not me?"

"I don't know. My profile's higher because of . . . you know, Rosa. Maybe that's it. Or maybe it's just because I'm a woman and they think that makes me more vulnerable."

"Why didn't you tell me before this?"

"I thought it was just crank stuff. Some of the same sort of thing happened to me after I found Rosa. In addition to a million wonderful notes I got from people thanking me, I also got some calls and a few letters that I'd prefer not to have received. It comes with the notoriety. It all faded after a while; I figured that this would fade, too."

"But?"

"The Suburban was parked down the street from Tom Clone's house last night. I saw it when I was pulling away."

"So you really did alibi Clone?"

She nodded and said, "Yes, I was with him. I don't really know any details of what happened to his grandfather—certainly couldn't tell you what time the assault occurred—but I told the SAC that I was with

Tom for almost three hours last evening. We had dinner, coffee. Went for a walk."

"And what time did you see the Suburban?"

"Nine-twenty. I left his house at nine-twenty. I remember looking at the clock on my dashboard just before I drove away." She also remembered that she'd looked at the clock because Tom Clone had asked her to. Kelda didn't tell Bill that part. She noticed the pedestrian light change to "Walk" a hundred feet in front of them and tugged Bill along with her so that they would have a chance to make the light at the corner.

"Did you tell the SAC all this?"

"Yes, I did. I even gave him a license plate number for the Suburban."

Bill raised an eyebrow. "You got the license plate? You're always thinking, Kelda. I like that."

They rushed across the intersection at Seventeenth Street.

Bill said, "Why are we hurrying? Do you have plate numbers on the Toyota that followed you, too?"

"We're not hurrying, I'm just trying to be sensitive to your schedule. You said that you had stuff to do. And no, the guy in the Toyota had his plates conveniently caked with mud."

"Did you tell the SAC about the other times you saw the Suburban? And about the Toyota and the phone calls?"

She took two more steps before she said, "Kind of."

He suddenly stopped walking, planting his feet so that she couldn't pull him along. "What does that mean?"

"What? What does what mean?"

"You didn't tell the SAC that you think you're being followed?"

"I . . . alluded to it. You know how he reacts to stuff like this, Bill. I can handle it myself. I'm being vigilant. I spotted the tails, didn't I?"

"Are you nuts? He reacts to 'stuff like this' because he doesn't want any of his agents ambushed, Kelda. Jesus, I can't believe you would . . . In case you haven't looked at a calendar lately, it's after September 2001. Way after."

"Bill, I—"

"You spotted the tails, Kelda? And how do you know what tails you might have missed? You could be putting other agents at risk by keeping this to yourself. You could . . ." The expression on his face went from concern laced with annoyance to something decidedly less sympathetic. He leaned back against the wall behind him and placed the sole of one shoe flat against the granite face of the building and shook his head.

"What?" she asked.

"Are you dating this guy, Kelda? Do you have feelings for this . . . this accused murderer, this, this—"

"Bill, it's . . ." She looked away from him. Her weak protest hung awkwardly between them.

"It's what?"

"It's complicated."

"Complicated? You bet it's complicated. Tom Clone is not an innocent man, Kelda. His conviction was thrown out. Thrown out, that's all. He wasn't suddenly found not guilty. He certainly wasn't exonerated. There's no evidence that he didn't kill that girl. You know the book in that murder case in Park County better than anyone but the detective who ran Clone down. One little break for the local cops and Clone could be rearrested at any time. You're putting a lot at risk personally and professionally by even being seen with the guy, let alone getting involved with him. And now, now look what's happened—the SAC knows that you're up to something and . . . it appears that somebody's following you . . . and you're Clone's alibi for—"

She stepped back from him. She told herself not to get defensive. The admonition didn't work. "Have you forgotten about the knife we found? You know, the one with somebody else's blood on it? Have you forgotten about that?"

"No," he replied. "I think about it every day."

The chill in his words slapped at her. "I know what I'm doing, Bill. I'm not sure why, but I have this need to understand him, to know how people could think him capable of what they think he did to—"

"It's not our job to understand them, Kelda. It's our job to catch them and convict them."

"I don't think I agree. Anyway, it's none of your business whom I'm seeing socially."

He turned his head away from her toward the Sixteenth Street Mall. "That little girl can't protect you from everything, Kelda. One of these times you're going to go to make a withdrawal from that account and you're going to find out that it's busted. Totally empty."

"What are you implying?" But she knew exactly what he was implying. He was reminding Kelda that her public heroics in rescuing Rosa Alija wouldn't insulate her forever.

"You know exactly what I mean," he said.

"Screw you, Graves. I do not need Rosa Alija to keep me out of trouble with the SAC."

"You don't? Tell me that after you get your ass reassigned to Billings. But please don't drag me up there with you. Denver's as cold as I ever want to get."

He stared at her for about ten seconds, pivoted, and started walking. His long strides were taking him away from the Sixteenth Street Mall, back in the direction of the Federal Building.

"Wait," Kelda called after him.

Bill Graves didn't slow. He broke into a jog and cut into a cloud of diesel exhaust hanging behind an RTD bus that was holding up traffic on Seventeenth.

CHAPTER

25

I woke feeling guilty about how I'd handled the phone call with Tom Clone the previous evening. Doubt about my own clinical judgment had once been a rare emotional state for me, but over the past year I'd begun to question my therapeutic decisions with increasing frequency and, unfortunately, I could argue, with increasing justification. The previous year my clinical missteps had cost some people their lives, and I was already beginning to suspect that the cavalier method with which I'd handled the emergency the night before might end up having similarly grave consequences.

While I was showering I tried to convince myself that my self-flagellation was nothing more than mindless catastrophizing. My behavior the night before might not have been an ideal clinical intervention, but it was hardly lethal. But my rationalization wasn't sufficient;

the guilt and regret that I was feeling didn't wash right off and disappear down the drain.

Lauren didn't know I was treating Tom Clone. That wasn't surprising—typically she didn't know any of my patients' names. It was therefore coincidence that she initiated a discussion over breakfast regarding the story in the *Daily Camera* about the assault on his grandfather. I made small talk in reply and succeeded in nudging our conversation away from Tom Clone and on to the ongoing dilemma of juggling our workdays and Grace's care, and negotiating which of us was going to be home first to rescue Viv, our daytime nanny.

The answer that day was Lauren.

She asked if my telephone emergency had turned out okay the night before. I told her it had.

And that was it.

I didn't tell her that the emergency patient was Tom Clone and that he had probably slept on a couch in the ICU waiting room at Community Hospital, but that he would have been much happier in our guest room. Nor did I mention that Sam Purdy was acting as though he suspected Tom of involvement in the assault on his grandfather. I didn't tell her that the heroic FBI agent who had rescued Rosa Alija was one of my patients and that she was apparently now dating the controversial man who had once been convicted of almost beheading his ex-girlfriend in Park County, and who was now—miraculously, it seemed—out of prison.

I didn't tell her that I was full of doubts about whether I was still capable of doing work that left people trusting me for insight into their lives.

What I told her was that I wished that the cast was off my arm and that I yearned to take her and Grace and both dogs and drive the Mini the whole length of the Peak to Peak Highway and maybe take it over Trail Ridge Road into Rocky Mountain National Park.

She told me that I was a good father and that she loved me, and I left for work with just enough warmth coursing through my veins to suspect that I would make it through another day as a psychologist.

Tom Clone's emergency appointment was that afternoon at three. He showed up right on time.

He and I were alone in the waiting room, so I greeted him by saying, "How's your grandfather doing, Tom?"

"A little better, they think. He's resting better anyway. But I'm worried. His EEG is showing some anomalies, he lost more blood than anybody his age can really afford to lose, and his kidney functions are screwy. I'm afraid his kidneys are going to shut down. That would kill him, for sure."

As I processed the technical sophistication of his remarks, I reminded myself that Tom Clone had been only months away from completing medical school when he was incarcerated for almost decapitating his girlfriend in Park County.

I consciously reminded myself that he hadn't done it. He hadn't killed that girl. The DNA said so.

"Come on back to the office," I said.

After we settled on our chairs, I waited for him to choose a place to start.

He scanned the perimeter of the office once before he said, "I was with that FBI agent last night. The one I told you about who picked me up from prison. The one who found the knife."

That FBI agent. Kelda.

I said, "When your grandfather was assaulted? That's who you were with? The FBI agent?"

"Yeah. She called out of the blue and asked me out, bought me dinner. We were down on the Mall most of the evening. We were having a great time—I thought we were, anyway—but once we got back to my place she was, I don't know, gone. Cold. You know, distant."

I waited.

"She said she was tired. That her leg was sore. Why would she drive to town, take me to dinner, and then suddenly go cold on me? The night just . . . ended. I don't get it. Maybe I'm just out of practice, but I think it's bullshit."

I thought a little reality testing might be in order. "Maybe, Tom, she was tired and her leg was sore."

He scowled at me. "No, you weren't there. It wasn't like that. Everything was great, perfect, and then suddenly, everything wasn't. She just said she was leaving, got in her car, and left. I don't know why I bothered."

His voice had sharpened and I realized that the events of the previous evening with Kelda had become overdetermined for Tom—they'd taken on meaning beyond the simple progression of events. Along with that awareness, a thought one-hopped through my consciousness like a hard shot across the infield: If I hadn't mentioned Tom's grandfather in the waiting room, would Tom have brought up the old man's condition on his own? There was no way to answer that question and I kicked myself for putting my compassion in front of my clinical obligations.

I said, "And that left you feeling . . . how?"

At first blush his response was pure non sequitur. He said, "I'm starting work tomorrow at Kaiser. In the pharmacy? The lady in their personnel department knew my story, feels I've been screwed, and says I'm perfect for the job. To tell you the truth, I think I got lucky that I ran into somebody who feels that way. She's in the minority, believe me."

"Congratulations."

"Yeah. Anyway, their insurance won't pay for me to come here to see you. If I want to see somebody, I have to see somebody on the Kaiser staff. I don't know if my attorney will continue to pay for therapy if I can see somebody on my insurance plan for free. So I don't know what's going to happen."

I could have gone into a harangue about how long the waiting list was going to be to see a psychotherapist at Kaiser, or how restrictive the mental health treatment options were going to be. It would have made me feel better, but I didn't. I said, "You don't know what's going to happen about what?"

"What's the point?" His words were perilously close to a whine. "Why should I get something started with you when I'll just have to stop? What good is that going to do?"

Lightbulb time.

Duh. Remember a concept called transference, Dr. Gregory?

I said, "Tom?" and waited until he was focused on my words. "What you're describing right now? It's similar to what you're feeling with that FBI agent, isn't it?" I almost said "with Kelda," but I caught myself just as the back of my tongue was curling toward the roof of my mouth to form the K. I didn't think Tom Clone had ever used her name with me.

He replied, "What do you mean?"

If I dissected his reply, I thought I would find about an equal blend of "I don't understand" and "What the fuck are you talking about?"

In the face of an interpretation similar to the one I'd just made to Tom, the response of "What do you mean?" wasn't an uncommon one, especially in the early stages of psychotherapy. A major goal of insight-oriented psychotherapy is to increase self-awareness so that similarities between emotional reactions to prior events and emotional reactions to current ones, like the circumstance I was pointing out to Tom, become self-evident to the patient.

Responding to his innocuous-sounding "What do you mean?" meant that I had a clinical judgment to make: How far should I stretch the interpretation that I was making? I decided to go for broke. The worst that would happen is that he would consider the connections I was suggesting to be totally inane. The best that would happen is that he would begin to see himself as vulnerable to the gravity of emotional and historical forces that he hadn't previously recognized.

In other words, as human.

"Tom, you haven't been out of prison long. And you haven't been coming to see me for long. Yet in the brief time that you've been here, you've focused most of our time together on events where people become very meaningful to you and then seem to turn their backs on you."

He made a perplexed face. It wasn't just confusion, though. A healthy dose of skepticism was mixed with something I was interpreting as aggravation. He said, "I don't know . . . I don't know what you're talking about."

I caught enough hesitation in his voice that I thought he was at least curious about the point I was making.

"Your mother?" I continued. "When you were young and she'd get manic, she'd take you on these terrific E-ticket rides, on these grand adventures she concocted, and then suddenly her mania would crash into depression and she'd leave you stranded and alone."

He was staring at me.

I asked, "Still with me?"

"So far."

The two words carried a surprising modicum of warning.

I felt the caution—it was milder than my reaction to a dog baring its teeth, though not much—and I pressed on. "Then there's this FBI agent who shows up in your life. First she finds the evidence that gets you out of jail, then she picks you up to take you home from prison, and she takes you out for a wonderful meal in a romantic hotel. The next time you try to reach her, she acts as though you're nothing but a bother. Then . . . she calls out of the blue and takes you out to dinner. The evening is terrific. But when you try to extend your time together, she just disappears like the night had meant nothing to her." I thought I'd explained enough. I waited for Tom to reply.

He didn't oblige.

I asked, "Do you see a pattern?"

He snorted at me through his nose. "I don't know what the fuck you're talking about."

I nodded once, slowly. I'd swung for the fences and failed to make contact. It wasn't the first time I'd gone down swinging, and it certainly wouldn't be the last. At least, I consoled myself, I didn't get called out on strikes.

I said, "Okay."

As I figuratively made the stroll back to the dugout, I was recalling what Tom had said to me the previous night when he'd called and requested the extra appointment. He'd told me that he was feeling vulnerable, both in terms of his physical safety and in terms of his legal status. I wondered if he would get around to talking about either concern during this session.

He said, "You done with that other thing?"

I said, "Yes." I thought, *You bet.*

"Here's something weird for you. The last couple of times I slept in my grandfather's house, I heard doors clanging shut. It sounded just like when I was inside when the cell doors slammed."

"You were awake or asleep?"

"The first night I was asleep. The sound woke me up. I thought it was just a bad dream. The next night I was asleep the first time I heard it, but the next time was maybe an hour later and I was still awake. It made me jump. It sounded just like a cell door slamming. Exactly."

"What do you think it was?" I asked.

"I don't know. I'm jumpy. I have a lot on my mind. Maybe I'm just hearing things. But that never happened to me before, even when I was on death row." He sat forward on the edge of his chair with his elbows on his knees. "I was also wondering about post-traumatic stress. Wondered if you thought that was possible."

I'd been watching for signs of post-traumatic stress disorder since Tom Clone had stepped into my office for the first time. Like combat veterans, or abused spouses, or the tens of thousands of people trapped in lower

Manhattan on September 11, or hundreds of other categories of traumatized people, Tom's experiences in prison
had left him vulnerable for symptoms of post-traumatic
stress.

"It's certainly possible, Tom. PTSD could certainly
cause flashbacks like the ones you're describing. And
your experiences in the criminal justice system were
certainly severe enough stressors to place you at risk.
Did you have any other . . . sensations associated with
hearing the doors slam?"

"Like what? You mean anxiety symptoms, like that?
What else would I look for—rapid breathing, heart
palps, sweaty palms? That sort of thing?"

I nodded, although I was reluctant to provide a
shopping list of symptoms. The list was longer than the
one Tom had asked about, of course, but I didn't enu-
merate any of the alternatives. I generally wasn't eager
to suggest to Tom, or to any patient, that there were
symptomatic targets at which to take aim.

"No. Nothing like that. Just the damn doors slamming." He shivered. "Once you've heard it a few times
for real—and, believe me, it's real when you're the one
that they're locking up—you'll never, ever forget it. You
don't know what it's like, that sound."

I watched, eerily fascinated, as his eyes told me he'd
gone someplace else.

No, I thought, *I don't know what it's like.*

I asked, "Are you having any other experiences that
remind you of the time that you spent in prison?"

"Like what?"

"Flashbacks."

"What would they be like?"

"I wasn't there, Tom. I can only imagine what you

went through. You haven't told me much about what life was like for you inside, so I don't know specifically what to ask."

"I don't like to think about it. I don't think I'm ever going to want to think about it."

I waited thirty seconds or so for Tom to exit my office before I made the stroll to the waiting room for my next patient. As I greeted her, I could see through the front window that Tom was climbing on a bright red Vespa parked at a bike rack in front of my office.

I followed my new patient back down the hall to my office wondering how a man just released from the penitentiary could afford to have a motor scooter that looked brand new.

Kelda didn't comment about my cast at the beginning of her rescheduled session the following week.
And she didn't ask about the condition of my arm.

She was almost fifteen minutes late and seemed intent on using the remaining minutes of her allotted time
efficiently. She sat on her chair, released her hair from
confinement behind her head, and said, "That trip to
Hawaii I told you about? I didn't go on my own. Jones's
family was going over to get some closure after her
death. I went with them. They wanted to collect some of
her things that someone had found at the gallery where
she'd worked and meet the people who knew her at the
end. They invited me to go along. So when I went, I
went over with her mother and her brother."

I didn't know what parable I had just heard the pre-
amble to. So I waited patiently to hear the fable.

"She'd hadn't been in Maui long, you know, when she died. Jones hadn't. Yet she'd already done about a dozen paintings—acrylics—and twice that many watercolors. That was a remarkable output for her. Three dozen pieces would have been a year's work for her in Denver, maybe more. To me that meant that something was stimulating her there, driving her.

"I didn't get it at first—I told you I didn't understand why she'd gone to Hawaii at all. But when I walked into that co-op, that gallery where they'd found some of her old things, I think I finally began to understand what was going on with her.

"The gallery had found five pieces in this upstairs storage room they have. The pictures weren't even framed. Two acrylics, three watercolors. The watercolors were small, maybe each about the size of a book. The two acrylics were larger—they were square, maybe thirty inches on a side. Something like that." She exhaled audibly. The sound was almost a sigh.

"In each of the five paintings in that storage room, there was an 'Oh my God, I'm in Hawaii quality' to it. You know, ocean vistas, palm trees, old churches, Haleakala—that's the name of the volcano on Maui. The person who showed us her pictures at the gallery said that painting that stuff was like a rite of passage for newly arrived artists in Hawaii. The good ones, she said, are the ones who get past it. The artists who don't get past it end up smoking weed and selling thirty-dollar prints to tourists. She said that Jones—she called her Joan, of course—she said that it was clear from the start that Jones was technically good—you know, that she had talent—but that these early pieces never sold in the gallery because they were just Hawaiian clichés—the sort of thing you could find at every souvenir shop on the island."

Kelda laughed. "I remember thinking during the conversation, *The early pieces? What are we talking? The first week? Ten days?*" She shook her head. "The woman in the gallery said that once Jones started putting herself—her feelings, her life, her spirit, whatever Oprah's calling it these days—into her work, she'd immediately started selling paintings. At first the other artists at the gallery thought it was just because Jones was pricing her stuff for less than they were, but soon it was clear to everybody in the co-op that Jones was doing something special, and that the customers were responding to it."

I watched Kelda dab at the corner of her left eye with the tip of her finger. Evidence of a tear? It would have been the first I'd seen from her. But it was a speck of something less poignant than a tear that she was clearing from her eye.

"The woman said that once word got around that Jones had died, the remaining paintings sold within days, but that everybody had forgotten about the five that were in storage because Jones had pulled them from the gallery and hadn't wanted them displayed.

"I asked her if there was any way that I could see any of the paintings that the gallery had sold. Any of the later ones. The ones with Jones's spirit." Kelda smiled as she said "spirit." I couldn't read the grin and wondered whether she was being sardonic or sarcastic. "The woman said she didn't know, excused herself to go check some records, and joined us again in a few minutes. 'The invoices show that they went to people from the mainland, mostly,' she said. 'A couple of large ones went to a designer who was decorating a condo at Ka'anapali. We have the designer's name, but not the clients'. Mainlanders are our typical customers. And there is a local collector who lives in Makawao'—that's a little cowboy town up on the side of the volcano—'who has two paintings. And Joan traded one to her landlord for rent. So if M'loo—that's her landlord—didn't sell it, she has one.' She told us how to find M'loo, and Jones's mother made arrangements to have the five remaining pictures shipped to her home. We thanked the woman in the gallery and we turned to leave.

"The woman touched Jones's mother on her shoulder and said, 'I almost forgot. I have her kit, too. It has her sketchpad in it and some paints and brushes. A little journal she kept. Should I include those when I ship the paintings?'

"Mrs. Winslett said she would like that, and we started to go.

" 'And I have one,' the woman in the gallery called after us. 'I have one of the chasing pictures, too. I didn't want to tell you because I was afraid you'd ask to take it with you and I don't think . . . I can give it up.'

"Jones's mother—Mrs. Winslett—went back to New Hampshire a couple of days later. Jones's brother and I decided to stay and try to see if we could find some of the paintings that Jones had sold. He wanted to see if he could get somebody to sell one to him. It was really important to him."

I spoke for the first time since I had greeted Kelda that day. "The woman in the gallery called them the 'chasing pictures'? Did you and Jones's brother discover what that meant?"

Kelda nodded. "Over the next few days we ended up

seeing some of the paintings. Jones's old landlord turned out to be an absolutely obese Indonesian woman with this huge smile and a laugh that made your eyes quiver. She still had the painting that she'd traded for rent for the little shack where Jones had been living. And the woman at the gallery let us see the one she had. And . . . the collector she told us about, a guy who owns a protea farm on the side of the volcano up near Makawao, he had two. The ones in the condo in Ka'anapali we never got to see. We tracked down the designer who'd bought them, but the owners of the condo weren't on the island while we were there."

Kelda crossed her legs. "The paintings were very different from the ones we'd seen in the storeroom at the gallery. The Hawaiian landscape aspects were more abstract—more impressionistic is probably a better way to put it—than in the first paintings we saw. I'm no art critic, but that's the way it seemed to me.

"But the main difference was that in the later pictures there was always a figure, you know, a person. The paintings weren't just landscapes, but the person wasn't the focus, either. The person was secondary, not front and center, and in each painting there is always some force at her back. In every painting, it's always a woman. The force in one is the wind, almost blowing her over. In another, she's on a beach and the force is a big wave crashing unevenly against some rocks behind her. You know that the water is about to wash over her. In another one that's set on one of the two main roads in Paia, it's a car that's after her as she's trying to cross a street. It's clear she's not going to make it out of the way."

Stating the obvious, I said, "Something is always after her? The woman in the pictures? Chasing her?"

"Yes. The last one we saw? It's the one that her landlord has. It's the most disturbing of all of them. In that one it's the darkness that's chasing her. The woman in the painting is facing west at sunset in a field near the ocean. M'loo said the plants in the field are pineapples; she even offered to take us to see the field where Jones had painted it. It's outside of Paia on the road to Hana. The darkness is creeping up on the woman from behind. It's sneaking right out of the sugarcane fields like a thief."

Words entered my head an instant before Kelda spoke again. It turned out that the words that came out of her mouth were the exact same ones that had just materialized in my head.

She said, "Or a killer."

I felt as though I were mouthing the words as she spoke them, and I wondered what that meant.

"A killer?" I repeated.

"The painting felt . . . dangerous. They all did. The darkness wasn't going to surround her. It was going to consume her. That's how it looked to me."

"What are you saying, Kelda?"

"I'm not sure. She wasn't feeling safe. I know she wasn't feeling safe. I could see it in her art."

"Were the Hawaii paintings that different from the work she did in Colorado?"

"They were better, that's for sure. But the biggest difference was the tone. Her work here was light, energetic. The chasing pictures are dark, ominous. She was frightened."

I stated the obvious. It was my job. "Jones never felt safe, though, did she?"

"Of course she didn't, but . . . this was different. The Hawaii paintings told us she was in danger."

"From what?"

"I don't know. I just know she felt she was in danger."

"She suffered from multiple phobias, Kelda. She spent a good chunk of her life frightened."

"I have her journal, Alan. The one that she left in the gallery? I have it. She was afraid. That's what the darkness represents in the painting that M'loo has. That's what all the chasing pictures are about. Her fear of someone."

"Not something?"

"She was always afraid of something. But never someone. Jones loved people. That's not how her fears worked."

A suspicion was developing in my mind. It came into shape slowly, erratically, like a web page loading from a recalcitrant server. When I had enough pieces to identify it, I followed the hunch. "How do you feel about darkness, Kelda?"

"No," she said immediately. She swallowed and shook her head, looking down at her hands in her lap. "I've covered enough rough ground today, Alan. That will have to wait for another time."

Kelda sat in that same position for a minute or two after finishing her tale about Jones and the chasing pictures and evading my question about the darkness. The silence wasn't awkward. It wasn't even particularly poignant. Kelda seemed to be like a runner catching her breath, surprised that she was still standing after a race she hadn't been sure she could even complete.

Typically, I wouldn't end a protracted silence like that one—I would leave that choice up to my patient. But in this case, the stillness of Kelda's posture was a clue about something I felt was worth a little exploration. Finally, I asked, "How's your pain right now?"

Her eyes brightened a little. "Aren't you supposed to call it 'my discomfort,' Alan? Isn't that what shrinks are supposed to say? You don't want to be guilty of suggestion, do you?"

Kelda wasn't usually playful with me.

Rather than get sidetracked by her remark, which is what I suspected she intended and what would have been most comfortable for her, I rephrased my question. "So how is your discomfort right now?"

Her features softened. The little wrinkles in her forehead and at the corners of her eyes disappeared as though some recent Botox injections had just magically kicked in.

She said, "I don't hurt right now."

"What do you make of that?"

She closed her eyes. I could see her eyeballs moving below her eyelids. It reminded me of watching Lauren while she was dreaming.

"I don't see what this has to do with Jones." She opened her eyes.

"Neither do I. Together we may be able to find out, though. I think that's the point."

"Usually by this time of day, I'm in a lot of pain."

I nodded.

"I don't see what this has to do with Jones, Alan."

I repeated, "Neither do I."

I really didn't. I didn't have a clue.

• • •

She stood to leave a minute later. I was very aware that she hadn't mentioned Tom Clone or the assault on his grandfather or the fact that she and Tom had been spending time together.

Usually, as I proceed in psychotherapy with my patients I remain ignorant of their omissions. During the course of treatment I am able to observe the continuity of their thoughts and even recognize the nature of the associations that they make, consciously or unconsciously, as they move from one topic to another. I can chart the process of their behavior as though I'm taking notes on a piece of music. But I typically have no way to observe the exclusionary choices that they make.

That means that I have no way to know the important topics that they are *not* discussing.

With Kelda, because of Tom Clone's revelations and because of Sam Purdy's updates, I had a narrow channel by which to chance a look in the rearview mirror of Kelda's life. And in that narrow tunnel of vision I could see what she'd chosen to drive right on by.

I reminded myself, however, that Tom Clone, not Kelda James, was holding the mirror I was looking in, and that Tom was undoubtedly pointing it precisely where he wished.

Still.

Kelda stopped at the door and turned. Her eyes were aimed down near my abdomen. "How's your arm?" she asked.

"Good," I said. "Fine."

"Great. I'm glad. Next week regular time then?"

"Yes."

CHAPTER

27

I was out the door less than a minute after Kelda left my office. I considered it propitious that the sky was mottled gray and that I could hear the rumble of distant thunder. Maybe the monsoons were finally coming. But a moment's reflection told me that the early evening air was still quite warm and it was obvious that it didn't contain enough humidity to allow me the luxury of forgetting my lip balm.

A glance confirmed that no raindrops dotted the dust that coated the surface of my car.

So maybe the monsoons weren't arriving after all.

I climbed into my car, opened all the windows to air it out, and checked my rearview mirror a second time when I was about halfway down the driveway. I looked just in time to see Sam Purdy pulling into the driveway from Walnut Street. He saw me coming, stopped, and got out of his car. I shut off the engine and got out of mine.

I wondered if he'd seen Kelda leaving my office, wondered if he knew what Kelda looked like. Then I thought, *Of course he does. Everyone knows what Kelda looks like. They know because of Rosa Alija.*

"Your arm's still broken," he said.

"Imagine that. Hey, Sam, how are you doing?"

"You don't want to know how I'm doing. And a few seconds from now you're not going to be happy to see me."

"What makes you think I'm happy to see you now?"

"Cute."

He closed the distance between us until he was close enough that I could examine the stains from food he'd spilled on his tie. The spots weren't recent; as far as I knew, Sam owned only three ties and this one was the oldest in the collection. One particular spot had been there as long as we'd been friends. The stain was shaped like Idaho and was about the size of a healthy fava bean.

"Why won't I be happy to see you?"

Lowering his voice to a melodramatic whisper, he said, "Because I need to talk to you about Tom Clone."

I winced. "I can't. You know that."

"By telling me you can't, you're already telling me something you're not supposed to tell me. So why don't you just go ahead and tell me one or two other things that you're not supposed to tell me? That way I don't have to make threats and impugn your character and we can still be friends."

Damn. I consoled myself with the fact that Sam's tone was civil, so far. I held out hope he was willing to be playful. Otherwise this was going to degenerate into confrontation as quickly as Grace's naptime whimpers became tears. I said, "I don't know what you mean."

He sighed. "Okay, I'll explain it to you then. You just told me you can't talk about Clone. If you can't talk about him, that means he's your patient or your client or whatever the hell you're calling the unfortunate schmucks you work with these days. Well, the fact is you weren't even supposed to tell me *that*. So we've already crossed the line about you not telling me things. You've lost your confidentiality virginity, so to speak."

His deduction was, as always, sound. I smiled at him as a boom of thunder shook the air all around us.

Sam ducked. Why did he duck? I don't know. I would guess that he felt as though the heavens were getting ready to swat him upside the head. I wasn't at all sure he didn't deserve it.

I asked, "And in your mind that means I should just become a confidentiality slut?"

"Yeah, exactly. That would sure make my life easier." He turned and gazed at the western sky. "Why don't you come get in my car with me before we get fried by lightning?"

"No, you come down here and get in mine. If I get in your car, you'll take me hostage until I agree to sacrifice my chastity."

"It's not your chastity I'm after."

"We've been down this road before, Sam. You know I'm not going to tell you what you want to know."

"We'll see. Just sit with me for a minute."

He followed me back down the driveway to my car. As he settled on the seat he said, "I don't think it's really going to rain. The air is too dry. It'll just be thunder and more virga. The lightning will probably start a fire up there somewhere." He gestured to the west, up toward the mountains.

"You're probably right." I had enough things to argue with Sam about. I didn't need to argue with him about the weather.

"I can't find Tom Clone," he said.

"Really?" At his unexpected change of focus, I switched over to my parent voice. "Do you remember if you put him back where he belonged the last time you used him?"

He didn't bite. "He's gone missing. He hasn't been by the hospital to visit his grandfather for over twenty-four hours, and he's not at home. Neighbors haven't seen him. He's vanished. What I need to know from you is whether he has a job and if he does, where he works."

"That's it?"

Sam laughed. "No, but it's all I'm allowing myself to hope for."

"Have you tried his attorney?"

"Yeah, as a matter of fact, I have. He's in Kenya. I wish I were in Kenya. I could do a month·or two in Kenya communing with the animals without a problem. But it'll never happen. Want to know why? Fancy attorneys go to Kenya; cops go to Disneyland, if we're lucky. And then we spend two years making payments on our Visa to cover the trip. By the time we're done with the interest payments, we've paid enough that we realize we should have just gone to Kenya after all."

"Why do you want to talk with Tom Clone?"

"Come on, Alan, don't ask me stuff like that. Don't take advantage of the fact that I pretend to like you."

I sighed. "Just tell me if you want to arrest him or just want to talk to him."

Sam looked out the car window at the house that contained my office. "You own this place or do you rent?"

"I own it with Diane and Raoul and General Electric."

He continued to gaze on the little brick Victorian wistfully. Diane and I had been prescient enough, or savvy enough, or, most likely, just damn lucky enough to buy a building that was in the center of downtown on a good-sized piece of land with enviable zoning just before Boulder's property values went through the roof.

"Mortgage?" he asked.

"Yeah, that's the GE part. But we bought the place when the market was soft, so we're doing okay. I consider the place my retirement plan or Grace's college fund, whichever comes first."

"Doing better than okay with it, I bet," Sam said.

"Yeah, better than okay."

"I never told you, but Sherry and I own the shop where she sells her flowers. It's a retail/condo-type thing. We have a mortgage, too, but over the years, we've made more money on the real estate than she's made selling flowers."

"Sometimes," I said, "being lucky is much more lucrative than being smart."

I watched him as he reached into his shirt pocket and held up a flimsy piece of paper with a few rows of Powerball picks on them. He said, "Amen to that," and laughed. After he stuffed the lottery ticket back into his pocket, he raised his chin and yanked at the knot in his tie. Then he spent an inordinate amount of time undoing the top button of his shirt. I thought the difficulty could have had something to do with the fact that he appeared to be wearing a size-sixteen shirt on his size-seventeen-and-a-half neck.

My sense of self-preservation caused me to withhold comment on my observation.

"Here's the thing—if Clone walked up that sidewalk over there and climbed the stairs to your office door right this minute, I'd just want to talk to him. But the truth is that if he didn't answer some of my questions just right, I'm not too far away from arresting him. I'm trying to be honest with you here."

"For his grandfather's assault?"

Sam sighed. "I'm afraid so."

I felt sweat on my temple and started the engine so that the air conditioner would kick on. "Close your door," I said.

"We going somewhere?" Sam asked.

I said, "No, I'm not anyway. I just want to get the AC running. You think he did it?"

"What's 'it'? That murder in Park County? Or the assault on the grandfather?"

I'd already heard Sam's thoughts on Ivy Campbell's murder. "I'm talking about his grandfather."

"I think there are things he's not explaining adequately. Time-frame things, mostly."

"What happened to his alibi? When you called me the other night, you said he has an alibi."

"His alibi held up okay—actually pretty good—but it turns out that there're some outstanding questions about the time of the actual assault. It may have happened before his alibi kicks in. We're not sure."

I moved my hands to my face and rubbed my eyes. I suddenly felt tired. "I can't tell you where he works. I wish I could. I know you'll find out eventually anyway and I'd love to save you the hassle."

"Who else might know where he works?"

"His grandfather?"

"The old guy is still gorked."

Gork: God only really knows. Sam was using the hospital staff acronym to tell me that Tom Clone's grandfather was in no neurological position to reveal his grandson's employer. I felt even more tired than I had.

"I don't know who else might know. What about a parole officer?"

"Clone's not on parole, Alan. He's a free man."

Of course he was. I knew that.

Sam reached for the door handle. "For the record," he said, "I'm worried about him."

"Huh? You're worried about him? Why?"

"I don't like it when people go missing."

"Are you worried about what he's up to? Or are you worried that he may be in danger? Which is it?"

"Maybe both. Certainly the latter. I have to consider the possibility that it wasn't a stranger who assaulted the grandfather and that the grandfather wasn't the intended victim." He cracked open the door.

"Wait," I said. I forced a deep breath and asked, "Sam, is anyone else in danger in this situation? From Tom Clone? Are you keeping anything from me? Has he threatened anyone?"

Sam chuckled. "Of course I'm keeping things from you. But no, Clone hasn't threatened anyone that we know of." He opened his mouth to say something more but only said, "Oh," and winced before he closed it again. Finally, he added, "Danger? Yeah, maybe. Maybe someone else is in danger."

"Imminent danger?"

"Yeah, imminent danger. That's possible."

"But no specific threat that you're aware of?"

"No, no threat."

"Possible's not good enough." I took another deliberate breath. At some level of my awareness, I knew I was pausing to give Sam a chance to catch up with me. "But you think he might be in danger, Sam? Clone? Say he didn't assault his grandfather, but someone else did. Tom Clone might still be in danger from the same person who broke into the house and beat up his grandfather?"

Sam was beginning to get a feel for the melody of the tune I was humming, and finally started tapping his foot to the music.

"Yeah, absolutely," he said. "No doubt about it. Until we get this thing solved, you have to figure that anyone else who lived in that house with the grandfather is in danger. If Clone didn't do the assault, he could even be somewhere injured right now—hell, maybe that's why we can't find him. We're talking definite imminent danger." He paused. "Definite."

I wasn't looking at Sam. Yes, I was concerned for Tom Clone's safety, but I knew I'd been dangling clues that invited Sam to conspire with me to rationalize an indiscretion I absolutely shouldn't commit. Sam was a quick study and he'd read his lines just right. I said, "Kaiser pharmacy over on Thirteenth. You know it?"

Sam said, "It's where the clinic is? By Casey School?"

"Yeah."

"We take Simon there," he said. He opened the door and stepped out of the car. Slamming the door, he leaned down and looked across at me. "You'll take me for a ride in that funny little car of yours, right? Once your arm's okay?"

"Maybe, if you promise not to sneeze."

He said, "Thanks, Alan."

I said nothing. I watched Sam walk away, not feeling good about what I'd done. And I knew I wouldn't have felt good if I had done nothing. I also knew that a year before, I wouldn't have revealed what I'd just revealed.

So why did I do it? Here was my rationalization: I did it because the cost of my silence the last time a cop asked me to talk still weighed on me like wet shoes. I had stayed silent that time and one of my patients had ended up dying less than a hundred feet away from me.

Was what I just did with Sam ethical? Probably not.

Hell, definitely not.

Was it right?

I'd once thought that the question was one of blacks and whites, occasionally charcoal grays and off-whites. Now? Sometimes I couldn't tell at all any longer.

Was I growing more experienced? Or just more jaded?

I didn't know. That was the nature of the funk I was in those days.

Grace was squirming on the changing table in front of me. The little changing-table dance was something she often did just as I released the second taped tab from the diaper that was destined for the bin. Keeping her on the table while I fumbled to keep the contents of the old diaper inside the diaper was a significant challenge to my dexterity when I had two unbroken arms. With one arm encased in fiberglass, the task had become a bad vaudeville routine. That's why I didn't turn my head when I heard Lauren enter the room behind me and say, "Sam's on the phone."

I thought—okay, I hoped—that my wife would offer to take over the diapering operation, but a whiff of what awaited her had apparently made it across the room before she had a chance to be so magnanimous.

She tucked the cordless phone between my shoulder and my ear and whispered, "That looks like a two-hander you got there. Say hi to Sammy for me."

"What does she mean, 'a two-hander'?" Sam asked.

"I'm in the middle of changing Grace's diaper. That kind of two-hander."

"Oh, bad memories, I can call back."

"No, just give me a minute or two to finish up here." I set the phone down and gave Grace's hygiene a hundred percent of my attention until she smelled as fresh as a baby can smell. After I snapped her into a fresh pair of jammies, I handed her off to Lauren and returned to the phone.

"What's up, Sam?" I was afraid, of course, that he was about to remind me of my newly earned confidentiality-slut status and demand some fresh Tom Clone information from me.

His agenda, it turned out, was more generous than that. "I thought you deserved an update about what we discussed earlier. Well, here's the latest scoop from inside the halls of the Boulder Public Safety Building: Mr. Clone is officially still missing. A crack detective learned from unidentified sources that today was supposed to be his first day of work at Kaiser, but he didn't show up for his new job and he didn't call in. They don't know where he is and, by the way, they don't really care, because he no longer has a job."

I was too cynical to be surprised. I did feel a flush of unease over Tom Clone's well-being. Almost immediately, I started blathering. "There seem to be only a few possible explanations, Sam. One is that for some reason he doesn't want to be found. Two—"

"Wait," Sam interrupted. "If he doesn't want to be

found, I say it's because he's guilty of something. For argument's sake, something like beating the shit out of his grandfather. That's just my nature. But go on."

"Two is that something has happened to him—you know, like an accident—and he's incapacitated in some way and that's why he can't be found."

Sam grunted. The grunt did not indicate his assent to my speculation.

I pressed on. "Three, it turns out that he has been in jeopardy all along and somebody has . . . hurt him."

"Because I like you, I'm not even going to comment on the odds of number two. He's been hurt and he can't get to a telephone? Come on. And I'll trade you my winning Powerball ticket if you can help me come up with a motive for number three. Why would somebody want to hurt Clone?"

"Sorry, Sam. That would require speculation based on privileged information, and this slut is going into recovery. I've changed my evil ways."

He laughed. "Figured as much. You have a minute for a little story?"

"Like a parable? From you?" I sat down on the upholstered chair in the nursery. Instantly I could smell the aromas of my baby—the good smells—and my wife. I felt my blood pressure drop.

"Last week a neighbor knocked on my door late, maybe nine o'clock. Simon was in bed already. I know this guy to see him, but I don't know him personally at all—we're not even on a wave-to-each-other-when-you're-driving-by-and-the-other-guy's-mowing-the-lawn kind of basis. He's a stockbroker."

Sam said "He's a stockbroker" as though the man's choice of professions should have been an adequate explanation for why Sam and the neighbor weren't more friendly. I knew better. Sam was characterologically cranky and generally mistrustful of civilians. That was the reason he kept his neighbors—probably every last one of them—at arm's length. His wife, on the other hand, could probably quote chapter and verse of the first couple of branches of each of her neighbors' family trees.

"Guy is kind of nervous, says he doesn't want to bother me but he's had this client for years, some sweet old man who lives over in Martin Acres. The guy—the old guy—has a small portfolio of bonds and uses the income to supplement his Social Security.

" 'Small,' by the way, turns out to be two hundred and eleven thousand dollars. Was I away when two hundred and eleven thousand dollars stopped being considered real money? Anyway, over the last couple of months, the old guy has started to sell off some of his bonds, one by one. Tell me something, is it 'sell' or 're-deem'? I know from bad guys and I know from bratwurst; I don't know from bonds."

I said, "I'm not sure."

"Figures. Where was I? Oh yeah, this old guy who never does anything without his broker's advice apparently won't tell the broker why he's suddenly so interested in divesting himself of double-A sewer-improvement notes for the City of Thornton, even though it's jeopardizing his retirement income.

"And this neighbor of mine—did I mention *whom I hardly know*—wondered if I'd check it out."

"Check what out?"

"Exactly. That's what I asked. Last time I looked, it was still legal for people to sell their bonds and not tell their broker why they're doing it. I say that and the guy stuffs his hands in the pockets of his Bermuda shorts and sighs and backpedals on my little front porch until he finally—finally—tells me that the old guy's daughter moved back in with him a few months back and he—the broker—thinks that she might be mistreating him, maybe even shaking him down for the money. The one time the broker saw the old guy recently, he had bruises up and down one arm and seemed very uncomfortable talking about his daughter."

"Abuse of the elderly," I said.

"Yeah, bingo. Well, from a public safety point of view, that's a rib with some significant meat on it—that's something I can check out. So the next day I get a few minutes free and I drive out to Martin Acres. I hang my shield on my coat pocket and puff up my chest, and I knock on the guy's front door."

I savored the image.

"The old guy came to the door himself. I introduce myself right through the screen. He stares at my shield for maybe ten seconds, then he says, 'Are you here to arrest Dorothy?' "

"Wow," I said. "Just like that, Sam? You're good. God, you're good. I ever tell you that?"

"Yeah, your sarcasm aside, I know I'm good. But to get back to my story, just like that the old guy says, 'Are you here to arrest Dorothy?' When I don't reply to the man's question right away, he starts to cry. I figure it's tears of relief, you know, so I'm standing there feeling pretty good about myself and my neighbor the stock-broker."

"Did you arrest Dorothy?"

"Yeah. Dorothy and I sat down and chatted at her

daddy's kitchen table and she spilled the beans and I arrested her right then and there. I did."

Sam stopped talking. I waited for something else. It didn't come.

"I give up, Sam. I'm missing the parable. It just sounds like another sad story to me."

"Were you always this concrete? I used to think that you had a more abstract side to your personality. Isn't that like a requirement for people in your profession?"

"You going to tell me the point?"

"My neighbor, the broker? He had no right to tell me what he told me about this guy selling his bonds."

"Ah," I said. "So your neighbor is yet another confidentiality slut. But because of his indiscretion, an old man is safe. That's the message that's supposed to help me sleep better tonight? Thank you, Aesop."

"Close but not quite, Doc. This is where the parable gets even more heuristic."

It was at moments when Sam used words like "heuristic" that I was reminded about his master's degree in literature.

"See, the truth is the old man's life has turned to shit. He'd already sold off over half the bonds that he needed to supplement his Social Security income"—Sam's pronunciation of the words made them sound like "so-so security"—"and he'll never get that money back. None of it. What's worse, as far as I can tell, it all went up Dorothy's nose. If you can believe it, the old man even sold off two more bonds to pay for a lawyer for the bitch daughter after I arrested her.

"And that's not the worst. The worst is that now what's left of his family is fractured so badly that it will never recover. The man lost his money and his family turned to crap."

I said, "It would have been worse if Dorothy had been permitted to continue to abuse him, Sam."

"You never know that, though, do you? She managed to ruin things for him no matter what we did to try to help. That's the parable. In court the day she was arraigned, he told me that he wished she had just gone ahead and killed him. You just never know about these things."

I tried to be palliative. "You did what you thought was best."

"Did I? I go back to that day that I'm standing at his door, and I'm no longer sure that the tears I saw on his cheek were from relief. I think the guy realized that whatever good cards he'd been holding in his hand up until that point in his life, fate had just figured out how to trump him. He'd gone from king of the old retired guys at the Senior Center to being some beat-up old chump who knows bitterness like he knows the gap in his mouth where the tooth is missing."

I inhaled deeply, trying to recapture the aroma of my family. "This Tom Clone thing you're looking into isn't going to have a pretty ending either, is it, Sam?"

"Nope. Not a prayer."

"Good night, Sam. Thanks for the update."

"Yeah. Hey, one more thing."

I wasn't surprised there was one more thing.

"You know anything you can tell me about this female FBI agent? The one who alibied him that night? You never even commented on the fact that they were together. The other night, I told you that Clone's alibi was a female FBI agent and you didn't even say a single word about it. Not even a flinch from you. The detective part of me finds that just the slightest bit goofy."

I know a lot about the FBI agent, I thought. *Or I may only know a little; I'm not quite sure which.* But whichever it was, I couldn't tell Sam a thing about Kelda James and anything she might have to do with Tom Clone.

I don't like being trapped. With both his parable and his question, Sam had me trapped. I scrambled for a way out of the snare. Injecting my tone full of mock indignation for his benefit, I said, "What do you think I am?"

It was his turn to laugh. "We've already established that, haven't we?"

I didn't want to wake Sam's wife and son, so I used his pager number when I tried to reach him much later that night.

I held Lauren's little phone in my hand as I stood outside on the narrow deck off the living room listening to the sounds of the night. The usual nocturnal symphony was being poisoned by an eruption of noise that was something like a duel between a gasoline-powered leaf blower and a violin being played by a baboon. Just for the record, the sound of a cantankerous fox almost succeeds in causing the caterwaul of a feline in heat to sound like Mozart.

The phone vibrated in my hand. It was a good thing that it was set to vibrate. Had it only chirped, I might not have heard it over the fox's screeching and moaning. I flipped it open. "Hi, Sam. It's Alan."

He wasn't happy that I'd called. "Whose number is this?"

"Lauren's cell. I didn't want your call to wake her, so I'm out on the deck listening to a pissed-off fox."

"You woke me. What does a pissed-off fox sound like?"

I held the phone out into the night for about fifteen seconds before I returned it to my face and said, "Like that."

"It's awful. You guys have to listen to that every night? Is that the price of living in the country?"

"This is a rare treat. Listen, has Tom Clone been seen since Monday afternoon? Like midafternoon?"

I felt a brief hesitation from Sam before he said, "No."

"Then I may have been the last one to see him. I saw him climbing onto a red Vespa on Walnut Street at about three forty-five Monday afternoon."

My rationalization? Technically, this bit of news about my patient wasn't privileged information. Given the media coverage his release from prison had generated recently, Tom was, whether he liked it or not, a public figure, and I could tell Sam what I'd observed him doing outside the confines of my office. If I hadn't been worried about Tom's welfare, however, I never would have shared with Sam the fact that I'd watched Tom climb onto a Vespa.

Even though Sam knew very well that my office was on Walnut Street and he also knew exactly where I spent my weekday afternoons, he was wise enough not to editorialize on either fact.

He wasn't wise enough, however, to know what a Vespa was.

"A red Vespa? What the hell is a Vespa?"

"It's an Italian scooter."

"Like my kid's Razor? That kind of scooter?"

"No, not a kid's scooter. A motor scooter, the kind that cool people in Rome use to get around the city. That kind of scooter. Like a little motorcycle. I'm sure you've seen them."

"I haven't been to Rome lately. Why didn't you just say motorcycle?"

I didn't answer that. I silently counted to three before I said, "I thought you might want to know that Clone was on a . . . vehicle."

"You called because of my parable, didn't you? It got to you, my goofy little story about the old guy with the bonds got to you."

"No, I didn't call because of your parable. I haven't thought about your parable once since you told it to me."

After a delay of a few seconds, Sam asked, "This has kept you from sleeping, hasn't it? All this guilty knowledge you have about Clone?" His voice was uncommonly compassionate.

"Yes, it has."

"Well, go on back to bed. This should help us. Sometimes it's easier to find a motorcycle—excuse me, a Vespa—than it is to find a person."

When I pressed the button to end the call, all I could hear were the incessant chirps of a few dozen crickets. The fox had stopped its caterwauling.

PART THREE

Praying for Monsoons

What the . . ." Tom Clone mumbled as he realized he was waking up outdoors. The air tasted different and his nose was assaulted by a sharp scent of pine. A metallic taste coated his tongue. He raised his head and lowered it immediately, trying to quell the flash of pain that was connecting his temples as though a hot spike had been inserted between the two sides of his skull. "Shit," he said aloud, grimacing.

Grimacing hurt so much that he grimaced again.

He attempted to move his feet but they would only slide laterally a few inches. He felt the slick surface of ripstop nylon against the skin on his arms and realized that he was in a sleeping bag. *There's an explanation,* he assured himself. *There's a way to explain this. Where was I last night?*

Tom Clone wasn't one of those Colorado natives who

were more comfortable waking up in a mummy bag with his sleep-crusted eyes focused on the streaky skies of morning. Prior to his incarceration, his idea of roughing it involved staying in motels without air-conditioning.

His memory of the previous night was a black hole. Groaning, he rolled his head to the left and then ever so slowly to the right, half expecting to discover that he was sleeping next to someone, some girl he'd picked up and who'd convinced him against his better judgment to go camping.

Camping?

After so long, he thought, he'd have done anything to get laid. Even gone camping. But he didn't remember getting laid.

There wasn't another sleeping bag beside him. He was alone. Oddly, a chain-link fence rose from the ground parallel to the sleeping bag not ten feet from his right side. "God, I must have been drunk to even think about sleeping here," he mumbled. His tongue felt as though it had been lacquered during the night.

His brain was trying to answer the simple question of where "here" was. It failed.

He raised his arms out of the sleeping bag and noticed a pinprick and bruise on the inside of his left wrist. "I don't know," he said, as though he was trying to answer his next question. "What the hell did I do to myself?"

His eyes focused past the evidence of injury on his wrist, and he saw another fence. This one was on his left.

"What the . . . ?"

Tom sat up abruptly. Pain radiated out from his spine. "Damn," he moaned. "Shit," he added as he rotated at his waist and looked back in the opposite direction.

The fence surrounded him, creating a square of about twenty feet on a side. He scrambled out of the sleeping bag and yanked himself to his feet. He paced backward around the rumpled sack. The walls around him rose eight feet.

"What the fuck?" he said. "What the hell is going on? Where's the damn gate?"

He approached the links and then jogged all four sides of the interior perimeter. "There's no gate," he said. "There's no gate." He heard the panic in his voice.

He realized suddenly that his feet were in dirty white socks. He wasn't wearing shoes.

He dove down onto the bag and rooted around to find his shoes inside. They weren't there. He lowered himself so that he was sitting on the bag, raised his knees, and wrapped his arms around his legs.

"Think," he said. "Think, think, think."

He was in the mountains, and he was below timberline. A thick pine forest grew in all directions just beyond the fence. Not too far to the west—on the darker side of the dawn sky—a line of snowcapped peaks seemed close enough to touch. He knew there were plenty of Coloradans who would have been able to recognize the vista from memory. He wasn't one of them.

Had he been more experienced in the wilderness, the stunted height of the nearby pines would have been a clue that he was somewhere very high in the mountains. But he wasn't experienced.

Where was he?

He didn't know. It could be anywhere from Cortez to Steamboat Springs as far as he could tell. He could even be in Wyoming or Utah.

He tried to remember the night before.

Nothing. Not a thing.

Damn.

He hopped to his feet, moved toward the fence, and looked up to the top. From his years in prison, he was so accustomed to the glint of concertina that he expected to see endless coils of razor-sharp stainless steel above this fence, too. But the coils weren't there. This was just a fence.

Was this some kind of sick joke?

He allowed himself a sardonic smile and reached out with one hand to begin to scale the fence.

"*I wouldn't do that,*" an amplified voice said.

Tom froze, then spun a full 360 degrees to try to find the person who was speaking to him. He didn't see anyone. He took a deep, raspy breath and scanned the adjacent forest more carefully. Still nothing.

He reached again for the fence.

"*I wouldn't—*"

Tom crumpled in agony at the foot of the fence. He was temporarily paralyzed by the jolt of electricity that had ratcheted through his body. The bottoms of his feet burned like they were on fire.

He watched with surprise as a dark stain spread on the inside thigh of his trousers. The discoloration spread for at least ten seconds before he felt the warm moisture from his own urine against his skin.

"*Next time, listen to my suggestions. They are valuable. In the meantime, stay away from the fence. It's uncomfortable to touch it. But I guess you know that by now, don't you?*"

Tom rolled away from the fence. The voice was obviously male. But he had no associations to it in his memory. He demanded, "Who the fuck are you?"

"*I'm not surprised you don't recognize me, actually. You don't have much experience with people like me.*"

"What? You're my jailer. I know all about jailers."

"*No, Tom, I'm your conscience. And you don't know a damn thing about having a conscience.*"

Tom felt suddenly sick. "Where are you?" he asked.

"*I'm right here. Where are you?*"

"Fuck you. What are you doing to me? How did I get here? What the fuck do you want?"

"*I'll answer a couple of your questions. How did you get here? I drugged you and brought you up here. What do I want? Satisfaction. Now, no more questions. No more answers.*"

"Fuck you!"

"*You know, I've been told that thirst tends to improve attitude. I think we'll do a little empirical study and see if that turns out to be true. In case your internal altimeter isn't working, we're well over nine thousand feet above sea level right now, Tom. The weather forecast is for another hot and dry day. Even way up here, it'll be in the eighties by midafternoon. Humidity should be hovering around twenty percent. That's dry. Real dry. You enjoy your morning.*"

"Wait!" Tom yelled.

No reply.

"Come back!" he tried.

Nothing.

"Shit!"

He was back in prison. He felt it in every cell in his body.

CHAPTER

30

Kelda called Tom Clone at his grandfather's house over her lunch hour on Wednesday. She used a pay phone one block away from the Federal Building. Only after the phone rang six or seven times did she remember that he'd told her that he was starting work that week.

She called directory assistance and got the number for the pharmacy at Boulder's Kaiser clinic and dialed. After punching menu choices for about two minutes, she finally reached a human being, and asked the woman who answered if she could speak to Tom Clone.

"I'm sorry. We don't have anyone here by that name," was the reply. Kelda thought the woman sounded as if she was twelve years old.

"This is the pharmacy?"

"Yes."

Kelda explained, "I'm looking for the new guy. He just started yesterday, I think. He's, um—"

"Oh, him? He didn't show up yesterday. So, well," the woman giggled, "he doesn't, like, even work here. Somebody else has been hired. The new new guy is a friend of Jack's, I think."

"The first new guy didn't show up today?"

"No, he didn't; he didn't show up at all. Not yesterday, not today. So I can't help you, I guess. Would you like the extension for Human Resources? Maybe they know something."

"No. Thank you."

Kelda hung up and tried Tom's grandfather's house again. This time she listened to the drone of the phone for fifteen rings before she hung up. She fought a flush of dread. A beige haze masked the western horizon. In the distance, white clouds billowed high above the Divide. The pastiche looked like meringue on top of dirt.

She dug around in her purse for more coins and a business card and punched a number, another Boulder number, into her phone.

A distracted voice answered, "Detective Purdy."

"Detective? This is Special Agent Kelda James. You and I spoke about Tom Clone."

"Yeah, I remember," Purdy said. "Almost like it was yesterday."

Which it had been.

"Have you arrested him?" Kelda asked.

She could hear Purdy breathing, and wondered whether he was intentionally exhaling directly into the telephone. "Is this a request for professional courtesy, Agent James? If it is, I respectfully decline."

In her well-practiced I'm-a-federal-agent-don't-give-me-any-shit voice, Kelda said, "Look, Detective. I can't find Tom Clone. I'll stop looking for him if I know that you have him behind bars. It's a simple question."

In the silence that followed, Kelda assumed that the Boulder detective was considering the advantage she had just offered him. If Tom Clone had been arrested, the detective could play Kelda any number of different ways. If Tom Clone hadn't been arrested, Purdy was probably playing out the possibilities of why Kelda James wasn't able to find him.

One distinct possibility, she knew—and she knew that Purdy knew—was that Tom didn't want to be found. She tried to consider the ramifications if Tom had gone on the run.

"If he was under arrest, that would be public record," Purdy said.

"Yes."

"But he's not."

"Thank you," she sighed. She didn't even try to keep the exasperation out of her voice.

"Not at all. If you do find Clone, I'd like to talk with him. Would you tell him that for me?"

"Yes, I'll pass that along. You should probably tell his attorney that, you know."

"His office already knows," Purdy replied. "But the attorney has just left on a safari in Kenya."

"Oh."

While she was considering Tony Loving's trip to Africa, Purdy asked her, "You wouldn't happen to know anything about a red Vespa, would you? It's apparently like a motor scooter. Maybe it belongs to Clone?"

She momentarily toyed with being as much of an

asshole as Purdy was being. Instead, she decided to answer his question civilly in hopes of getting some coop-
eration in return. "Yes, I do know something about it,
actually. It belongs to his grandfather, not to Tom. His
grandfather has a bad hip, uses the scooter to get around
town. Apparently, he finds using it more comfortable than
getting in and out of cars."

"Grandfather probably isn't using it much right
now. Don't think they allow Vespas in the ICU."

The bolus of sarcasm from Purdy was disappointing
but not totally unexpected to Kelda. The legendary tension between federal agents and local cops wasn't just
myth. "I imagine not," she said, intentionally trying not
to aggravate the situation.

"Does Tom ever use it?" Purdy asked.

"I don't know. Why don't you ask him?"

"For the same reason you can't ask him whatever
you want to ask him. Because I can't find him either."

"Since when?"

"He was last seen Monday afternoon. Midafternoon,
to be specific. Did you hear from him after that?"

Without hesitation, she said, "No, I didn't. And why
do you want to know about the Vespa anyway? What
does that have to do with it? Did you find the Vespa
someplace?" She gave him a couple of seconds to respond. When he didn't, she prodded, "Come on. I've
been up-front with you."

She felt another echoing exhale in her earpiece before Purdy said evenly, "It's just a loose end. I'm sure
even FBI agents get them sometimes. Loose ends, I
mean. Not as often as someone like me investigating
assaults and minor crap like that in Boulder might get
them. But sometimes."

She wanted to scream at him. "Can we be frank, Detective?"

"That would be refreshing, Special Agent James. Dear God, that would be refreshing."

She had been about to divulge to Purdy that Tom Clone had been concerned about his safety, but suddenly her mouth hung open, she blinked her eyes twice, and she completely reconsidered what she had been about to say.

"Never mind," she said. "Good-bye, Detective."

She hung up the phone and shook her head. Nearby, she saw a couple of support personnel from the Bureau walking along the sidewalk. If she had been alone, she would have thrown something or slammed the receiver against the phone—or something—and she would have screamed, "You goddamn shit!"

Instead, she adjusted her shoulder bag and pulled her sunglasses down in front of her eyes and crossed the street just as the light changed. The pace she took to the lobby of the Hotel Monaco would have forced almost anybody trying to stay with her to jog.

She dropped two coins into the lobby pay phone and punched in a familiar number.

No answer.

She retrieved the two coins and punched in another familiar number.

After only one ring, she heard the beginning of a recording from the veterinary practice of Dr. Ira Winslett. The practice, she learned, was temporarily closed due to a family emergency. The doctor's calls were being taken by—Kelda slammed the phone down before she learned what other vet was covering for Ira. She didn't really care.

She cursed under her breath, stepped away from the phone, and closed her eyes, trying to compose herself.

When she opened her eyes again, she saw the fleeting image of a man in a dark suit moving rapidly along the sidewalk in front of the hotel.

She thought it might have been Bill Graves.

"Oh damn," she whispered.

CHAPTER

31

The amplified voice said, *"In case you're wondering, it's one o'clock. How's your attitude?"*

Tom Clone was sitting with his legs crossed. He was holding the sleeping bag above his head as a shelter against the sun, but the heat was almost intolerable. In reply to the voice, he lifted his right hand out from beneath the bag and raised his middle finger to the sky.

"Thirsty?" the voice inquired.

Tom lifted his left hand so he could flip his captor the bird with both hands. The sleeping bag slipped to the ground behind him. A few clouds were forming above the Divide, but to him the sky didn't portend rain. He thought wistfully that he'd settle for some cloud cover and a little shade.

"Now catch!" The quality of the voice had changed dramatically. It was no longer amplified.

"What?"

"Turn around."

Tom did.

"I said, 'Catch!'" A figure wearing a bulky canvas suit with fat gloves and a helmet with a screen over the face stood on the edge of the pine forest. In one hand the person held a wooden box about eighteen inches square with a handle on the top. In the other hand he carried a shopping bag with a flat bottom.

Tom perused the disguise and had to admit it was pretty good camouflage. He couldn't identify whoever was wearing the suit. He still thought the voice had been a man's.

"Catch what?" Tom asked.

The man took a half-dozen steps forward until he stood only ten feet from the fence. He set the box down on the dirt, reached into the bag, and removed a half-liter bottle of water. He tossed it over the fence.

Tom jumped back a yard or so and caught it.

His ears picked up a droning noise, as though someone was operating a lawn mower a hundred yards away. *Were they that close to civilization?*

The thought gave him hope.

"Now put down the bottle and catch this." The man in the canvas suit reached back into the bag and lifted an orb about the size of a softball. He held it up above his head so that Tom could examine it. Then, with an exaggerated underhanded motion, he tossed it high over the fence.

Tom dropped the bottle and braced to catch the orb. It was coming straight at him. The second it hit his hands the ball disintegrated and he found himself instantly enveloped in a cloud of fine yellow powder. All that remained of the ball in his hands was a crumpled pile of cheesecloth, flat toothpicks, and a little bit of tape.

He coughed and tried to spit the yellow dust out of his mouth, "What the fuck was that?"

"Pollen."

"Pollen?"

"Yes, Tom, pollen. You like pollen?"

"Not particularly. I'd rather have a sandwich."

"You know who likes pollen?"

"Mary Poppins?"

"Bees like pollen, Tom. And to make them like it even more, I chopped up a few queen bees and mixed them up with the pollen. The scent of the queen bees draws the worker bees like naked girls draw adolescent boys. And these particular bees are a tad on the aggressive side, anyway."

Tom's heartbeat accelerated and, without thinking, he brushed at his bare arms. The dust, as fine as cake flour, coated him like paint. Brushing it only seemed to force the yellow pigment into his skin.

He stared at the man. With monumental alarm, his mind recognized the purpose of the canvas suit the man was wearing.

It wasn't a disguise.

It was a beekeeper's outfit.

"No!" Tom screamed. He started a frantic dance, flailing his legs, maniacally rubbing his hands over his skin and clothing. "Are they killer bees? Are they going to kill me?"

The man reached down and grabbed the handle on the wooden box.

"No, you can't!" Tom yelled, still swiping at the yellow powder that covered his body.

The man lifted the box and began to swing it front to back.

The droning noise grew louder.

"Wait! Tell me what you want! You can't do that!" Tom implored.

The length of the arc of the box increased a little bit each time the man swung it. It reminded Tom of a child climbing progressively higher on a swing.

The humming sound permeated the clearing.

Tom ran to the farthest corner of the enclosure. It felt futile, but he didn't know what else to do.

Near the top of its forward arc, the man released the wooden box from his hand. It accelerated as it shot into the air, easily clearing the top of the fence before falling and crashing to the dust about five feet into the pen.

The wooden box collapsed upon impact, and the sound of the furious swarm of bees escaping their confinement was the scariest thing Tom had heard since the night in prison when . . .

The bees were upon him before he could complete the thought.

No, they're not killer bees," the man said. "And I do hope you're not allergic." He didn't think Tom Clone heard him.

The funny thing was, his words were totally sincere.

CHAPTER

32

Kelda almost didn't have to fake it. Ten minutes after she'd left the lobby of the Hotel Monaco, she felt almost as sick as she was pretending to be when she took the elevator back up to the FBI Field Office and told the young guy at the reception desk that she had just thrown up her lunch and was going to take the rest of the day off.

Bill Graves watched her collect her things and stuff them into her shoulder bag. "Where are you going?" he finally asked.

"Home. I'm not feeling well. I just puked up my lunch."

"Oh," he said. "I hope you feel better. Anything I can do? Do you need a ride someplace?"

She forced a smile. "Thanks, but no. I'm sure I'll be fine. It's just a stomach bug, probably."

"Please don't tell me you ate at that Italian place at the Hotel Monaco? Panzano? I really like that place, wouldn't want to think it made you sick."

His words caused her to hold her breath. Bill *had* seen her in the lobby of the Hotel Monaco. And he wanted her to know that he'd seen her. The question was: Why did he want her to know?

· Was he warning her about something?

"No, no. There was too long a wait at the restaurant, and I didn't have time. I just ended up grabbing something from a street vendor. Just my luck, it came right back up." She regretted the lie even as she was telling it. If Bill had been following her, he would know that she hadn't really stopped at any of the sidewalk stands for lunch.

He'd know she was lying. And he'd conclude she had a reason to lie.

After a moment's contemplation, he said, "Well, I do hope you feel better. Take care."

· "Thanks, Bill. You're a sweetheart, you know that?"

"I keep telling you that, Kelda."

She slipped her bag over her left shoulder and headed toward the bank of elevators.

When the car arrived, Kelda stepped in, moved to the back corner of the elevator, and leaned against the wall. The sudden swoosh of the rapid descent flipped her empty stomach, and she wondered if she really was going to throw up. As the car stopped about halfway down the building to pick up additional passengers, she suddenly realized why Bill Graves had told her that he'd seen her standing in the lobby at the Hotel Monaco.

He wanted her to know she was being followed.

Kelda bolted out of the elevator just before the door

closed on the eleventh floor, and hustled down the hall to the staircase. Descending the stairs to the building's lobby, she used a delivery door that a UPS driver had left propped open and made her way out to the alley.

The tail that Bill Graves was warning her about could have been unofficial—it could have been nothing more than Bill being curious or intrusive. That was worrisome, but Kelda was confident she could lose any tail Bill put on her if he was acting alone. But . . . if the tail was something that had been mounted by the SAC with full Bureau resources, that was something else altogether. If that was the case, Kelda couldn't risk using her car to leave downtown. She couldn't even risk renting a car with her own ID.

The air was hot and still. A block from the Federal Building, she checked her wallet and counted her cash. Thirty-seven dollars. She backtracked half a block and withdrew four hundred dollars from an ATM. If her colleagues wanted to know she'd collected money from her account, she knew that they could get the information easily. But it wouldn't tell them anything important about her location. She was exactly where they thought she would be, less than a block from the field office.

Kelda convinced herself that no helicopters—they couldn't want to know what she was up to *that* badly—were involved in tracking her, and she flagged down a cab. She told the driver to drop her at the corner of Thirty-second and Speer, just across Federal Boulevard on the other side of Interstate 25. At the conclusion of the ten-minute ride, she gave the driver one of the fresh bills that she'd just gotten out of the ATM and

told him to keep the change. She waited on the corner
until the cab was out of sight. After carefully examining
the area for signs that her colleagues had managed to
track her—she didn't notice a thing—she headed on foot
toward Highland Park.

It only took her two minutes to get to the address
she was seeking on Grove Street, less than a block from
the park. The home was a bungalow with a tiny lawn
and impeccably maintained landscaping. Kelda climbed
three wooden steps to the front porch and touched the
bell.

"Please be home, please be home," Kelda murmured as she fished in her change purse for a couple of
Percocet. Still waiting, she popped them into her mouth
and swallowed them dry.

Seconds later, Maria Alija answered the door. She
was dressed in a simple print dress and open-toed shoes.

Kelda asked, "May I come in, Maria?"

A storm of alarm rose in Maria's eyes. "Is my baby
okay?"

Kelda raised both palms. "Rosa's fine. She's fine."
The panic in Maria's eyes didn't ebb. Kelda said, "You
believe me, don't you, Maria?"

"*Sí.*"

"I need a favor from you, *por favor*. Can I borrow
your car? It's kind of an emergency."

Without hesitation, Maria Alija reached into her
purse and held out her keys to Kelda. "I was just heading back to work. You can have it as long as you want.
Overnight, whatever you need. Anything for you. You
are family."

"And you are a saint, Maria. I'll drop you off at your
work," Kelda said. "How's that?"

Maria worked in a dentist's office that was about a mile north of her home. A couple of minutes later, as Kelda pulled Maria's old Ford Contour into the lot, she asked, "One more favor, Maria? Another big one."

"*Sí.*"

"Do you carry a cell phone?"

"*Sí*, for Rosa. She worries."

"May I borrow it?"

Maria smiled. "Kelda, I would give you a kidney, gladly."

You shouldn't have swatted at them. It only pisses them off. If you had just stayed still, I don't think you would have been stung so often. Maybe not even at all. But, although I wouldn't know, I bet that's hard to do when a thousand bees are buzzing around your head."

The voice was once again amplified.

Tom could hear it, clearly. As far as he could tell, he hadn't been stung on his ears. He would have said, "Fuck you," but his lips were already so swollen he didn't think it was worth the agony it would cause to try to speak.

"The point wasn't the stinging. It was the fear. Did you experience the fear, Tom? Did you?"

Tom nodded. A few bees still buzzed around the enclosure. The faint noise they made sounded to Tom like a dentist's drill hovering above his unanesthetized molar.

"*What? Did you say something?*"

"I could ha'e gone into shock and died. You could ha'e killed 'e."

"*That's true. I took that risk.*"

Tom had already poured half the bottle of water that the man had thrown to him over his skin. The other half he'd poured down his throat, trying not to touch the rim of the bottle to his lips. "It really 'ucking hurts. The stings. They 'ucking 'urn and they 'ucking sting."

"*I bet they do.*"

"One got inside 'y 'outh. I even ha'e a sting in 'y arm'it."

"*Really? One stung you inside your mouth? That's why you're talking so funny. And you have one in your armpit? Ouch.*"

"Why?" Tom pleaded.

"*Why? Why am I doing this? You tell me. Why? Why would someone do this to you? Terrify you half to death? Why?*"

Tom was fighting tears. "I don't know. Why?"

"*You don't know yet? I guess we're not done, then. The lessons will just have to continue. You keep working on an answer, okay? Tom? It's important. I hope you get this right, because if you don't understand the lessons, I promise that you won't want to take the final.*"

"No 'ore 'ees. No 'ore 'ees. 'ease." Tom Clone had made it through all his years in the penitentiary without begging. But he was begging.

"*Just tell me then, why would someone do this to you? Just tell me and we'll move on to another lesson.*"

Tom could barely create a coherent thought through the volume of agony he was suffering from the plethora of fresh bee stings. *Another lesson? Oh God.* He shook his head, mute and helpless.

"*Hey,*" the voice coaxed, "*listen to this.*"

For almost a minute, Tom heard nothing. What he was listening for was the drone of the distant lawn mower, which to him would mean the advent of another swarm of bees and more agony. What he finally heard was even more frightening: the unforgettable sound of steel doors slamming.

Prison doors.

"Oh 'an. You 'ucker," Tom said. "It was you. You 'ade those 'oises in 'y house."

"*Yes, I did. I actually recorded them right off the DVD of* The Green Mile. *You probably missed it, but it was a pretty good Tom Hanks movie about death row. Then I cleaned them up digitally a bit. It's a cassette recorder on a timer up in the attic. I think the effects sound pretty good. Do you agree?*"

Tom didn't reply.

"*Good. I'm just going to keep playing that loop for a while. I have it set up so that the doors seem to close at random. Just like it must have been for you when you were inside. You just never know what's coming. That can't be pleasant. Could make you fearful.*"

Tom felt his heart pop in his chest, and his mind flashed on a lesson from his senior psychiatry rotation. *Learned Helplessness,* maybe. An orange book. Someone named Seligman—or something like that—wrote it.

It was about the connection between despair and the inability to control negative consequences in life. *This is what life was like for those rats and dogs,* he thought. *I'm helpless. There's nothing I can do to stop this madman.*

"I'm behind you now, Tom." The voice was natural again, lacking amplification. "You should turn around."

Tom crawled to his knees. Slowly, he rotated to face his captor.

The man was ten feet from the fence. He was wearing faded blue jeans, a polo shirt, and lightweight hiking boots. A motorcycle helmet—a full one, with chin and jaw protection and a dark visor—totally hid his face. In his left hand he carried another wooden box with a handle on top. This box was about eighteen inches long and a foot high. The man wore heavy leather gloves.

" 'ore 'ees?" Tom's voice was burdened with so much dread he could barely get the sounds out of his throat.

"More bees? No." The man shook his head, hefting the box slightly. "Snakes this time. Vipers."

"What?"

The man repeated himself. "I said, 'Vipers.' It's a terribly misunderstood species of snake."

He moved forward and placed the wooden box flush against the chain-link fence, reached down, and lifted the side that was closest to the fence straight up and away from the box.

Ten seconds later, a glistening head about the size of a small egg emerged from the shadows and extended through one of the galvanized diamonds in the mesh of the fence.

"It's about fear, Tom. Do you get it yet?"

Tom was incredulous. He couldn't take his eyes off the box and the snake that was emerging from the darkness. " 'i'ers?" he asked. "That's a 'i'er?"

"Yes, Tom. Vipers. That's a viper."

"Hel'! Hel'!" He scrambled to his feet and backed away, dragging the sleeping bag with him across the enclosure.

"No one's going to help you, Tom. Do you know what that's like? Not to have anyone help you when you're afraid? To have someone know that you're afraid and be in a position to help you but refuse you help? Can you imagine what that is like, Tom? You know, I bet you can."

"Hel'! Hel'!" Tom's voice cracked as he screamed. His parched throat couldn't generate the volume that his lungs were demanding.

"You don't have to wonder what it's like to be stalked anymore, Tom. The vipers are stalking *you* now."

The snake surged forward so that about a foot of its body extended out of the wooden box. There it stilled, its sleek head frozen in space about ten inches above the dirt.

The man said, "He hasn't eaten in well over a week."

"Hel'!"

A second head emerged from the box, protruding through a different diamond in the mesh.

"Neither has that one," said the man, who turned and walked back toward the forest. He paused and said, "Remember, Tom. It's about fear. It's all about fear. *Feel the fear.*"

Just then a prison door slammed in the middle of the Colorado wilderness.

CHAPTER

One of the two snakes had slithered about halfway across the enclosure toward Tom when he came to the sudden realization that the man in the beekeeper's suit and the motorcycle helmet wasn't Detective Prehost.

Why would Prehost want to teach him lessons about fear?

In Tom's experience, Prehost's motivations had no heuristic undertones. Prehost's scheme was devoid of pretense. He simply wanted Tom poisoned to death in the execution chamber at the Colorado State Penitentiary. He wouldn't bother to engage in theater to torment Tom about the meaning of fear.

So, Tom wondered, if the man in the motorcycle helmet wasn't Fred Prehost, who the hell was he?

While Tom desperately pondered the identity of his captor, the second snake cleared the fence and stretched down to the dry earth. The dark natural camouflage of the two vipers failed to disguise them in the pale dust of Colorado's high country. As the snakes slithered across the open space in the fenced-in pen, they were as visible to Tom as shark fins in a swimming pool.

Tom tried to remember what he'd read you were supposed to do if you confronted a snake.

Run or not run?

Stay still or back away?

Act big or act small?

He couldn't remember. At that moment he wasn't sure he could remember how to tie his shoes. If he had shoes. "Hel' 'e," he whispered. "Oh God, 'ease hel' 'e."

He wondered if he could use the electricity in the fence against the snakes. But how?

The second of the two vipers to exit the box began making up for lost time. Edging forward, it overtook the first snake and seemed to be on a direct line for where Tom stood in the corner. He took two sideways steps toward the west.

The physician in Tom Clone noticed that he wasn't sweating at all, and he began to wonder about heat-stroke. He was oddly comforted by a sudden thought: Growing delirious from heatstroke might be preferable to whatever these snakes might do to him.

That's what he was thinking about when he heard the rattle.

He growled, "Rattlesnakes! These are rattlesnakes! I thought you said they were 'i'ers!"

The amplified voice responded, *"Most people don't know that rattlesnakes are part of the viper family. But they are. Technically, these two are western diamondback rattlesnakes. Native to this region, but never seen at this altitude unless someone like me gives them a lift. One real cold night up here and these guys will be toast. Or ice, as the case may be. But I didn't actually mislead you, rest assured that these are indeed vipers."* He paused. *"Would you have preferred a pair of puff adders or a couple of copperheads instead? I can oblige, I assure you."*

Tom couldn't take his eyes off the black-brown ropes slithering in his direction. He cried, "They'll kill 'e!"

"Well, obviously we'll have to wait and see about that. They're certainly capable of it. These western diamondbacks aren't the most aggressive of the vipers, but neither are they the most docile. They're quite venomous, though; you absolutely wouldn't want to be bitten by one. They have fangs from hell—a true marvel of bioengineering. Bye now, Tom."

"No! No!"

"I'll check back in a while and see how things turned out. Remember the lesson: It's all about fear."

A cell door slammed in the distance.

Tom felt his stomach roil. He doubled over in dry heaves.

CHAPTER

35

Ira lived in a tract home half a mile from the Boulder Turnpike in the nondescript suburban landscape where Arvada became Westminster became Broomfield. In the years that they had known each other, Kelda had never asked him in which town he actually lived, because she couldn't see how it really mattered to anyone but the mailman, the tax collector, and maybe the guy who drove the UPS truck. For everybody else, "Denver's western suburbs" sufficed.

Given that almost all the streets around Ira's house had the exact same name—Dudley—distinguished only by different suffixes: Parkway, Lane, Way, Street, Place, Circle—Kelda found it amazing that anyone ever found a specific address in Ira's neighborhood. She knew how to get there. That was all that was important to her.

The ride to Ira's house took her fifteen minutes after

she dropped Maria off at work on North Federal. Ira's home was the one on the cul-de-sac with the siding that was painted the darkest shade of putty permitted by the covenants of the homeowners' association. The distinctive waffle-batter-with-too-much-vanilla color—as opposed to the predominant sky-on-a-hazy-day color—was the only way Kelda was able to identify Ira's dwelling from a distance. Once she was close enough to the house, she could confirm it was indeed Ira's by spotting the menagerie of animal sculptures that he'd hidden amongst the shrubs and bushes of the otherwise association-approved landscaping. Her favorite statue was the brass baboon that peeked out from behind the rose of Sharon by the front door.

Ira had told her once that if any of his neighbors complained, he would be forced to remove the sculptures. Apparently, they were a violation of an association covenant that was intended to protect the burg against an invasion of lawn jockeys and pink flamingos. She'd had to break the news to him that not even the FBI could do anything about the covenant.

During her rare evening visits to Ira's house—they both preferred her place in the disappearing open country around Lafayette—she usually saw children playing on the wide asphalt course at the fat end of the cul-de-sac. But on that scorching weekday afternoon the neighborhood looked more like a modern ghost town. Not a single car was parked along the curb, not even an air-conditioning repair truck or a plumber unplugging a stopped-up drain. The lawn sprinklers were all off, the garage doors were all closed, and the miniblinds and curtains were all pulled to ward off the summer sun. The kids, she figured, must all be away at camp. The lawn service companies must have been busy on another block.

She pulled into Ira's driveway and walked to his door as though she were expected. She didn't bother to knock. Instead, she slipped her key into the lock and let herself inside. The air-conditioning in the house was off and the air inside was still and warm.

"Ira," she called in a sardonic honey-I'm-home voice. "Ira, it's Kelda. Are you here?"

She knew he wasn't.

She continued to the back of the house. The kitchen had the model-home quality of a room that wasn't accustomed to use. She couldn't recall ever seeing Ira prepare food there. In the center of the island counter was a tape recorder. On it was a yellow sticky note that read "Kelda."

She sat on a stool adjacent to the island and hit the button marked "play." As she touched the button, she said, "Hi, Ira," and was almost surprised at how pleasant her greeting sounded.

She wondered how he would word it, what tone he would take.

She didn't wonder what the message was going to say.

Ira's voice was as casual as it always was. *"Hi, babe,"* he started. *"Knowing you, I'm guessing that it didn't take long for you to figure out what was going on and that it's Wednesday morning that you're listening to this. It doesn't really matter. Maybe you were even quicker than I thought you'd be. It doesn't make any difference. If you're listening to this, I'm gone, and if I'm gone, you won't find me until I'm done. Don't even waste your energy looking."*

Kelda said, "Actually, I'm a little slow catching up with you, Ira. I think maybe it's the drugs."

Ira didn't wait for her to finish her thought. *"I don't know whether it's fair or not—even whether it's warranted or not—but I've lost faith in your commitment to our . . . plan. I've been keeping an eye on you since our boy got free, and it seems that you've been keeping some things from me. Sooo, I've decided to accelerate things a bit. Okay, I've accelerated things a lot. You and I never exactly agreed about the delay you wanted before we got things started. . . . Hey, what can I say? I changed the plans. Your doubts aren't my doubts."*

Kelda heard the sound of a ringing phone emerge from the recorder. Ira responded by saying "Damn" and shutting off the machine.

A second or two later the recording continued and he said, *"Where was I? Oh yeah.*

"Anyway, babe, I'm off on our adventure and obviously I'm . . . flying solo. I won't muck it up, I promise. Look around, everything's been sanitized. And this way your hands stay clean. That's good, right? You know that I love you, Kelda. Go ice your legs, babe, put on a fresh patch, and pray for the monsoons."

She hit "stop," then "rewind," and a few moments later, "eject." She plucked the tape from the machine, placed it in her purse, poured some water into the ficus by the back door, checked to make sure the parakeets, Oliver and Lee, had seeds and water, and headed back toward the front of the house. She stopped just before she reached the door and stepped into the tiny room by the entryway that the developer of the neighborhood generously referred to in his marketing materials as "an executive study." The two big aquariums inside the room were empty. She bent at the waist so that she could be sure that the snakes hadn't burrowed deep beneath the shredded newspaper in their glass homes.

They hadn't.

No surprise.

She ran down the stairs to the unfinished basement. It was as empty as it had been the day Ira had moved in. All the equipment was gone.

As she climbed the stairs back up to the first floor, she realized that her feet were on fire. The sharp needles she usually walked on by this time of almost every day had become so fiery hot they felt as if they were glowing. The pain of their sharpness was indistinguishable from the pain of their heat. She closed her eyes and tried to breathe through the pain.

It didn't help.

She locked the front door of Ira's house with the key when she left. Once in the car she phoned Tom Clone's grandfather's number again. She didn't expect an answer and she didn't get one.

She was at a loss.

Gary Cross, her first supervising agent in the Denver Field Office, had told her that there was only one thing to do when she reached a dead end during an investigation.

"What?" she'd asked.

"Something else," he'd replied.

She stared at Maria's cell phone and tried to decide what exactly that something else might be. In the meantime, she searched her shoulder bag for her stash of Percocet.

Lunch for psychotherapists is a moveable feast.
What that means in reality is that it is usually moved
until midafternoon.

Midday appointments are a coveted commodity for
most clinical mental health professionals. Few working
people are able to steal forty-five minutes from their
workday once or twice a week for an appointment with a
therapist, so "meeting over lunch" is a common solution
to the dilemma. On some days those "lunch" appointments begin as early as eleven and end as late as two.

That's why I was walking out the door of my building at a few minutes after two o'clock to get something
to eat.

I was halfway down Walnut to Ninth when I heard
a female voice call my name. Not "Dr. Gregory," but
"Alan, Alan." I looked over at the sound.

The woman in the car who was calling for me was Kelda James. She lowered her sunglasses and leaned toward the open window so that I could see her face. "Do you have a second?" she asked.

"Do we have an appointment?" I replied, suddenly flustered by the possibility that I really wasn't actually free for lunch, but that I had another scheduled appointment that I'd forgotten to record.

"No, no. But can we talk for a second?"

I was almost broadsided by a young man—he definitely wasn't a kid—on a skateboard who zoomed past me before he disappeared around the corner onto Ninth. I stepped off the sidewalk onto the street and leaned down toward the window of Kelda's car.

"Thank you," she said.

"Is this an emergency?" I asked. Translation: *Is this more important than me eating lunch?*

She nodded. "Yes, I'm afraid it is."

"Go on."

"I'm not sure I know how to ask this but . . . I need to know if you know where I can find Tom Clone."

I pressed my tongue against my teeth for a moment before I untangled my mouth enough to say, "What?" I admit that my first thought was to uncomplicate my afternoon and simply say, "No."

Kelda repeated, "Do you know where I can find Tom Clone?"

If I said I couldn't respond, I would be acknowledging that Tom was my patient. That was the trap that Sam Purdy had set for me with the exact same question. If I said I didn't know where he was, I was coming perilously close to flouting Tom's confidentiality.

"Kelda, I'm . . ." I watched a huge tractor-trailer fail

to complete the turn from Ninth onto Walnut. Traffic in both directions was totally blockaded by the truck's trailer, which extended across the width of Ninth. "What are you asking me? You want to know if I know where someone you referred to me for psychotherapy is right now?"

"This isn't just my curiosity, Alan. This is an emergency. A serious emergency."

I shaded my eyes against the afternoon sun. "Are you asking this question as my patient or as an FBI agent?" Unlike Kelda, I *was* just being curious with my question. It made no difference to me whether Kelda was acting personally or professionally. My hands were tied with the same ethical twine regardless of the hat she was wearing while she asked the question.

"I don't know."

I thought she looked quite despairing.

"But it's serious?"

She nodded.

"Then go ahead and park your car. I'll meet you back at my office in a minute or two."

She sighed—I interpreted it as frustration, not relief—and said, "Thank you."

It's a long story," she said. She hadn't even settled onto the chair. Her shoulder bag was still clutched in her hand. I suspected that she wasn't convinced that I was really going to insist that she explain what was going on.

I sat and crossed my legs. "I have another patient at three," I replied evenly. "You should probably get started telling your long story."

My curiosity and my concern for Tom Clone had almost eclipsed my hunger. Almost.

"I shouldn't spend the time"—I could tell she almost said "waste the time"—"telling you all this. I wish you would trust me that it would be better for Tom if you would just tell me what I need to know. Then I could go do whatever it is I can do to . . . help him."

"Sorry, Kelda, but we're going to have to do this my way. Why don't you sit down? There are very limited circumstances that permit me to divulge privileged information."

She fell heavily onto the chair. The shoulder bag clunked to the floor as though it were stuffed with a shot put. The fingertips of her left hand almost immediately began kneading her quad. "I think Tom's in danger," she said.

"Go on," I said. I was thinking that my cast felt heavy.

CHAPTER

37

Tom? Where did the snakes go?" The voice blew out of the speaker with an uncertain timbre.

"O'er there." Tom's heart didn't even leap at the sound of his captor's voice. He pointed in the direction of the line of lodgepole pines south of the enclosure. He was standing within six inches of the fence on the north side of his prison. "I think they got hot. They needed the shade."

"That happens with snakes. They're too hot; they're too cold. Who knows, they may be back, right? Tonight for instance. Who knows? It may be too cold in there for them, and they'll have to come looking for warmth. Like from you, or from your sleeping bag. Or—maybe—you in your sleeping bag."

"Yes," Tom agreed. In the hour or so since the man had first opened the box and the two vipers had edged through the diamond links of the fence, Tom had decided that he was much more worried about the snakes than he was about the bees. Much more worried.

"When you fall asleep tonight I may just throw a few lame mice in there with you. They like mice. The vipers do. I don't want them to get too hungry."

" 'i'ers. 'ice," Tom repeated numbly. " 'lease don't. No la'e 'ice. I think I already know all a'out 'ear."

"You do? That's terrific. I'd love to hear, so please tell me what you know about fear. No, no, no. Instead tell me why . . . tell me why it's important that you know all about fear."

Tom didn't know. " 'Cause it's i'ortant."

"Duh. Good guess. Why is it important?"

" 'Cause . . . 'cause . . . uh . . ."

"Think about girls you've known, Tom? Does that help?"

"Huh?"

"Dingdong. Ring a bell, Tom? Girls, girls, girls. Hello."

Tom was tired. He was hot. He was dehydrated. His brain was almost fried from fear. His adrenals were parched from depositing gallons of hormones into his bloodstream. He had enough histamines in his system from the bee stings to thwart the effects of a tanker-truckload of Benadryl. No matter how hard he was trying, he couldn't manage to fire the synapses that were necessary to help him figure out why the hell some guy was imprisoning him in the mountains and what some girl from his past had to do with the bees and the vipers.

"Girls? Girls I dated?"

"Think, Tom. Think about girls you've dated. Any

blond girls? Real pretty, beautiful even. Why are we here today, Tom?"

"To learn a'out 'ear."

"Very good."

Tom said, "Girls. 'ear. They go together." He wasn't sure where the thought had come from, but he knew it was right. He suddenly felt like an A student.

"Oh yes, some girls know about fear. Some girls know about fear the way that bees know about honey."

" 'ees," Tom said. His pulse raced at the word.

The man suddenly appeared through the trees from the west. Once again he was wearing the motorcycle helmet with the visor. On this approach he was dragging a huge canvas bundle behind him through the forest. The bundle was so heavy that the man needed both hands to get it over the rough spots on the forest floor.

"What is that?" Tom asked. He waited for the big sack to move on its own and for a mountain lion or a black bear to pop out of the bag like a crazed stripper emerging from a cake at some old-time bachelor party.

The man didn't answer. He let go of the bundle and disappeared back into the woods. A minute or so later, he returned, dragging another canvas bundle. He left it beside the first and immediately took long strides toward the fence. Once again he threw a half-liter bottle of water over the fence. Tom hopped out of the way, not even trying to catch it.

He shifted his eyes from the bottle to the canvas sacks and back again. "What's in those 'ags?" A tremor caused his voice to twang.

"These?" The man's voice was oddly hollow behind the dark visor. "Growing a little wary, Tom? Paranoia setting in? These are just supplies I need for the lessons. The fear lessons."

" 'ear lessons." He stepped back a solitary step. After looking over his shoulder to see how close he was to the chain-link, he stepped back once more. "I know a'out 'ear. No 'ore lessons. 'lease."

"Drink, Tom. It's just water in the bottle, I promise. If you don't want it, just throw it back over. I don't want to litter."

Tom leaned down and lifted the bottle from the dust. He examined the bottle to make certain the seal was intact.

The man made a *tsk, tsk, tsk* sound behind the dark visor. "You going to drink it or send it out for a lab analysis?"

Tom unscrewed the cap. He smelled the contents before he raised it to his lips. He drained the entire bottle. He wanted more.

"Thank you," he said.

The man tossed a sealed foil bag over the fence. Tom examined it without lifting it. He had no idea what it was. As soon as he was done with the examination he returned his eyes to the two canvas sacks.

The man said, "It's high-energy food, Tom. A new thing called energy gel. High in carbs and proteins. Rip a corner off the bag and just suck it down. Don't worry, it goes down good."

Tom read the small print on the bag for a few seconds, then did as his captor instructed.

"I need you hydrated and nourished," the man explained. "The lessons aren't over. There's always more to learn about fear."

"Girls," Tom said.

"Yes," the man agreed. "Girls. Specifically, a girl."

Just then Tom thought he began to get it.

"Oh shit," he said. His adrenals cramped and squeezed and dumped their remaining bounty, and within seconds Tom knew all over again exactly what fear was.

"Is it Joan?" he whimpered. The question roared in his head but little sound escaped his swollen lips.

"What?" the man said. "I can't hear you, Tom."

38

Kelda opened her mouth with so much reluctance that for a moment I felt not like a psychologist but like a dentist brandishing a gleaming hypodermic full of Novocain. She said, "Jones's journal? The one I told you about that was with the things we picked up in Maui?"

"Yes," I said.

"A few years ago, I got a chance to read it."

"Yes," I said. I thought, *I bet it wasn't pretty.*

"Someone was after her. That's really why she went to Hawaii. To get away from him."

A pan-phobic woman writing in her diary about someone being after her, I thought. *Now there's a surprise.* My frustration was only exceeded by my fatigue and hunger. I waited about ten seconds before I said, "The CliffsNotes version won't suffice, Kelda. I need to know what's going on before I can decide how to help you."

She looked away, then back at me. "Okay. A guy she started dating after I left for Australia threatened her. And then he followed her to Hawaii when she moved. According to her journal his name was Tom Clone."

Oh boy.

"She had just started seeing him when the news media began to link him with the murder of Ivy Campbell."

I thought, *I bet that's when she got spooked. Really spooked.*

Kelda continued. "For whatever reason, Jones was convinced that she was going to be his next victim. She felt . . . threatened. A week or two later, she got the offer to go join the co-op in Paia, and she went. For her to do that—to get on a plane by herself and go to Hawaii—she must have been seriously frightened."

"But he found her there?"

"Yes. She wasn't sure how he found her. But he did. He followed her over to Maui."

"This is all in her journal?"

"Yes, it is. And he told her that she made him want to dance."

Tom had used the phrase with me once, describing Ivy. Or had it been describing Kelda? I wasn't sure, though I was sure it wasn't a coincidence that I was hearing it now from her. I said, "He did? That's important?"

"To me it is."

"Go on."

"What?"

I waited. Godot never came.

Finally, I said, "And you think that he killed her? That Tom Clone pushed Jones off that cliff?"

"I go back and forth on that, actually. Some nights, I'm lying awake and I think he literally pushed her. Other nights, I think he just went there and scared her to death. That he figuratively pushed her. Either way . . ."

Some reality testing seemed in order. Gently, I asked, "Why, Kelda? Why would he do that?"

"She broke up with him. She left him. Just like what happened with Ivy Campbell."

I thought that it had been Tom who had broken up with Ivy, not the other way around. But I knew that arguing the facts with Kelda wasn't the correct therapeutic move. This conversation wasn't about facts. I said, "That's it? She broke up with him?" I wanted Kelda to hear the fragility of the motive for murder she was proposing.

"Yes."

"And you think he went to Hawaii to . . . ?" I let my uncasted hand float to express the lethal void at the end of the sentence. "And . . . you hold him responsible for her death?"

"That's not important."

It's not? But I nodded, processing her denial.

"It is quite a coincidence," I said.

"What?"

"That all these years later, you turn out to be instrumental in getting him off death row for the first murder. The same guy who threatened your friend."

"Yes," she agreed. Her eyes never wavered from mine. "It is quite a coincidence."

"Where do I come in?" I suspected that the answer was that I was supposed to be willing to be played for the fool. One of the many nice things about my friend Sam Purdy was that Sam never pretended to be squeezing my ass while he tried to pick my pocket. He just went right for my wallet.

Kelda wasn't being quite so straightforward. She was enticing me with the story about Tom Clone and Jones's diary. That was hot breath in my ear. All she actually wanted to do was to rifle my files.

"What do you mean?"

"You referred Tom to me, Kelda. Why? If you hold him responsible for your friend's death, why would you do that?"

"I was half asleep when he asked for a name. I've regretted it ever since. I regret it right now, I guarantee you that."

"And you think it's that simple? You were half asleep so you gave him my name?"

"Yes," she said. Her tone had become defiant. My impression was that she wasn't particularly eager to entertain any alternative hypotheses, although I had come up with two or three without breaking a sweat.

I tried a gentle confrontation. "I think you wanted me in the middle of this, whatever it is."

"Why would I do that?"

I didn't know what to say, so I said nothing. I'm not always wise enough to do that.

"You want to know how you come in now, Alan? You can tell me whether you know where I can find him. That's where you come in."

"Is he in danger?" I asked. If she told me he was, and I decided the threat was serious and imminent, all the rules about confidentiality changed. I assumed that

Kelda, a law enforcement officer—albeit a federal one—knew that. I was eager to hear her response to my question, but tried not to show it.

"Let's just say I'm worried about him. Very worried. Will that suffice?"

"Worried personally or professionally?"

"Let's just say . . . worried."

For the first time in days I felt a dull ache in my humerus. I curled my fingers around the end of the cast, but that didn't change the pain.

She shook her head in frustration and said, "You're not going to tell me, are you? I'm just wasting my time here."

"You're assuming I know something, Kelda. All this visit has assured me of is that I know much less than just about everybody else."

"That's what this is about? You're upset because everybody hasn't shared their secrets with you? How petty."

Was that what it was all about? I hoped not. I said, "I'm sorry if you see it that way."

She squeezed her eyes shut. I watched the muscles tighten in her jaw. Wearily, she demanded, "Just tell me. Where is he?"

Almost involuntarily I shook my head. I asked, "How's your pain right now, Kelda?"

She said, "Fuck you," and stood to leave.

39

Kelda stood on the sidewalk outside Dr. Gregory's office for a moment, feeling disoriented. She didn't immediately recognize the keys that she held in her hand; she couldn't even remember what kind of car she was driving.

Her dead end had just become a brick wall.

"Something else," she said aloud. "Something else. What is my 'something else'?"

Behind her she heard someone say her name.

With a name like Kelda, she didn't even entertain the possibility that the person might be talking to someone besides her.

CHAPTER

40

I sat immobile on my chair, staring at the door she'd left open, half expecting her to return.

She didn't.

I walked out to the waiting room and stood at the front window, my good hand in my trousers pocket, my casted arm hanging at its constantly useless angle. Kelda was standing on the sidewalk. A man in a gray business suit was walking toward her. His lips were moving.

Concerned that she would spot me spying on her, I stepped back from the window. I sat at my desk for a few seconds, stood right back up, walked to the rear window, and immediately returned to the desk. I picked up the phone and punched in Sam Purdy's number at the police department, expecting to hear the greeting from his voicemail. Instead, I listened as he said, "This is Purdy."

"Sam, it's Alan. Hi."

"Hi, Alan."

"Listen, I only have a minute between patients, but I was wondering something. Have you found Tom Clone?"

"No," he said. I thought that there was some incongruous levity attached to the solitary word.

"No sign of the Vespa?"

Again Sam's voice carried a little lilt as he said, "Turns out that there're Vespas all over town. Did you know that? Some new trendoid thing that's going on in Boulder. I see them all the time now that I know what they are. I just didn't know what those whiny little things were called."

"Yeah, I've heard they're getting popular. But any sign of the grandfather's Vespa in particular? The red one?"

"No. No sign of it. Don't get me wrong, we're looking, but finding Tom Clone and the Vespa are not the most important things the Boulder Police Department is doing right now. Basically, that case is an unsolved assault on the elderly. It's not a nice thing, but it's not the end of the world from a law enforcement perspective. You know what I mean? We have rapes, we have unsolved murders, we have—"

"Yeah, yeah. I understand. Life goes on."

After a few seconds of silence, my friend asked, "Have you heard from Tom Clone, Alan?"

"Sorry, Sam."

"Sorry you can't tell me? Or sorry you haven't heard from him?"

"Take your pick. I'm sorry about a lot of things these days."

"You know, you don't sound too good." His voice had softened. "You want to tell me what's going on?"

"Nothing . . . nothing. I was just curious about your progress with the investigation. Thought I'd call and see how everything was going."

"Middle of the afternoon and you just have this undeniable urge to know where Clone is? You really want to think your public servants are goofy enough to believe that? That's what I'm supposed to believe?"

"Yes, Sam. That's exactly what I would like you to believe."

I heard him sigh before he said, "You know, I might actually be tempted to go along with you if you were the first person to call me this afternoon trying to find Tom Clone. But since you aren't, I'm a little more suspicious than usual."

"Who else called?"

He laughed. "You think I'm going to tell you that? Though it probably doesn't matter whether I do or I don't. I think you already know the answer."

Kelda, I thought. *God, she called Sam trying to find Tom. What the hell is going on?*

Sam said, "If you have another minute or two before your next victim shows up, maybe we could talk a little more about that Fed you never seem to want to talk about. Remember her? The one I told you about who alibied Clone? We could do that. After we have that conversation, I fervently believe that both of us would feel better."

I didn't know what to say.

"Alan, you still there? I don't hear you. Are we breaking up? Are you on a cell phone or something?"

"I'm, uh . . . I'm, uh . . . Oh shit, Sam. I don't know what the hell I am."

He chuckled. "Why don't you call me sometime when you're in a better mood," he said, and he hung up the phone.

I wanted to hit redial and tell Sam about Jones and Paia and Kelda and the fact that everybody seemed to want to know where Tom Clone was.

I wanted to but I couldn't.

Right at that moment I hated the work I did.

CHAPTER

41

Politically, Colorado is a bastion of western conservatism. As a result, the vast majority of Coloradans view the decidedly less-than-conservative city of Boulder either as an amusing curiosity or, less benignly, as an irritating oddity. For many of the state's residents, Boulder is too idiosyncratic, too idealistic, too liberal, too pretty, too different, and too weird.

And, ironically enough, that is almost exactly how the majority of Boulder residents view the little town of Ward.

Although it is within the high western boundary of Boulder County—barely, some would point out—Ward, Colorado, attracts a different breed of residents than most of the county's mountain towns. Many people have been lured to Ward over the years by its laissez-faire reputation, by its spectacular but isolated location high in the eastern shadows of the Continental Divide, and by its defiant municipal independence. Although many have been lured to attempt to live in Ward, the process of natural selection routinely whittles down the population to a manageable number. The rigors associated with spending Rocky Mountain winters in an infrastructurally challenged, socioeconomically marginal community at an elevation well in excess of nine thousand feet rapidly separate the hardy from the foolhardy.

The combination of isolation and altitude ensures that for nine months a year life isn't easy in Ward, but its residents tend to be the kind of people who would find life intolerable almost anyplace else.

Founded in 1860 by Calvin Ward, who was drawn to the area by its rich veins of minerals, the town has endured the collapse of its mining backbone, the evaporation of its brief status as a tourist mecca, the departure of its only railroad, and two devastating fires, which some locals still argue were actually arsons instigated by envious folk from down the road in Central City. The Ward that has survived these trials is an anachronistic village that is still housed in many of the frame or stone buildings that somehow escaped the last of the big fires at the end of the nineteenth century.

Remove a few of the newer structures, cut down some utility poles, and cart away the rusting hulks of a few hundred abandoned motorized vehicles of all descriptions, and it wouldn't take much else to make Ward appear something as it did a hundred years earlier. The mine tailings that sit above town look just as they did in photos from the 1890s, a series of unbroken rust-colored waves frozen in ominous time above the village.

Ward is a town where self-sufficiency and independence are prized and a generous dose of tolerance isn't questioned; it's assumed.

If the town of Ward were the type of place that cared to have a motto—which it isn't—its motto might well be "Leave Us Fucking Alone."

Living in Park County fifty miles due south of Boulder County, Fred Prehost was accustomed to mountain people, but after five minutes in Ward he knew he wasn't in Park County anymore. The few people who were walking the town's streets appeared to consist primarily of refugees from the original Woodstock or extras from some postapocalyptic movie that nobody ever saw twice. Human residents seemed to be outnumbered by canine residents by at least two to one, and the canines appeared to be much better fed than the *Homo sapiens*.

As his car was circled by a pack of four dogs, Prehost was thinking that, apparently, in Ward, obeying leash laws was considered optional.

"Hey, Hoppy," he said. "Any ideas?"

The two friends were sitting in the front seat of Prehost's old Suburban, which, other than being a bit too well cared for, actually looked right at home on the streets of Ward.

"We need to talk to some people, I guess, find that car I saw them in. My best advice would be for us to forget that we're cops. One, this isn't our county. Two, I figure the folks that I'm looking at around here"—Hoppy gestured with a nod at an obese, bald man with a snake tattoo curling up around his ear and an old poncho over his shoulders—"are dispositionally more likely to be fond of strangers than they are to be fond of strangers who are cops."

Prehost snorted. "You think Boulder County has ever sent a building inspector to this place? I mean, like, ever? Look at these buildings. That one there is half 1950s Greyhound bus, half God-knows-what. I don't think there's a section in the building code that covers that."

"Got me, Fred."

"But this is where you lost Clone, you're sure? Right here? You know that much?"

"Yeah, the guy in the green Pathfinder flagged him down on North Broadway in Boulder. They talked for a few minutes and then they came right up here in the Pathfinder without stopping."

"And they took Left Hand Canyon, not Boulder Canyon?" Fred Prehost knew all this already but he had the detective disease that made him want to hear everything two or three times, even when he was talking to another detective.

"That's right."

"Go on."

"Like I said, I was worried that they'd figure out I was following them, so when they pulled into town I was giving them some space—I was maybe a quarter mile behind. When I chugged into town the Pathfinder had vanished. I looked for them for a while, and when I couldn't find them, I went back down the hill and waited back at his grandfather's house in Boulder, but Clone never came back down. He may not be here anymore, but this is the last place I saw them."

"And the motorbike is where he left it? You actually checked that? You're not just assuming?"

"It's still parked at the Mental Health Center on Iris. Right where he left it."

Prehost had run the plates on the green Pathfinder himself. A couple of phone calls revealed that the tags had been stolen from a new Hyundai Santa Fe that was parked nights in an apartment building lot in Arvada and days in the huge lot of the MCI service center in Glendale. Other than the fact that the owner of the truck felt he needed stolen tags, the information wasn't helpful at all: Plate picking would have been a piece of cake in either location.

"So we need to find somebody who can tell us who around here might have a nice green Pathfinder," Prehost said.

"Yep."

"We do it together or separate?"

"Us? Separate. Definitely separate. We don't want to look like cops, and we don't want to look like queers," said Hoppy.

"What's our cover?"

"Don't look at me."

Prehost scratched his chin for a moment. "What about we say we were visiting relatives in Nederland and somebody in a Cadillac—no, even better, make that a Mercedes—so somebody in a big black Mercedes hit our car—no, no, no, somebody in a big black Mercedes hit our *dog*—and we think the guy in this Pathfinder saw the whole thing and may be able to be a witness for us, and somebody in Nederland said that they thought they recognized the Pathfinder and that they thought that the guy who owned it lived some-where near Ward. How about that?"

"I think you're a genius, Fred. You just come up with that right now? What kind of dog?"

"A Lab, everybody loves Labs. Or maybe a golden retriever. What do you think?"

"Lab. Did the dog die in the accident?"

"Hell no. You ruin the story if you have the dog die. People get morose, then they don't want to talk to you. Our dog's in the hospital; he needs surgery to walk again. It's going to be expensive, some experimental thing that has to be done by specialists at the veterinary school in Fort Collins. We need to find the guy in the Pathfinder so we can make sure the guy in the Mercedes pays through the nose so our dog isn't crippled for the rest of his life."

"Is it your dog or my dog?"

"Let's make it your dog, Hoppy. You're better at looking miserable than me. You head that way." Prehost pointed through the windshield. "I'll do the other side of the street. I want to know what Clone and this guy with the stolen tags are up to. Maybe we'll find them in a meth lab or something. That would be sweet. With the slightest bit of luck, we'll have Clone back in jail by dinnertime."

Hoppy pushed his door open and began to climb out. Then he stopped. "What's his name? My dog?"

Prehost was already thinking about something else. He said, "What? Oh. D.P. His name is D.P."

"Huh? T.P.? Toilet Paper?"

"No, D.P.—Death Penalty. The dog's name is D.P."

Hoppy laughed. "Gotcha."

• • •

Fifteen minutes later, Fred Prehost found Hoppy standing at something vaguely resembling a counter at the Ward General Store having a cup of coffee with an earth-mother type. For a moment, Prehost thought that the woman was somebody he'd busted in Cripple Creek for tipping over slot machines, but memory told him that woman was a size-ten felon, and this one was at least a sixteen.

"This building's original, Fred. Did you know that? It's been a general store just like this for over a hundred and forty years. Survived all the fires. This is Clara, by the way."

Prehost pretended he was tipping the hat he wasn't wearing. "Hello, Clara. Nice to meet you."

Clara smiled. "Coffee? Fresh a few minutes ago. We roast the beans ourselves. Best in town." She laughed heartily and pointed to a gorgeous old roaster in the corner of the store. "Store" was a generous assessment of the establishment. A few shelves harboring a sparse collection of foodstuffs separated the part of the structure where things were sold from the part where people lived. Or hung out. To Prehost, it wasn't at all a clear demarcation.

"No, thank you, I'll pass."

Hoppy said, "It turns out that Clara has a Lab, too, though hers is one of those golden ones, not a black one like old D.P. And she knows the car we're looking for, even knows the guy who drives it to see him, but doesn't know where he lives. She thinks he's just up here occasionally, isn't really a local, but that we should keep asking. She's sure someone in town will know where to find him."

"Well, Clara, you do know what you're talking about.

The guy down at the—what is that down there a little ways? Is that a junkyard? Anyway, the guy with the hair that's all—"

"Lootie," Clara supplied. "With the cornrows."

"Yeah, that's his name. Lootie. Anyway, Lootie knew the vehicle right away. He gave me pretty good directions to the cabin this guy's been fixing up, says the man's real pleasant."

Clara nodded and said, "He is a pleasant man." She snapped her stubby fingers. "What *is* his name?"

"Oliver. Lootie said he calls himself Oliver."

"I'll remember that now. Next time I see him I'll remember to call him Oliver. Like the book, *Oliver Twist*. Or the movie. My memory is trouble, especially with names. I do okay with faces, but names . . ." Clara shook her head, smiled, and added, "You ask me, I think it was all the acid I took."

After they thanked Clara for her hospitality, Hoppy carried his coffee and a couple of muffins back to the Suburban. As he settled onto his seat, he asked, "So where are we going?"

"That way," Prehost responded. He pointed up the hill to the west before he looked down at his little pocket notebook. "We head up something Lootie called the Brainard Lake Road. He said we should go out Morning Star to Chatham and we'll run into the Brainard Lake Road. When we get near Left Hand Creek apparently it all gets complicated. But I got it all written down."

"You act like you know this place."

"Ward? Hardly." He was quiet for a moment. "But I do get the feeling that being a cop here would be like shooting ducks in a pond. I bet the half of the town that's not using right now still has adequate blood levels of illegal substances in their bodies from the sixties and seventies. Local cops would just have to line everybody up on Main Street or whatever the hell they call it and hand out urine cups. The rest would be up to the guys with the test tubes and the white coats."

"Clara?" Hoppy said.

"Clara, indeed."

"This guy Lootie seem to have all his brain cells?"

"Mostly. Lootie seemed all right. Actually, if you get past his looks and the smell from his rotting teeth, he's the sort of guy you'd like to have a beer with. I think the directions he gave me will get us to Oliver's cabin. In fact, I smell Mr. Clone already. Ten dollars says that this Oliver guy is somebody that Clone knows from inside and what they're working up here is a meth lab or an ecstasy dump."

"I like my money too much to take that bet. Your instincts are good on this shit, Fred."

"What time you have?"

Hoppy checked his watch. "Almost five. Do we have enough time before it gets dark?"

Prehost said, "Sure, plenty. I like approaching at dusk anyway. Reminds me of my infantry training. Ducks in a pond," he repeated softly.

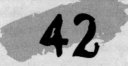

I s'ell gas," Tom said.

"You do? You sell gas? You work in a gas station? I thought you'd be able to get a better job than that," the man said absently. His words were muffled by the helmet and visor.

"*No!* I don't sell gas, I s'ell gas." Tom was looking all around, pivoting on one foot, trying to identify the source of the odor.

"You smell gas? Natural gas?"

"No, no. Gasoline. I s'ell gasoline. Don't you s'ell it? Where is it? What are you doing?"

The man unfolded the sides of one of the canvas bags to reveal an old Coleman cooler. The cooler was dark blue with a white plastic top.

The man stood and faced Tom. "The smell is coming from in here, Tom."

"What is that?"

"Here, see for yourself."

The man flipped off the lid of the cooler, reached inside, and removed an orb about the size of a softball. Small tubes stuck off the sides. The man raised the device and held it up so that Tom could see it.

"What is it?"

"It's a latex glove, Tom. Filled with my own little recipe for napalm. You know napalm, Tom?"

"What?" Tom was incredulous. His mouth hung open and his eyes grew wide. "Na'al'? Why?" he cried. But he knew why.

"Fear, Tom. Remember, it's all about fear. You afraid of fire?"

Tom's voice cracked as he whined, "Every'ody is a'raid o' 'ire. Don't 'urn 'e. 'lease!"

The man underhanded the orb over the fence. The latex ball hit the dirt about ten feet from Tom and imploded upon impact. A green transparent gel splashed up and out from the wrist hole, which had blown open as soon as the glove hit the ground. "Watch," the man said.

The man lit an entire book of matches and placed it in a small metal basket at the end of a telescoping aluminum pole that Tom recognized as a device for retrieving golf balls from water hazards. Once he pushed the basket through the fence, the man extended the pole until the basket hovered two feet above the splash of napalm.

"No!" Tom wailed. He turned, ran to the far corner of the enclosure, crouched, and raised his hands to his face.

The man tipped the basket over and the book of

flaming matches fluttered toward the stained soil. A huge *whoosh* of flames jumped from the ground and engulfed the matchbook before gravity could help it complete its descent toward the fuel.

Tom yelped.

The fire settled. The blue-yellow flames licked across the ground like slithering insects.

The man reached into the cooler and grabbed two more puffy surgical gloves. One by one he tossed them over the fence. Each imploded upon impact. Each was closer to Tom than the first.

Tom called out, "Let's talk a'out girls and 'ear."

The man was retracting the aluminum pole. "You want to talk about girls and fear? Now? Because you're afraid of fire?"

Tom nodded dramatically.

The man paused and faced Tom.

"Fear kills, doesn't it, Tom?"

Desperate, Tom tried frantically to guess what it was that the man wanted to hear. "I guess it can. Yes, 'ear can kill. Are you going to kill 'e?"

The man didn't answer. He shook his head. Tom couldn't tell whether it was an expression of disdain or denial.

Finally, the man said, "Did it kill any girls, Tom? Or did you?"

"What?" Tom said.

"Well?" the man's voice taunted.

"*What?*"

"After you killed Ivy, Tom, was another girl next?"

"*What?*"

The man readied another book of matches. Before he set it afire, he paused and retrieved two more little napalm bombs and tossed them toward Tom. One bomblet hit six feet from him, splashing gel onto his feet.

The man returned his attention to the flaming matches in the basket of the telescoping pole.

"I didn't kill I'y. I' innocent. The DNA! The DNA! You 'ust ha'e heard a'out the DNA."

The man stopped what he was doing. His voice flattened as he said, "Heard about it? Have I heard about it? You know whose blood was on that knife, Tom? The one that the FBI agent found?"

"No. Who?"

The man lit the matches. He placed the little ball of fire in the basket at the end of the pole.

The sun completed its drop behind the Continental Divide, and thunder exploded in the western sky.

A few fat drops of rain plopped and cratered on the dust inside the enclosure.

The man raised his hands and looked up toward the sky. "So are you a lucky man, Tom? Are the monsoons coming today? No reason to be afraid of fire in a thunderstorm, is there?"

More thunder clapped; lightning snapped a bolt of fire a second or two later. For an instant, the lightning was so bright that it muted the brilliance of the flames from the napalm.

Tom squirmed and said, " 'e? Lucky?"

The man inserted the basket through the fence. He lit the puddle of napalm closest to Tom. A breeze picked up the flames and immediately blew them to the other pool of fuel.

Tom hurried to brush dirt into the gel on his feet as he watched black-brown smoke snake upward.

The flames jumped to a puddle of napalm even closer to Tom.

The man readied a couple of more bombs to throw over the fence. He said, "If I hit you with one of these, it's not going to be pretty. But I'm going to try."

All around Tom, the dirt looked as if it was covered with flaming Sterno.

"*God!*" he implored. "*God?*"

Bill," Kelda said.

Bill Graves stood on the sidewalk outside Dr. Gregory's office with his hands in the pockets of his suit trousers. His thin lips were in a flat line but she thought a hint of triumph flickered in his eyes.

"How did you find me? Are you on your Harley? Is that how I missed you?" Kelda asked.

"No, I'm not on my bike. It wasn't hard finding you, Kelda. I followed you all the way from downtown." His voice was warm, almost teasing. "You're not as clever as you think. You almost spotted me when you stopped at that house on the west side to get that crappy little car that you're driving, but after that it's been a breeze to stay with you."

"Why?"

His eyes narrowed a little. "Because I like you, Kelda.

And because I think you may be wading into something that's a shade deeper than you thought it was."

Because I like you. Kelda's mind flashed on the empty picture frame on her colleague's desk.

"And what I'm wading into is your business, Bill?"

"I think it might be."

"Once more, why?"

"Once more, because I like you. But also—and this is a guess—I think the situation you're in has something to do with Clone and that knife we found. That makes it my business."

Above Bill's head an immense thunderhead was crowning the peaks of the Divide. She didn't even consider the possibility that it would blow down and cool the Front Range. This was one of those summers where the storms only taunted and teased.

"Can we talk, Kelda?"

"I don't think that's a good idea."

"But whatever you're up to is?"

"You're a nice guy, Bill. You don't really want to know what's going on. Trust me, you don't want a piece of this."

"You telling me that because you like me, too?"

She said, "Maybe."

"Was that Bureau work you were doing in there?" He nodded toward the building she'd just exited. "Or did you have an appointment with a shrink?"

The pain flared in her legs. She closed her eyes for a second, then turned and walked away from her colleague. After two steps she stopped and looked back over her shoulder. "I can lose you. Don't bother to try to follow me."

"Are you trying to be a hero again, Kelda? Is this—whatever the hell you're doing—is this about that little girl?"

She spun and faced him. "Rosa Alija? Is that the little girl you're talking about?" Her words popped from her lips and she regretted the intensity.

"You have to move on. It's been a long time, Kelda."

"Since what? Since I saved her life? Since I put three slugs into the chest of a monster? You think I want to do that again? Is that what you're saying? Is that what you think of me?"

"You know what people say, Kelda. In the Bureau. People talk, you know that."

"No. What? What do people say in the Bureau?" She knew what other agents thought and she knew what they said behind her back. But she discovered that she didn't want to believe that Bill thought it, too.

"It must be hard being a hero and then . . . not . . . being a hero. You and I chase numbers. It's not too glamorous. It has to be hard for you after—"

Tears filled her eyes. "I don't know what I'm doing today, Bill. But I can promise you that it has nothing to do with being a hero."

CHAPTER

44

Hoppy was in charge of the arsenal.

While Prehost drove up the Brainard Lake Road toward Oliver's cabin, Hoppy checked both their handguns and loaded Prehost's twelve-gauge shotgun with buckshot. Hoppy already knew that the little pistol in his ankle holster was ready to go. It always was.

Hoppy asked, "How does this go down? If we're going to do this on our own, we have to get him back to Park County, right?"

"We'll see. Depending on what we find, it may be better just to turn things over to Boulder County. If we decide to take it back home, we'll do something with the green Pathfinder. We'll make it look like we followed it down the Peak to Peak Highway and then back home. Then we'll make sure that's where everything will go down."

"What about this Oliver guy?"

Prehost didn't hesitate. "Depends what his involvement is. I doubt if he'll make the trip south. But we'll have to see."

Following Lootie's directions, Prehost didn't make a single wrong turn on the way to the little log cabin on the hillside above Left Hand Creek. The green Pathfinder was parked twenty feet from the front door.

Prehost stopped his Suburban. "Here we go, Hoppy."

"You want the shotgun?"

"Put it on the seat so we can reach it easily. We'll say hello first. But let's take a look inside that car before we do."

Hoppy approached the Pathfinder with the barrel of his handgun pointing skyward. "Some supplies in the back, Fred. Boxes and shit. I don't see any weapons or anything."

Thunder shook the sky. First a sharp crack, but the rumble that followed was long and low. Raindrops dotted the dusty metal on the hood of the green Pathfinder.

Prehost said, "Good. Pop the hood."

"Doors are locked."

Prehost walked over to the driver's door and slammed the butt of his handgun through the glass. "Not anymore. Pop the hood."

Hoppy did.

As thunder roared and echoed off the mountains, Prehost yanked at some wires in the engine compartment, eased the hood of the Pathfinder shut, then took long strides toward the cabin. He didn't hesitate at the door. With his handgun at waist height he walked right into the cabin. Hoppy stayed a few steps behind.

A fancy little red enamel woodstove dominated the single room. On one side was a full-size bed in an iron frame, and a rocking chair. On the other side was an oak table with two chairs, a hot plate, and a small microwave.

"Guy's a neat freak," Prehost said as he lowered his gun.

Hoppy poked his head in the door. "This ain't no meth lab, Fred."

"Nope, it's not. But there might be another building someplace where they keep the equipment, you know? Damn stuff stinks. What's this?" He kicked at a heavy canvas suit that was folded on the floor near the door. A helmet with a mesh front topped the pile.

Hoppy took two steps into the cabin and focused his attention on the canvas suit. He said, "I don't know."

Prehost said, "Where do you think our two guys are?"

A fresh burst of lightning lit the inside of the cabin, and thunder boomed off the log walls. Both men glanced toward the windows.

Hoppy shook his head. "We could wait for them. Darkness might be our friend. You know they'll be back by dark, right? Maybe even sooner if this thunderstorm sticks around. I wouldn't want to be outside up here in a lightning storm like this."

"I would think that's the case. But let's take a closer look outside again first. Make sure our friends don't have another way out of here."

"Wait, Fred. What's this?" Hoppy walked over to a small portable television that sat on the oak table.

"It's a TV, Hoppy. You don't have one at home?"

"Fred, it has a cable attached to the back. There's no cable up here. You're telling me that this Oliver guy went to the trouble of installing a satellite dish just to feed this crappy little nine-inch set?"

Prehost stepped back and waved his hand at the TV. He said, "Wait, wait, wait. This isn't from a satellite dish. There's no receiver here. Those dishes require that you have a receiver. You know, to process the signal. You see a receiver?"

"Fred, screw the receiver. There's no power here. This cabin doesn't even have electricity. This TV must be running on batteries or a generator or something. Something's fishy."

"Did you see a generator outside? There has to be a generator for the TV and the microwave."

"No, I didn't see a generator."

"Solar?"

"Did you see panels on the roof? I didn't."

Hoppy lifted the thin black cable from the TV and tracked it out the nearest window. Even in the dying light of dusk he could tell that the cable snaked along the dusty path that disappeared into the pine woods behind the cabin to the north. He cringed as a bolt of lightning flashed on the Divide.

Prehost looked over Hoppy's shoulder and said, "I think this might be some kind of closed-circuit feed, Hoppy. That's why there's no receiver."

"What the hell?"

Prehost said, "Turn it on, Hoppy. Turn on that set."

Hoppy moved to the front of the television and pushed the tiny button marked "Power."

An image flickered to life on the screen. Hoppy said, "This thing must be using batteries. Has to be."

The two cops immediately lowered themselves onto the wooden chairs that were beside the table and leaned toward the little appliance while they tried to make sense of what they were seeing on the TV. The colors of the image were muted to tinted grays and pastels.

"What is that? Is that a fence? What's that fence for? Is that like a corral or something?" Hoppy asked.

"No, I don't think so. That's a person outside there, closest to the camera, with his back to us. He's wearing like a . . . helmet or something. And over there, see, that's a person inside crouching on the far side, inside the fence. See that, right there. That's a person."

"Is that Clone?"

"Which one?"

"Inside."

"I can't tell," Prehost said. "Maybe."

"Me neither. But I think it might be."

"Whoa! What was that flash? Turn up the sound."

The screen momentarily went almost totally white before the flash narrowed to a spot that was close to the human who was crouching inside the fence.

Hoppy asked, "Was that lightning that did that, Fred? What made the TV do that?" He kept his fingertip pressed to the "Volume $\wedge$" button, but he heard nothing come from the speaker of the TV set.

"No, I don't think so, Hoppy."

"It looks like fire."

"Is this live? What are we watching?" asked Fred.

"I can think of one good way to find out." Hoppy stood from the table and moved toward the door.

Prehost watched the screen as the guy outside the

enclosure underhanded something over the fence. Whatever he threw landed within feet of the person inside the enclosure and seemed to deflate. Prehost said, "Wait! Look!"

"You go ahead. I'm going to follow that cable, Fred, see where it goes. This is too weird for me."

Prehost watched until another flash turned the screen white. He wasted a moment trying to figure out what he had just seen before he took off after Hoppy. Once he was outside he stopped at the Suburban to grab the shotgun.

Hoppy already had it. Fred snagged his big flashlight out of the backseat and jogged out behind the cabin to find the cable so he could follow his partner into the woods.

Rain had started falling steadily. Prehost decided it was a really shitty time for the arrival of the monsoons.

45

Kelda waited until Bill Graves got in his car and drove away before she returned to Maria Alija's car. Graves's words echoed in her head. *"Are you trying to be a hero again, Kelda?"*

Maybe I am, she thought as she recalled how it all started.

It was that the-shock-is-wearing-off-and-I've-never-been-so-tired-in-my-life week after the jetliners crashed into the buildings in New York City and Washington, D.C.

She was with Ira for the first time since that morning. He was sitting on the sofa in Kelda's living room, and she was on the floor, her legs resting on a carefully arranged array of bags of frozen peas. She'd worked almost nonstop for over a week as part of a task force of FBI accounting specialists that was trying to follow the money trail the hijackers had left behind.

She considered it the equivalent of tracking scat.

After a week of relentless activity and almost no sleep, the pain in her lower legs was close to intolerable. She silently compared it to the suffering of strangers in New York and Washington, knew that her pain was nothing, and shifted her weight on the peas.

Ira shook a copy of the *Denver Post* at her and said, "No, no! It's too good for him."

"What is?" Kelda said. Her attention was focused on CNN. Jeff Greenfield was talking to Gary Hart. She still wasn't sure why.

"Bush said he wants bin Laden dead or alive. That's too good for him. Killing him is too easy a way out for him after what he did to us. Putting him on trial or putting him in jail? What good does that do?"

"What?" She lowered the volume on the television. Jeff Greenfield's lips kept moving. "I'm sorry. What?"

He repeated his argument.

She reached out and caressed the long muscles of his calf. "I know," she said. "I know."

Ira didn't want to be comforted. "No, Kelda. Don't put me off about this. I mean it."

She turned her head to face him. "Okay. I believe you mean it. But we don't even know where bin Laden is yet."

Ira dropped the paper onto his lap. His eyes were bleak. "We can't do anything about him, can we? Can we even find him?" She knew he was asking her the questions as an FBI agent, not as a girlfriend.

"I don't know," she said. "It's not easy." On the screen across the room, a wall in a firehouse in New York City was covered with photographs of young men holding small children, of young women hugging their families. Even without any commentary, Kelda knew that the pictures were of those who had never made it home from the World Trade Center.

She started to weep.

What about Tom Clone?" Ira whispered a couple of hours later as he lay beside her in bed.

"What about him?" Kelda said.

"Is 'dead or alive' good enough for him?"

She didn't reply.

"He terrorized Joan," Ira argued. "What did we do? All we did was put him in prison. Whatever happened to 'an eye for an eye'? Where's the retribution? Where's the justice?"

When she replied, she spoke into the darkness. He was taking her someplace she didn't want to go, and her voice was as tired as she was. "He's on death row, Ira. He's eventually going to die for what he did to Ivy Campbell."

"Is that enough? He thinks we don't even know about Joan."

She counted to three. "He can only die once no matter how many women he killed."

"He terrorized her. Imagine her fear at the end. When he was stalking her. When she was on that cliff. Imagine what she felt. He'll die not even knowing that he's being punished for what he did to Joan. He'll die not knowing what she felt when she died."

Kelda thought about Jones. About that moment on the cliff in Maui.

Ira pulled himself up on his elbows. "Wouldn't you like a week alone in a room with bin Laden?"

What? "Yeah. Of course I would. I'd take an hour alone with him. Hell, give me ten minutes."

"I can't give you that. I wish to God I could. But maybe I can get you ten minutes alone in a room with Tom Clone. We could force-feed him some of the agony that Joan felt. We could force-feed him some of Joan's fear. Wouldn't you like that?"

"Ira, what on earth are you talking about?"

"I'm not sure," he said. "But I think I have an idea."

She swung her legs to the floor. "I have to pee."

Ira called after her as she crossed the room. "We could get even, Kelda. We could get even. How many times can people say that they really, really got even?"

The next morning, Kelda was up and ready to leave the house before dawn. She had dreamed about Jones. Jones was the woman in the chasing pictures. In Kelda's dreams the paintings came to life and Jones was the one running, running, running.

Kelda shook Ira awake before she left. He'd been sleeping on his back and he woke up without moving. Only his open eyelids betrayed the fact that he'd abandoned his dreams.

"What would I have to do?" she asked him, her lips inches from his. She could taste his sour breath.

His heart rate quickened. "All you have to do is get into the property room in Park County and get some of Ivy Campbell's blood. A piece of the clothing she was wearing the day she was killed, something like that. I don't need much. Some, a scrap, but it has to have her blood on it. There was lots of blood. We only need a little. We'll do it together."

She thought about the implications of his words. She thought about her dreams the night before. About Jones's nightmare on the cliff's edge. "I can do that," she said.

"I know you can," he said.

He kissed her. "I'll do the lab work. That's my thing. But we'll do the time alone in the room with Clone together."

"I'll get my ten minutes?"

"Minimum."

She stared into his eyes trying to detect bravado or hesitation or doubt. "Once I go to Park County and . . . you know, there won't be any turning back, Ira."

"No turning back, Kelda."

She pulled the covers from his naked body and straddled him. He reached below her skirt but didn't take his eyes from her face.

Kelda literally jumped when her cell phone rang. She took her hands from the wheel of Maria Alija's car, fumbled for her phone, not Maria's, and checked the number on the screen. The call had originated from a Boulder exchange, and although the number seemed vaguely familiar she wasn't sure who it was.

"Hello," she said.

A male voice said, "I'm looking for an FBI agent named James. Is she at this number?"

She recognized the voice. "Hello, Detective Purdy. You've found her."

"I figured that. I've also found a red Vespa. You interested in taking a look at it with us?"

"Absolutely. Yes, yes. Where are you?"

"You know Boulder?"

"Well enough."

"I'm in the parking lot of the Mental Health Center at Iris and Broadway. Know where that is?"

"I know where Iris is and I know where Broadway is. The Mental Health Center is right on the corner?"

"Yeah. Northeast corner. Red brick building. One story. You'll see us. We're the ones with the police cruisers and the yellow crime-scene tape."

She closed her eyes and shook her head at his sarcasm before she regained her composure and said, "It turns out that I'm in Boulder right now, Detective. I'll be there within minutes."

"Why am I not surprised to hear that you're in town? You're where exactly? Like the vicinity of Walnut Street maybe? Up by the Mall?"

She thought, *How the hell does he know that?* "Ten minutes, Detective Purdy. Ten minutes."

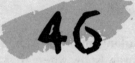
Prehost caught up with Hoppy about a hundred feet into the woods. Hoppy was standing still, straddling the black cable that led from the log cabin window. A second cable, bright yellow, and fatter than the video feed, came from the other direction and disappeared into the boarded-up entrance of an old mine. Thick timbers that were deeply creviced from a century of exposure to the elements outlined the mine entrance. From somewhere deep inside the mine, they could hear a muted, rhythmic rumble.

The rain was still falling in intermittent fat drops. Occasional thunder shook the trees.

Hoppy whispered, "Fred, that there's a power cable." He pointed at the entrance to the mine. "And that's a generator running inside there, I bet. He has the entrance insulated for sound."

Prehost nodded. "Let's go. I want to see what the hell is going on with that fence."

Hoppy moved the shotgun into his right hand and stepped back. "You first, Fred. This one's yours."

They walked another hundred feet into the aspen trees and lodge-pole pines before they saw an eruption of flames through the trees and heard someone wail, "I know a'out 'ear! I know a'out 'ear! No 'ire! No 'ore 'ire!"

"Then tell me about the girl."

"I didn't kill any girl. I didn't. You ha'e to 'elieve 'e!"

"I know who killed the girl, Tom."

Hoppy whispered, "What the hell is he talking about? He knows who killed what girl?"

Prehost looked back and glared at him while he raised an index finger to his lips. He mouthed, "Quiet, we may learn something."

"He knows who killed what girl? What's he saying, Fred?"

"Shut up."

The light was more dusk than day but Prehost could see the man with the motorcycle helmet standing between the forest and the fence. On the far side of the enclosure another man crouched in the corner.

A crack of lightning lit the sky all around them. The person in the motorcycle helmet spun at the rumble from the storm, then dropped to his hands and knees.

Hoppy hissed, "Shit, he saw us."

Prehost shook his head. "Stay still."

The rain accelerated. The drops grew smaller and dozens were multiplied by thousands. Around them the aspen leaves flickered from their impact. In the enclosure, the dirt began to turn dark.

The person in the helmet continued to stare into the forest.

His voice as quiet as he could make it, Hoppy told his partner, "He has something in his hand."

"Shhh."

Inside the enclosure, the flames that had erupted moments before became smaller, mostly licking the ground.

"Watch it, Fred," Hoppy whispered. "He has something in his hand."

The person in the helmet suddenly underhanded whatever he was holding in his hand. The object hit a spindly aspen tree twenty feet or so in front of the Park County cops and immediately burst apart.

Both men dropped to the ground.

Seconds passed and Hoppy felt a bitter tingle in his nose. He said, "Shit. That's gas. Run, Fred, run."

As they scrambled to their feet they could see that the person in the helmet was trying to light matches in the rain.

The two cops sprinted in opposite directions.

Prehost yelled, "Police! Drop your weapons! Raise your hands!"

From the enclosure came the unbelieving cry of a reply. " 'olice? 'olice? Really? 'olice?"

The person in the helmet stopped fumbling with the matches. Instead, he reached down and grabbed something out of a cooler on the ground. He spotted Hoppy running away through the woods and immediately threw the object at him.

Hoppy saw the projectile coming and flung himself

to the wet earth of the forest floor. He pulled the shotgun close to his body and covered his head with his other arm. When he thought it was safe to look up again, he discovered that his face was fifteen inches from the onyx eyes of a pissed-off snake.

Purdy's tie was tucked into his trousers and his shield wallet hung open on his overtaxed belt. He had the end of the earpiece of a pair of cheap reading glasses stuck between his teeth while he was leaning over and staring at the red Vespa as though he were deciding how best to cook it.

Kelda had never actually met Sam Purdy, but she intuitively picked him out of the cluster of people at the scene. She flashed her FBI identification to a patrol officer so that he would let her get close enough to Purdy to say, "Detective Purdy? I'm Special Agent Kelda James."

He turned his head to look at her. At seeing how pretty she was in person, he mumbled, "Figures."

"Excuse me?" she said.

He pulled the glasses from between his teeth. "Nothing. Nice to meet you. This look like the Vespa?"

"It does."

He turned his attention back to the red scooter. "Do you know these things don't even need real license plates? When they have these whiny little 50cc engines they're not even considered motorcycles. The state just gives them that little sticker right there." He pointed at the rear fender. "See it? That thing. A square inch, maybe. If you didn't know to look for it, you'd miss it for sure."

"Yes," she said. She was wondering what his act was all about and was not even considering the possibility that it wasn't an act. She was determined to remain his audience and not become his foil.

Purdy went on. "So, I was wondering, was your friend using the services of the . . . you know, county?" He tilted his head in the direction of the red brick building that housed the Boulder County Mental Health Center.

The sky to the west was dark gray and lightning was jumping off the high peaks between Boulder and the Divide. From Boulder and its vantage so close to the mountains, approaching thunderstorms sometimes appeared suddenly as the huge wave of an approaching airborne tsunami. This was one of those times. The blustery air out in front of the storm smelled of rain.

"Was Tom Clone a client of the Mental Health Center? Not that I know of."

"So why was he here?"

She made a perplexed face for his benefit but her concentration was focused on the puzzle of how Ira had managed to get Tom off the Vespa and into his Pathfinder. She guessed that Ira had used her as bait.

To Purdy, she said, "Clone was looking for work. Maybe he was here trying to get some kind of job. Have you talked to the people inside the building? He may have filled out an application."

Purdy smiled just enough to let her know that he'd recognized her joust. He tapped his watch. "It's a little late in the day, unfortunately. The Human Resources people are gone for the day. The staff people that are still in there after hours are the, um, clinical types." He tucked his lower lip so that it disappeared below his mustache. "You ever try to get help with an investigation from a shrink, Agent James? It's not pretty. It's just not pretty."

She noticed that he was managing to maintain the smile in his eyes.

"I take it that nobody saw Tom drive it here? And that nobody recognizes the Vespa as his?"

"That's right. Nobody but you."

A profound clap of thunder echoed off the mountains. Purdy didn't react to it, but he stepped around to the front end of the scooter and spread an open palm over the Vespa as though he were a magician who was about to levitate it one-handed. "Want to make a guess where this was seen last? I mean before today?"

She almost cursed aloud at his question and her best guess about the answer, but managed to say, "No. Why don't you just tell me where it was?" She knew he was going to tell her that it had been outside Dr. Gregory's office.

He did. "It was on Walnut Street. Just west of Ninth.

Do you know the neighborhood? It's mixed residential and offices. Nice, but a little too close to Canyon Boulevard for my taste."

Yes, Gregory's office. What was she supposed to say next? Her eyes jumped to a bolt of lightning that seemed to elevate from the hogbacks on the western edge of town. "I think it's finally going to rain," she said.

Purdy looked toward the mountains. His eyes registered surprise, as though he hadn't noticed the approaching thunderstorm before. He nodded and said, "Yep, it's that time of year. Monsoon season. So why do you think this Vespa was on Walnut Street?"

"How would I know?"

"Just thought you might."

"When was it seen there?" she asked. She didn't really think Purdy would answer her.

He did. "Day before yesterday."

"Who was driving it on Walnut Street?"

"Your friend."

Ah, she thought, *here it comes.* "Maybe he had business over there."

"Business? Like an appointment? That kind of business?"

"Sure. Like an appointment."

"Yeah, that's it. Maybe he was buying life insurance. Or setting up a blind trust with a tax attorney or something."

"Cut the crap, please, Detective. I don't know what Tom was doing over there. I don't keep his Day-Timer. I barely know him."

"Bullshit. You know him better than you're letting on. And you know exactly what he was doing there. But that's okay. Because I do, too—I know what he was do-ing there. I know all about his appointment on Walnut Street. I just wanted to see how we were doing on the honesty scale, here. You and me. Local cop and federal agent. *Mano a womano.*"

She was speechless.

Rain started pelting the ground. A patrol officer was standing ready to cover the Vespa with a tarp.

Purdy indicated the officer should go ahead and drape the scooter, then he wrinkled his nose and looked at Kelda. "Have you seen Clone or talked to Clone since he was last seen on this scooter the day before yesterday?"

"No, I haven't."

"In case you're wondering—on that honesty scale I was talking about, we're not doing too well," he said, while he rubbed his temples with his fingertips. "This is giving me a headache. You got any Tylenol or anything? I noticed you were limping."

To herself, she said, "Shit."

She hoped that her lips hadn't moved.

CHAPTER

48

Hoppy thought, *So that's what that sound is.*

The snake was coiled up on a rock for warmth, but its rattle had begun clattering and the snake had raised its head in ominous alert. To Hoppy the viper's eyes looked like charred grains of rice.

He was wondering if there were rules that prescribed what he was supposed to do in his current predicament.

Do I move or do I not move?

If I move, do I go fast or do I go slow?

Hoppy slid his finger onto the trigger of the shotgun. The plan he was formulating in his head was simple: Get to his feet as fast as he could and shoot the damn snake to smithereens with buckshot. He told himself he'd do it on the count of three. His eyes frozen on the snake, he silently counted, "One . . . two . . ."

The snake moved first. It was a quick little jerk of its head. Off to the right, maybe an inch. That was it.

Hoppy never got to "three." He didn't pop to his feet. Once his eyes registered the movement of the snake his finger squeezed the trigger on the shotgun.

The flash from the barrel was as bright as lightning and the roar many times louder than any thunder he'd ever heard. He was so startled by the noise and the light and what the recoil had done to his elbow and by the intense stinging he felt on his scalp that he momentarily forgot all about the snake.

Then, a second or two later, he remembered, and he scrambled backward and leaped to his feet. He managed to get the barrel of the gun aimed directly at the rock where the snake was coiled.

About eight inches of snake remained on the rock. The beady black eyes were gone but the rattle end was intact. Rain was pelting the bare stone.

Hoppy thought the rattle was silent but he couldn't be sure because he really couldn't hear a thing. His ears hadn't recovered from the decibel concussion of the shotgun blast. The sharp pain on top of his head had him truly concerned that the snake might have sunk his fangs into his flesh before the buckshot turned the reptile into ground chuck.

He called out, "Fred! Fred!" having temporarily forgotten about the man in the motorcycle helmet with the little balloons full of God-knows-what, not to mention that guy inside the fence with the speech impediment.

• • •

The rain, so intense for a few minutes, had eased to something that only a generous meteorologist would call a drizzle. A thin ribbon of dark blue and orange sky lit the tops of the Divide.

The only person that Fred Prehost could spot was his buddy, Hoppy, who was standing in a small clearing in the woods pointing his shotgun at a rock. Prehost couldn't see the guy in the motorcycle helmet, and he couldn't see the guy who was in the enclosure.

He still couldn't figure out who the hell Hoppy had decided needed shooting.

Prehost hissed, "Hoppy, get down! Hoppy! Get down!" But Hoppy wasn't responding.

Prehost crawled closer. From twenty feet away, he said, "Down! Get down! Jesus."

Nothing.

Prehost threw a small rock at his friend's feet. As the stone hit his boot, Hoppy spun with the shotgun ready. Prehost waved his hands and said, "It's me. It's me." But he was thinking, *Shit, he's going to shoot me*.

Finally, Hoppy recognized his friend and lowered the barrel of the gun. Fred made a dramatic motion with both hands, urging him to get down; Hoppy lowered himself to a crouch.

In a voice that was at least a couple of measures too loud, he declared, "I shot a snake."

"You what?"

Hoppy saw Fred's lips move but didn't hear him. He shook his head and said, "It was a rattlesnake."

"Up here? No way, buddy."

Hoppy pointed at his ear with his free hand and shook his head. He said, "I can't hear you. My ears."

From the direction of the enclosure, Prehost heard, " 'olice? Hel'! 'olice? Hel'! Hel'!"

Prehost held a hand up to Hoppy.

"Hel'! Hel'!"

Hoppy said, "I heard that."

Fred said, "Let's go. Careful. We don't know where the other guy is."

Hoppy said, "Okay." The two men made their way the last few yards through the woods.

Prehost said, "Cover me." When his friend didn't respond, he added, "You hear that?"

Hoppy nodded and raised his shotgun again. "I got you."

Prehost checked the woods in all directions before he approached the enclosure. He barely recognized the man inside the fence. "Clone? Is that you?"

"Yes! Yes!"

"Who did this? Who put you in here?"

"A guy. 'ear! 'ear! It's all a'out 'ear and so'e girl."

Prehost had no idea what Clone was talking about. He stepped closer to the pen. "What? There's no gate? Can you climb out? Do you think you can climb the fence?"

Tom yelped, "Don't touch the 'ence! Don't touch the 'ence! It's electric. You'll get a shock!"

"Oh," Prehost replied and withdrew his hand. He walked to the corner of the enclosure and examined the connection where the cable from the mineshaft was wired to the steel of the fence. He turned back to Hoppy. "We okay, here? You watching the woods?"

Hoppy gave him the thumbs-up. Prehost grabbed the orange cable with his left hand and with a single hard pull yanked it free of the fence. He raised the loose cable in the air and shook it. "It's not going to shock you anymore, Clone. Can you climb out now?"

"I think so."

"Then do it. Wait a second. First, where did he go? The helmet guy?"

Clone pointed back in the direction of the cabin. "That way. He ran down that way."

"You know who he is?"

He said, "No. No. I don't. I think I saw hi' yesterday in 'oulder, 'ut I don't re'e'er anything until I woke u' u' here."

"Why is he doing this?"

Tom said, " 'ear. It's all a'out 'ear. And so'e girl."

Prehost said, "Ears?"

Tom Clone groaned.

Hoppy stepped forward. "Fred, we should leave Clone here while we find the guy. He'll get in the way if he comes with us. He's safe inside there. We don't want to lose him."

Prehost said, "You're right." He turned to Tom. "Change of plans. I want you to stay here for a few minutes while we round that other guy up. I want to talk to him and find out what he knows about who killed the girl. We'll be back for you real soon."

Tom screamed, "No! No!"

Prehost lowered the orange power cable and touched the frayed end to the wiring that was still attached to the fence post. Fiery sparks lit the dusk as the electrical connection bridged the wires. "Yes, yes, I'm afraid," Prehost said. "I wouldn't touch that fence if I were you."

"No!"

"Don't worry, we'll be back. You sit tight." Prehost turned to Hoppy. "Are you getting your hearing back?"

"Little by little, Fred."

"What are those marks on your head?"

Hoppy's dirty fingertips grazed the skin near his hairline. "I'm thinking maybe he got me. The snake. How long will the poison take, Fred? Do you know how long it takes?"

"A rattlesnake, huh? You say you shot a rattlesnake?"

"I did. It's back there. I'll show you the rattles."

"No way, Hoppy. Not up here. I think you're seeing things. Those are blast burns on your head from the shotgun. It looks like you almost blew your own damn head off trying to kill that imaginary rattlesnake."

Fifty feet away Tom Clone listened to the whole exchange with his mouth hanging open in exasperation. Finally, his voice swollen with defeat, he interjected, " 'i'er . . . It was a 'i'er."

"Huh? Hyper?"

" 'i'er! 'lease don't 'orget a'out 'e. 'lease."

Prehost stopped and faced the man in the enclosure. "Forget about you, Tom? All I can say is watch what you wish for. Didn't your momma ever teach you that? Watch what you wish for."

CHAPTER

49

Lauren had the afternoon off from work at the district attorney's office. After the conclusion of Grace's afternoon nap, my two girls were planning on coming downtown to run some errands before we all met for dinner. The gray light streaming in my office windows and the sounds of distant crackling thunder indicated that a thunderhead seemed to be descending on Boulder from the mountains, so the plans were subject to change. I stepped into the backyard of the building through the French door on the south side of my office to get a closer look at the approaching storm. Although the eastern skies were cobalt, the western view was nothing but gray waves undulating above the inert mass of the mountains.

Something was blowing in off the Divide and it was blowing in fast.

I stepped back inside and phoned Lauren on her cell.

"Hi, sweetie," I said after she answered. "How are my girls?"

"We're good. It looks like we're finally going to get some rain. Did you see this storm?"

"I sure did. Where are you two?"

"Nordstrom. I'm waiting to pay for some things for Grace. Are you done already?"

Nordstrom meant Flatiron Crossing, a shopping mecca east of Boulder. The new mall made me crazy. When I got within a mile of it, my blood pressure went crazy, my pulse raced, and whatever patience I possessed evaporated. The allure of Nordstrom's baby department aside, shopping excursions to suburban malls were Lauren's exclusive domain, one that I always thought she embraced with a little too much enthusiasm.

I said, "Yeah, I am. My last patient canceled. You want to change plans and just have dinner at home? That way you and Grace don't have to drive all the way back into town in the weather."

"Will you cook?"

"Cook? I'll make sure there's food on the table. I'm thinking takeout."

"Can you kill fifteen or twenty minutes?" she asked. "Let's see how the storm develops. I think I'd still like to go out to dinner. So would Grace."

"You have enough energy?" My question was a small curtsy to Lauren's multiple sclerosis. An afternoon of shopping was often more than enough to do her in for the rest of the day.

"So far, so good."

"Then, sure, I can stay busy here for a little while.

Why don't you call me back when you decide what you want to do?"

"Grace says she loves you."

"Sure she does. Tell her I love her and her mother, too."

I busied myself with patient charts, making some fresh case notations in terms that were as obscure as I could manage, caught up on some filing that dated back months, and I waited for the phone to ring.

Diane poked her head in the doorway to say good night. I told her that I'd lock up the building.

After a half hour passed and the return call didn't come, I moved to the window. The storm was fierce overhead but clearing skies to the west told me that this wasn't the advance guard of the summer monsoons. It was a routine Rocky Mountain afternoon thunderstorm cell that would pass into the plains within minutes. Tomorrow the relentless summer heat would be back.

My pager vibrated on my hip. I pulled it from its holster and saw a number I didn't recognize.

I punched in the number I used to retrieve my voicemail. The most recent message played first.

A frantic voice spoke. "Dr. Gregory? This is To' Clone? Can you hel' 'e? 'lease? I was kidna'ed and 'ut inside a 'ence and so'eone is trying to kill 'e. 'ear lessons! 'ear lessons! Call 'e 'ack right away. Hurry, 'lease. I need hel'!" He left the same number that was on the screen of my pager.

"Tom?" I said aloud. "What the hell?"

The number that he'd left was busy. I waited for half a minute and tried again. Still busy. I paced the office for another thirty seconds, then tried one more time. The phone rang twice before someone answered.

"Tom?" I said.

A sonorous male voice, not Tom's, replied calmly, "Just a second. Your friend is right here. You hold on."

Tom answered by saying, "Dr. Gregory? Hel' 'e."

I was using my therapist's demeanor, but it felt an odd fit for the circumstances, given Tom's obvious alarm. "Sure, Tom. I'll do whatever I can to help you. Where are you right now?"

"In the 'ountains." Away from the phone, I heard him say, "Where a' I, 'oca?" A second later, he spoke to me again. "I' near Ward. It's in the 'ountains. You know where that is? Indian 'eaks."

"Yes," I said. "I know where Ward is. Do you need an ambulance? I can send an ambulance."

"No!"

"Then you need to call the police, Tom. They'll help you. Whatever trouble you're in, they'll help."

"No!" he barked. "No 'olice. I didn't do anything. Nothing. So'eone kidna'ed 'e to teach 'e 'ear lessons! You ha'e to co'e and get 'e, 'ut you can't call the 'olice! They're the ones trying to kill 'e. Will you co'e get 'e?"

He sounded as desperate as anyone I'd ever spoken with. "Yes, Tom. I'll come get you. Can someone there give me directions?"

"Yes. Here's 'oca."

"Oka? His name is Oka?"

"No! 'oca. Here he is."

The deep voice returned to the phone. "This is Boca. Your friend's a mess. It's pitiful. I'd hurry if I were you."

"What's wrong with his voice? Why can't he talk?"

"He's been stung all over his body by bees. His face, and inside his mouth. He smells like gasoline and he keeps talking about vipers and napalm and electric fences. And fear? He goes on and on about fear, and fear lessons. He looks like he's been through a damn war. I've been to one or two, so I know how people look after they've been in the shit."

Bees and snakes and napalm? I didn't know whether Tom needed a trauma surgeon or an IM injection of Haldol. "Are you in a position to drive him someplace?"

"My truck is in town being repaired. I hit an elk down near Allenspark. All I have is my mountain bike."

I suspected there was a story there. I didn't have time for it, though.

"How do I get to you?"

When he was done dictating directions, I repeated what I'd written down. He made one correction. I said, "Boca, could you ask Tom something for me?"

"Shoot."

"Ask him if he's ever been to Hawaii."

"What?"

"I know it sounds strange. Just please ask him if he's ever been to Hawaii."

I could hear Boca repeat my question to Tom and I could hear Tom say, "Wha'? No."

I said, "I heard him. Never?"

Boca said, "Never?"

Tom said, "Ne'er. I'e ne'er 'een to Hawaii."

Tom had no reason to lie. None. Given the stress he was under he couldn't possibly have guessed why I was asking the question. Even if he had, my clinical intuition was that he wouldn't be able to lie with such facility in those circumstances. I said, "Thanks, Boca."

Ten seconds after I hung up, while I was contemplating what it meant that Tom Clone had never flown across the Pacific to Hawaii, my private line rang. Lauren said, "It's me. Grace is cranky. We're going to head home after all. We'll see you there, okay? You'll pick something up for dinner?"

"Change of plans. I have an emergency brewing with one of my patients. It looks like I have to make a house call. Sorry."

"You're kidding?" She wasn't happy.

"I wish I was. It's up in the mountains. I could be late."

"A house call? Really? You make house calls?"

"In rare circumstances, I guess I do. Give Grace a kiss. I love you guys. I'll call when I know what's going on."

CHAPTER

50

Prehost and Hoppy were walking side by side down the trail that led back to the cabin. Prehost said, "I say he went to the car and when he discovered he couldn't drive it, he took off down that road on foot. He's probably trying to make it back to Ward so he can catch a ride out of here. Somebody in that crazy town will help him no matter what he's done."

Hoppy replied, "Sounds possible, Fred. But I think we should do a quick check on that boarded-up mine first. It would be his first place to hide. He may have thought we were right on his tail. Maybe he didn't try to make it all the way back to the car or the cabin. He probably thinks we don't know about the mine."

"Maybe."

"We have to be careful, though. He could have guns or God-knows-what stashed in there."

Prehost chuckled. "Or maybe another rattlesnake."

Hoppy didn't respond.

The rain had stopped and the night held a chill. Prehost said, "Bet the summers are even shorter up here than they are in Park County. Don't you think?"

"This doesn't feel like summer to me. What do you think, Fred? Should we check the mine?"

"Yeah, okay, we'll take a quick look at the mine."

"Yeah. A quick look."

Prehost said, "Who the hell is this Oliver guy? What the hell was he doing back there with that . . . that . . . thing where he had Clone? What was that, like a, I don't know, a corral? What was that?"

Hoppy answered just as they reached the clearing that led to the mine entrance. "Got me. More like a prison camp, I think. How you want to do this?"

"Can we pull that door off?"

Hoppy tugged lightly at it. "Yeah, it'll come right off. It's not bolted or anything like that. It's just there for soundproofing, I think."

"Well, let's do that, first." Prehost held up the flashlight so his friend could see better. "Then we'll see what we have inside there."

The door on the shaft entrance was just a sheet of plywood lined on both sides with rigid foam insulation. It wasn't even secured to the entrance; it just rested against the opening. Prehost tossed it aside by himself. The insistent throb of the generator seemed to roar from the cave.

Prehost peered into the opening. "He's not in there, Hoppy. Let's go."

"Damn it, Fred, we're here. Let me at least look. It'll just take a minute. Give me the flashlight."

Prehost handed the light to Hoppy, who lowered his head and stepped into the rough-framed opening that led to the mine. "Be quick, Hoppy. That mine has to be full of carbon monoxide from that generator. And he ain't in there. I'm damn near sure of it. We're losing time."

The darkness inside the mine swallowed Hoppy after three or four steps. Seconds later, Prehost couldn't even see the glow from the beam from his partner's flashlight. He cursed softly.

A minute or so later, he saw the flashlight beam reemerge from the darkness, and seconds later, he spotted Hoppy. He was breathing with his mouth open, like a dog on a hot day. He gasped for ten or fifteen seconds, unable to speak. Finally, he managed to say, "You gotta see this."

"He's in there?"

Hoppy nodded. He rested the shotgun across his knees and leaned over it, wheezing. "You gotta see it."

Prehost said, "I don't like caves and shit. How far in is it? Do I really have to go in there and see what you found?"

"It's no big deal getting in. Thirty feet in there's like a room. You can walk the whole way, just have to bend over. But you have to see what he had going, Fred. You have to."

"Did he shoot himself?"

Hoppy shrugged. "Couldn't tell."

"Blood?"

"It's a mess. But you have to see the setup. What he had planned inside that mine."

"Meth lab?"

"I don't know. Maybe you'll know what all that stuff is."

"Shit. Show me the way."

Hoppy leaned the shotgun against the mineshaft door, took a noisy breath of clean air, and stooped low to reenter the cave. Prehost was a step behind him. The smell of gasoline exhaust in the narrow tunnel was as thick as fog.

After eight or nine feet the shaft took a forty-five-degree turn to the right. The timbers that supported the tunnel were as rotten as tomatoes still on the vine after the first freeze. Prehost said, "I hate this shit, Hoppy."

"Not too much farther, Fred. The generator's in a little alcove right ahead. Five more feet. His body's right past it."

Sure enough, the generator was roaring exactly where Hoppy said it would be. He warned, "Stay on the right side for the next few feet. It's a low ceiling on the left."

Prehost said, "I really hate this shit, Hoppy." But he stayed right, just as he was told.

Seconds later, Hoppy turned and flashed the beam of the light above Prehost's head. "Okay, you can stand up now, Fred. There's headroom here."

Prehost felt queasy and a fierce headache was burning up the back of his neck. He figured he was already starting to suffer from the first signs of carbon monoxide poisoning. "Let's hurry, Hoppy. We're going to die in here. This is poison we're sucking."

Hoppy said, "You're half right. One of us is going to die in here. I'm real sorry, Fred."

Prehost said, "What?" just as he spotted the little pistol in his friend's left hand.

"If Oliver really knows who killed the girl, I just can't risk you ever finding out. I'm so sorry, Fred."

"Hoppy, what the hell—"

The little gun made a huge roar in the cave. Prehost took a hasty step back as though he'd concluded that the bullet from the gun was a punch he could absorb better from a distance. His brain registered the earth disappearing from beneath his back foot before it noted the slug that had pierced the firm flesh of his upper abdomen. His last words as he disappeared into the void of a deep vertical shaft were a surprised "Oh shit, Hoppy."

Hoppy watched Prehost disappear into the mineshaft and counted to two before he heard the dull punctuation of a thud.

He retraced his steps to the opening of the mine. Once outside, he stumbled forward into a somersault and came up gasping for air, tears in his eyes.

Aloud he said, "I'm so sorry, Fred."

After a minute he raised himself to his feet and looked down the trail toward the cabin. Then he looked in the other direction back toward the fenced pen that imprisoned Tom Clone. Hoppy wasn't sure which way to go. Finally, he said, "Oliver, I'll get you later. Hel-lo, Tom."

Hoppy took half a dozen steps toward the trail before he remembered the shotgun that he'd leaned next to the entrance to the mine.

He spun and returned to grab the gun. To his amazement, he saw that it was gone.

"Damn," he said. "Damn." He aimed the flashlight into the woods all around him but saw no one lurking. He carefully checked his service weapon and reloaded a round into the pistol from his ankle holster before he trotted down the trail to the enclosure.

He could tell before he'd even made it out of the woods that the fenced pen was empty.

Tom Clone was gone.

A closer examination revealed that the orange power cable was separated by almost a foot from the wiring that led to the fence post. Clone had somehow managed to sever the connection that Prehost had reset, and then he had scaled the fence to freedom.

Tom Clone was gone.

The shotgun was gone.

Oliver was gone.

Fred Prehost, Hoppy's only ally, was long gone.

Hoppy stepped back into the woods to reconsider his plan.

At least, he reassured himself, the damn rattlesnake was dead.

He allowed himself the comfort of that thought for a few seconds before he realized that he should have asked Fred Prehost for the keys to the Suburban before he sent him to the bottom of the mineshaft.

That was an oversight, for sure.

PART FOUR

A Step into Darkness

CHAPTER

51

The section of Boulder Canyon Road that is closest to town is a curvy two-lane wonder of engineering that hugs the irregular contour of Boulder Creek as the river carries snowmelt from the highest reaches of the Rockies down the Front Range toward the plains. Even within a few hundred yards of town, the deepest parts of the canyon are perpetually bathed in the shadows of imposing vertical rock walls. Depending on the season, the canyon draws hordes of hikers, bikers, picnickers, rock climbers, ice climbers, and sightseers from the city.

On a typical summer evening, the cars cruising Boulder Canyon Road are most likely to be driven by residents commuting home to the mountain towns up the hill, or gamblers heading farther south up to the high-country gaming meccas in Blackhawk and Central City.

As she climbed the unfamiliar road out of Boulder, Kelda was keenly monitoring the cars that lined up behind her, wary about being followed. The pavement was still wet from the thunderstorm, and she was driving cautiously, unsure of the handling of Maria Alija's car, and hoping her slow speed would bring any potential tails into sight of her rearview mirror. As she passed the Red Lion Inn she spotted two cars lined up behind her: a big SUV with headlights as bright as lasers and, behind it, a four-door sedan. She guessed it was a Mitsubishi something, but she wasn't really sure.

She counted a single passenger in the SUV, and no passengers in the sedan. Within minutes a third car—she thought it was a Lexus sports car—joined the parade up the hill. Kelda kept her pace moderate—fast enough to get her to the top of the canyon as soon as possible, slow enough to keep the traffic lining up behind her. The Lexus driver wasn't satisfied with Kelda's pace, however; she blew past all three vehicles in front of her on a straightaway so short that the double yellow line never broke into dashes.

Twenty uneventful minutes later, after completing a climb to eight thousand feet above sea level, Kelda approached Barker Reservoir near Nederland, the funky little town that guards the top of Boulder Canyon. A third and fourth car had joined the uphill procession, but darkness kept Kelda from identifying makes or models. She assumed that the lights of Nederland would allow her to gather all the information she needed to know about the cars behind her.

The big SUV that had been tailgating her since

Boulder pulled into the parking lot of a restaurant in Nederland. Moments later, both of the unidentified cars at the rear of the pack headed south on Highway 72. Only the sedan that Kelda thought was a Mitsubishi stayed with her after she turned north toward the town of Ward. The car kept a steady position about a hundred yards behind her. If this was a tail, she decided, whoever was doing it should be involuntarily retired from law enforcement.

She was thinking it was Bill Graves. And she was thinking that he wanted her to know he was there.

Little traffic impeded her progress toward Ward. Nighttime traffic north of Nederland on 72 is typically light. But then, so is daytime traffic. She fumbled to review the map on the seat beside her and almost missed her turn onto Chief Street, finally braking hard to manage the left-hand turn that seemed to lead directly into the wilderness between Ward and the Continental Divide.

She thought there was a fifty-fifty chance that the sedan would stay right behind her.

It did.

Kelda said, "Damn you, Bill. This is none of your business."

As she cleared a bend and was temporarily invisible to the driver of the sedan, she floored Maria's car and sped through a second turn and a third, finally putting the car into a skid that left it sideways across the narrow lane. She hopped out of the car and ran, crouching in a ditch at the side of the road, most of her body shielded by a big boulder. Her Sig Sauer was in her hand, light as a feather.

What if it isn't Bill?

Seconds later a different car—not the sedan that had been following her—skidded to a stop. The driver stepped into the darkness. It was a man in gray pants. He hesitated, apparently befuddled at the sight of the empty car with the open driver's door blocking the road in front of him.

Kelda couldn't identify the man in the darkness. Everything about his silhouette said Bill Graves, with one exception: The man's left hand was empty. Bill Graves would never walk into an obvious ambush without his weapon.

Unless, she scolded herself, he knew that it was Kelda who had set the trap. Which, if he was following her, he did know.

She pulled herself from the drainage ditch and crept behind the man as he slowly approached Maria's car. Three feet from his back she hissed, "On your knees."

The man dropped to his knees as though he were a Catholic who'd just recognized he was standing in front of the Pope.

"Now lie down, on your face. Leave your hands where I can see them," she ordered.

He did.

She saw the red cast and said, "Oh no."

Alan Gregory said, "God, I hoped it was you. Can I get up now?"

After leaving Sam Purdy and the red Vespa at the Boulder County Mental Health Center, Kelda had stopped at the Ideal Market on North Broadway to get something to eat while she pondered what "something else" she was going to do next. She sipped at a bottle of iced green tea and took tasteless bites of a turkey sandwich on wheat while sitting in Maria Alija's car in the grocery store lot. The car was facing south and the sky above the Flatirons was dark but clear. The brief storm was history.

Her phone chirped in her shoulder bag.

The number she saw on the tiny screen shocked her. Just in case someone else was using his phone, she answered, "Kelda James."

His voice a tense whisper, Ira said, "It's me, babe. I think I've really screwed things up. Some guys showed up with guns and shit and I had to run, and I think he got out. Got away."

"Who? Who got out?"

"You know. The guy. Our ten-minutes guy. He got out."

"Out of . . . the room?"

"Yes. Out of the room. Things are a mess and I need your help, Kelda. I really need your help."

"What do you need?" She felt surprisingly calm. Her heart was lingering on the fact that both Ira and Tom Clone were alive.

"Come get me," Ira pleaded.

"Where are you?"

"Up near Ward, on the Peak to Peak. I have a cabin up there I never told you about."

"That's the room where you were . . ." She swallowed. "You know . . . alone with him?"

"Yes. That's the room. It's close to the room. The room is actually outside. It's complicated, Kelda."

"But you're at your cabin?"

"No, no. I'm in the woods. I'm afraid they're watching the cabin. I'm sure they're watching the cabin. They disabled my car."

"Who were the two guys with the guns?"

"I don't know. They just showed up behind me and a minute later one of them started shooting."

"Did they see you?"

"Not my face. But they saw my cabin, and my car."

"And the car?"

"Dead."

"The . . . guy? He got away?"

"I'm pretty sure he did. Either that or the other two

guys who showed up have him. That's possible. I don't know."

"Does the guy know who you are?"

"No. I've been careful."

Yeah, right, she thought. "What do they look like? The two guys with the guns?"

"I barely saw them. It was getting dark and it was raining. Everything happened real fast. White guys. Not young."

"Cops?"

"I don't know. Maybe."

"Did they identify themselves as police officers, Ira?"

Kelda noted hesitation before he said, "No."

"No?"

"No."

She immediately reasoned that if the two guys were cops, Ira wouldn't tell her. He'd be worried that she would be even more reluctant to get further involved in his predicament.

"Ira, tell me something. Did you have anything to do with what happened to . . . the guy's grandfather?"

She felt Ira's second hesitation like a flash of agony up her legs.

"He walked in on me. I didn't mean to . . ."

"Ira, tell me how to find you."

"I didn't want to hurt the old guy. You believe me?"

"Tell me how to find you."

"Do you know how to get to Brainard Lake? It's in the Indian Peaks above the Peak to Peak."

"I've been there once, I think. Camping."

"Well, you have to get to Ward, first. Then here's

what I need you to do." He gave her directions and concluded with "You have your gun?"

"You know I do. Ira, you need to do something for me, too."

"Anything."

"While I'm on my way up there, you need to figure out what comes next, okay? I don't know what you've done. So, you need to decide the next step."

"I can do that. You know I can. I love you, babe."

She folded the phone and pulled out her *Pierson Guides* atlas. A quick glance at the map told her she could take either Left Hand Canyon or Boulder Canyon up the mountains to Ward. Left Hand was more direct and probably had less traffic. But she knew the Boulder Canyon road.

Kelda had never taken the road up Left Hand and she didn't trust Maria's car, so she pulled left on Broadway in the direction of Canyon Boulevard and the entrance to Boulder Canyon.

She was stopped at a red light at Pine Street when her phone rang a second time. She figured it was Ira calling again and answered without checking the ID screen.

A frantic voice said, "Kelda, it's 'e! To'. Hel' 'e! 'lease hel' 'e! Can you hel' 'e?"

After I confessed to Lauren that I was making a
house call, I fumbled with my files, dropped my car
keys, and then momentarily couldn't find my cell phone
in the clutter on my desk. The cherry red cast on my arm
seemed to be mocking me, and I dreaded the prospect of
trying to drive the curves of Boulder Canyon with one
hand. *Two hands and my new Mini—sure.* The prospect
brought a smile. Briefly.

It's only a block from my office on Walnut Street to
Canyon Boulevard. Nine blocks past downtown the
boulevard narrows to two lanes and quickly begins to
adopt the contour of the curvy, steep mountain passage
that is Boulder Canyon. Just before I reached the mouth
of the canyon, I reconsidered my impulsive plan. I turned
off onto Pearl Street so I could make a phone call. In
the best of circumstances, I'm not the most coordinated

human being in the Western Hemisphere. With the cast on my arm, the odds of my successfully juggling a cell phone while driving with my knees through Boulder Canyon were on the low side. Anyway, the cell reception in the confines of the canyon was miserable.

"Diane," I said after the call clicked through. "It's Alan." Diane Estevez wasn't just a wonderful friend and a good business partner. She was a heck of a clinical psychologist. I valued her counsel.

"You're breaking up," she whined.

On the negative side, she wasn't always the most patient person I knew.

"I'm not surprised. I'm up at Eben Fine Park. I need some advice."

"Sure, here's some advice: Don't try to make cell phone calls from mountain canyons. It doesn't work."

"Thanks. This is serious, okay? I need some consultation from you. You have a second?"

"I'm busy trying to decide what kind of takeout I want Raoul to pick up for dinner. What's up?"

"A patient just called me and said that he's been hurt by . . . some people . . . you know, injured—that kind of hurt—and he says that he's still in danger from them and he wants me to come get him. He's up in the mountains, way up in the mountains, like near Ward. A guy who's helping him confirms that he's in bad shape. The thing is that my patient's telling me that some of the people who are after him are the police, so I can't call the cops for help."

"How the hell do you get in situations like this, Alan? I swear, I don't know anyone else—"

"Diane, that's not helpful. Please be helpful. I know you have it in you."

"Is he paranoid?"

"Fearful. Let's say fearful. But he has some reasons to be fearful. His circumstances are very unusual."

"Psychological reasons? Or practical reasons?"

"Both."

She made an I-don't-believe-what-I'm-hearing kind of noise before she asked, "Does he have any reason to try to get you mixed up in something crazy? Think about this one before you answer."

I hesitated. "Kind of."

I could hear her mumble, "Shit." After an audible exhale she asked, "Is he in imminent danger?"

"All the evidence I have says yes, he probably is."

"Why can't this guy who's helping him take him someplace safe?"

"He doesn't have a car."

"You want advice? Here's advice: Call the police. Don't go up there. Don't do it, Alan. The presence of imminent danger gives you the freedom to do what you need to do regarding confidentiality."

"That's what I thought you'd say."

"You're not going to listen to me, are you? You have a baby, Alan. Alan! Don't even—"

"I'm thinking."

"You're breaking up on me. Don't go. I swear I'll—"

A burned-out therapist, one who didn't care, would have eagerly heeded Diane's caution.

I didn't want to be that therapist, the one who didn't care.

Each recent morning as I climbed out of bed, I'd been more and more terrified of being that therapist.

The connection to Diane was crappy, but not so crappy that I couldn't have continued the conversation.

I closed the phone anyway. Seconds later, I reopened it and speed-dialed Sam Purdy at home.

His wife heard something in my tone and handed the phone immediately to Sam.

"Yeah," he said.

"I found Tom Clone, Sam. Or he found me."

His voice flat as a good pool table, he replied, "Cool. The good news is that you win the scavenger hunt; the bad news is that the prize fund is empty. Why are you calling me? You want to gloat? You know you're not going to tell me where Clone is. But do tell him this for me when you see him, would you? If he wants his little motorbike back, he's probably going to have to come down and fill out some paperwork. Tell him it should take about a week."

"Sam, I'm calling because I need your help with something . . . goofy." "Goofy" was Sam's Minnesota word. It seemed apropos to the current situation.

It took me a couple of minutes to explain about Tom Clone's phone call from Boca's cabin. Sam was especially interested in the part about the fear lessons and the bees and the snakes and the napalm. He asked quite a few questions that I couldn't answer to his satisfaction.

One of them was "And he's absolutely sure cops are involved in this torture?"

"He says he's sure that the two guys who showed up at the end identified themselves as police."

"What do you think?"

Sam, I knew, was asking me about the quality of Tom's thinking. "Some Park County cops have been hounding him since he got out of prison, Sam. You know, over the Campbell murder."

"Why don't I know about this?"

"Clone didn't report it to anyone. Considering the circumstances, he didn't think anybody would believe him. He was really trying to keep a low profile with law enforcement."

"He reported it to you, though, right?"

"Yes."

"And in your wisdom, you decided to keep it to yourself?"

"Sam, please."

"Do you believe Clone? Come on. I need something to work with. You're serving me nothing here."

"Some of what he said, yes, I believe him."

"And this guy he's with right now in Ward? He sounded legit?"

"Yeah. He was coherent, well spoken. He implied that he had been in the military. I'd say he's reliable. He said that it looked to him like Tom had been worked over by someone or something."

"Yeah?"

"Clone's apparently covered with bee stings and smells like gasoline. I can tell you from my brief conversation with him that he can barely talk. He apparently has bee stings on his lips and inside his mouth."

"Shit. You said he's in Ward, right? You ever been to Ward, Alan? It's like a rest stop on a road trip to Mars."

"Yeah, I've been to Ward. Last time I was there, I actually found it kind of charming."

"You wouldn't find it charming if you were a cop," he scoffed. "Where are you right now?"

"Eben Fine Park. Apparently I'm about to make a rest stop on a road trip to Mars."

"And you're going to take Boulder Canyon?"

"I was."

"Don't be a fool. Take Lee Hill to Left Hand. Less aggravation, less traffic. Save you ten minutes, easy."

"I'm already at the mouth of Boulder Canyon, Sam."

"I don't care. You'll be behind all the commuters in Boulder Canyon. With your luck you'll get stuck behind a propane truck, or even worse a septic truck, the entire way up the hill. You don't want that. I know; I've done it. Cut across town on Ninth. You'll be glad you did."

"I'll think about it."

"You want me to come with, don't you?" Sam asked me. It wasn't really a question, more like an accusation.

"Yes. I'd be grateful."

"Ward's out of my jurisdiction, Alan. Way out of my jurisdiction. I can't just sit tall in the saddle and ride right into town with my six-guns blazing."

I had no time to savor the image Sam was painting for me. "Just call the sheriff and tell him that you're following a lead in the assault on Clone's grandfather. He'll give you permission to talk to anybody you want in Ward and you know it. He probably won't even insist on sending a deputy along to babysit you."

He harrumphed.

"The best part is that it's not even a lie."

"If your wife wasn't an assistant DA, you wouldn't know any of this, would you? You're not that smart, you know."

He was begging for a wise-ass retort. I declined.

Sam said, "I need ten minutes here. I want to lay my eyes on my kid and he's not home from his baseball game yet, but he's due back soon. I'll pick you up in what, fifteen minutes, maybe twenty. Or even better, you can just stop here on your way to Lee Hill. You'll come right by me."

I couldn't shake the intensity of Tom Clone's desperation from my imagination. "I'm going to head up there now, Sam. I'll meet you in Ward. That'll give me a few minutes to prepare Tom for your arrival. You got something to write with? I want to give you the directions to Boca's cabin."

"The guy's name is Boca? What kind of name is that? What's his last name?"

"You want to run his name, don't you?"

"Of course I do. I run just about everybody's name. It's a hobby of mine."

"I don't have his last name, just Boca. He lives in Ward, Sam, remember."

"Right, I forgot. I should just go to NCIC and run 'Boca in Ward.' That should work real well. What is 'Boca'? What kind of name is that?"

"I don't know. I think it's Spanish for 'mouth.'"

"Mouth? Who calls themselves Mouth?"

"Sam, you want the directions?"

"Listen, I won't be long here," Sam said when I'd given him the route to Boca's cabin. "Simon's due home any minute from his baseball game. I'd rather you wait for me or come by here and get me. You know if you go up there by yourself, you're going to—"

"I'm going to what, Sam?"

"You know, Alan."

"What?"

"You're going to get in trouble. People will get shot. Bombs will go off. Plagues will start. Something. It's a karma thing with you."

I couldn't argue with him. My track record where

mayhem was concerned wasn't exemplary. "To be honest, Sam, I'd rather not go at all, but I think I have to. It's the right thing to do. I'll see you in Ward."

"I didn't think you'd wait for me."

"You're a good man for doing this, Sam Purdy."

"No," he said. "What I am is a moron."

I took Sam's advice and backtracked across town on Ninth Street, passing within a couple of blocks of Sam's house. I was tempted to stop, but I didn't.

As he predicted, there was almost no traffic as I climbed on Lee Hill Road. Thirty minutes and three thousand plus feet of altitude later, Kelda James ordered me to my knees.

CHAPTER

After she lowered her gun and permitted me to get up from the ground, I followed Kelda's car as she drove the final few minutes to Boca's cabin, which was near Left Hand Creek down an unmarked dirt lane off the main road to Brainard Lake.

Neither Kelda nor I was driving a vehicle suitable for maneuvering up the steep, rutted, rock-pitted passage that Boca probably called his "driveway," so we parked at the bottom and hiked the last fifty yards or so up to the cabin. Although the trees at this altitude tended to be stunted by the arid, harsh climate, the pine forest was surprisingly thick, the sky was frosted with stars, and the air was so clean it tingled. I thought, *This must be why people live up here.* As we neared the front door of the neat frame cabin, my lungs were aching from the brief climb, as though my body was intent on reminding me that the difference between the east and west boundaries of Boulder County was, vertically at least, over a half a mile.

Kelda wasn't as winded as I was. But I thought she was limping. Between gasping inhalations I asked, "How are your legs?"

She shook her head, opened her mouth to speak, and then allowed her lips to close back together. After a quick breath, she said, "My legs hurt. It doesn't mean I'm going to sit down. It doesn't mean I'm going to go home. They hurt. They usually hurt. Let's go get Tom."

"Okay," I said, digesting her animosity. I was closest to the cabin, so I pounded on the door with the side of my fist.

A stunningly handsome black man answered the door. His upper cheeks were peppered with faint freckles, and his dark eyes expressed an inner warmth that seemed to surround him with a glow. He held out his hand and said, "Hello, I'm Boca. Won't you please come in? You must be the doctor." He looked past me out the door. "And you must be the FBI agent. Tom told me about both of you."

Kelda said, "Nice to meet you." Something about him—his beauty? his eyes? his manner?—had softened her like room temperature softens butter.

I added, "It's a pleasure. We're very grateful for all you've done to help Tom." I took the man's right hand with my left. He glanced briefly at my cast. My breathing was almost back to normal.

"I didn't do anything but offer a man in need some courtesy. May I see some identification from the two of you? Please don't be offended."

Kelda's FBI badge was a better statement than my driver's license, but both sufficed. Boca required reading glasses to check the fine print. The glasses were hung on a chain around his thick neck. After he was satisfied with our ID, he said, "Thank you. But I'm afraid Tom's gone."

It was Kelda who said, "What?" It was part exclamation, part resignation. She hadn't expected this part of her evening to go smoothly.

Boca fingered the graying hair on the side of his head and spent a moment examining Kelda and me as though he was trying to decide whether he could really trust us. Although he'd invited us into his cabin, he hadn't removed his significant mass from the doorway. "A man came to my door about five minutes ago. When I stepped outside to speak with the gentleman, Tom decided it was a good idea to go out the back window."

"Did the man introduce himself?"

"No, he did not."

"Tell me about him, please. Everything you remember." Kelda did the talking.

When Boca responded, each word was measured and intonated gorgeously, as though he'd memorized lines. "He was a thin man with new blue jeans and a plain gray sweatshirt. He was quite dirty." He paused. "And he had frog eyes."

"Frog eyes?"

"They stuck out, bulged. The way frogs' eyes do. And, oh yes"—with the "oh yes" his voice moved momentarily from tenor to baritone—"he had powder burns on his head."

Kelda's head tilted a fraction of an inch before she

asked, "Where exactly?" I couldn't understand why the precise location was important.

Boca spread his big hand a few inches into the hair-line above his forehead and dragged his fingers over his temple and right ear. "This area, ma'am."

"Why do you think they were powder burns?" she pressed.

"Because they were. And because I could still smell it on him. The residue from the gunpowder. I have a nose for it."

Kelda said, "Can you describe him? The man at the door? Was he a strong man? With biceps like . . . like that firewood there?" She pointed at the trim pile of as-pen logs stacked a few feet from the cabin. Each white-barked log was six to eight inches in diameter.

"No. He was not a strong man. Quite the opposite."

"Was he tall? Thin?"

"Yes, but not as tall as the doctor." He nodded slightly in my direction.

"His hair? Long, short? What?"

"Short. Combed over."

I was acutely aware that Kelda was asking questions that indicated that she had suspects in mind. How was that possible? What had Tom told her during their con-versation that he hadn't told me?

"Did he introduce himself?" Kelda asked Boca.

"No. He merely said he was lost and he asked to use my telephone. He was trying to look past me into the cabin."

"Was he armed?"

Boca reached behind him and removed something from the back pocket of his trousers. He held it flat across his palm. His hand was so large that the gun in it looked like a toy. "He was carrying this on his ankle. It made me uncomfortable, so I removed it from him."

Kelda said, "You took it from him? Just like that?"

"I know some martial arts, ma'am. What I did was, I encouraged him to lose his balance. From that point on, the removal of the weapon was not particularly difficult. As I said, he was not a strong man."

"May I take the gun from you? Do you mind?"

"I wish you would."

She lifted the gun from his hand, checked to see that it was loaded, and placed it in her shoulder bag.

"Where is this man now?"

"After I removed his weapon, he wriggled away from me and ran back into the woods. I suspect that he never really wished to use my phone."

"What about Tom? Was he armed?"

Boca stared hard at her before he answered, as though he was looking for something specific in her eyes. Some assurance. Something. Finally, he said, "He has a shotgun with him, ma'am."

"Boca?" I asked. "We'd like to know everything Tom said to you. Will you spend a few minutes going over that?"

Kelda said, "I've got to find Tom. I can't be late for this." She faced Boca. "I'm in a borrowed car and I don't have my equipment. Do you have a flashlight I could borrow?"

I wanted to ask what she meant by that, what she meant when she said she couldn't be late.

But Boca said, "Yes, ma'am." And Kelda took the flashlight and went silently into the night.

• • •

Before Kelda disappeared into the woods behind the cabin, she called back at me, admonishing me not to call anyone for help.

When I opened my mouth to argue with her, she said, "There are things going on that you don't know anything about."

The understatement almost made me laugh.

Boca's home was a single room. An alcove on the far side functioned as a bathroom; an expensive-looking high-tech toilet was visible through a hanging curtain. The entire wall adjacent to the entry door was covered with books. Mostly paperbacks. Not one appeared unread. A lamp by the bed was the sole illumination in the space.

Boca took a minute to tend a fire in a stove in the corner before he said, "Please have a seat."

I took a chair at an oak table. Boca sat on the edge of his bed. The bed was neatly made. I don't know why I found that odd, but I did. If I lived halfway to heaven all by myself, I didn't think I'd make my bed.

I think he saw me looking at the lamp by the bed. "I have solar panels on the roof. And I have a gasoline generator for backup electricity. I read a lot. I listen to jazz. Besides that, I have little use for power. There is ample wood for heat."

"It's beautiful up here," I said.

"Yes," Boca said. "You broke your arm?"

"I tripped over my dog. I can be a klutz."

His eyes softened. "You're a psychologist, right? That's what Tom said."

"Yes, sir, I am. I'm a clinical psychologist."

He leaned forward and rested his elbows on his

knees. "Is Tom . . . you know, unbalanced? Is that why he's—"

I didn't want him to ask me something I couldn't reveal about Tom. Before he could finish his thought, I interrupted and said, "Tom told you . . . what he's been through?"

"Kind of. I knew some things already. I read newspapers when I'm in town. He told me some other things."

"Well, he's been through a lot. And when you've been through the kind of trauma that he's been through, well, it tends to take its toll on people."

My words seemed to strike my host almost like a physical blow. After he regained his composure he slowly rolled up the sleeves on his shirt. First the left, then the right. As the cuff of his right sleeve reached his elbow, I saw a tattoo that he'd uncovered on his dark skin. The art was simple. In inch-tall black letters it read "IX-XI." From the bottom of each Roman numeral flowed a bright red tear.

A focused pressure formed in my chest, as though a dense weight were tugging on my heart. I swallowed and nodded once, my eyes glued to the rippling forearm of this dignified man who, without saying a thing, had just whispered volumes about a chapter in the life he'd lived.

I said, "You're new in Colorado, Boca?"

He almost smiled as he said, "Yes. Yes, sir, I am. Less than a year. I once lived in . . . on the East Coast."

I recalled his story about disarming the man at the door and guessed, "Policeman?"

He shook his head.

"Firefighter?"

He nodded.

I thought, *Oh my God*.

Boca didn't travel two-thirds of the way across the country to live by himself nearly nine thousand feet above sea level so that a stranger could pepper him with questions about the reason for his exile. That's what I told myself, anyway. Call it intuition.

I said, "Tom's not crazy, Boca. He's trying to adjust to some monumental events. I imagine after what he's been through the past few days that he'll have some more adjusting to do."

Boca shifted his weight back, resting his hands on the mattress. "You're not sure about him, though, are you?"

"I don't know exactly what you're asking." I knew what he was asking. I just didn't want him to be asking it.

Boca didn't deign to dance with me. I was getting the impression that if he ever knew the steps to the prevarication dance, he'd forgotten them before the dust settled in September 2001. He said, "You're not convinced that he didn't kill that girl. That's what you're not sure about."

I wanted to ask, *Which girl is that? The one in Park County or the one in Maui that her friend calls Jones?* But I didn't. I still knew the steps to the prevarication dance. I knew them well. So I danced with him. "I can't talk about that, I'm sorry. Confidentiality. I'm sure you understand."

But Boca's suspicion was right. Despite his assertion that he'd never been to Hawaii, I wasn't at all sure about Tom Clone. Kelda's disclosures that afternoon about Jones's journal and her fears about Tom Clone had haunted me since I'd heard them. Sam Purdy's suspicions had aggravated my own. My doubts about Tom, which had germinated shortly after I'd first met him, had spent the past few hours growing with the alacrity of Jack's beanstalk.

"With all due respect, Doctor, Tom needs your help. Your own doubts aside."

"I know he does." I did know that Tom needed my help. In my heart, though, I wasn't certain that the sentiment I expressed to Boca was as sincere as my words.

Boca said, "People . . . sometimes have to do things even when they're not sure. For the sake of humanity, sometimes we must reach out a hand. Sometimes we all must step into the darkness. The step may lead nowhere, but sometimes we all must take it."

My breathing stopped. "Thank you," I said.

"Yes," he replied.

He scratched absently at his forearm.

I considered the possibility that Boca was inviting me to comment further on his tattoo, and maybe, maybe, to hear about one time that he'd reached out a hand and stepped into the darkness, but I decided that in the absence of a more direct summons from him, the best thing I could do was to move on.

Some distant thunder echoed through the Indian Peaks.

I said, "We get monsoons each summer. Did you know that? Sometimes people who are new to Colorado don't know about the monsoons."

He raised his eyebrows. "Monsoons? Like in India? It rains all the time, that kind of monsoon?"

"Not all the time, but it rains. Every July the storms come up from the Gulf of Mexico and the Gulf of

California. I thought for a while that the storm that passed through here earlier this evening was the start of the monsoons. It's been dry on the Front Range so far this summer."

"Monsoons?" he mused. "Everybody's been warning me about winter. I didn't know about the monsoons."

"You don't have to worry about the monsoons unless you're a farmer. Too few are bad. Too many are bad. Hail is bad. The lightning can be a problem up here. But for most of us they come and they go. They're just summer storms. They just . . . are."

He was staring into the blackness beyond his window as though he half expected to see the monsoons coming over the Divide right that minute.

"So do you have neighbors up here, Boca?"

He looked at me with some suspicion. I thought he was puzzled by my small talk.

"The closest cabin is almost a half mile away. A guy comes up on weekends and works on it. Other than that, his cabin's empty. Next closest neighbor is a quarter mile past him." He smiled. "May I offer you some tea? It will just take a moment. The stove's hot."

"No, thank you. Do you know the guy who's fixing up the cabin?"

"No, sir, I do not. He's a young man who drives a green SUV that he washes frequently. People in town tell me that his name is Oliver. He and I have not spoken. Not once."

"Did Tom say anything else while you were waiting for us to get up here? Anything that would help us understand what we should do next?"

"The older I get, the fewer truths I know. But one truth I know well is the face of fear. When he walked in my door, Tom had that face." Boca's voice moved again from tenor to baritone. "His eyes were hooded with dread. His words sang the song of disbelief. His spirit sagged under the burden of despair."

He was reciting something, I thought. Some stanzas from some anthem he'd read or written once after a personal sojourn in hell. I thought I knew the hell. At least I knew it the way I knew about things like Tora Bora and the Gaza Strip.

I'd seen it on television.

When he went on, it was as though he could hear my thoughts. "Tom was a man who'd walked halfway to hell and he wasn't sure yet whether or not he was going to make it back out."

"That bad?"

"He kept saying that he spent the last few days getting fear lessons."

"Fear lessons?"

"Yes, sir. Have you had fear lessons yet in this life? Tom had his lessons right on this mountain. I could see it in his face. And the good Lord knows I've had mine."

"I don't know . . . what you mean."

"You will. When the time for your fear lesson comes, you'll know it."

A sharp *craaaack* punctured the night.

I jumped. Boca didn't. But his eyes filled with tears. He said, "I'm afraid that was a gunshot."

"Shotgun?" I asked.

"I'd say a handgun."

He stood and walked to the corner of the large room.

I noted that he was as far as possible from the door.

I said, "I'm going to go check on Kelda and Tom."

"If you don't mind, I'm going to stay here." He reached into a drawer and pulled something out. A whistle. He handed it to me. "Blow that once or twice and I'll call nine-one-one. I'm sorry but it's the best I can do."

He'd said, *"When the time for your fear lesson comes, you'll know it."*

As I closed the door behind me, I had an inkling.

55

The thunderstorm that passed earlier in the evening had temporarily transformed the mountain air from arid to almost humid. I felt a chill as I stepped away from Boca's cabin.

I allowed my eyes a moment to adjust to the blackness and my ears to adjust to the silence. Since the shot had fractured my illusion of safety, I hadn't heard another sound from outside. Not a call for help, not a whelp of pain, not labored breath, or careless footsteps.

I could hear my own heart beating. I could also hear Diane's admonition: *"You have a baby, Alan. Don't go!"*

The alternative? Not going.

Not going meant allowing my two patients—Kelda and Tom—to survive this puzzle on their own. My job, I reminded myself, was to help them survive *after* they'd survived this trial. Or the next trial. Or the one after that.

What had Diane said? The goal isn't to help patients get better, but rather to help them get better equipped. How did this fit?

I didn't know.

I was tempted to go back to my car and wait for Sam Purdy to arrive. I fingered the whistle. A single blow and a fraction of an hour later some fine deputies of the Boulder County Sheriff's Office would descend on these woods.

But Tom Clone didn't trust them.

And Kelda James had been clear that she didn't want them around.

Who did I trust?

Not Tom, not Kelda. My gut said I could rely on Boca. But if push came to shove—and push was perilously close to coming to shove—I was planning to trust the Boulder County Sheriff.

I clambered down the steep driveway and listened some more for some indication of where anybody might be.

The roar of a second gunshot splintered the night. Almost simultaneously, I thought I heard the distinctive ping of a slug impacting rock. My breath snagged in my chest.

Fear lesson, I thought. *Is this my time?*

It was. Boca was right. I knew.

Without another moment of hesitation I raised the whistle to my lips. I blew.

The second I stopped, a tattered voice called out, "Who's there?"

Tom Clone was still alive.

Wishing I had Boca on my flank, I moved in the direction of his voice.

It was my step into the darkness.

56

The burning in Kelda's lower legs was so intense that she could no longer tell if the sensation was one of searing heat or freezing cold, and the bones in her legs felt as though someone had been pinging them with a ball-peen hammer. The two Percocet she'd swallowed on the way up Boulder Canyon had had about as much impact on her pain as a couple of M&M's.

She was trying to maneuver down the dirt road near Left Hand Creek without using the flashlight that Boca had given her. She stopped every few steps to listen for a sound to guide her.

She desperately wanted to escape the darkness, to flick on the flashlight, but she knew that the beam of precious light would act as a magnet for the black hole at the end of the barrel of every gun in the forest. She attempted to quell her fears by trying to decide whom she hoped to find first.

Tom? She absolutely had to find Tom, but she was worried about what he knew. What had he figured out on his own? What had Ira told him?

Ira? Oh, Ira. Baby. What would she do when she found Ira? Even the brief conversation with Boca left her concerned that Ira hadn't covered his trail well. The trail to Ira would lead back to her.

That trail would destroy her.

And the guy who'd come to the door of Boca's cabin? She thought he was one of the Park County cops who had tried to roust Tom and her on their way from the penitentiary. But where was the other one? The one with the big arms and the attitude? Prehost? Where was Prehost?

Kelda figured that when she stumbled on one of the cops, she'd find the other. Despite the fact that Boca had managed to get the backup gun from one of them, she figured they were still pretty well armed.

The first sound that alerted her was the snap of a twig. She flattened herself into a ditch by the dirt path.

Deer? Bear? Lion?

She wished. She knew she wasn't that lucky.

The second sound was a man groaning as though he'd been punched high in the gut.

Kelda held her gun steady, pointed into the night in the direction of the groan. The Sig weighed as much as a watermelon.

Five seconds passed. Ten. Her legs throbbed. She imagined a bed of frozen peas.

A sudden wail rapidly swelled into a scream as a person sprinted from the evergreen forest onto the road about thirty yards in front of her. Kelda's brain was trying to make sense of the noise and the shadows and the silhouettes.

The runner seemed to be turning toward her.

A breathless voice came from the shadows. "Stop, damn it! I'll fucking shoot you. I will."

The voice wasn't Ira's. And she didn't think it was Tom's. She thought she recognized it, though; it was the voice from the green Toyota pickup that had followed her home to Lafayette two weeks before.

The voice of the man who had said, "Evening, darlin'."

Now she figured that it was one of the Park County cops—probably the one called Hoppy—or somebody else who was up here that she didn't even know about.

The charcoal silhouette on the trail froze. From the silhouette came the plea, "Okay, okay. Don't shoot."

Kelda knew it was Ira. And she knew from his voice that Ira was scared to death.

On her hands and knees, she edged closer to him. She stopped abruptly as a second figure emerged at the very edge of the forest and said, "Don't fucking move! Got it?"

Kelda thought that was the "Evening, darlin' " cop.

"Okay, okay. Don't shoot." Ira's dread chilled her.

"Who are you?"

The cop was scared, too.

Ira hesitated before he said, "Oliver Lee."

Kelda recognized the name—Oliver and Lee were Ira's parakeets.

"What the hell were you doing back there? With Clone and that fence? What was that?"

"Just a prank. A thing. You know."

"Do I sound like I fucking know? What kind of prank thing?"

"You know, we were . . . getting even."

"Who's 'we'?"

"Me. Not we. Me."

"You said 'we.' "

"I meant me."

"Getting even for what?"

"Something Clone did before he went to prison. An old . . . grudge. That kind of thing. Come on, let me go. Let me go. I won't do it again. I got even. But now I'm all done. Let me go."

"Where's my shotgun?"

Ira said, "I don't know."

"You don't have it?"

"No."

"You lying?"

"No."

Kelda could see enough of his silhouette to know that Ira was holding out his hands to show that he didn't have the gun. She wondered how the cop had managed to lose both his shotgun and his backup gun in the same evening. She also wondered where the cop's partner was.

"Keep your hands out like that."

Kelda thought that the cop was trying to act as if he was in control, but all he was succeeding in doing was showing how frightened he was.

Ira kept his hands out.

The cop asked, "What'd he do? Clone? What do you want revenge for?"

"He killed a girl."

"Yeah, he was in prison for that. What's your grudge? What are you getting even for?"

Ira said, "He killed another girl. Someone . . . I knew."

Kelda worried how far Ira was willing to go with the story. The disclosures he'd made so far wouldn't allow the cop to figure out who he really was. But if he offered much more . . . She mouthed, "Be careful, baby. Be careful."

She was, she guessed, twenty yards from Ira, twenty-five from the Park County cop. She considered moving closer but decided not to risk being discovered.

"No shit? He killed another girl?" the cop asked.

Kelda noted that the man's tone had changed. Ira's revelation about another murder interested him.

"Yes, a few weeks after Ivy Campbell was murdered."

"What?" the cop asked. To Kelda's ear, the question was a defiant "Are you crazy?" kind of "What?"

Ira explained, "Clone was dating her, the other girl. She was living in Denver when she broke up with him. He threatened her, then he followed her to Hawaii, and . . . he killed her there."

The cop was silent for ten seconds. Finally, he said, "No, he didn't. He didn't go to Hawaii and kill any girl. You're wrong, you don't know what the hell you're talking about."

"He did," Ira said.

Kelda thought she heard the slightest fissure emerge in Ira's voice.

"Then why haven't I heard about this? Where's your evidence? What do you have?" the cop asked.

"Her journal. He was, like, stalking her. It says he was going to come to Hawaii to kill her. Then it says that she saw him there. And then . . . then she was dead."

"He cut her throat?"

"No, no. He, he . . ."

Kelda thought, *Don't, Ira! Don't!*

"He didn't cut her throat."

The "Evening, darlin' " cop thought about something for almost half a minute before he said, "You're saying he killed her in Hawaii?"

Ira said, "Yes, yes."

The man grew silent again. When he broke his silence, his tone was even more skeptical than before. He asked, "And this was when?"

"Just after Ivy Campbell was killed in Park County. Like I said, a few weeks. Nineteen days later to be precise. That's all, just nineteen days."

The cop laughed. "You don't know what the hell you're talking about. You got the wrong guy. Clone didn't do it. He didn't kill any girl in Hawaii. Are you making all this up for me?"

It was Ira's turn to say "What?" Kelda could tell that he was befuddled. It was easy for her to tell because she was, too.

The cop said, "We were watching Clone the whole time after Ivy Campbell was killed in Park County. He was our prime guy from almost the beginning. He'd been dating her, he lied to us about being up there, his fingerprints were places they shouldn't have been. From day two on, we were watching him. We might have lost him for a few hours here and there, or left him alone while he was at work, or asleep, but we never lost him long enough for him to get on a plane and fly to Hawaii and kill some girl. How long was he supposed to be there? In Hawaii."

"A few days, three or four. Less than a week."

"No way," the cop said. He laughed some more. "You've been torturing the wrong asshole."

Kelda almost gasped for air. She hadn't even realized she was holding her breath.

"No! He did it. He killed her," Ira sputtered.

The "Evening, darlin' " cop kept laughing.

We've been torturing the wrong asshole? Kelda thought. *Is that really possible? Ira?*

"Sorry," the cop said. "You're full of shit. You set all this up for the wrong guy. You're as pitiful as he is."

Kelda wanted to yell, "No way, no . . . way!" Instead she struggled to still her heart as she listened to Ira's reply.

"No, it's true. It is. I've seen the investigation from the Park County detectives. The file they put together. There's nothing in there about anybody following Clone around during those first few weeks. He had time to go to Hawaii. He even had time off from work during the few days he was gone. I read the file. I read the whole . . . thing. I checked the timeline myself. He did it. He did."

Kelda thought, *Oh shit. Careful, Ira, careful. Don't fall into his trap. Don't go there. Don't reveal too much.*

She wished she knew where the second cop was. If

she knew where the guy with the big arms was, it would really increase her options on how to intervene if Ira started revealing too much, which it appeared he was about to do.

The cop asked, "How did you get a chance to read it? The murder book? How did you get ahold of it? That's not public information. You can't just walk in the door and get a copy of the murder book."

Ira's breathing changed. He stammered, "Somebody showed it to me."

"Somebody?"

"A friend from . . . there."

"Park County?"

"Yeah."

"Well, I'm from there. Park County. In fact, I'm the one who followed Clone about half the time between the murder and the day we arrested him. There wasn't a twenty-four-hour period during the weeks before he was arrested that I didn't lay my own eyes on Clone. He didn't take any trips to any island paradise while I was watching him, I promise you that."

"You're wrong. That's not . . . It's not in the . . . the . . . file. There's nothing in the file about anybody following him. I read it. I checked all the dates. He had time off. He was free."

"You're right about one thing. There's nothing in the file. Because maybe I didn't put it in the file. Maybe I did it on my own because I wanted to catch the creep . . . that bad."

We've been torturing the wrong asshole? Kelda thought, once again.

Ira tried to mount an offensive. He said, "Why are

you here? Tonight? Why are you up here? What do you want with me?"

"We're not up here for you."

Kelda noted that he'd said "We."

Ira again. "Then what do you want with Clone?"

Kelda thought, *Good, Ira. Keep thinking. Keep thinking. Keep the pressure on him. Make him talk.*

"We're cops. He's a perp. Beyond that, you'll never know the answer, asshole."

Ira said, "You're wrong. You don't know what Clone did. I know what he did."

The cop exploded in rage. "*I'm* wrong? *I'm* wrong? You little fuck, you don't know who the hell you're messing with. I'm going to make you so sorry—"

Her vision had adjusted a little more to the darkness and, with the cop's outburst, she registered a flurry of movement on the edge of the woods.

Ira must have noticed the movement, too.

Suddenly, the silhouette that was Ira disappeared in a blur.

Across from where Ira had been, the muzzle blast of a handgun flared in the darkness on the forest edge. The sound of footsteps followed, sparking yet another fiery blast from the handgun.

The footsteps stopped.

Behind her, from the direction of Boca's cabin, Kelda heard the rattling shrill of a whistle.

Seconds later her cell phone chirped.

Damn!

She dove into the forest and tried to find the phone so she could quiet the thing. Another shot ripped through the darkness.

This one was aimed at her.

She hunched behind a tree and got the phone to her ear. "What?"

Ira whispered, "I heard the phone ring. I know you're here, babe. And I really, really need your help."

She took a deep breath and yelled, "I'm a special agent of the FBI! Everybody drop your weapons! Everybody!"

The sharp crack of a semiautomatic weapon answered her command. At the same instant a slug buried itself in the soft soil a yard from her legs. She hunkered even closer to the tree.

The Park County cop knew she was FBI. He was shooting at her anyway.

Why?

From somewhere in the woods, not close, not too far away, Tom Clone called, "Kelda?"

Kelda heard Ira yell, "I'm really exposed out here," an instant before another shot flared from the handgun.

Ira's words and the clap from the handgun were followed a second or two later by Tom Clone's distinctive slur. "You're the 'ear lessons guy! You're the 'ear lessons guy!"

That earned another shot from the handgun.

The disproportionate roar of a shotgun blast swallowed the handgun's echo.

In the silence that followed, Kelda heard the characteristic hiss of a gasping exhale.

Whose?

She didn't know.

She felt almost paralyzed by fear.

Who had guns? Who was shooting?

Who were the good guys? Whom could she trust?

The darkness had surrounded her and doubt was eating away at her soul. She turned her head toward the dirt road and thought, *Is that Death Row?*

CHAPTER

58

While I heard the shots from the handgun, I was crouching low, picking my footfalls carefully, trying to progress through the woods in the direction of Tom's voice. Each time a gunshot sounded, I froze. But when the reverberations of the shotgun blast bounced off the mountainside, I fell hard to the earth, pushing my cheek into the soil. A mini-landslide of dirt slid inside my cast.

In the silence that followed I could hear my own blood rushing in my ears, and the breeze sluicing through the pines, but nothing else.

Tom's last call before the boom of the shotgun had been, "You're the 'ear lessons guy!"

Fear lessons.

What had Boca said? When the time comes for the fear lessons, I'll know it?

The time had come.

When the series of gunshots sliced through the darkness the way a machete slices through flesh, I knew it.

After an eternity, a voice said, "I'm standing up and going into the middle of this road here. Don't shoot anymore. I'm dropping my weapon."

I couldn't see him, had no way to know whether he was doing what he said he was doing. And I had no way to know who he was.

After twenty more seconds, Kelda said, "Tom? Are you there?"

In front of me, I guessed maybe twenty or thirty yards, Tom Clone, breathless, replied, "Yes."

Then she said, "Anybody else here?"

No one else responded.

Kelda said, "I'm a special agent of the FBI and I'm not dropping my weapon. I want everybody on that dirt road. You have ten seconds. You got it?"

Tom said yes. The other male voice echoed the word.

I could hear someone—Tom?—creeping into the woods. He was brushing branches and crushing twigs as he made his way to the road.

Fingers closed over my ankle and someone cautioned, "Shhh. Not a sound."

My heart felt as though it instantly doubled in size. I snarled, "Damn you, Sam."

His lips so close to my ear that I could feel his breath, he said, "Sorry I'm late. Simon's game went long. This thing here? This is the goofiest thing I've ever heard. How long you been here?"

"Maybe ten minutes," I whispered. "I think somebody was just shot."

"Yeah, the shotgun. I got that. You stay right here, understand? I'm feeling like my services are needed."

CHAPTER

59

Sam called my name another ten minutes later.

I'd been watching flashlight beams crisscrossing in the woods in the distance. I hiked toward them.

I was almost close enough to Sam to begin to question him about what had happened when the *thwap-thwap-thwap* of an approaching helicopter drowned out every other sound that the night was manufacturing in the Indian Peaks.

Sam waved me closer with one hand while with the other he painted light patterns in the sky with the flashlight. I thought that he was providing guidance to the helicopter pilot who was hovering above.

Kelda stood in a caricature of catatonia on a narrow dirt lane about ten yards from Sam. She was holding a flashlight, too. The beam in her hand was locked in place at her feet, highlighting the torso of a man I didn't recognize. Sprawled on his side, legs splayed, he too was still. Crimson shadows of blood darkened his neck and face.

Kelda wasn't tending to him.

To me, that meant that he was dead.

I wanted to ask someone who he was. How he had died. Who had killed him. And why. But the helicopter rotors insisted on my silence.

I kept walking closer to Sam until I saw another man.

He was sitting against the base of an aspen tree, his arms circled around the trunk behind him. Another step and I could see that his wrists were shackled with a plastic band. His head was bowed.

Suddenly, a beam of light burst from the helicopter with an intensity that felt obscene, illuminating the tiny piece of the forest where I stood.

That's when I spotted Tom. Or someone who I guessed was Tom.

He was curled in a ball on the forest floor about five feet away from Sam.

He looked like a pile of rags that had been dumped in the woods.

No, more accurately, he looked like a pile of rags that a passing motorist had used to cover, unsuccessfully, the carcass of some roadkill that had been dumped in the woods.

I said, "Sam? Is Tom dead?"

I stepped closer to them both.

The helicopter rotors answered, *"Thwap-thwap-thwap."*

The obscene light slid away and the helicopter disappeared over the ridge near Boca's cabin.

"Sam," I repeated. "Is that Tom Clone? Is he okay?"

I was ducking clumsily beneath the low branch of an aspen tree.

"The Flight for Life chopper is for him. He'll be okay, I think. Stop right there, Alan. I don't want you any closer for now. Do you understand?"

Sam's voice told me he wasn't kidding.

I stopped, and then I took a step back for good measure. "Who's the guy in the road?" I asked.

"No ID on him. Best I can piece together so far, he's the guy who was torturing Mr. Clone."

"And the guy cuffed to the tree? He shot the guy on the road?"

"The guy cuffed to the tree says he's a Park County Sheriff's deputy, if you can believe it."

"Why did he shoot the guy on the road?"

"He didn't. Clone shot him. Clone had the shotgun."

I glanced at Kelda. She still hadn't moved. Not a muscle.

I barely reacted to Sam's recitation. Apparently, I was all out of adrenaline; I felt bone tired.

I'd stepped into the darkness and found fear.

Had I accomplished anything else?

Boca had said that sometimes the step into the darkness leads nowhere.

That, I decided, was the step I took. The one that led nowhere.

PART FIVE

Seeking Higher Ground

The Boulder County Sheriff's investigators completed the first round of questioning with Kelda and me at about the same time, about ten minutes before midnight.

I could hear her a few steps behind me as I trudged back up the hill toward Boca's cabin and my car.

"Can we meet?" she asked slightly breathlessly. Her catatonia had disappeared along with the helicopter that had ferried Tom Clone down the Front Range to a hospital in Boulder.

"Sure," I said into the blackness. "Call my office tomorrow. We'll work out a time." My mind was elsewhere—the reverberation of the shotgun blast continued to echo and the darkness continued to shroud my vision—and I was tired. I told myself that I would have been more gracious to her if I weren't so tired.

She came abreast of me and touched my arm. "What about now, Alan? Right now?"

"It's the middle of the night, Kelda."

"I know what time it is. I think we should talk about . . . what happened here. I think there are some things that . . . you should be aware of. Things you didn't see down there. It could change things for you . . . tomorrow."

"Change things how?"

She looked behind her. "Not here, Alan."

"It can't wait?"

"I don't think it should. I think you need to know everything that happened up here tonight."

Bees and snakes and napalm. Fear lessons, darkness. Shotguns and death, I mused.

"That's funny," I said. "I was just thinking that maybe it would be better if I never knew what happened up here tonight."

"You don't mean that."

I did mean that, but I said, "You obviously have someplace in mind. What are you thinking?"

"I was thinking, I don't know, that Boca might loan us his cabin for a short while. We could talk there."

I shook my head. "Boca's been dragged into enough. I don't want to intrude on him again. He moved up here to get away from . . . situations like this. From people like us."

"How about a restaurant in Nederland?"

At that hour, all that would be open would be a bar, and Nederland's bars were a little too notorious for my taste. "It's not appropriate for us to meet in a restaurant."

I expected her to argue with me. She didn't. It was apparent that she had a long string of options prepared.

"Then how about your office? Say, half an hour, forty minutes?"

"You're sure that this can't wait?"

"I'm not going to have any free time tomorrow and I don't think you are either. I think we should do it now. If the sheriff calls for another interview before we get a chance to talk . . ." She let the thought hang provocatively.

"What if he does?"

"You should hear what I have to say before you talk to him again. That's all."

"You want to influence what I say to the sheriff?"

"Not at all. I want to talk about some things we both experienced tonight. Tell you my impressions."

"This makes it sound like this meeting you want will be therapy?"

"Yes. Therapy."

I took three more steps. "Okay. My office. I guess I'll see you in Boulder, then."

I don't know whether it was a function of the hour or her casual dress or what we'd just been through up near Ward, but Kelda kicked off her shoes in my office and positioned herself on the sofa as though she were curling up to watch TV at home. Her fingertips immediately found a quad muscle to knead.

I waited. Although for some reason I wasn't as tired as I'd been an hour earlier, I would have much preferred at that moment to be inhaling the aroma of my little girl as I kissed her good night on the way to join my wife in bed.

Kelda wasn't looking at me when she finally began.

"Could Jones really have made it all up? All that stuff she'd written in her journal about Tom following her to Hawaii?"

Given the events of the evening, and the prologue Kelda had offered up near Boca's cabin, I'd expected something more profound.

I considered how a clinical psychologist at the top of his game might respond to her question. Whatever the proper response might have been, I'm sure mine wasn't it. I answered, "I don't think she exactly made it up, Kelda. Jones wasn't well. You know that. After she heard that the guy she'd been dating was a suspect in almost beheading a girl who was not that different from her in age, appearance, circumstances—"

She finished my thought, "That's when her paranoia took over."

I leaned forward, closing the distance between us by a third, and made my voice soft. "Yes, that's probably when her paranoia took over. Looking back, it seems as though she may have developed a delusion that was centered on Tom Clone, or he conveniently stepped into one that she was developing anyway. Given her predisposition to paranoia, given the absence of her primary emotional support—you—given what she was hearing in the news about Ivy Campbell's murder, given some tension that may have existed in her relationship with Tom—all the pieces were in place for her to suffer some deterioration in her emotional balance, which was precarious at best, anyway.

"I think it's a safe assumption that her reality testing was quite impaired at the end. Once she got to Hawaii, probably even before she left, she began to see Tom Clone where he wasn't, and she totally convinced herself that he was after her. So . . . to answer your question, no, Jones didn't make it up. I'm sure she believed that Tom was after her. Remember the paintings. The chasing pictures. Her fears—the danger she felt—were her reality." I added firmly, "But that doesn't mean that any of it actually happened."

"She was sweet, Alan. If you could get past her fears, she had a terrific heart underneath."

"I don't doubt that, Kelda. Jones had an illness. Not a nice illness. The fears weren't real. But Jones was."

She smiled faintly at me, as though she was grateful that I wasn't going to ask her to give up her love for her friend.

Although I still hadn't heard anything that convinced me that this emergency session was necessary, I reminded myself to be patient. I decided to try to plant a seed even though I didn't expect to see anything sprout from it anytime soon. "I'm thinking that Jones wasn't the first girl that you tried to rescue, Kelda."

"What?"

I allowed a few seconds to drip away before I responded. "So much of what we've talked about since you first came into my office has to do with Jones and with Rosa Alija. In a way, your life has been very much consumed with your efforts to save those two people, and the consequences of those efforts."

I expected her to brush me off. She didn't.

"I . . . um. I . . ." She looked away from me.

"Go on, Kelda," I said.

She wrinkled her nose in an expression I'd not seen before. She said, "I've never told you much about . . . growing up."

Here we go, I thought. *Here we go.* "No, you haven't. You haven't spoken about your family much at all."

"You've guessed, though, haven't you? Do you already know?"

"Do I know what happened when you were growing up? No, I don't. I don't have any idea. Have I imagined that something did happen? Yes, I have. We all have history."

She grew silent and stayed quiet for a length of time that stretched into minutes. Her hands stilled and she ceased massaging her legs. It was by far the longest period of contemplation—or escape?—that I'd witnessed since I started seeing her for psychotherapy.

If you had asked me to bet, I would have bet that Kelda was going to take a protective stroll away from any examination of her past. I would have bet that her defenses would rise to protect her like her gun rising from her holster. A quick-draw.

I would have bet wrong.

"We had a tree house," she said. "My little sister and I. My dad built it for us. A really, really special tree house. With a shingled roof and curtains and rugs. We loved it. It was our favorite place.

"I could climb all the way from my bedroom window, out onto the roof, down some long limbs, and into the tree house. Sometimes I'd sneak up on my sister and scare her when she was there by herself. One time."

Kelda didn't pause after she said "One time."

She stopped.

I did the therapist's equivalent of putting a hand on her back and shoving. "Go on," I said.

She took a long, slow breath to steel herself. "One time, one night, when I was eleven and she was eight, I went out my window after dinner and snuck up on her and I found her in the tree house with the boy who lived two doors down from us." She closed her eyes. "You know the rest."

"No, I don't."

"Her shorts were down. He was touching her. That's the rest."

"No. It's not."

She opened her eyes. The glare was incendiary. I fought an impulse to pull away from her fury.

She swallowed once and went on. "I pushed him out the door. He fell, and landed on his neck. That's it."

"You saved her?"

"Are you kidding? I was too late to save her. I'm always too late. But I punished him. He hasn't taken a step since that day. Not one."

Clarity. A little girl molested by a neighbor. A culprit punished.

Clarity?

Hardly.

"That's not all, though, is it?" I asked.

"What?"

"The fall paralyzed him. But that wasn't all, was it?"

"No, that wasn't all. He had brain damage, too. He couldn't talk. He couldn't communicate."

The fire had left her eyes and Kelda's voice was cold.

I stated the obvious. Often it was the most important part of my job. "Which meant that he couldn't tell you why he did it. He couldn't tell you what made him tick."

"No. He couldn't."

"And that left you feeling . . . what?" I asked.

Her nostrils flared just a tiny bit. "So," she said flatly, "Tom Clone didn't have anything to do with Jones's death."

The change in direction was so abrupt that I felt as though I'd just been subjected to inhumane g forces. I managed to say, "No. It appears he didn't. You changed the subject, Kelda."

"Did I? That leaves—"

My phone rang in my pocket. I guessed it was Lauren wondering where the hell I was, so, despite the poignancy of the therapeutic moment, I took my attention away from Kelda and glanced at the caller ID on my cell. I was wrong about the identity of the caller. "I'm sorry to interrupt, but, given the circumstances, I should get this," I told Kelda.

"I understand."

I stood, moved behind my desk, and turned my back on Kelda. I considered walking out into the hallway to take the call but didn't want to leave Kelda alone in the office with my phone logs and files. I said, "Hi."

Sam said, "You knew it was me, didn't you? I hate caller ID. Listen, there's something I thought you'd want to know. This Park County cop we have up here? He's a guy named Bonnet, George Bonnet, calls himself Hoppy for some reason. Thing is, after sitting quiet for almost three hours, he just confessed to killing Ivy Campbell."

I opened my mouth, closed it, and finally managed to say, "You're kidding, right?"

"No, I'm not. One of the sheriff's guys leaned on him a little—not hard. Well, not too hard—and he just started talking. Then he led us all to this mineshaft and showed us where he killed his friend—another Park County cop named—just a second—named Prehost. Says he shot Prehost and let his body go down an old mineshaft. It's going to be a bitch to recover."

"He killed his friend, too?"

"Yeah. Apparently the two of them had been following Clone, trying to get the focus of the old murder case back on him, and then, then . . . well, then something totally screwy happened up here. There's some weird prison fence thing out in the forest and Tom Clone was trying to tell everybody he was kidnapped and attacked by bees and snakes and shit. Goofiest thing I've ever seen in my life." He paused. "Well, almost."

"But you're sure about Ivy Campbell's murder?"

"I'm sure Bonnet confessed, if that's what you're asking. I heard it myself. Is it legit? Who the hell knows? But this cop says he did it. I can't come up with a reason why he'd confess if it wasn't true."

"Was the other cop part of it?"

"Hoppy says not. He says the other cop thought Clone was guilty of the old murder the whole time. Hoppy killed him because he was afraid that the guy who was torturing Tom might say something that would let his partner figure out that Hoppy was involved in Ivy's murder."

"Wow."

Sam's voice changed a little. "You don't know anything about any of this, do you, Alan?"

I was grateful that the answer was that I didn't.

I said, "Just what I heard from Boca at the cabin. Just what I heard from Boca. The same stuff you've probably heard about the kidnapping and the fence thing and the fear lessons. The bees and snakes. And the gasoline. There was something about gasoline. I told you that earlier on the phone. Remember?"

I looked over my shoulder at Kelda. Her attention to my conversation was rapt. She mouthed, "What?"

A minute too late, I walked out into the hall and closed the door behind me.

Sam said, "Boca's great. I like Boca. Yeah, we got all that, the gas part, too—found a cooler full of some na-palm stuff out by this fenced-in pen. Had to get the HazMat guys out of bed to deal with it. But you don't know anything about this guy Hoppy and the Campbell girl? That's news to you, right?"

"Absolutely."

"Hoppy says the guy who was shot up here had been babbling about some old murder in Hawaii. You know anything about that?"

"A murder in Hawaii?" I managed. In a split second I spied the trapdoor that was hidden in a dark corner of Sam's question. Without much hesitation, I lifted the lid and slithered into the blackness. By uttering a few additional words—"I don't know anything about a mur-der in Hawaii"—I pulled the door shut over my head.

"No?"

"No."

I know about a girl who died at the base of a cliff near Paia. But no murder. No. The girl I know about jumped. Or maybe she fell. But no murder. No. "What was Hoppy's motive?"

"He says Ivy offended him in a bar. He says she 'dis-respected' him in a bar the night before. He followed her to where she was staying and then went back out there the next day and demanded an apology from her. He says he was drunk, that he used to have a problem with alcohol. She responded by disrespecting him again. Things deteriorated from there, apparently."

"That's it? Jesus."

"This Hoppy guy was assisting on the murder investigation from day one. He made sure that Clone was framed like a picture in a museum. He was in a perfect position to do it."

"I guess."

One more time, Sam asked, "Is there anything you want to add, Alan? This Hawaii thing, maybe? You don't know anything about it, you're sure? Last chance. I have to go."

"Nothing. Nothing. I don't know anything about any murder in Hawaii. Not a thing."

He was silent. His silence felt like a big fat hand shoving me insistently in the back. I was glad he couldn't see my face. I said, "Thanks for calling. Thanks for everything you've done tonight."

"If you decide you know something, you have my cell number, right?"

What did he think I knew? Worse, what did he know I knew? "Yes, I know the number. But I don't know anything."

He hung up. I folded the phone, returned to my office, and sat back down. Kelda didn't appear to have moved.

Kelda said, "What's going on?"

I tried to remember where we'd left off. "You had just changed the subject. You'd been talking about your sister and the tree house and then you said that Tom didn't have anything to do with Jones's death."

"That was Purdy, wasn't it? What did he just tell you?"

When totally off balance, I tend to fall back on the rules. It's not one of my more endearing traits. I said, "This is therapy, Kelda. I don't discuss my personal phone conversations in therapy."

She didn't hesitate. She said, "You're joking, right?"

"No. I'm serious."

"Then you're fired."

"What?"

"You're fired. You're not my therapist anymore. So what did Purdy just tell you? Answer me or I'll go get my phone and find out for myself. You know that if I have someone call the Boulder Sheriff, they'll tell us what's going on."

I was too tired to care about the rules. "Hoppy Bonnet? The Park County cop? He just confessed to murdering Ivy Campbell."

She blinked twice as though she had to translate my words from English before she could process them. Then she gasped and her hand flew to her mouth. After fifteen seconds or so, she started to weep.

"Can I start therapy again?" she asked.

With that as a prelude, I definitely wanted to hear whatever she was planning to say next. Cynical? Sure. Was it the right clinical course to jump back and forth into a therapeutic relationship, given the events of the night? Probably not, but I didn't think about it long enough to come to a thoughtful conclusion. I was too determined to hear what was going to come next.

I said, "Yes."

"Right now? We're in therapy again? This is confidential?"

"Yes."

She said, "I planted the knife that got Tom Clone out of prison. It wasn't the real murder weapon."

"You . . ."

"The man who was killed up there tonight is Ira Winslett. Ira is Jones's brother. He and I planted the knife that got Clone freed from prison."

My mouth hung open.

"I came up with a ruse to get into the property room in Park County, and I stole a section of her bloody clothing out of evidence. Ira doctored the knife with the blood that was dried on the clothes. We hid the knife, and then I went and pretended to find it."

I actually said, "I'm speechless." I was that incredulous.

"Once our lab determined that some of the blood on the knife wasn't Tom Clone's, I anonymously let the attorney who was handling Tom's appeals know that the anomaly had shown up. That got everything going. He contacted the Bureau; the courts took another look at the case. . . . It all took some time, but we got Tom out of prison."

"Why, Kelda? Why did you do it?"

"Ira and I wanted to get him out of jail so we could punish him for what he did to Jones."

"Punish him? He was on death row, for Christ's sake." I didn't feel I had to add, *For a crime it turns out he didn't commit.* So I didn't.

"He was on death row for what he did to Ivy Campbell. We wanted time alone with him for what he did to Jones."

"Oh my God," I said as I finally comprehended what Kelda and Jones's brother had been doing.

"Yeah," she agreed. "Oh my God."

"That's what the thing was with the fence and the fear lessons and the snakes and the bees and—"

"Yes, yes, yes. But that was all Ira. He cut me out of all the planning a while ago. He didn't trust me anymore. Maybe he never really trusted me. Maybe he just needed me to get Tom out of prison. Right now, I don't know what to think."

"That's why you've been frantically looking for Tom? Because you knew that Ira had him? And you guessed what he was going to do to him? No, you didn't guess, you knew?"

She nodded and wiped away a tear that had migrated to her chin.

"That's why you referred Tom to me, isn't it?"

She cocked her head and looked at me. "What do you mean?"

"You wanted me to stop you. To interfere with this . . . this plot you were cooking up with Ira."

"No. No. Giving him your name that day . . . it was just a . . . brain cramp. That's all."

"I don't think so. Think about it, Kelda. You wanted me in the middle of this. You must have wanted me to stop you."

"No," she said.

"You were dating Tom, Kelda."

I watched her try to chase the thought away. "That was . . . I don't know . . . tactical."

"How?"

"At first, I wanted to know how he was most vulnerable. How to get to him . . . most effectively. That's what I told myself, anyway. But then . . . I don't know. I started to want to know what made him tick, to understand how he could have done what he did to Ivy

Campbell and to Jones. I wanted to find his weak spot, the way he found theirs." She shifted on the sofa, crossing her legs beneath her. "But after a while . . . the last couple of times . . . I wasn't so sure at all why I was spending time with him. Something had changed."

I said, "This time, you wanted to know him before you pushed him out of the tree house?"

"Maybe that's it. I don't know. I've thought about it that way. I just don't know."

"Prisons take different forms, don't they, Kelda?"

"What do you mean?"

"The kid you pushed out of the tree house? He's in one, isn't he?"

"Yes, he is."

"Are you in a prison, too, Kelda?" I asked.

"Are you?" she shot back, after half a heartbeat's delay.

I considered pressing her further, upping the ante. Instead, I asked, "Tom was being tortured, wasn't he?" The t-word was Sam's, but it seemed to fit. "Jones's brother took him up to Ward to imprison him and to torture him?"

"I never used that word. But, yes," she said, "that was his plan. Our plan. We wanted ten minutes alone in a room with Clone. That's what we called it. 'Alone in a room.' "

"Ten minutes?"

"Metaphorically."

"You got Tom Clone out of prison to torture him, Kelda?"

"We wanted him to know what she felt. What she wrote about in her journal. Her agony. Her terror. We wanted him to know what anguish he caused her. We wanted him to know it, to *feel* it."

"Revenge?" My incredulousness had hardly abated.

"Retaliation. Revenge. Retribution. Vengeance. I've found lots of words for it since it all started. But they were all just different ways of saying that we were teaching him a lesson, we were getting even. It's all been about getting some satisfaction, Alan. I never felt any satisfaction after saving Rosa, because the way it ended was too easy for the guy who molested her. I didn't want that to happen again. So that's what it's been about for me. I wanted some satisfaction."

"Did you feel satisfaction after you pushed the boy from the tree house?"

She glared at me. "At least he knew my sister's helplessness, didn't he? After that, he knew exactly what vulnerability was. Didn't he? Didn't he?"

I didn't know what to say. *Of course he did.*

Kelda wasn't burdened by any doubts. "He got what was coming to him. And I got satisfaction."

I repeated the last word silently before I opened my mouth to speak. But words to describe my feeling were as elusive as the summer monsoons.

Kelda leaned forward. "Oh, don't be so naïve—think about it, Alan. Think about September 11. If you offered the families of the people who died that day ten minutes alone in a room with bin Laden, you don't think they'd take it? What about the Oklahoma City victims and McVeigh? Of course they'd go for it. All of them. In a New York second. Well, Ira and I decided to take our ten minutes. We saw a way to do it and we were going to get our time alone with Clone."

"Fear? The 'fear lessons'? This is what the fear

lessons were about? You were making him as frightened as she was?"

"I wanted him to stand on the edge of that cliff with Jones and feel the thrust of a hand on his back. I wanted him to feel what that boy felt after he fell from the tree house. I wanted that second or two he spent in the air before his neck snapped to last for infinity."

"The boy didn't fall from that tree house, Kelda. You pushed him. Not to punish him, but to save your sister."

"Whatever."

"Tom Clone didn't kill anybody, Kelda," I said. My outrage was barely in check. "He didn't kill Ivy Campbell and he didn't have anything to do with Jones's death. Nothing."

I could see the muscles in her jaws tighten into ropes.

"We didn't know that. Yes, we manufactured the evidence that got him out, Ira and I, but we were working under the assumption that he really had killed Ivy Campbell. The system said he did it. A jury said he did it. The evidence said he did it.

"And we were absolutely sure that he killed Jones. Her journal made that as clear as day."

I wanted to scream at her. I settled for packing my words in ice. "Tom Clone has never been to Hawaii, Kelda. Never."

She swallowed. "He hasn't? You're sure about that?" I could tell that she wasn't truly surprised by my revelation. The tenor of her questions told me she had already come to the conclusion that Tom had never followed Jones to Hawaii.

"Yes, I'm sure. I asked him on the phone earlier tonight. After you told me about what you read in Jones's journal, I had Boca ask him if he'd ever been there. I didn't tell him why I was asking. I just asked him if he'd ever been. Well, he said he hadn't. I don't think he even knows that Jones moved to Maui.

"He didn't have anything to do with what happened in Paia. Nothing at all. Jones fell off that cliff. Or she jumped. Or someone else pushed her. But Tom Clone didn't do it."

She looked away from me. "You have to believe that I didn't know that before tonight. I didn't know . . . that he didn't kill Jones."

"He didn't kill anyone." I made sure that I ladened my voice with as much irony as it could bear when I added, "Until tonight, anyway."

"Ira and I thought what we were doing was right. That our crusade was just. We were sure . . ." Her voice trailed off.

I half expected a knock on the door. A loud knock, pounding fists. A sheriff with a warrant for her arrest.

I asked, "Are you going to get away with this, Kelda?"

"I'm not sure. It depends on what Ira said before he was killed. There's no evidence down here. If Ira was careful up there . . . maybe. Nobody can even tie Tom to Jones's death. Without doing that, why would they look for Ira or me? Nobody knows what we were planning but you."

The weight of the knowledge that I was the keeper of the secrets plastered me to my chair. I could barely fill my lungs, the burden on my heart felt so great.

"Now it turns out that we got Tom out of prison for all the wrong reasons, but I'm beginning to think that maybe it was the right thing to do after all. Is that possible? That the right thing happened? If Ira and I hadn't gotten Tom out of prison, he'd still be on death row, right? He'd be scheduled to die in Cañon City. No matter what Ira did to him up there, it's better than that, isn't it? It's better than Tom dying from a lethal injection, right?"

I chewed her words reluctantly and tried to swallow the rationalization even though I knew that every bit of it was rotten. My capacity for empathy deserted me and I thought, *How am I supposed to feel right now?*

Before I could get too far lost in that egocentric miasma, Kelda said, "I can't believe what I did to Tom. And . . . I can't believe that Ira is dead. He was my lover. I never told you that. Maybe you guessed. It doesn't matter. Now he's dead and there's a hole right here"— she thumped a fist between her breasts—"where he used to be. I don't know what to think anymore." Her voice sharpened. "What am I supposed to feel, Alan? Tell me, please. I'm . . . lost. Now that this is over, what am I supposed to feel?"

A single word emerged in my head.

Satisfaction?

CHAPTER

61

Only a few lights were on in the Denver Field Office. A solitary special agent was on night shift handling the after-hours FBI phone duty. When Kelda stepped off the elevator and said hello to the agent at the phones, a new guy she barely recognized, he told her that the shift, thus far, had been slow.

"Hope it stays that way," Kelda said.

One of the lines rang just then and the agent brought his hands together like an altar boy in prayer before he reached for the receiver. Although she thought she'd seen a flicker of recognition in his eyes, he didn't say a thing to her about the events in Ward the night before.

Were she planning on staying with the FBI, she would have remembered him for his discretion.

Kelda made her way to her desk and began packing

her things into a couple of cardboard file boxes. She expected to collect the few personal items she kept at work and to be back in the elevator in ten minutes.

She almost made it.

As she was completing a final search of the drawers of the desk, someone approached her from behind so silently she didn't hear his footfalls until the last few steps.

Without turning to face him, she said, "You need to change whatever it is you use on your hair, Bill. It precedes you like a toxic wave."

"Thanks for the tip, Kelda. I've been wondering why I've been striking out with so many women. I had been worried that it's a character flaw. It's nice to know it's merely a question of bad hair gel. My favorite problems in life are the ones that can be solved for less than five bucks."

"Hint: Spend more than five bucks. It will probably smell better. How did you know I'd be here?"

"After what happened last night up in the mountains with Clone and those Park County cops, I bugged the SAC all day today. He handed me a bunch of bullshit before he finally admitted that you were going on leave, but he wouldn't tell me why.

"Knowing you, I figured that you'd try to sneak out of here without saying good-bye to anyone. I told Carter at the desk that I'd owe him one if he'd give me a heads-up if you showed your face while he was covering the phones. I was killing time down at Panzano when he called. Great *fritto misto*. The bartender is keeping a couple of seats warm at the bar for me. Why don't you come on down? I'll buy us a bottle of Barolo."

Kelda glanced at the empty section in the hinged frame on Bill's desk.

"I don't think so, Bill."

"Come on, finish packing up. I'll help you carry that stuff to your car. Then we'll go have some wine."

She said, "Your calamari will already be cold by the time we get back to the restaurant." She didn't really want to put him off; she merely wanted to gauge his persistence.

"I suspect they'll fry some up fresh if we ask them to. I just got my tax refund check. Come on, I'm celebrating."

She lowered herself to her desk chair, thinking that it would be the last time she would sit in the Denver Field Office, and she allowed her eyes to close. Her legs didn't hurt, and for an extended moment, she wondered why. Finally, she opened her eyes and looked up at Bill Graves.

"What?" he asked. "What's that face?"

"Is your cousin really the governor of Kansas? Tell me the truth. No bullshit this time."

He didn't smile. He said, "We've known each other for a long time, Kelda. We're colleagues. We're friends. We wouldn't lie to each other, would we?"

She tasted his words for irony, but couldn't quite decide.

The *fritto misto* was terrific, as advertised, and the wine that Bill picked was so supple and rich that Kelda thought that if red grapes could actually bleed, they would bleed this Barolo.

Bill held his wineglass in front of his face and

looked at Kelda through the tannic legs that rippled down from the rim on the inside of the glass. "You know somebody set us up," he said.

"What?"

"That knife we found up in the mountains? Somebody set us up. If it wasn't the real murder weapon—and the Park County cop who now says he killed that girl is telling everybody that it wasn't—then somebody set us up to find what we found."

"Yes?" She focused on spearing a ring of calamari.

"Doesn't that piss you off?"

She didn't trust that she could make her face a good enough mask, so she poked the squid into her mouth before she gazed at the surface of the wine in her glass. She could see a distorted reflection of Bill Graves in the mahogany surface of the wine. Finally, she said, "I guess."

"Why would somebody do that?"

"Somebody wanted him off death row, I suppose. You know as well as I do how many fanatics there are out there about . . . capital punishment."

"Why us, though? Why the Bureau? Why didn't they just use the local cops as their patsies?"

"Does it matter? They didn't do it to us personally, Bill. We were just somebody's tools."

"I know that. I'm wondering why someone would conspire to get him out of jail. That's what I don't get."

"Maybe it was somebody who knew that he was innocent. That's why they did it. Whatever the reason, it appears that . . . justice was done. If we hadn't retrieved that knife, Clone would have been executed for a crime he didn't commit. So we did a good thing, right?"

"I know, I know. But who would've known that for

sure? The real murderer. Nobody else. And I can't see that Park County cop they arrested arranging this whole charade. It doesn't add up. What would be in it for him?"

She leaned in close to him, hoping to dissuade his interest in the topic. "Why do people do half the shit they do, Bill?"

"You know, I really thought Clone did it," Bill said, ignoring her subtle flirtation. "I thought he killed Ivy Campbell. Eighty percent of the people on death row were convicted on less evidence than there is against Clone."

"I did, too," Kelda replied, sitting back again. "I thought he did it."

"Right from the start, I had reservations about what we did to help Clone get out of the penitentiary. I know we were just doing our jobs—you and me—but given the evidence against the guy, I wasn't sure he should be free. No, that's not true. The truth is that I *was* sure he *shouldn't* be set free."

She speared a tiny scallop, dipped it in some fiery red sauce, lifted it to her mouth, and took a long sip of wine before she said, "I had doubts, too. About getting him out." She thought that the words were one hundred percent honest, and because they were she liked the feel of them as they slid across the contour of her lips.

"So why were you up there last night?"

"In Ward?"

"Yes, in Ward."

"Clone called me and asked for help. He sounded desperate. That's why I went. He didn't know where else to turn."

"Why didn't you get some backup?"

She thought that Bill was trying to sound nonchalant, nonjudgmental. She liked him for that. She knew some of her colleagues would have blasted her with "What the hell were you thinking going up there alone?"

"He thought that there were some cops involved in whatever it was that was going on. He asked me not to call anybody, said it would only make things worse. I went along with him."

After a moment spent digesting her rationale, Bill asked, "Why didn't you get Bureau help?"

"Maybe I should have," she replied. But she knew that Bill's question was ripe with subtext. What he really wanted to know is why she didn't call *him*. "He didn't call me until after you and I talked in Boulder, Bill. I didn't shut you out. If I'd known what was going to go down, I would have called you."

The last lie wasn't necessary. She immediately regretted it.

To her, he seemed to be processing her words as though he were checking the addition on a column of figures. After a few minutes, he said, "Clone was being tortured up there. That's what I hear."

"I didn't see that part. It was dark when I got to Ward, and everybody was already running around the forest. I didn't actually see Tom up close until he was being loaded into the chopper. But I can tell you that he looked awful. I believe that something terrible happened to him up there. Maybe torture."

She thought of Ira's vipers and his bees and the laboratory in his basement.

Bill said, "Well, I hear he was being tortured. That's what the local cops are telling the SAC."

"Bill, I really don't want to talk about this. Is that okay? Do you mind? The wine's nice. Let's enjoy it."

"No," he said, his voice suddenly stern. "House wine is nice. This bottle of Barolo is as lovely as you are."

She forced a smile in reply.

"What are you going to do, Kelda? Now that you're gone from the Bureau."

"It's only a leave of absence. I've had some health problems. I need to get some things with my health . . . under control. I don't think I'll make any decisions until I make some progress on that."

"You want to tell me about the health problems?"

She eyed him for a while, deciding.

"I've had problems with my legs for a long time, but it's been unclear what's been going on. Just this morning I got word that an MRI I had last week shows a little lesion on my spinal column. The radiologist thinks that could explain a lot of my problems. My neurologist was pretty surprised by the news."

"Why?"

"I think he was beginning to believe that it was all in my head. And I think I was beginning to agree with him."

"A lesion? That sounds like it could be serious."

"That's exactly what I said to my doctor."

"Well, is it? Serious?"

"He says he doesn't know yet. He wants to do more tests to see what it really is. You know how it goes with doctors."

"You'll keep me informed?"

"Maybe."

He shook his head gently. "It's not just a leave. You know it isn't. You won't be coming back to work."

She raised an eyebrow. "You're so sure?"

"I have radar for some things. It's the way I knew that Cynthia was screwing her boss. This is one of the things I have radar for."

"I'm not screwing my boss, Bill."

He found something funny in whatever image he conjured of the SAC and Kelda romantically entwined. "Thank God for that, Kelda. But you are sneaking out the back door. Whether you admit it to yourself or not, you're leaving. There'll be somebody fresh at your desk next week. Some frigging new guy."

She was tempted to argue with him. Didn't. Tacitly granting his point, she said, "I like forensic accounting, and I'm pretty good at it. I think I can find some work if I need to."

"I suspect you can," he said, pouring some fresh wine into his empty glass. "And you'll probably make enough to afford to drink this stuff whenever you want."

"It'd be nice to make some money for a change."

He looked into his wine as he asked, "Are you still going to see him, Kelda?"

She stopped breathing. She was thinking, *I can't see Ira anymore, he's dead.* Her grief had almost erupted through her façade when she realized that Bill wasn't talking about Ira at all.

"Tom Clone?" she asked. "You mean date him?"

"I guess that's what I mean."

"I don't know. We haven't talked. You know, since . . ." She thought about Tom for a few seconds and repeated, "I don't know."

"But you were dating him? That's what that was that you two were doing?"

"I don't even know that for sure. Maybe. It was just

one of those things. We went out. I didn't let myself think about what it meant. I was more curious than interested, if that makes any sense. It didn't feel romantic. I felt that I needed to be with him for some other reason. There was a connection to him because of . . . the knife . . . and everything. And I wanted to understand him. That was part of it. What he'd been through, you know? I was curious."

"Like with Rosa?" he said. "That kind of connection? The way you still see her sometimes?"

The irony and innocence of the question almost caused Kelda to lose her balance on the stool. "Yes," she managed. "Kind of like that. But maybe it was more like the way that I always wished I'd had a chance to get inside the head of the guy who kidnapped her. To know evil like that. I didn't know what it was going to be with Tom, what I was going to discover about him. But I had to look, you know? Like at a traffic accident?" She liked the sound of the rationale. "Yeah, more like that."

They sat in silence until Bill said, "In my head, Kelda—and this is just me—this right here"—he waved an index finger between her stool and his—"right now, is my first date since I kicked Cynthia out of the house. I thought you should know that I feel that way, so there's no confusion. I haven't felt I could trust anybody since she did what she did to me."

Kelda almost blurted, "And you trust *me*?"

She didn't.

But she thought it was likely that Bill Graves was about to make the same mistake with her that he'd made with Cynthia. The poor guy still didn't know whom he could trust. Just the slightest encouragement on her part, she figured, and she and Bill would be done talking about Tom Clone for a while.

She looked away long enough to consider the likelihood that Dr. Gregory would tell her that accepting Bill's advances might be a repetition of the pattern with Ira, and man after man before him. What had Alan said? That her romantic relationships always seemed to mix business with pleasure? Yes, that she chose boyfriends because of something they could do for her.

But Dr. Gregory's comments made no more sense to her then than they had when he'd first uttered them.

Yeah, she thought. *Even if he's right, what's so wrong with that?*

Forcing a smile onto her face, she looked up and touched Bill's hand. She felt a sudden camaraderie with him. It surprised her. Warmth flushed her skin, and she knew she couldn't blame it on the wine.

Not totally, anyway.

I'd cleared my schedule and had a day free of patients. It seemed like the right thing to do.

First thing that morning, in return for a promised turn behind the wheel, the orthopedist who was treating my broken arm fitted me with a new cast that he thought would allow me to drive my still-virgin Mini. He had me sit in a plastic chair in his casting room with my arm extended at just the right angle, and then he proceeded to fit the fiberglass and plaster onto my hand in such a way that we both thought I could grasp an imaginary gearshift.

It was amazing what difference a little geometry made. As I drove home to Spanish Hills in my old car, I felt like a new man.

My very first spin in the reincarnated Mini was a

solitary jaunt over the route of the famed Morgul Bismarck bicycle-racing course in the eastern side of the county, not far from my house. My arm ached from the effort when I was done, but the drive was worth every second of discomfort.

Lauren was working only until noon and we were planning to meet for lunch. She was surprised when I called and said that I would pick her up at the district attorney's office instead of meeting her at a downtown restaurant. She was shocked to see me pull up at the front doors of the Justice Center in the red and white Mini.

"New cast," I said, lifting my color-coordinated arm.

A big smile on her face, she asked, "How is it?" She was talking about the car, not the cast.

"I'll show you. Get in."

The thing purred like a big cat as I motored north on Broadway before pulling up Lee Hill Road into the deep cavern behind one of the many hogbacks that line the long center stretch of Colorado's Front Range. Omit the previous forty-eight hours and I couldn't recall the last time I had been up Left Hand in a car, though I'd probably done the climb a dozen times on my bike in the past couple of years, so I knew the road with the intimacy of a cyclist. I skipped the bypass to Olde Stage and stayed on Lee Hill all the way up to Left Hand Canyon, where I turned west to go even farther into the mountains.

Halfway up the climb Lauren said, "So are we eating or just motoring?"

I said, "Eating, eventually. Motoring, definitely. Other things, too."

"Other things?"

"Indeed."

"What about Grace?"

"Viv will stay with her until we get home. I offered her twenty bucks on top of the extra hours she'll get. She thought about it for a second or two before she said yes."

"So do you like your car?"

"Watch."

With a short thrust of my casted arm, I downshifted. The little box on wheels hopped to attention and I maneuvered it through the curving canyons as though it had already memorized every turn.

Ten minutes later, high in the Rockies, at the very top of Left Hand Canyon, we approached the anachronistic town of Ward. I said, "This is where it all happened the other night."

Lauren was still angry about the danger I'd put myself in for Tom Clone. But she nodded because she already knew that this is where it had all happened.

I slowed to a crawl to allow a trio of dogs to cross the road. None of the dogs' gene pools had been contaminated with an AKC specimen in many generations.

She said, "You needed to come back, didn't you?"

I said, "Yes," but I didn't say more.

A turn to the south on the other side of Ward would have brought us down the Peak to Peak toward Nederland, Barker Reservoir, and the upper reaches of Boulder Canyon. But I pulled north instead, leaving the little town of Ward behind us before I cut off onto the washboard dirt track of Gold Lake Road and meandered a few miles to the entrance to the remote Gold Lake Resort.

"What's this?" my wife asked.

"A little treat for us. A thank-you for the car. A thank-you for being you. An apology for how . . . distracted I've been."

She gazed out at the pristine meadows and the pine and aspen forests that were spread in the wilderness below the Divide before her eyes settled on the log cabins clustered on a gentle hillside. "I didn't even know this place was here."

"Good. Then it will be a surprise for you. It was once a camp for affluent girls from St. Louis. Now it's something else."

"Affluent girls," she repeated absently. I watched her eyes and could tell she was transfixed by the reflection of Sawtooth Mountain in the still waters of Gold Lake. "Something else indeed," she said.

Twenty minutes later, after we changed out of our clothes in one of the resort's tepees, we were sitting in a stone-lined hot pool on the uncluttered banks of Gold Lake. The summer wonder of the Indian Peaks Wilderness towered above us to the west, the cold face of Longs Peak's glaciers dominating the sky to the north. As sublime as the setting was, I knew our stay in the pool would be brief; Lauren's MS severely reduced her tolerance to hot water.

"Can I break the mood?" I asked.

"Only if you really, really have to."

"What's going to happen to Tom Clone? Did you hear anything at the office this morning?" I'd called Tom a few times at Community Hospital, but the police weren't permitting him to receive calls, at least not from the likes of me.

Lauren's eyes were closed, the water lapping at the skin of her throat and steam enveloping her dark hair. "Physically, he's going to be okay. I heard that he'll be ready to leave the hospital today, and nobody in the office seems to think he'll be arrested when he gets out. Given everything we know about what happened up there that night—I guess it's up *here* that night, isn't it?—I don't think he's going to be charged with any crimes. Unless the sheriff's investigators develop something new, what we have so far would never stand up to a jury. You've read the *Camera*, Alan; public sentiment is definitely to set Tom Clone free. He's done thirteen years already for a crime he didn't commit. Nobody wants to see him go back to prison for whatever part he played in whatever the hell happened two nights ago. Call the shooting self-defense, call it whatever you want, but, after what he went through up here, I think he's going to walk out of that hospital something resembling a free man. For once in his life, everybody seems to want to grant him the benefit of the doubt."

"So he really gets to start from square one? A new life. A clean slate."

"In theory. But after what he's been through, he's probably starting from square minus four or five. He'll have his grandfather to lean on, though. I heard this morning that he's doing better, is out of the ICU."

"That makes me happy."

She opened her violet eyes wide and looked at me. She said, "Show me where everything happened."

My new cast high in the air, I floated to the other side of the pool and pointed west and slightly south toward the Continental Divide, in the direction of the lodgepole and aspen forests that surround Brainard Lake.

"Right over there," I said. "No more than a couple of miles from here. Just a little bit west and south of Ward."

"This side of the Peak to Peak or the other side?"

"The other side."

She floated over beside me and seemed to stare directly at the spot in the wilderness where I was pretty sure Boca's cabin stood. Below the surface of the pool, her hand found the soft skin adjacent to my navel.

She said, "Are you going to keep seeing him for therapy?" Although I'd never said a word to Lauren about treating Tom Clone, events had made it crystal clear exactly who had been the recipient of my house call.

I didn't answer right away, trying to conjure an ethically appropriate way to respond. Finally, I said, "Usually when a patient wants to continue in therapy, it's fine with me, too."

"And there's no reason to think that this case would be unusual?"

I almost laughed at the thought that this case wasn't unusual. But I said, "No. There's no reason to think that."

"I'm glad," she said. "I'm sure he needs you."

I didn't know how to respond to that. Didn't know whether to tell her about the bricklayer who was afraid he'd grown to despise the bricks. Nor did I want to admit to her my own failure to grant Tom the benefit of the doubt.

She said, "Just don't do it again, okay? Something stupid like the other night? Just don't do it."

I'd already prepared my defense. "I want Grace to know the difference between right and wrong. I want her to know that people matter. Given the work we do, you and me, sometimes . . . we're going to need to be part of the lesson."

"Well, I want Grace to know her father."

"Okay," I said. I'd been trumped. I knew that if Lauren and I debated this fifty times, I would win exactly none of the contests.

Zero.

I cupped some water in my good hand and watched it slip through the cracks between my fingers. "I can't argue with you. I don't know that what I did was right. It's like justice. Just when you think you have a good way to hold on to it, it leaks out someplace and flows away."

"Welcome to my world," Lauren said. "You balance yourself on top of the fence. You look in both directions and eventually you pick a side, and you jump off. That's it. I'm sure you did what you thought was best. And that's all you can do." She rested her fingers on my cast. "I just need to know that you'll always, *always,* consider Grace and me high in your equation."

I nodded as I lofted some more water and watched it spill away. But I wasn't satisfied. "Aren't there times when you think you know better, though? Times when you think that the justice you could create would be better than the justice the system dishes out?"

"Of course there are those times," Lauren said. "Frequently."

"Then what do you do?"

"I let the system work."

"Even when you know it's inadequate?"

"Sure. But it's inadequate almost by definition. Ultimately, by choosing to live in a civilized world, we trump any sense of ultimate justice. Truly satisfying justice—where the punishment really, really fits the crime—would demand that we do things that civilized societies can't risk doing. It's just the way it is. The system is imperfect."

I cupped one more handful of water. It took a second or two longer, but it, too, dripped away. Lauren seemed so at peace with the imperfections.

"Hey, when's lunch?" she asked. I figured she'd spotted the log cabin splendor of Alice's Restaurant in the main lodge when we checked in.

"I left my watch in the tepee. Half an hour or so is what I would guess. You have a facial scheduled after that. And then a foot massage in another one of the tepees."

My wife adored foot massages. "Really? A foot massage in a tepee?"

"Really."

"What are you going to do while I get my massage?"

"I thought I'd go for a hike. Or maybe see exactly how hard it is to paddle a canoe with one arm in a cast."

She smirked. "There, that's the answer to your question: That's what justice is like—paddling a canoe with one arm in a cast. But we still have half an hour or so before lunch?"

I nodded.

"That should be enough time," she said.

"For what?"

I felt her fingers move south.

Every muscle in her body stilled for a moment as she said, "We all go through bad times."

"And usually we survive them?" I asked.

"Yes," she said. "We do."

ACKNOWLEDGMENTS

Writing is an individual endeavor. In my case, it's me, maybe one or two dogs, and an otherwise empty room. Publishing, however, is a team sport, and I'm lucky to have a team of all-stars behind me. Kate Miciak and Nita Taublib edit the old-fashioned way, and I'm a better writer because of it. Irwyn Applebaum, in his inimitable fashion, asked a simple question at the beginning of this project that sharpened its focus. Others at Bantam Dell—Susan Corcoran, Elizabeth Hulsebosch, Deborah Dwyer—do their job as well as or better than anybody in this industry. Thanks so much to you all.

I'm not naïve enough to think that it stops there. Every player has his or her own team. Some of them I know well (thanks to Loyale Coles and Samantha Bruce-Benjamin), others I barely know, or have never met. But I know that they've left their mark on this book. My gratitude goes out to them.

My agent, Lynn Nesbit, is backed up by a great team, too. Specific thanks to Amy Howell and Richard Morris. And I don't want to forget Eileen Hutton and her staff at Brilliance Audio.

In the early summer of 1997, I was invited by Paula Woodward of KUSA-TV in Denver to witness an interview she was conducting on Death Row at the Colorado State Penitentiary with a condemned prisoner named Gary Davis. In many ways the seeds of *The Best Revenge* were planted that day. I thank Paula for the unique opportunity she afforded me.

Early readers of this manuscript helped me polish it. Elyse Morgan and Al Silverman continue to honor me with their critiques and their friendships. Jane Davis is the webmaster behind www.authorstephenwhite.com. She's as good as they come, both as webmistress and human being. Nancy M. Hall's astute eyes eliminated many errors in the final book. And, although this career of mine is extending into its second decade, I try not to lose sight of the beginning, when Patti and Jeff Limerick kicked open the first door for me.

A delightful trend in fiction publishing is the practice of authors donating naming rights for a character to a worthy charity that in turn auctions off the opportunity to have a character named after a real-live person. This time the process resulted in a strange outcome. The high bidders at the auction were Mark Reese and his wife Martha Graves Reese, who is the sister of Kansas Governor Bill Graves. She asked me to create a character using her brother's name. I did my part (I actually included the real governor *and* a fictional counterpart, in addition to finding a role for Martha), and I thank Martha and Mark Reese and Governor Bill Graves for their graciousness and generosity.

Special thanks to some other writers. Candice DeLong (*Special Agent*), Christopher Whitcomb (*Cold Zero*), and David Fisher (*Hard Evidence*). Their nonfiction books were especially helpful for background research and—for any readers interested in learning more about the unique culture of the FBI—the books were illuminating and entertaining, as well. Any damage done to the facts should be blamed on me, not them.

Finally, I thank my friends and my family. To say this work wouldn't be possible without them is trite, but true. My mother, Sara, is more excited about each new book than even I am. And my wife, Rose, and my son, Xan, inspire and energize me in ways that are as essential as oxygen.

If you enjoyed

Stephen White's
The Best Revenge

turn the page for an
exciting preview

of

Blinded

by

Stephen White

*Coming in hardcover from
Delacorte Press in February 2004*

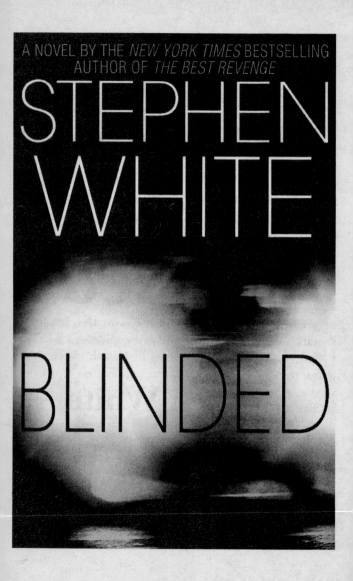

A NOVEL BY THE *NEW YORK TIMES* BESTSELLING
AUTHOR OF *THE BEST REVENGE*

STEPHEN
WHITE

BLINDED

Blinded
On sale February 2004

Sam

Every cop knows the taste and the odor that assault the senses when tenderness and evil collide. It's a baby coddled in a bassinet in a fume-filled meth shack. It's the fractured face of someone's grandma after a purse-snatcher has done his thing. It's a pregnant woman bloodied and dead on the floor.

I'd been a cop a long time. I knew the aroma. And I knew the taste.

I did.

It may sound goofy, but I also believed that on good days I could smell the spark before I smelled the fire and I could taste the poison before it reached my lips. On good days I could stand firm between tenderness and evil. On good days I could make a difference.

• • •

What the heck is it about a woman sleeping? Okay, a woman who isn't your wife of double-digit years.

A woman was sleeping right beside me, no more than half a foot away. The spice of her perfume tickled the back of my throat and the fire from inside her radiated right through my clothes. Yeah, I was paying attention to a thousand things I should have been ignoring. The intimacy of her breathing. The edginess of her eyes darting below their lids. The pure power of the rise and fall of her chest. The vulnerability of her slightly parted legs. They were all way too distracting to me.

Guilt about it all? A little maybe. Not that much. Not given what had happened already.

Still, I should have been looking in the other direction, out the window. I should have been watching for the signs of the inevitable collision—for the arrival of the evil—because I knew that it was coming. I did. I could taste it in one tiny spot on the back of my tongue. Left side, all the way back where an oral surgeon having a very bad day had once hacked out one of my wisdom teeth.

I allowed myself a last greedy inhale of her tenderness—just one more taste—before I forced my attention outside. Had I missed something? Didn't look like it, no. But when I cracked open the window I instantly detected tenderness in the air out there, too. Outside right on in, the tenderness was being swept along on the glorious aroma of a roasting Thanksgiving turkey.

I even thought I knew the bird. It was a big tom, twenty-two pounds. Traditional stuffing like my mom used to make.

Tenderness in here. Tenderness out there.

So where was the evil?

Where?

I could taste the turkey as though it was already on my lips, and I could taste her spice as though her sleepy head was resting on my chest. But I could also taste that tiny spot of evil on the back my tongue.

She moaned just a little.

Inside, I did too.

one

Alan

Nine-fifteen on Monday morning. My second patient of the day.

Gibbs Storey hadn't changed much in the ten years since I'd last seen her. If anything, she appeared to be more of a model of physical perfection than she'd been in the mid-nineties. I guessed yoga, maybe Pilates. Her impeccable complexion hadn't suddenly become pocked with acne or ravaged by psoriasis, nor had her high cheekbones dropped to mortal levels. Her blond hair was shorter, but no less radiant, and her eyes were the same sky blue I remembered. The absence of any wrinkles radiating around them caused me to wonder about a recent Botox poke, but I quickly surmised that Gibbs's fair skin would probably never be susceptible to the tracks of age. She'd be in possession of some magic gene and she'd be immune.

She'd always had beauty karma. Along with popularity karma. And the ever-elusive charm karma.

She didn't have marriage karma, though.

I'd first met Gibbs and her husband, Sterling, when they came to see my clinical psychology partner, Diane Estevez, and me for therapy for their troubled relationship. Diane and I saw them conjointly—a quaint, almost anachronistic therapeutic modality that involved pairing a couple of patients with a couple of therapists in the same room at the same time—for only three sessions. Ironically, with therapy fees being what they are, and managed care being what it is, Diane and I hadn't done a conjoint case together since that final session with Gibbs and Sterling Storey.

After they'd abruptly canceled their fourth session and departed Boulder—"Dr. Gregory, Sterling got that job he wanted in L.A.! Isn't that wonderful!" Gibbs informed me breathlessly in the voicemail she'd left along with her profound thanks for how helpful we'd been—neither Diane nor I had heard a word from either of them. That was true, at least, until Gibbs called, said she was back in town, and asked me for an individual appointment.

Gibbs call requesting the individual appointment had come ten days before, on a Friday. My few free slots the following week didn't meet any of her needs, so we'd settled on the Monday morning time. At the time, she had accepted the week and a half delay graciously.

In the interim between her call and her first appointment, I'd pulled her thin file from a box in the storage area that was stuffed with the records of old, inactive cases, and examined my sparse notes. The few lines of intake and progress reports that I'd scrawled after the conjoint sessions told me less than did my memory, but I didn't need copious notes to remind me that Diane and I hadn't been all that helpful to Gibbs and Sterling.

Couples therapy is not individual therapy with two people. It is a whole different animal, more closely akin to group therapy with a radioactive dyad. Issues within couples aren't subjected to the simple arithmetic of doubling; problems seem to be susceptible to the more severe forces of logarithmic multiplication. Therapeutic resistance in couples work, especially conjoint couples work, isn't just the familiar dance between therapist and patient. Instead, a well-choreographed routine between husband and wife takes place alongside every interaction between either client and either therapist. Each marital partner knows his or her steps like an experienced member of a ballroom dancing pair. She retreats as he aggresses. He surely demurs as she swoons.

A couples therapist needs to learn everyone's moves before he or she can be maximally effective.

My memory of the Storeys' conjoint treatment was that Diane and I had only just begun to recognize their peculiar tango when they terminated the therapy and moved to California.

The first conjoint session had been a typical "what brings you in for help" introductory. "Communication" was the buzzword of the day in the care and feeding of relationships, and that's the culprit the Storeys identified as the reason they had entered into our care. Each maintained that they desired assistance "communicating" more effectively with each other. He was, perhaps, a little less certain than she of his motivation.

Neither Diane nor I had believed either of them. No, we didn't entertain the possibility that they were out and out lying to us—at least I didn't; I could never be a hundred percent certain about Diane—but rather we were waiting for them to approach the revelation that they might be lying to themselves, or to each other, about their reason for being in our offices. "Communication problems" was a socially acceptable entrée to treatment—an acceptable thing to tell their friends.

But Diane and I weren't at all convinced at the time that it was the reason we were seeing the Storeys.

Hi, Dr. Gregory," Gibbs said as she settled on the chair in my office for her first individual appointment. Her greeting wasn't coy exactly, but it wasn't not-coy exactly either. "Long time," she added.

Her fine hair was pulled back into a petite ponytail. She smiled in a way that almost dared me not to notice how together she looked.

I nodded noncommittally. My practiced chin dip could have been measured in millimeters.

"I'm sure you're wondering why I'm here," she said.

Another microscopic nod on my part. Most days while doing my work as a psychologist, if I were paid by the word I'd go home a pauper. But Gibbs was right, I was wondering why she'd come back to see me after so many years. I had a guess—I was wagering that she'd divorced Sterling and had moved back to Boulder to start a new life. It was a scary journey for most people. Me? I was going to be the tour guide.

That was my guess.

"You remember Sterling? My husband?"

Husband? Okay, I was wrong. The Storeys were separated then, not divorced.

I spoke, although it being Monday morning I failed to assemble a complete sentence. "Yes, of course," I said.

Gibbs raised her fingertips to her lips and leaned forward as though she were whispering a profanity and was afraid her grandmother would overhear. She said, "I think he murdered a friend of ours in Laguna Beach."

Okay, I was wrong twice.

two

The previous weekend.

I decided that I couldn't stand watching her struggle with the damn halo.

It just wasn't natural.

She hated it. And, even for something as unearthly as a halo, it didn't look right on her. Maybe it was the size—did the thing really have to be that big?—or maybe it was the way it seemed to block her off from the world. Was that the intent? And tight spaces? No way. If she could squeeze through a narrow pathway headfirst at all, she ended up making enough of a clanging racket that she emerged hanging her haloed head in shame. I wasn't sure exactly what she hated most about wearing the damn thing, but I was absolutely sure that she hated it.

Still, I'm a psychologist not only by training but also

by demeanor and I was determined to help her live with the halo. Taking it off wasn't an option.

We had our orders.

I wondered, why not transparent material instead of opaque? Wouldn't that be an improvement? Maybe a rearview mirror would be nice. Or . . . wouldn't the plastic cone be more tolerable if it were just smaller?

And there was always duct tape. Couldn't I create some alternative with duct tape?

The ultimate solution hit me at a quarter to three in morning in the utter darkness that divides Saturday from Sunday as I was soothing my year-old daughter back to sleep on the upholstered rocker in her room.

A paw umbrella.

I had to figure out a way to make Emily a paw umbrella. If I could shield her paw from her mouth, then she wouldn't have to wear a bizarre plastic Elizabethan collar to shield her mouth from her paw. A little over a week before, her veterinarian had excised a basal cell carcinoma from the top of her front left paw. Now the dressing was off so that the excision could be exposed to the air. Emily's only job was to let the wound heal without the aid of her big tongue and her copious saliva, a state of affairs absolutely in contradiction to a Bouvier's instincts, which dictated that her drool was the finest salve on the planet.

The halo effectively prohibited her from licking the wound. But the bizarre collar was making our dog morose. A paw umbrella was the obvious alternative. How hard could that be?

• • •

I explained my project to my friend, Sam Purdy, who'd come over for a late-morning bike ride. We were sitting at the kitchen table in my Spanish Hills home. The Thanksgiving decorations embellishing all the stores in Boulder and the naked trees below us in the valley at the foot of the Rockies screamed late autumn, but the day promised to read more like late spring. Bright sun, clear skies, gentle breezes, and the guarantee of an afternoon in the seventies.

"I decided—I think it was some time around four o'clock this morning—that I needed to use rigid foam to make the doughnut piece," I said. Sam didn't answer me. I thought he was trying to swallow a belch. The surprising part was that he was trying to swallow it; Sam didn't usually allow social decorum to interfere in his digestive processes.

I proceeded to trace a circle about five inches in diameter and then began cutting a hole in the gardener's kneeling pad that I'd swiped from my neighbor's barn. "It has to hold its shape," I explained. "This foam will be perfect."

"Lauren won't care that you're cutting up her stuff?" Sam knew me well enough to know that if it had to do with gardening, it couldn't belong to me.

"It's not Lauren's. I stole it from Adrienne's shed. But even if were Lauren's she wouldn't care. It's for a good cause." Sam was a Boulder police detective, so I was demonstrating a modicum of trust by coping to a misdemeanor before lunch.

Adrienne was my urologist neighbor, and the keeper of a sizeable vegetable garden. Our unofficial deal was this: For the right to steal goodies from her plot at will, each August, using her tomatoes, I made a year's supply of fresh tomato sauce and roasted tomato salsa for her freezer.

Her tomatoes and basil and chilis, my kitchen labor. Communal living at its most pure. I figured that the foam rubber I swiped would somehow become part of the annual accounting.

I cut a Bouvier-ankle–sized hole in the center of the disc of foam and then sliced from the center to the outside so I could close the contraption around Emily's ankle like a handcuff, or more accurately, paw-cuff. The thing I'd created was the size of a DVD, more or less, but the hole in the center was larger, more like the circle in the middle of an old 45rpm record.

"Is Adrienne home?" Sam asked.

I was almost so distracted by my veterinary appliance manufacturing that I failed to notice his fingers pressing up under his rib cage. Almost.

"Why?" I asked. Adrienne was a good neighbor— she lived with her son in a big house across the dirt lane—and a great friend, but what I suspected was more germane to this discussion was the fact that she was also a fine urologist who had once treated Sam for a kidney stone.

"Nothing," he said. "I was just wondering."

I began laying out some rigid plastic craft strips that I'd swiped from Lauren's craft cupboard. Lauren wasn't particularly crafty; supplies tended to age indefinitely once they made it into crafts storage. There was some Elmer's glue in there that I bet dated back to Jimmy Carter's administration.

The plastic strips I chose were about two inches by four. To accomplish my design I'd figured I would need to cover about two hundred and seventy degrees of the foam circle with the plastic strips. With a pair of kitchen shears I began to turn my circle into a rough octagon to accommodate the attachment of the flat strips.

Sam rotated his neck. Up. Side-to-side. Back. His fingertips disappeared below his ribs again.

"Nothing?" I asked. "You sure?"

"I'm thinking I may be developing another damn stone."

I tried not to act obvious as I began using filament tape to attach the plastic strips to the octagon of foam, but I was watching Sam too. Sam was usually stressed out, he was chronically overweight, he frequently ignored the diet that Adrienne had recommended after his first stone, and he didn't get enough exercise unless I dragged him along on an occasional bike ride somewhere. All in all, he was a prime candidate for a return trip down the river of agony that carried sharp little stones from the kidneys to the hellish port of *Oh My God!*

"I'm sorry. Does it feel like the last one?" I asked. I'm quite adept at keeping alarm out of my voice. I think I kept the alarm out of my voice.

"Not exactly. But then I've worked hard to repress the memory of the last one. Who knows?"

"Suppress. Not repress. If you have to work hard at it, you're suppressing. Repression is an unconscious act."

He snorted at me and shook his head. "Work on your damn paw umbrella. Don't insult me with your psychobabble."

I used a totally benign please-pass-the-salt voice to inquire, "How is it different this time?"

"I don't know."

He stood up but didn't go anywhere. He craned his chin upward, then side-to-side.

"Is your neck stiff?"

His face said it was. He added, "I must have slept on it funny."

"Adrienne's already gone for the day. She and Lauren took Jonas and Grace to the zoo in Denver. But I can probably reach her on her cell. Do you want me to give her a call?"

"Nah. I'll be fine. You almost done with that thing?"

I was taping the plastic strips together, sealing the gaps between them with filament tape. I figured any slender gap was a potential escape route for Emily's wily Houdini of a tongue. "Why don't you sit, Sam?"

To my surprise, he did. I noticed beads of sweat dotting his wide forehead like drizzle on a car windshield.

"You don't look too good. Let's bag the bike ride. Why don't I . . . I don't know, take you somewhere? Go see a doctor. If you're passing a stone you're going to need some drugs. Given how bad you felt last time, some serious drugs."

"I'll be okay. If it doesn't go away in a minute, I'll take some Tylenol or something."

Yeah, that should help. And when you're done, I thought, *why don't you go put out a forest fire by pissing on it?*

He grimaced and twisted his neck some more. "Put that thing on her. I want to see how it works."

Taping the device to Emily's left front paw proved more challenging than manufacturing it had been. She didn't fight me; the halo was so humiliating to her that a multicolored, Clydesdale hoof–shaped paw umbrella was little additional insult to her doggie fashion sensibilities. I needed two different adhesive tapes from the first-aid kit and then had to reinforce the harness with an astonishing quantity of filament tape. But the thing ultimately held together and stayed where it was supposed to stay on her lower leg.

I told Emily to stand.

She didn't. She sighed.

I took the damn plastic halo off her collar and told her to stand.

She stood.

The umbrella hung over her wounded paw. The plastic strips stopped half an inch above the floor. Without delay her instincts emerged and she leaned over to lick her open wound.

She couldn't.

She lay back down to lick her wound.

She couldn't.

She got back up and took a few tentative steps, offering a quick disciplinary lick at our other dog, a miniature poodle named Anvil. Anvil hadn't done anything to warrant the discipline. Emily attempted to discipline him at irregular intervals because she could, and, she believed, she should.

Anvil, as always, was unfazed. I'd recognized long ago that he didn't recognize discipline in any form.

"You know Jonas? Adrienne's son?" I asked.

Sam grunted in reply.

"He has trouble saying Anvil so he renamed him, calls him Midgeto. I think it fits, don't you?"

Sam's eyes were shut tight. Apparently so were his ears.

Emily returned her attention to the multicolored umbrella on her paw. She walked in a circle as though she were trying to determine if the thing was really going to stay with her.

After a careful appraisal from multiple angles she stared at me, gave a little flip of her bearded head, and uttered a familiar, guttural, all-purpose murmur of approval. To the untrained ear the noise probably sounded like an insincere growl. But since I spoke a little Bouvier, I knew differently.

Rarely in history have members of two different species been so enamored of the same invention. I loved the paw umbrella. Emily, our big Bouvier des Flandres, loved her paw umbrella.

Sam's opinion of the paw umbrella was more difficult to discern.

When I turned back to him to share our joy, I finally realized that he was having a heart attack.